TALES OF MYSTERY &

General Editor: D.

CHILDREN OF THE NIGHT
Classic Vampire Stories

CHILDREN OF THE NIGHT

CLASSIC VAMPIRE STORIES

selected and introduced by
David Stuart Davies

WORDSWORTH EDITIONS

In loving memory of
MICHAEL TRAYLER
the founder of Wordsworth Editions

1

Readers who are interested in other titles from
Wordsworth Editions are invited to visit our website at
www.wordsworth-editions.com

For our latest list and a full mail-order service contact
Bibliophile Books, 5 Thomas Road, London E14 7BN
Tel: +44 0207 515 9222 Fax: +44 0207 538 4115
e-mail: orders@bibliophilebooks.com

This edition published 2007 by
Wordsworth Editions Limited
8B East Street, Ware, Hertfordshire SG12 9HJ

ISBN 978 1 84022 546 4

Typeset in Great Britain by Antony Gray
Printed by Clays Ltd, St Ives plc

CONTENTS

INTRODUCTION

Children of the night . . . what music they make.
[*Dracula*, by Bram Stoker]

Of all the creatures that haunt supernatural fiction, the vampire is the most fascinating. These dark children of the night not only feed on our lifeblood but also on our fears. Once bitten by a vampire we are doomed to a life that is not life but is not death either. Sleeping during the day, the vampire is compelled to rise at sundown to slake his thirst for blood, the sustenance of his unholy existence. The concept both frightens and fascinates us. There is something darkly romantic and erotic about the vampire. The bloodsucker has held sway in supernatural writings for over two hundred years.

The vampire's impact on our imagination may well stem from reality, for the key features of the vampire story are actually based on fact, in legends and folk tales that date back to antiquity. From the earliest times vampires have been reported in many cultures throughout the world. However, it is in Europe where the cult of the undead has received most attention and it is here that the image of the bat-like creature which flits across the night sky in search of blood as portrayed in many horror movies has been established.

Accounts of the vampire's nefarious activities have been recorded and passed down from generation to generation. For example, on 7 January 1732, an official report was signed by Regimental Field Surgeon Johannes Fluckinger of the Austrian government (and three of his assistants) detailing their investigation of vampirism in Serbia. The report related local accounts of several sudden and unusual deaths in the village of Meduegna five years earlier, which were blamed on a man named Arnold (Paole) Paul, who had claimed to have been bitten by a vampire and subsequently died. Some believed that he had risen from the grave and was perpetrating these murders. When his body was disinterred, it appeared unusually well preserved, and, more shockingly, blood was flowing from its head and more blood spurted out when it was staked. The field surgeon and his assistants continued their investigations into further alleged vampiric attacks in the region, and other suspected vampires were unearthed and examined. Eight bodies which were thought to appear unnaturally fresh were burned.

Within a short time, accounts of the vampire Arnold Paul appeared in several European publications, apparently reaffirming the actual existence of such creatures. It is believed that the word 'vampire' or 'vampyre' (taken from the Serbian usage) first entered the English language when the story was printed in two English periodicals, the *London Journal* and the *Gentleman's Magazine*, in 1732.

The case of Arnold Paul is just one of many accounts of a similar nature that found themselves in respectable publications, but it was the writers of fiction in the nineteenth century, attracted by the gothic appeal of such blood-sucking night visitors, who enhanced the notoriety and popularity (if that is the right word) of the vampire.

The line between reported fact and fiction is demonstrated effectively in 'The Vampire of Croglin Hall'. This is one of the most well-known of the supposedly factual vampire stories in Britain. The actual story first appeared in a book called *In My Solitary Life* by Augustus Hare (1834–1903), in which the incident is told to the author by a Captain Fisher. There is some doubt as to the actual date of the events that took place at Croglin Hall, a lonely dwelling in Cumbria which overlooked a graveyard. Peter Haining, in his *The Dracula Centenary Book* (1997) suggests 1848, but research carried out by others indicates that this case may in fact have taken place as early as some time between 1680 and 1690. In the end, the date is of no great importance; what is more interesting is the fact that the incident 'dramatised' by Hare in his tale is regarded as true and has become one of the enduring vampire legends of England.

It is generally accepted that *The Vampyre* (1819) by John Polidori (1795–1821) is the first notable work of fiction featuring a vampire. The story's conception is as interesting as the tale itself. In 1816 Lord Byron, the famous literary bad boy, planned a trip across Europe, intending to stay a while in Switzerland with his friends, the poet Shelley and his wife, Mary. Byron was accompanied on the trip by his own physician, Dr John Polidori, who proved an irksome and at times quarrelsome travelling companion. Part of Polidori's trouble stemmed from his feelings of inferiority when in the company of such bright, witty and inventive individuals. Byron joined his friends at Villa Diodati on the shores of Lake Geneva. True to form, Polidori took an instant dislike to Shelley and sulked ostentatiously through the group's many discussions about poetry and the arts.

Then came the famous night of the storm when, housebound because of the inclement weather, Byron suggested that each of them should write a ghost story. The most famous result of this challenge was, of course, Mary Shelley's *Frankenstein* (1818). Shelley himself quickly lost interest in the project and wrote nothing, but Byron penned a brief fragment in his notebook. Mary Shelley noted that poor Polidori 'had a terrible idea about a skull-headed lady'.

Polidori's behaviour deteriorated further. He even challenged Shelley to a duel on one occasion. By the end of the summer, Byron, tired of the physician's tedious behaviour, dispensed with his services. The unhappy Polidori received some kind of revenge by taking Byron's bare bones of a plot for his ghost story and writing his own version of it. The villainous vampire, Lord Ruthven, the central character in the tale, has more than a passing resemblance to Byron himself. Indeed, when the story was first published in the *New Monthly Magazine* for April 1819 it was attributed to Byron. The next month's issue contained a letter from Polidori in which he claimed the story as his own work, while admitting that it was based on a piece that Byron had begun in Geneva in 1816 but had never finished. The provenance of authorship was never satisfactorily resolved although it would seem that Polidori told the truth in his letter: that he was re-working and adding elements to a basic premise created by his old master Lord Byron.

The Vampyre remains an important work not just because it was the first vampire story in English fiction, but also because it provides many of the elements that became standard features in such tales: explicit sexual innuendoes, foreign settings, Gothic curses, passionate heroes and the unsettling necrophiliac attraction of the undead state.

James Malcolm Rymer's (1814–1881) *Varney the Vampyre* (1846), a marathon penny dreadful of 220 chapters, was the next major contribution to the literature. The subtitle of the piece, 'The Feast of Blood', is a clear indication of tone and content. The central character, Francis Varney, a satanic ladies' man, the possessor of fiery eyes, taloned hands and savage teeth, anticipates Dracula in appearance at least. The novel, chaotic in construction because of its episodic presentation – it appeared in 109 weekly instalments – cannot claim to be fine literature, but nevertheless it caught the public's imagination and became the most successful of the penny weeklies in the mid-nineteenth century. We provide a satisfyingly chilling and gruesome taster of the novel in this collection.

It was in the late 1840s that Count Alexis Tolstoy (1817–1885), the elder cousin of Count Leo Tolstoy, wrote 'The Curse of the Vourdalak', which the cultural historian Christopher Frayling regards as 'one of the most impressive vampire stories ever written'. Alexis Tolstoy had a great passion for Gothic horror stories, but such literature was out of vogue in the Russia at this time, and his fiction was regarded as somewhat suspect and the result 'of an overindulgence in opium'. As a result, the story was not published until 1884, nine years after the author's death by suicide after taking an overdose of morphine.

Strangely, despite its brilliance, 'The Curse of the Vourdalak' is not a well-known vampire tale. Nevertheless, it exudes an atmosphere of primitive terror which is sustained from the beginning to the end.

Meanwhile in Britain, after *Varney the Vampyre*, readers had to wait until 1871 for a well-constructed, finely-written vampire story, and the publication of *Carmilla*, by Sheridan Le Fanu (1814–1873). In this story the author presents us with a female bloodsucker as the main character in order to explore the sexual nature of the vampire. Indeed, as many critics have noted when discussing *Carmilla*, the female vampire's fascination with Laura and the general's daughter, an attachment 'resembling the passion of love', has more than passing lesbian overtones, a notion that was dealt with explicitly when Hammer Films came to make *The Vampire Lovers* (1970), which is probably the most faithful version of the Le Fanu story.

Certainly Bram Stoker (1847–1912) was influenced by Le Fanu's story when he came to create his vampire masterpiece *Dracula* (1897), particularly in his treatment of the trio of female vampires who attack Jonathan Harker on his first night at Castle Dracula – a section of the novel that is included in this collection. Similarly, Le Fanu's vampire expert, Baron Vordenburg, can be seen as a forerunner of Stoker's Professor Van Helsing. Le Fanu also established certain 'rules' concerning vampire lore in fiction: these creatures have superhuman strength, can transform themselves into various animals – Carmilla's favourite shape was that of a cat, rather than a bat or a wolf which became more usual in later works, including *Dracula*.

Le Fanu also maintained that the mere bite of a vampire did not kill you or turn you into a vampire. The vampire fed off the victim over a period of time until they wasted away. The victim thus fulfilled both the vampire's daily need for blood and its fascination for a particular person whom it chose as a victim, an idea that has been exploited greatly in numerous vampire movies.

It was towards the end of the end of the nineteenth century that Bram Stoker's *Dracula* was published. It is perhaps the greatest, certainly the most famous and seminal of all vampire novels. The author researched his subject thoroughly and was to some extent influenced by earlier tales including Polidori's *The Vampyre*, Rymer's *Varney the Vampire* and, as has been noted, Le Fanu's *Carmilla;* but nevertheless he managed to create a work of sparkling originality featuring the archetype of evil. Count Dracula is both a frightening but also a disturbingly attractive character whose vampiric life very quickly assumed mythic status in popular culture, which is the key to his everlasting appeal.

Stoker added to vampire lore by creating new rules, including the concept of the vampire needing to lie in a coffin with native soil during daylight hours, requiring an invitation to enter a building and casting no reflections in mirrors. These rules have been adhered to in countless stories and movies.

Much of the novel's immediate success was due to Stoker's innovative use of a contemporary setting. Readers were able to identify with the modern English scene, which provides the backdrop for the bulk of the narrative, and which is contrasted wonderfully with the gothic aura infused into the early section of the novel set in Transylvania. It is from these opening scenes that we take our illustrative extract when the innocent clerk Jonathan Harker arrives at Castle Dracula and we meet the Count for the first time.

It is interesting to note that after the publication of *Dracula* in 1897, few vampire novels were published for quite some time. It was as though writers realised that they could not top this masterpiece.

That is not to say these fiends have been neglected by writers of fiction, but, apart from a few exceptions, they have been most effectively portrayed in short stories; a number of the best of them feature in the remainder of this volume. However they are, in the main, stories in which the author attempts to ring the changes on the vampire myth as established by the writers already mentioned.

F. Marion Crawford (1854–1909) was an American author who produced a small but effective output of supernatural fiction including our story 'For the Blood is the Life', which is one of his best. Again we encounter a female vampire, Cristina, in a tale that is as poetic in mood as it is frightening.

Mary Elizabeth Braddon (1835–1915) had a brief career on the stage before she took up writing for a living, and her theatrical experience is mirrored in the bright, realistic dialogue in 'Good Lady Ducayne'. The story of a young girl seeking a position as a lady's companion begins in a lively, almost comic fashion and then, after the appearance of the title character, darkens and becomes more and more unsettling.

M. R. James (1862–1936) needs no introduction to readers of supernatural fiction. His ghost stories are amongst the best and most chilling of the genre. In 'An Episode of Cathedral History' we are in familiar James territory, the world of academics, ancient documents and dark dusty cloisters which harbour secret terrors. James's vampire is an ephemeral being which is not only terrifying to the central character but to the reader also.

Guy De Maupassant (1850–1893) wrote 'The Horla' just six years before he died of syphilis in an insane asylum, and there is a touch of inspired madness about this weird story, a kind of hallucinatory glimpse into the unknown. 'The Horla' is a fascinating blend of the gothic and science fiction. Once more we are dealing with a psychic vampire, but this time the entity is unseen, an invisible intelligence that is vampirising the living. We are left wondering whether the narrator is mad or in possession of a horrific truth.

'Bewitched', by Edith Wharton (1862–1937), is a tale set in rural New England in the early days of the settlers when the belief in vampirism was strongly held. Wharton, who was a friend of Henry James, once observed that although she didn't believe in ghosts, 'I'm afraid of them'.

Finally, we return to the 'traditional' vampire tale with a twist with 'The Welcome Visitor', which I wrote especially for this collection. If nothing else, it shows that a vampire does not have to be a tall, dark, handsome fellow or a beautiful and voluptuous young woman to frighten you.

The vampire remains one of literature's most potent bogeymen, as you will soon realise when you begin reading this carefully chosen collection. And remember to take care on those dark chill evenings, when the clouds float across the moon and the errant breeze shakes the branches against your window pane, for the children of the night will be abroad in search of blood.

DAVID STUART DAVIES

CHILDREN OF THE NIGHT

Classic Vampire Stories

The Vampire of Croglin Hall

AUGUSTUS HARE

'Fisher,' said the Captain, 'may sound a very plebeian name, but this family is of a very ancient lineage, and for many hundreds of years they have possessed a very curious old place in Cumberland, which bears the weird name of Croglin Grange. The great characteristic of the house is that never at any period of its very long existence has it been more than one storey high, but it has a terrace from which large grounds sweep away towards the church in the hollow, and a fine distant view.

'When, in lapse of years, the Fishers outgrew Croglin Grange in family and fortune, they were wise enough not to destroy the long-standing characteristic of the place by adding another storey to the house, but they went away to the south to reside at Thorncombe near Guildford, and they let Croglin Grange.

'They were extremely fortunate in their tenants, two brothers and a sister. They heard their praises from all quarters. To their poorer neighbours they were all that is most kind and beneficent, and their neighbours of a higher class spoke of them as a most welcome addition to the little society of the neighbourhood. On their part, the tenants were greatly delighted with their new residence. The arrangement of the house, which would have been a trial to many, was not so to them. In every respect Croglin Grange was exactly suited to them.

'The winter was spent most happily by the new inmates of Croglin Grange, who shared in all the little social pleasures of the district, and made themselves very popular. In the following summer there was one day which was dreadfully, annihilatingly hot. The brothers lay under the trees with their books, for it was too hot for any active occupation. The sister sat on the veranda and worked, or tried to work, for in the intense sultriness of that summer day, work was next to impossible. They dined early, and after dinner they still sat out on the veranda, enjoying the cool air which came with the evening, and they watched the sun set, and the moon rise over the belt of trees which separated the grounds from the churchyard, seeing it mount the heavens till the whole lawn was bathed in silver light, across which the long shadows from the shrubbery fell as if embossed, so vivid and distinct were they.

'When they separated for the night, all retiring to their rooms on the ground floor (for, as I said, there was no upstairs in that house), the sister felt that the heat was still so great that she could not sleep, and having fastened her window, she did not close the shutters – in that very quiet place it was not necessary – and, propped against the pillows, she still watched the wonderful, the marvellous beauty of that summer night. Gradually she became aware of two lights, two lights which flickered in and out in the belt of trees which separated the lawn from the churchyard, and, as her gaze became fixed upon them, she saw them emerge, fixed in a dark substance, a definite ghastly something, which seemed every moment to become nearer, increasing in size and substance as it approached. Every now and then it was lost for a moment in the long shadows which stretched across the lawn from the trees, and then it emerged larger than ever, and still coming on. As she watched it, the most uncontrollable horror seized her. She longed to get away, but the door was close to the window, and the door was locked on the inside, and while she was unlocking it she must be for an instant nearer to it. She longed to scream, but her voice seemed paralysed, her tongue glued to the roof of her mouth.

'Suddenly – she could never explain why afterwards – the terrible object seemed to turn to one side, seemed to be going round the house, not to be coming to her at all, and immediately she jumped out of bed and rushed to the door, but as she was unlocking it she heard scratch, scratch, scratch upon the window. She felt a sort of mental comfort in the knowledge that the window was securely fastened on the inside. Suddenly the scratching sound ceased, and a kind of pecking sound took its place. Then, in her agony, she became aware that the creature was unpicking the lead! The noise continued, and a diamond pane of glass fell into the room. Then a long bony finger of the creature came in and turned the handle of the window, and the window opened, and the creature came in; and it came across the room, and her terror was so great that she could not scream, and it came up to the bed, and it twisted its long, bony fingers into her hair, and it dragged her head over the side of the bed, and – it bit her violently in the throat.

'As it bit her, her voice was released, and she screamed with all her might and main. Her brothers rushed out of their rooms, but the door was locked on the inside. A moment was lost while they got a poker and broke it open. Then the creature had already escaped through the window, and the sister, bleeding violently from a wound in the throat, was lying unconscious over the side of the bed. One brother pursued the creature, which fled before him through the moonlight with gigantic strides, and eventually seemed to disappear over the wall into the churchyard. Then he rejoined his brother by the sister's bedside. She was dreadfully hurt, and her wound was a very definite one, but she was of strong disposition, not ever given to romance or superstition, and when she came to herself she said, "What has happened is most extraordinary and I am very much hurt. It seems inexplicable, but of course there is an explanation, and we must wait for it. It will turn out that a lunatic has escaped from some asylum and found his way here." The wound healed, and she appeared to get well, but the doctor who was sent for to her would not believe that she could bear so terrible a shock so easily, and insisted that she must have change, mental and physical; so her brothers took her to Switzerland.

'Being a sensible girl, when she went abroad she threw herself at once into the interests of the country she was in. She dried plants, she made sketches, she went up mountains, and, as autumn came on, she was the person who urged that they should return to Croglin Grange. "We have taken it," she said, "for seven years, and we have only been there one; and we shall always find it difficult to let a house which is only one storey high, so we had better return there; lunatics do not escape every day." As she urged it, her brothers wished nothing better, and the family returned to Cumberland. From there being no upstairs in the house it was impossible to make any great change in their arrangements. The sister occupied the same room, but it is unnecessary to say she always closed the shutters, which, however, as in many old houses, always left one top pane of the window uncovered. The brothers moved, and occupied a room together, exactly opposite that of their sister, and they always kept loaded pistols in their room.

'The winter passed most peacefully and happily. In the following March, the sister was suddenly awakened by a sound she remembered only too well – scratch, scratch, scratch upon the window, and, looking up, she saw climbed up to the top-most pane of the window, the same hideous brown shrivelled face, with glaring eyes, looking in at her. This time she screamed as loud as she could. Her brothers rushed out of their room with pistols, and out of the front door. The creature was already scudding away across the lawn. One of the brothers fired and hit it in the leg, but still with the other leg it continued to make its way, scrambled over the wall into the churchyard, and seemed to disappear into a vault which belonged to a family long extinct.

'The next day the brothers summoned all the tenants of Croglin Grange, and in their presence the vault was opened. A horrible scene revealed itself. The vault was full of coffins; they had been broken open, and their contents, horribly mangled and distorted, were scattered over the floor. One coffin alone remained intact. Of that the lid had been lifted, but still lay loose upon the coffin. They raised it, and there – brown, withered, shrivelled, mummified, but quite entire – was the same hideous figure which had looked in at the windows of Croglin Grange, with the marks of a recent pistol-shot in the leg: and they did the only thing that can lay a vampire – they burnt it.'

The Vampyre; a Tale

JOHN POLIDORI

It happened that in the midst of the dissipations attendant upon a London winter, there appeared at the various parties of the leaders of the *ton* a nobleman, more remarkable for his singularities than his rank. He gazed upon the mirth around him, as if he could not participate therein. Apparently, the light laughter of the fair only attracted his attention, that he might by a look quell it, and throw fear into those breasts where thoughtlessness reigned. Those who felt this sensation of awe, could not explain whence it arose: some attributed it to the dead grey eye which, fixing upon the object's face, did not seem to penetrate, and at one glance to pierce through to the inward workings of the heart; but fell upon the cheek with a leaden ray that weighed upon the skin it could not pass. His peculiarities caused him to be invited to every house; all wished to see him, and those who had been accustomed to violent excitement, and now felt the weight of ennui, were pleased at having something in their presence capable of engaging their attention. In spite of the deadly hue of his face, which never gained a warmer tint, either from the blush of modesty or from the strong emotion of passion, though its form and outline were beautiful, many of the female hunters after notoriety attempted to win his attentions, and gain, at least, some marks of what they might term affection: Lady Mercer, who had been the mockery of every monster shown in drawing-rooms since her marriage, threw herself in his way, and did all but put on the dress of a mountebank, to attract his notice – though in vain – when she stood before him, though his eyes were apparently fixed upon hers, still it seemed as if they were unperceived – even her unappalled impudence was baffled, and she left the field. But though the common adultress could not influence even the guidance of his eyes, it was not that the female sex was indifferent to him: yet such was the apparent caution with which he spoke to the virtuous wife and innocent daughter, that few knew he ever addressed himself to females. He had, however, the reputation of a winning tongue; and whether it was that it even overcame the dread of his singular character, or that they were moved by his apparent hatred of vice, he was as often among those females who form the boast of their sex from their domestic virtues, as among those who sully it by their vices.

About the same time, there came to London a young gentleman of the name of Aubrey: he was an orphan left with an only sister in the possession of great wealth, by parents who died while he was yet in childhood. Left also to himself by guardians, who thought it their duty merely to take care of his fortune, while they relinquished the more important charge of his mind to the care of mercenary subalterns, he cultivated more his imagination than his judgment. He had, hence, that high romantic feeling of honour and candour, which daily ruins so many milliners' apprentices. He believed all to sympathise with virtue, and thought that vice was thrown in by Providence merely for the picturesque effect of the scene, as we see in romances: he thought that the misery of a cottage merely consisted in the vesting of clothes, which were as warm, but which were better adapted to the painter's eye by their irregular folds and various coloured patches. He thought, in fine, that the dreams of poets were the realities of life. He was handsome, frank, and rich: for these reasons, upon his entering into the gay circles, many mothers surrounded him, striving which should describe with least truth their languishing or romping favourites: the daughters at the same time, by their brightening countenances when he approached, and by their sparkling eyes, when he opened his lips, soon led him into false notions of his talents and his merit. Attached as he was to the romance of his solitary hours, he was startled at finding that, except in the tallow and wax candles that flickered, not from the presence of a ghost, but from want of snuffing, there was no foundation in real life for any of that congeries of pleasing pictures and descriptions contained in those volumes, from which he had formed his study. Finding, however, some compensation in his gratified vanity, he was about to relinquish his dreams, when the extraordinary being we have above described, crossed him in his career.

He watched him; and the very impossibility of forming an idea of the character of a man entirely absorbed in himself, who gave few other signs of his observation of external objects than the tacit assent to their existence implied by the avoidance of their contact: allowing his imagination to picture everything that flattered its propensity to extravagant ideas, he soon formed this object into the hero of a romance, and determined to observe the offspring of his fancy, rather than the person before him. He became acquainted with him, paid him attentions, and so far advanced upon his notice, that his presence was always recognised. He gradually learnt that Lord Ruthven's affairs were embarrassed, and soon found, from the notes of preparation in — Street, that he was about to travel. Desirous of gaining some information respecting this singular character, who, till now, had only whetted his curiosity, he hinted to his guardians, that it was time for him to perform the tour, which for many generations has been thought necessary to enable the young to take some rapid steps in the career of vice towards putting themselves upon an equality with the aged, and not allowing them to appear as if fallen from the skies, whenever scandalous intrigues are mentioned as the subjects of pleasantry or of praise, according to the degree of skill shown in carrying them on. They consented: and Aubrey immediately mentioning his intentions to Lord Ruthven, was surprised to receive from him a proposal to join him. Flattered by such a mark of esteem from him who, apparently, had nothing in common with other men, he gladly accepted it, and in a few days they had passed the circling waters.

Hitherto, Aubrey had had no opportunity of studying Lord Ruthven's character, and now he found, that, though many more of his actions were exposed to his view, the results offered different conclusions from the apparent motives to his conduct. His companion was profuse in his liberality – the idle, the vagabond, and the beggar received from his hand more than enough to relieve their immediate wants. But Aubrey could not avoid remarking, that it was not upon the virtuous, reduced to indigence by the misfortunes attendant even upon virtue, that he bestowed his alms – these were sent from the door with hardly-suppressed sneers; but when the profligate came to ask something, not to relieve his wants, but to allow him to wallow in his lust, or to sink him still deeper in his iniquity, he was sent away with rich charity. This was, however, attributed by him to the greater importunity of the vicious, which generally prevails over the retiring bashfulness of the virtuous indigent. There was one circumstance about the charity of his Lordship, which was still more impressed upon his mind: all those upon whom it was bestowed, inevitably found that there was a curse upon it, for they were all either led to the scaffold, or sunk to the lowest and the most abject misery. At Brussels and other towns through which they passed,

Aubrey was surprised at the apparent eagerness with which his companion sought for the centres of all fashionable vice; there he entered into all the spirit of the faro table: he betted, and always gambled with success, except where the known sharper was his antagonist, and then he lost even more than he gained; but it was always with the same unchanging face with which he generally watched the society around: it was not, however, so when he encountered the rash youthful novice, or the luckless father of a numerous family; then his very wish seemed fortune's law – this apparent abstractedness of mind was laid aside, and his eyes sparkled with more fire than that of the cat whilst dallying with the half-dead mouse. In every town, he left the formerly affluent youth, torn from the circle he adorned, cursing, in the solitude of a dungeon, the fate that had drawn him within the reach of this fiend; whilst many a father sat frantic, amidst the speaking looks of mute hungry children, without a single farthing of his late immense wealth wherewith to buy even sufficient to satisfy their present craving. Yet he took no money from the gambling table; but immediately lost, to the ruiner of many, the last gilder he had just snatched from the convulsive grasp of the innocent: this might but be the result of a certain degree of knowledge, which was not, however, capable of combating the cunning of the more experienced. Aubrey often wished to represent this to his friend, and beg him to resign that charity and pleasure which proved the ruin of all, and did not tend to his own profit; but he delayed it – for each day he hoped his friend would give him some opportunity of speaking frankly and openly to him; however, this never occurred. Lord Ruthven in his carriage, and amidst the various wild and rich scenes of nature, was always the same: his eye spoke less than his lip; and though Aubrey was near the object of his curiosity, he obtained no greater gratification from it than the constant excitement of vainly wishing to break that mystery, which to his exalted imagination began to assume the appearance of something supernatural.

They soon arrived at Rome, and Aubrey for a time lost sight of his companion; he left him in daily attendance upon the morning circle of an Italian countess, whilst he went in search of the memorials of another almost deserted city. Whilst he was thus engaged, letters arrived from England, which he opened with eager impatience; the first was from his sister, breathing nothing but affection; the others were from his guardians, the latter astonished him; if it had before entered into his imagination that there was an evil power resident in his companion, these seemed to give him sufficient reason for the belief. His guardians insisted upon his immediately leaving his friend, and urged, that his character was dreadfully vicious, for that the possession of irresistible powers of seduction rendered his licentious habits more dangerous to society. It had been discovered, that his contempt for the adultress had not originated in hatred of her character; but that he had required, to enhance his gratification, that his victim, the partner of his guilt, should be hurled from the pinnacle of unsullied virtue, down to the lowest abyss of infamy and degradation: in fine, that all those females whom he had sought, apparently on account of their virtue, had, since his departure, thrown even the mask aside, and had not scrupled to expose the whole deformity of their vices to the public gaze.

Aubrey determined upon leaving one whose character had not yet shown a single bright point on which to rest the eye. He resolved to invent some plausible pretext for abandoning him altogether, purposing, in the meanwhile, to watch him more closely, and to let no slight circumstances pass by unnoticed. He entered into the same circle, and soon perceived, that his Lordship was endeavouring to work upon the inexperience of the daughter of the lady whose house he chiefly frequented. In Italy, it is seldom that an unmarried female is met with in society; he was therefore obliged to carry on his plans in secret; but Aubrey's eye followed him in all his windings, and soon discovered that an assignation had been appointed, which would most likely end in the ruin of an innocent though thoughtless girl. Losing no time, he entered the apartment of Lord Ruthven, and abruptly asked him his intentions with respect to the lady, informing him at the same time that he was aware of his being about to meet her that very night. Lord Ruthven answered, that his intentions were such as he supposed all would have upon such an occasion; and upon being pressed whether he intended to marry her, merely laughed. Aubrey retired; and, immediately writing a note to say, that from that moment he must decline accompanying his Lordship in the remainder of their proposed tour, ho ordered his servant to seek other apartments, and calling upon the mother of the lady, informed her of all he knew, not only with regard to her daughter, but also concerning the character of his Lordship. The assignation was prevented. Lord Ruthven next day merely sent his servant to notify his complete assent to a separation; but did not hint any suspicion of his plans having been foiled by Aubrey's interposition.

Having left Rome, Aubrey directed his steps towards Greece, and crossing the Peninsula, soon found himself at Athens. He then fixed his residence in the house of a Greek; and soon occupied himself in tracing the faded records of ancient glory upon monuments that apparently, ashamed of chronicling the deeds of freemen only before slaves, had hidden themselves beneath the sheltering soil or many-coloured lichen. Under the same roof as himself existed a being, so beautiful and delicate that she might have formed the model for a painter wishing to portray on canvas the promised hope of the faithful in Mahomet's paradise, save that her eyes spoke too much mind for anyone to think she could belong to those who had no souls. As she danced upon the plain, or tripped along the mountain's side, one would have thought the gazelle a poor type of her beauties; for who would have exchanged her eye, apparently the eye of animated nature, for that sleepy luxurious look of the animal suited but to the taste of an epicure. The light step of Ianthe often accompanied Aubrey in his search after antiquities, and often would the unconscious girl, engaged in the pursuit of a Kashmere butterfly, show the whole beauty of her form, floating as it were upon the wind, to the eager gaze of him who forgot the letters he had just deciphered upon an almost effaced tablet, in the contemplation of her sylph-like figure. Often would her tresses falling, as she flitted around, exhibit in the sun's ray such delicately brilliant and swiftly fading hues, as might well excuse the forgetfulness of the antiquary, who let escape from his mind the very object he had before thought of vital importance to the proper interpretation of a passage in Pausanias. But why attempt to describe charms which all feel, but none can appreciate? It was innocence, youth and beauty, unaffected by crowded drawing-rooms and stifling balls. Whilst he drew those remains of which he wished to preserve a memorial for his future hours, she would stand by, and watch the magic effects of his pencil, in tracing the scenes of her native place; she would then describe to him the circling dance upon the open plain, would paint to him in all the glowing colours of youthful memory, the marriage pomp she remembered viewing in her infancy; and then, turning to subjects that had evidently made a greater impression upon her mind, would tell him all the supernatural tales of her nurse. Her earnestness and apparent belief of what she narrated, excited the interest even of Aubrey; and often as she told him the tale of the living vampyre, who had passed years amidst his friends and dearest ties, forced every year, by feeding upon the life of a lovely female, to prolong his existence for the ensuing months, his blood would run cold, whilst he attempted to laugh her out of such idle and horrible fantasies; but Ianthe cited to him the names of old men, who had at last detected one living among themselves, after several of their near relatives and children had been found marked with the stamp of the fiend's appetite; and when she found him so incredulous, she begged of him to believe her, for it had been, remarked, that those who had dared to question their existence always had some proof given, which obliged them, with grief and heartbreaking, to confess it was true. She detailed to him the trad- itional appearance of these monsters, and his horror was increased, by hearing a pretty accurate description of Lord Ruthven; he, how- ever, still persisted in persuading her, that there could be no truth in her fears, though at the same time he wondered at the many co- incidences which had all tended to excite a belief in the super- natural power of Lord Ruthven.

Aubrey began to attach himself more and more to Ianthe; her innocence, so contrasted with all the affected virtues of the women among whom he had sought for his vision of romance, won his heart; and while he ridiculed the idea of a young man of English habits marrying an uneducated Greek girl, still he found himself more and more attached to the almost fairy form before him. He would tear himself at times from her, and, forming a plan for some antiquarian research, he would depart, determined not to return until his object was attained; but he always found it impossible to fix his attention upon the ruins around him, whilst in his mind he retained an image that seemed alone the rightful possessor of his thoughts. Ianthe was unconscious of his love, and was ever the same frank infantile being he had first known. She always seemed to part from him with reluct- ance; but it was because she had no longer anyone with whom she could visit her favourite haunts, whilst her guardian was occupied in sketching or uncovering some fragment which had yet escaped the destructive hand of time. She had appealed to her parents on the subject of Vampyres, and they both, with several present, affirmed their existence, pale with horror at the very name. Soon after, Aubrey determined to proceed upon one of his excursions, which was to detain him for a few hours; when they heard the name of the place, they all at once begged of him not to return at night, as he must necessarily pass through a wood where no Greek would ever remain, after the day had closed, upon any consideration. They described it as the resort of the vampyres in their nocturnal orgies, and denounced the most heavy evils as impending upon him who dared to cross their path. Aubrey made light of their representations, and tried to laugh them out of the idea; but when he saw them shudder at his daring thus to mock a superior, infernal power, the very name of which apparently made their blood freeze, he was silent.

Next morning Aubrey set off upon his excursion unattended; he was surprised to observe the melancholy face of his host, and was concerned to find that his words, mocking the belief of those horrible fiends, had inspired them with such terror. When he was about to depart, Ianthe came to the side of his horse, and earnestly begged of him to return ere night allowed the power of these beings to be put in action – he promised. He was, however, so occupied in his research, that he did not perceive that daylight would soon end, and that in the horizon there was one of those specks which, in the warmer climates, so rapidly gather into a tremendous mass, and pour all their rage upon the devoted country. – He at last, however, mounted his horse, determined to make up by speed for his delay: but it was too late. Twilight, in these southern climates, is almost unknown; immediately the sun sets, night begins: and ere he had advanced far, the power of the storm was above – its echoing thunders had scarcely an interval of rest – its thick heavy rain forced its way through the canopying foliage, whilst the blue forked lightning seemed to fall and radiate at his very feet. Suddenly his horse took fright, and he was carried with dreadful rapidity through the entangled forest. The animal at last, through fatigue, stopped, and he found, by the glare of lightning, that he was in the neighbourhood of a hovel that hardly lifted itself up from the masses of dead leaves and brushwood which surrounded it. Dismounting, he approached, hoping to find someone to guide him to the town, or at least trusting to obtain shelter from the pelting of the storm. As he approached, the thunders, for a moment silent, allowed him to hear the dreadful shrieks of a woman mingling with the stifled, exultant mockery of a laugh, continued in one almost unbroken sound – he was startled, but, roused by the thunder which again rolled over his head, he with a sudden effort forced open the door of the hut. He found himself in utter darkness: the sound, however, guided him. He was apparently unperceived; for though he called, still the sounds continued, and no notice was taken of him. He found himself in contact with someone, whom he immediately seized, when a voice cried 'Again baffled!', to which a loud laugh succeeded; and he felt himself grappled by one whose strength seemed superhuman: determined to sell his life as dearly as he could, he struggled, but it was in vain: he was lifted from his feet and hurled with enormous force against the ground – his enemy threw himself upon him, and kneeling upon his breast, had placed his hands upon his throat – when the glare of many torches penetrating through the hole that gave light in the day, disturbed him – he instantly rose, and, leaving his prey, rushed through the door, and in a moment the crashing of the branches, as he broke through the wood, was no longer heard. The storm was now still; and Aubrey, incapable of moving, was soon heard by those without. They entered; the light of their torches fell upon the mud walls, and the thatch loaded on every individual straw with heavy flakes of soot. At the desire of Aubrey they searched for her who had attracted him by her cries; he was again left in darkness, but what was his horror, when the light of the torches once more burst upon him, to perceive the airy form of his fair conductress brought in a lifeless corse. He shut his eyes, hoping that it was but a vision arising from his disturbed imagination; but he again saw the same form, when he unclosed them, stretched by his side. There was no colour upon her cheek, not even upon her lip; yet there was a stillness about her face that seemed almost as attaching as the life that once dwelt there – upon her neck and breast was blood, and upon her throat were the marks of teeth having opened the vein – to this the men pointed, crying, simultaneously struck with horror, 'A Vampyre! a Vampyre!' A litter was quickly formed, and Aubrey was laid by the side of her who had lately been to him the object of so many bright and fairy visions, now fallen with the flower of life that had died within her. He knew not what his thoughts were – his mind was benumbed and seemed to shun reflection, and take refuge in vacancy – he held almost unconsciously in his hand a naked dagger of a particular construction, which had been found in the hut. They were soon met by different parties who had been engaged in the search of her whom a mother had missed. Their lamentable cries, as they approached the city, forewarned the parents of some dreadful catastrophe. – To describe their grief would be impossible; but when they ascertained the cause of their child's death, they looked at Aubrey, and pointed to the corse. They were inconsolable; both died broken-hearted.

Aubrey being put to bed was seized with a most violent fever, and was often delirious; in these intervals he would call upon Lord Ruthven and upon Ianthe – by some unaccountable combination he seemed to beg of his former companion to spare the being he loved. At other times he would imprecate maledictions upon his head, and curse him as her destroyer. Lord Ruthven chanced at this time to arrive at Athens, and, from whatever motive, upon hearing of the state of Aubrey, immediately placed himself in the same house, and became his constant attendant. When the latter recovered from his delirium, he was horrified and startled at the sight of him whose image he had now combined with that of a Vampyre; but Lord Ruthven, by his kind words implying almost repentance for the fault that had caused their separation, and still more by the attention, anxiety, and care which he showed, soon reconciled him to his presence. His lordship seemed quite changed; he no longer appeared that apathetic being who had so astonished Aubrey; but as soon as his convalescence began to be rapid, he again gradually retired into the same state of mind, and Aubrey perceived no difference from the former man, except that at times he was surprised to meet his gaze fixed intently upon him, with a smile of malicious exultation playing upon his lips: he knew not why, but this smile haunted him. During the last stage of the invalid's recovery, Lord Ruthven was apparently engaged in watching the tideless waves raised by the cooling breeze, or in marking the progress of those orbs circling, like our world, the moveless sun – indeed, he appeared to wish to avoid the eyes of all.

Aubrey's mind, by this shock, was much weakened, and that elasticity of spirit which had once so distinguished him now seemed to have fled for ever. He was now as much a lover of solitude and silence as Lord Ruthven; but much as he wished for solitude, his mind could not find it in the neighbourhood of Athens; if he sought it amidst the ruins he had formerly frequented, Ianthe's form stood by his side – if he sought it in the woods, her light step would appear wandering amidst the underwood, in quest of the modest violet; then suddenly turning round, would show, to his wild imagination, her pale face and wounded throat, with a meek smile upon her lips. He determined to fly scenes, every feature of which created such bitter associations in his mind. He proposed to Lord Ruthven, to whom he held himself bound by the tender care he had taken of him during his illness, that they should visit those parts of Greece neither had yet seen. They travelled in every direction, and sought every spot to which a recollection could be attached: but though they thus hastened from place to place, yet they seemed not to heed what they gazed upon. They heard much of robbers, but they gradually began to slight these reports, which they imagined were only the invention of individuals whose interest it was to excite the generosity of those whom they defended from pretended dangers. In consequence of thus neglecting the advice of the inhabitants, on one occasion they travelled with only a few guards, more to serve as guides than as a defence. Upon entering, however, a narrow defile, at the bottom of which was the bed of a torrent, with large masses of rock brought down from the neighbouring precipices, they had reason to repent their negligence; for scarcely were the whole of the party engaged in the narrow pass, when they were startled by the whistling of bullets close to their heads, and by the echoed report of several guns. In an instant their guards had left them, and, placing themselves behind rocks, had begun to fire in the direction whence the report came. Lord Ruthven and Aubrey, imitating their example, retired for a moment behind the sheltering turn of the defile: but ashamed of being thus detained by a foe, who with insulting shouts bade them advance, and being exposed to unresisting slaughter, if any of the robbers should climb above and take them in the rear, they determined at once to rush forward in search of the enemy. Hardly had they lost the shelter of the rock, when Lord Ruthven received a shot in the shoulder which brought him to the ground. Aubrey hastened to his assistance; and, no longer heeding the contest or his own peril, was soon surprised by seeing the robbers' faces around him – his guards having, upon Lord Ruthven's being wounded, immediately thrown up their arms and surrendered.

By promises of great reward, Aubrey soon induced them to convey his wounded friend to a neighbouring cabin; and having agreed upon a ransom, he was no more disturbed by their presence – they being content merely to guard the entrance till their comrade should return with the promised sum, for which he had an order. Lord Ruthven's strength rapidly decreased; in two days mortification ensued, and death seemed advancing with hasty steps. His conduct and appearance had not changed; he seemed as unconscious of pain as he had been of the objects about him: but towards the close of the last evening, his mind became apparently uneasy, and his eye often fixed upon Aubrey, who was induced to offer his assistance with more than usual earnestness – 'Assist me! You may save me – you may do more than that – I mean not my life, I heed the death of my existence as little as that of the passing day; but you may save my honour, your friend's honour.' – 'How? Tell me how? I would do anything,' replied Aubrey. – 'I need but little – my life ebbs apace – I cannot explain the whole – but if you would conceal all you know of me, my honour were free from stain in the world's mouth – and if my death were unknown for some time in England – I – I – I – but life.' – 'It shall not be known.' – 'Swear !' cried the dying man, raising himself with exultant violence, 'Swear by all your soul reveres, by all your nature fears, swear that for a year and a day you will not impart your knowledge of my crimes or death to any living being in any way whatever may happen, or whatever you may see.' – His eyes seemed bursting from their sockets: 'I swear !' said Aubrey; he sunk laughing upon his pillow, and breathed no more.

Aubrey retired to rest, but did not sleep; the many circumstances attending his acquaintance with this man rose upon his mind and, he knew not why; when he remembered his oath a cold shivering came over him, as if from the presentiment of something horrible awaiting him. Rising early in the morning, he was about to enter the hovel in which he had left the corpse, when a robber met him, and informed him that it was no longer there, having been conveyed by himself and comrades, upon his retiring, to the pinnacle of a neighbouring mount, according to a promise they had given his lordship, that it should be exposed to the first cold ray of the moon that rose after his death. Aubrey, astonished, and taking several of the men, determined to go and bury it upon the spot where it lay. But when he had mounted to the summit he found no trace of either the corpse or the clothes, though the robbers swore they pointed out the identical rock on which they had laid the body. For a time his mind was bewildered in conjectures, but he at last returned, convinced that they had buried the corpse for the sake of the clothes.

Weary of a country in which he had met with such terrible misfortunes, and in which all apparently conspired to heighten that superstitious melancholy that had seized upon his mind, he resolved to leave it, and soon arrived at Smyrna. While waiting for a vessel to convey him to Otranto, or to Naples, he occupied himself in arranging those effects he had with him belonging to Lord Ruthven. Amongst other things there was a case containing several weapons of offence, more or less adapted to ensure the death of the victim. There were several daggers and ataghans. Whilst turning them over, and examining their curious forms, what was his surprise at finding a sheath apparently ornamented in the same style as the dagger discovered in the fatal hut – he shuddered – hastening to gain further proof, he found the weapon, and his horror may be imagined when he discovered that it fitted, though peculiarly shaped, the sheath he held in his hand. His eyes seemed to need no further certainty – they seemed, gazing, to be bound to the dagger; yet still he wished to disbelieve; but the particular form, the same varying tints upon the haft and sheath were alike in splendour on both, and left no room for doubt; there were also drops of blood on each.

He left Smyrna, and on his way home, at Rome, his first inquiries were concerning the lady he had attempted to snatch from Lord Ruthven's seductive arts. Her parents were in distress, their fortune ruined, and she had not been heard of since the departure of his lordship. Aubrey's mind became almost broken under so many repeated horrors; he was afraid that this lady had fallen a victim to the destroyer of Ianthe. He became morose and silent; and his only occupation consisted in urging the speed of the postilions, as if he were going to save the life of someone he held dear. He arrived at Calais; a breeze, which seemed obedient to his will, soon wafted him to the English shores; and he hastened to the mansion of his fathers, and there, for a moment, appeared to lose, in the embraces and caresses of his sister, all memory of the past. If she before, by her infantine caresses, had gained his affection, now that the woman began to appear, she was still more attaching as a companion.

Miss Aubrey had not that winning grace which gains the gaze and applause of the drawing-room assemblies. There was none of that light brilliancy which only exists in the heated atmosphere of a crowded apartment. Her blue eye was never lit up by the levity of the mind beneath. There was a melancholy charm about it which did not seem to arise from misfortune, but from some feeling within, that appeared to indicate a soul conscious of a brighter realm. Her step was not that light footing which strays where'er a butterfly or a colour may attract – it was sedate and pensive. When alone, her face was never brightened by the smile of joy; but when her brother breathed to her his affection, and would in her presence forget those griefs she knew destroyed his rest, who would have exchanged her smile for that of the voluptuary? It seemed as if those eyes – that face – were then playing in the light of their own native sphere. She was yet only eighteen, and had not been presented to the world, it having been thought by her guardians more fit that her presentation should be delayed until her brother's return from the continent, when he might be her protector. It was now, therefore, resolved that the next drawing-room, which was fast approaching, should be the epoch of her entry into the 'busy scene'. Aubrey would rather have remained in the mansion of his fathers, and fed upon the melancholy which overpowered him. He could not feel interest about the frivolities of fashionable strangers, when his mind had been so torn by the events he had witnessed; but he determined to sacrifice his own comfort to the protection of his sister. They soon arrived in town, and prepared for the next day, which had been announced as a drawing-room.

The crowd was excessive – a drawing-room had not been held for a long time, and all who were anxious to bask in the smile of royalty hastened thither. Aubrey was there with his sister. While he was standing in a corner by himself, heedless of all around him, engaged in the remembrance that the first time he had seen Lord Ruthven was in that very place – he felt himself suddenly seized by the arm, and a voice he recognised too well sounded in his ear – 'Remember your oath. ' He had hardly courage to turn, fearful of seeing a spectre that would blast him, when he perceived, at a little distance, the same figure which had attracted his notice on this spot upon his first entry into society. He gazed till, his limbs almost refusing to bear their weight, he was obliged to take the arm of a friend, and forcing a passage through the crowd, he threw himself into his carriage, and was driven home. He paced the room with hurried steps, and fixed his hands upon his head, as if he were afraid his thoughts were bursting from his brain. Lord Ruthven again before him – circumstances started up in dreadful array – the dagger – his oath. – He roused himself, he could not believe it possible – the dead rise again! – He thought his imagination had conjured up the image his mind was resting upon. It was impossible that it could be real – he determined, therefore, to go again into society; for though he attempted to ask concerning Lord Ruthven, the name hung upon his lips, and he could not succeed in gaining information. He went a few nights after with his sister to the assembly of a near relation. Leaving her under the protection of a matron, he retired into a recess, and there gave himself up to his own devouring thoughts. Perceiving, at last, that many were leaving, he roused himself, and entering another room, found his sister surrounded by several, apparently in earnest conversation; he attempted to pass and get near her, when one, whom he requested to move, turned round, and revealed to him those features he most abhorred. He sprang forward, seized his sister's arm, and, with hurried step, forced her towards the street: at the door he found himself impeded by the crowd of servants who were waiting for their lords; and while he was engaged in passing them, he again heard that voice whisper close to him – 'Remember your oath!' – He did not dare to turn, but, hurrying his sister, soon reached home.

Aubrey became almost distracted. If before his mind had been absorbed by one subject, how much more completely was it engrossed, now that the certainty of the monster's living again pressed upon his thoughts. His sister's attentions were now unheeded, and it was in vain that she entreated him to explain to her what had caused his abrupt conduct. He only uttered a few words, and those terrified her. The more he thought, the more he was bewildered. His oath startled him – was he then to allow this monster to roam, bearing ruin upon his breath, amidst all he held dear, and not avert its progress? His very sister might have been touched by him. But even if he were to break his oath, and disclose his suspicions, who would believe him? He thought of employing his own hand to free the world from such a wretch; but death, he remembered, had been already mocked. For days he remained in this state; shut up in his room, he saw no-one, and ate only when his sister came, who, with eyes streaming with tears, besought him, for her sake, to support nature. At last, no longer capable of bearing stillness and solitude, he left his house, roamed from street to street, anxious to fly that image which haunted him. His dress became neglected, and he wandered, as often exposed to the noon-day sun as to the midnight damps. He was no longer to be recognised; at first he returned with the evening to the house; but at last he laid him down to rest wherever fatigue overtook him. His sister, anxious for his safety, employed people to follow him; but they were soon distanced by him who fled from a pursuer swifter than any – from thought. His conduct, however, suddenly changed. Struck with the idea that he left by his absence the whole of his friends with a fiend amongst them, of whose presence they were unconscious, he determined to enter again into society, and watch him closely, anxious to forewarn, in spite of his oath, all whom Lord Ruthven approached with intimacy. But when he entered into a room, his haggard and suspicious looks were so striking, his inward shudderings so visible, that his sister was at last obliged to beg of him to abstain from seeking, for her sake, a society which affected him so strongly. When, however, remonstrance proved unavailing, the guardians thought proper to interpose, and, fearing that his mind was becoming alienated, they thought it high time to resume again that trust which had been before imposed upon them by Aubrey's parents.

Desirous of saving him from the injuries and sufferings he had daily encountered in his wanderings, and of preventing him from exposing to the general eye those marks of what they considered folly, they engaged a physician to reside in the house, and take constant care of him. He hardly appeared to notice it, so completely was his mind absorbed by one terrible subject. His incoherence became at last so great, that he was confined to his chamber. There he would often lie for days, incapable of being roused. He had become emaciated, his eyes had attained a glassy lustre – the only sign of affection and recollection remaining displayed itself upon the entry of his sister; then he would sometimes start, and, seizing her hands, with looks that severely afflicted her, he would desire her not to touch him. 'Oh, do not touch him – if your love for me is aught, do not go near him!' When, however, she enquired to whom he referred, his only answer was, 'True! true!' and again he sank into a state whence not even she could rouse him. This lasted many months: gradually, however, as the year was passing, his incoherences became less frequent, and his mind threw off a portion of its gloom, whilst his guardians observed, that several times in the day he would count upon his fingers a definite number, and then smile.

The time had nearly elapsed, when, upon the last day of the year, one of his guardians entering his room, began to converse with his physician upon the melancholy circumstance of Aubrey's being in so awful a situation, when his sister was going next day to be married. Instantly Aubrey's attention was attracted; he asked anxiously to whom. Glad of this mark of returning intellect, of which they feared he had been deprived, they mentioned the name of the Earl of Marsden. Thinking this was a young Earl whom he had met with in society, Aubrey seemed pleased, and astonished them still more by his expressing his intention to be present at the nuptials, and desiring to see his sister. They answered not, but in a few minutes his sister was with him. He was apparently again capable of being affected by the influence of her lovely smile; for he pressed her to his breast, and kissed her check, wet with tears flowing at the thought of her brother's being once more alive to the feelings of affection. He began to speak with all his wonted warmth, and to congratulate her upon her marriage with a person so distinguished for rank and every accomplishment, when he suddenly perceived a locket upon her breast; opening it, what was his surprise at beholding the features of the monster who had so long influenced his life. He seized the portrait in a paroxysm of rage, and trampled it under foot. Upon her asking him why he thus destroyed the resemblance of her future husband, he looked as if he did not understand her – then seizing her hands, and gazing on her with a frantic expression of countenance, he bade her swear that she would never wed this monster, for he —— But he could not advance – it seemed as if that voice again bade him remember his oath – he turned suddenly round, thinking Lord Ruthven was near him, but saw no-one. In the meantime the guardians and physician, who had heard the whole, and thought this was but a eturn of his disorder, entered, and forcing him from Miss Aubrey, 'esired her to leave him. He fell upon his knees to them, he implored, he begged of them to delay but for one day. They, attributing his to the insanity they imagined had taken possession of his mind, ndeavoured to pacify him, and retired.

Lord Ruthven had called the morning after the drawing-room, nd had been refused with everyone else. When he heard of Aubrey's ll-health, he readily understood himself to be the cause of it; ut when he learned that he was deemed insane, his exultation and pleasure could hardly be concealed from those among whom he had gained this information. He hastened to the house of his former companion, and, by constant attendance, and the pretence of great affection for the brother and interest in his fate, he gradually won the ear of Miss Aubrey. Who could resist his power? His tongue had dangers and toils to recount – could speak of himself as of an individual having no sympathy with any being on the crowded earth, save with her to whom he addressed himself – could tell how, since he knew her, his existence had begun to seem worthy of preservation, if it were merely that he might listen to her soothing accents – in fine, he knew so well how to use the serpent's art, or such was the will of fate, that he gained her affections. The title of the elder branch falling at length to him, he obtained an important embassy, which served as an excuse for hastening the marriage (in spite of her brother's deranged state), which was to take place the very day before his departure for the continent.

Aubrey, when he was left by the physician and his guardians, attempted to bribe the servants, but in vain. He asked for pen and paper; it was given him; he wrote a letter to his sister, conjuring her, as she valued her own happiness, her own honour, and the honour of those now in the grave, who once held her in their arms as their hope and the hope of their house, to delay but for a few hours that marriage, on which he denounced the most heavy curses. The servants promised they would deliver it; but giving it to the physician, he thought it better not to harass any more the mind of Miss Aubrey by, what he considered, the ravings of a maniac. Night passed on without rest to the busy inmates of the house; and Aubrey heard, with a horror that may more easily be conceived than described, the notes of busy preparation. Morning came, and the sound of carriages broke upon his ear. Aubrey grew almost frantic. The curiosity of the servants at last overcame their vigilance, they gradually stole away, leaving him in the custody of a helpless old woman. He seized the opportunity, with one bound was out of the room, and in a moment found himself in the apartment where all were nearly assembled. Lord Ruthven was the first to perceive him; he immediately approached, and, taking his arm by force, hurried him from the room, speechless with rage. When on the staircase, Lord Ruthven whispered in his ear – 'Remember your oath, and know, if not my bride today, your sister is dishonoured. Women are frail!' So saying, he pushed him towards his attendants, who, roused by the old woman, had come in search of him. Aubrey could no longer support himself; his rage not finding vent, had broken a blood-vessel, and he was conveyed to bed. This was not mentioned to his sister, who was not present when he entered, as the physician was afraid of agitating her. The marriage was solemnised, and the bride and bridegroom left London.

Aubrey's weakness increased; the effusion of blood produced symptoms of the near approach of death. He desired his sister's guardians might be called, and when the midnight hour had struck, he related composedly what the reader has perused – he died immediately after.

The guardians hastened to protect Miss Aubrey; but when they arrived, it was too late. Lord Ruthven had disappeared, and Aubrey's sister had glutted the thirst of a VAMPYRE!

Varney the Vampyre
[an extract]

JAMES MALCOLM RYMER

The solemn tones of an old cathedral clock have announced midnight – the air is thick and heavy – a strange, death-like stillness pervades all nature. Like the ominous calm which precedes some more than usually terrific outbreak of the elements, they seem to have paused even in their ordinary fluctuations, to gather a terrific strength for the great effort. A faint peal of thunder now comes from far off. Like a signal gun for the battle of the winds to begin, it appeared to awaken them from their lethargy, and one awful, warring hurricane swept over a whole city, producing more devastation in the four or five minutes it lasted, than would a half-century of ordinary phenomena.

It was as if some giant had blown upon some toy town, and scattered many of the buildings before the hot blast of his terrific breath; for as suddenly as that blast of wind had come did it cease, and all was as still and calm as before.

Sleepers awakened, and thought that what they had heard must be the confused chimera of a dream. They trembled and turned to sleep again.

All is still – still as the very grave. Not a sound breaks the magic of repose. What is that – a strange, pattering noise, as of a million of fairy feet? It is hail – yes, a hail-storm has burst over the city. Leaves are dashed from the trees, mingled with small boughs; windows that lie most opposed to the direct fury of the pelting particles of ice are broken, and the rapt repose that before was so remarkable in its intensity, is exchanged for a noise which, in its accumulation, drowns every cry of surprise or consternation which here and there arose from persons who found their houses invaded by the storm.

Now and then, too, there would come a sudden gust of wind that in its strength, as it blew laterally, would, for a moment, hold millions of the hailstones suspended in mid air, but it was only to

dash them with redoubled force in some new direction, where mor
mischief was to be done.

Oh, how the storm raged! Hail – rain – wind. It was, in very truth
an awful night.

There is an antique chamber in an ancient house. Curious an
quaint carvings adorn the walls, and the large chimney-piece is
curiosity of itself. The ceiling is low, and a large bay window, from
roof to floor, looks to the west. The window is latticed, and filled
with curiously painted glass and rich stained pieces, which send in
a strange yet beautiful light, when sun or moon shines into the
apartment. There is but one portrait in that room, although the
walls seem panelled for the express purpose of containing a series of
pictures. That portrait is of a young man, with a pale face, a stately
brow, and a strange expression about the eyes, which no-one cared
to look on twice.

There is a stately bed in that chamber, of carved walnut wood is
it made, rich in design and elaborate in execution; one of those works
of art which owe their existence to the Elizabethan era. It is hung
with heavy silken and damask furnishing; nodding feathers are at its
corners – covered with dust are they, and they lend a funereal aspect
to the room. The floor is of polished oak.

God! how the hail dashes on the old bay window! Like an occasional discharge of mimic musketry, it comes clashing, beating, and
cracking upon the small panes; but they resist it – their small size
saves them; the wind, the hail, the rain, expend their fury in vain.

The bed in that old chamber is occupied. A creature formed in all
fashions of loveliness lies in a half-sleep upon that ancient couch –
a girl young and beautiful as a spring morning. Her long hair has
escaped from its confinement and streams over the blackened cover-
ings of the bedstead; she has been restless in her sleep, for the
clothing of the bed is in much confusion. One arm is over her head,
the other hangs nearly off the side of the bed near to which she lies.
A neck and bosom that would have formed a study for the rarest
sculptor that ever Providence gave genius to, were half disclosed.
She moaned slightly in her sleep, and once or twice the lips moved as
if in prayer – at least one might judge so, for the name of Him who
suffered for all came once faintly from them.

She has endured much fatigue, and the storm does not awaken
her; but it can disturb the slumbers it does not possess the power to
destroy entirely. The turmoil of the elements wakes the senses,
although it cannot entirely break the repose they have lapsed into.

Oh, what a world of witchery was in that mouth, slightly parted, and exhibiting within the pearly teeth that glistened even in the faint light that came from that bay window. How sweetly the long silken eyelashes lay upon the cheek. Now she moves, and one shoulder is entirely visible – whiter, fairer than the spotless clothing of the bed on which she lies, is the smooth skin of that fair creature, just budding into womanhood, and in that transition state which presents to us all the charms of the girl – almost of the child, with the more matured beauty and gentleness of advancing years.

Was that lightning? Yes – an awful, vivid, terrifying flash – then a roaring peal of thunder, as if a thousand mountains were rolling one over the other in the blue vault of Heaven! Who sleeps now in that ancient city? Not one living soul. The dread trumpet of eternity could not more effectually have awakened anyone.

The hail continues. The wind continues. The uproar of the elements seems at its height. Now she awakens – that beautiful girl on the antique bed; she opens those eyes of celestial blue, and a faint cry of alarm bursts from her lips. At least it is a cry which, amid the noise and turmoil without, sounds but faint and weak. She sits upon the bed and presses her hands upon her eyes. Heavens! what a wild torrent of wind, and rain, and hail! The thunder likewise seems intent upon awakening sufficient echoes to last until the next flash of forked lightning should again produce the wild concussion of the air. She murmurs a prayer – a prayer for those she loves best; the names of those dear to her gentle heart come from her lips; she weeps and prays; she thinks then of what devastation the storm must surely produce, and to the great God of Heaven she prays for all living things. Another flash – a wild, blue, bewildering flash of lightning streams across that bay window, for an instant bringing out every colour in it with terrible distinctness. A shriek bursts from the lips of the young girl, and then, with eyes fixed upon that window, which, in another moment, is all darkness, and with such an expression of terror upon her face as it had never before known, she trembled, and the perspiration of intense fear stood upon her brow.

'What – what was it?' she gasped; 'real, or a delusion? Oh, God, what was it? A figure tall and gaunt, endeavouring from the outside to unclasp the window. I saw it. That flash of lightning revealed it to me. It stood the whole length of the window.'

There was a lull of the wind. The hail was not falling so thickly – moreover, it now fell, what there was of it, straight, and yet a strange clattering sound came upon the glass of that long window. It could

not be a delusion – she is awake, and she hears it. What can produc
it? Another flash of lightning – another shriek – there could be no
no delusion.

A tall figure is standing on the ledge immediately outside the long
window. It is its fingernails upon the glass that produces the sound s
like the hail, now that the hail has ceased. Intense fear paralyses th
limbs of that beautiful girl. That one shriek is all she can utter – with
hands clasped, a face of marble, a heart beating so wildly in her bosom
that each moment it seems as if it would break its confines, eyes
distended and fixed upon the window, she waits, frozen with horror
The pattering and clattering of the nails continue. No word is spoken
and now she fancies she can trace the darker form of that figure
against the window, and she can see the long arms moving to and fro
feeling for some mode of entrance. What strange light is that which
now gradually creeps up into the air? Red and terrible – brighter
and brighter it grows. The lightning has set fire to a mill, and the
reflection of the rapidly consuming building falls upon that long
window. There can be no mistake. The figure is there, still feeling for
an entrance, and clattering against the glass with its long nails, that
appear as if the growth of many years had been untouched. She tries to
scream again but a choking sensation comes over her, and she cannot.
It is too dreadful – she tries to move – each limb seems weighed down
by tons of lead – she can but in a hoarse faint whisper –

'Help – help – help – help!'

And that one word she repeats like a person in a dream. The red
glare of the fire continues. It throws up the tall gaunt figure in hideous
relief against the long window. It shows, too, upon the one portrait
that is in the chamber, and that portrait appears to fix its eyes upon the
attempting intruder, while the flickering light from the fire makes it
look fearfully life-like. A small pane of glass is broken, and the form
from without introduces a long gaunt hand, which seems utterly destitute of flesh. The fastening is removed, and one-half of the window,
which opens like folding doors, is swung wide open upon its hinges.

And yet now she could not scream – she could not move. 'Help –
help! – help!' was all she could say. But, oh, that look of terror that
sat upon her face, it was dreadful – a look to haunt the memory for a
lifetime – a look to obtrude itself upon the happiest moments, and
turn them to bitterness.

The figure turns half round, and the light falls upon the face. It
is perfectly white – perfectly bloodless. The eyes look like polished
tin; the lips are drawn back, and the principal feature next to those

dreadful eyes is the teeth – the fearful-looking teeth – projecting like
those of some wild animal, hideously, glaringly white, and fang-like.
It approaches the bed with a strange, gliding movement. It clashes
together the long nails that literally appear to hang from the finger
ends. No sound comes from its lips. Is she going mad – that young
and beautiful girl exposed to so much terror? She has drawn up all
her limbs; she cannot even now say help. The power of articulation is
gone, but the power of movement has returned to her; she can draw
herself slowly along to the other side of the bed from that towards
which the hideous appearance is coming.

But her eyes are fascinated. The glance of a serpent could not have
produced a greater effect upon her than did the fixed gaze of those
awful, metallic-looking eyes that were bent on her face. Crouching
down so that the gigantic height was lost, and the horrible, pro-
truding, white face was the most prominent object, came on the
figure. What was it? – what did it want there? – what made it look so
hideous – so unlike an inhabitant of the earth, and yet to be on it?

Now she has got to the verge of the bed, and the figure pauses. It
seemed as if when it paused she lost the power to proceed. The
clothing of the bed was now clutched in her hands with unconscious
power. She drew her breath short and thick. Her bosom heaves,
and her limbs tremble, yet she cannot withdraw her eyes from that
marble-looking face. He holds her with his glittering eye.

The storm has ceased – all is still. The winds are hushed; the
church clock proclaims the hour of one: a hissing sound comes from
the throat of the hideous being, and he raises his long, gaunt arms –
the lips move. He advances. The girl places one small foot from the
bed on to the floor. She is unconsciously dragging the clothing with
her. The door of the room is in that direction – can she reach it?
Has she power to walk? – Can she withdraw her eyes from the face
of the intruder, and so break the hideous charm? God of Heaven!
is it real, or some dream so like reality as to nearly overturn the
judgment for ever?

The figure has paused again, and half on the bed and half out of it
that young girl lies trembling. Her long hair streams across the
entire width of the bed. As she has slowly moved along she has left it
streaming across the pillows. The pause lasted about a minute – oh,
what an age of agony. That minute was, indeed, enough for madness
to do its full work in.

With a sudden rush that could not be foreseen – with a strange
howling cry that was enough to awaken terror in every breast, the

figure seized the long tresses of her hair, and twining them round his bony hands he held her to the bed. Then she screamed – Heaven granted her then power to scream. Shriek followed shriek in rapid succession. The bed-clothes fell in a heap by the side of the bed – she was dragged by her long silken hair completely onto it again. Her beautifully rounded limbs quivered with the agony of her soul. The glassy, horrible eyes of the figure ran over that angelic form with a hideous satisfaction – horrible profanation. He drags her head to the bed's edge. He forces it back by the long hair still entwined in his grasp. With a plunge he seizes her neck in his fang-like teeth – a gush of blood, and a hideous sucking noise follows. *The girl has swooned, and the vampyre is at his hideous repast!*

[Young Ringwood – fiancé of the late Clara Crofton – has heard strange tales about nocturnal happenings in the village church. He suspects that his beloved may have become a vampyre (through contact with Varney) and decides to see for himself . . .]

Yes, it was twelve o'clock, that mysterious hour at which it is believed by many that

> Graves give up their dead,
> And many a ghost in churchyard decay,
> Rise from their cold, cold bed
> To make night horrible with wild vagary.

Twelve, that hour when all that is human feels a sort of irksome dread, as if the spirits of those who have gone from the great world were too near, loading the still night air with the murky vapours of the grave. A chilliness came over Ringwood and he fancied a strange kind of light was in the church, making objects more visible than in their dim and dusty outlines they had been before.

'Why do I tremble?' he said, 'why do I tremble? Clouds pass away from before the moon, that is all. Soon there may be a bright light here, and lo, all is still; I hear nothing but my own breathing; I see nothing but what is common and natural. Thank heaven, all will pass away in quiet. There will be no horror to recount – no terrific sight to chill my blood. Rest Clara, rest in Heaven.'

Ten minutes passed away, and there was no alarm; how wonderfully relieved was Ringwood. Tears came to his eyes, but they were the natural tears of regret, such as he had shed before for her who had gone from him to the tomb, and left no trace behind but in the hearts of those who loved her.

'Yes,' he said, mournfully, 'she has gone from me, but I love her still. Still does the fond remembrance of all that she was to me, linger at my heart. She is my own, my beautiful Clara, as she ever was, and as, while life remains, to me she ever will be.'

At the moment that he uttered these words a slight noise met his ears.

In an instant he sprang to his feet in the pulpit, and looked anxiously around him.

'What was that?' he said. 'What was that?'

All was still again, and he was upon the point of convincing himself that the noise was either some accidental one, or the creation of his own fancy, when it came again.

He had no doubt this time. It was a perceptible, scraping, strange sort of sound, and he turned his whole attention to the direction from whence it came. With a cold creeping chill through his frame, he saw that that direction was the one where was the family vault of the Croftons, the last home of her whom he held still in remembrance, and whose memory was so dear to him.

He felt the perspiration standing upon his brow, and if the whole world had been the recompense to him for moving away from where he was he could not have done so. All he could do was to gaze with bated breath and distended eyes upon the aisle of the church from whence the sound came.

That something of a terrific nature was now about to exhibit itself, and that the night would not go off without some terrible and significant adventure to make it remembered he felt convinced. All he dreaded was to think for a moment what it might be.

His thoughts ran on Clara, and he murmured forth in the most agonising accents –

'Anything – any sight but the sight of her. Oh, no, no, no!'

But it was not altogether the sight of her that he dreaded; oh no, it was the fact that the sight of her on such an occasion would bring the horrible conviction with it, that there was some truth in the dreadful apprehension that he had of the new state of things that had ensued regarding the after-death condition of that fair girl.

The noise increased each moment, and finally there was a sudden crash.

'She comes! She comes!' gasped Ringwood.

He grasped the front of the pulpit with a frantic violence, and then slowly and solemnly there crossed his excited vision a figure all clothed in white. Yes, white flowing vestments, and he knew by their fashion that they were not worn by the living, and that it was some inhabitant of the tomb that he now looked upon.

He did not see the face. No, that for a time was hidden from him, but his heart told him who it was. Yes, it was his Clara.

It was no dream. It was no vision of a too excited fancy, for until those palpable sounds, and that most fearfully palpable form crossed his sight, he was rather inclined to go the other way, and to fancy what the Sexton had reported was nothing but a delusion of his overwrought brain. Oh, that he could but for one brief moment have found himself deceived.

'Speak!' he gasped. 'Speak! speak!'

There was no reply.

'I conjure you, I pray you though the sound of your voice should hurl me to perdition – I implore you, speak.'

All was silent, and the figure in white moved on slowly but surely towards the door of the church, but ere it passed out, it turned for a moment, as if for the very purpose of removing from the mind of Ringwood any lingering doubt as to its identity.

He then saw the face, oh, so well known, yet so pale. It was Clara Crofton!

' 'Tis she! 'tis she!' was all he could say.

It seemed, too, as if some crevice in the clouds had opened at the moment, in order that he should with an absolute certainty see the countenance of that solemn figure, and then all was more than usually silent again. The door closed, and the figure was gone.

He rose in the pulpit, and clasped his hands. Irresolution seemed for a few moments to sway him to and fro, and then he rushed down into the body of the church.

'I'll follow it,' he cried, 'though it lead me to perdition. Yes, I'll follow it.'

He made his way to the door, and even as he went he shouted: 'Clara! Clara! Clara!'

He reached the threshold of the ancient church; he gazed around him distractedly, for he thought that he had lost all sight of the figure. No – no, even in the darkness and against the night sky, he saw it once again in its sad-looking death raiments. He dashed forward.

The moonbeams at this instant being freed from some dense clouds that had interposed between them and this world, burst forth with resplendant beauty.

There was not a tree, a shrub, nor a flower, but what was made distinct and manifest, and within the church, such was the almost unprecedented lustre of the beautiful planet, that even the inscriptions upon the old tablets and tombs were distinctly visible.

Such a refulgence lasted not many minutes, but while it did, it was most beautiful, and the gloom that followed it seemed doubly black.

'Stay, stay,' he shouted, 'yet a moment, Clara; I swear that what you are that will I be. Take me over to the tomb with you, say but that it is your dwelling-place, and I will make it mine, and declare it a very palace of the affections.'

The figure glided on.

It was in vain that he tried to keep up with it. It threaded the churchyard among the ancient tombs, with a gliding speed that soon distanced him, impeded, as he continually was, by some obstacle or another, owing to looking at the apparition he followed, instead of the ground before him.

Still, on he went, heedless whither he was conveyed, for he might be said to be dragged onward, so much were all his faculties both of mind and body intent upon following the apparition of his beloved.

Once, and once only, the figure paused, and seemed to be aware that it was followed, for it flitted round an angle made by one of the walls of the church, and disappeared from his eyes.

In another moment he had turned the same point.

'Clara! Clara!' he shouted. ''Tis I – you know my voice, Clara, Clara.'

She was not to be seen, and then the idea struck him that she must have re-entered the church, and he too, turned, and crossed the threshold. He lingered there for a moment or two, and the whole building echoed to the name of Clara as, with romantic eagerness, he called upon her by name to come forth to him.

Those echoes were the only reply.

Maddened – rendered desperate beyond all endurance, he went some distance into the building in search of her, and again he called.

It was in vain; she had eluded him, and with all the carefulness and all the energy and courage he had brought to bear upon that night's proceedings, he was foiled. Could anything be more agonising than this to such a man as Ringwood – he who loved her so, that he had not shrunk from her even in death, although she had so shrunk from him.

'I will find her – I will question her,' he cried. 'She shall not escape me; living or dead, she shall be mine. I will wait for her, even in the tomb.'

Before he carried out the intention of going actually into the vault to await her return, he thought he would take one more glance at the churchyard with the hope of seeing her there, as he could observe no indications of her presence in the church.

With this view he proceeded to the door, and emerged into the dim light. He called upon her again by name, and he thought he heard some faint sound in the church behind him. To turn and make a rush into the building was the work of a moment.

He saw something – it was black instead of white – a tall figure – it advanced towards him, and with great force, before he was aware that an attack was at all intended, it felled him to the ground.

The blow was so sudden, so unexpected, and so severe, that it struck him down in a moment before he could be aware of it. To be sure, he had arms with him, but the anxiety and agony of mind he endured that night, since seeing the apparition come from the tomb, had caused him to forget them.

[*Ringwood recovers. The assailant is, of course, none other than Varney, the Vampyre, protecting his bride. Meanwhile, the villagers – after a 'grand consultation at the ale-house' – have decided to take matters into their own hands . . .*]

'The vampyre, the vampyre,' cried the blacksmith, 'death to the vampyre – death and destruction to the vampyre.'

'Hurrah!' cried another, 'to the vaults – this way to Sir George Crofton's vault.'

There seemed to be little doubt now, but that this disorderly rabble would execute summary vengeance upon the supposed nocturnal disturber of the peace of the district.

Ever and anon, too, as these shouts of discord, and of threatening vengeance, rose upon the night air, there would come the distant muttering of thunder, for the storm had not yet ceased, although its worst fury had certainly passed away.

Dark and heavy clouds were sweeping up from the horizon, and it seemed to be tolerably evident that some heavy deluge of rain would eventually settle the fury of the elements, and reconcile the discord of wind and electricity.

Several of the rioters were provided with links and matches, so that in a few moments the whole interior of the church was brilliantly illuminated, while at the same time it presented a grotesque appearance, in consequence of the unsteady and wavering flame from the links, throwing myriads of dancing shadows upon the walls.

There would have been no difficulty under any ordinary circumstances in finding the entrance to the vault, where the dead of the

Crofton family should have lain in peace, but now since the large flagstone that covered the entrance to that receptacle of the grave was removed, it met their observation at once.

It was strange now to perceive how, for a moment, superstition having led them on so far, the same feeling should induce them to pause, ere they ventured to make their way down these gloomy steps.

It was a critical moment, and probably if any one or two had taken a sudden panic, the whole party might have left the church with precipitation, having done a considerable amount of mischief, and yet, as is so usual with rioters, having left their principal object un-accomplished.

The blacksmith put an end to this state of indecision, for, seizing a link from the man who was nearest to him, he darted down the steps, exclaiming as he did so –

'Whoever's afraid, need not follow me.'

This was a taunt they were not exactly prepared to submit to, and the consequence was, that in a very few moments the ancient and time-honoured vault of the Crofton's was more full of the living than of the dead.

The blacksmith laid his hand upon Clara's coffin.

'Here it is,' he said, 'I know the very pattern of the cloth, and the fashion of the nails. I saw it at Grigson's the undertaker's before it was taken to the Grange.'

'Is she there – is she there?' cried half a dozen voices at once.

Even the blacksmith hesitated a moment ere he removed the lid from the receptacle of death, but when he did so, and his eyes fell upon the face of the presumed vampyre, he seemed rejoiced to find in the appearances then exhibited some sort of justification for the act of violence of which already he had been the instigator.

'Here you are,' he said, 'look at the bloom upon her lips. Why, her cheeks are fresher and rosier than ever they were while she was alive; a vampyre my mates, this is a vampyre, or may I never break bread again; and now what's to be done?'

'Burn her, burn her,' cried several.

'Well,' said the blacksmith, 'mind, it's as you like. I've brought you here, and shown you what it is, and now you can do what you like, and of course I'll lend you a hand to do it.'

Anyone who had been very speculative in this affair, might have detected in these last words of the blacksmith, something like an inclination to creep out of the future consequences of what might next be done, while at the same time shame deterred him from exactly leaving his companions in the lurch.

After some suggestions then, and some argumentation as to the probability or possibility of interruption – the coffin itself was, with its sad and wretched occupant, lifted from the niche where it should have remained until that awful day when the dead shall rise for judgment, and carried up the steps into the church, from thence they passed into the graveyard, but scarcely had they done so, when the surcharged clouds burst over their heads, and the rain came down in perfect torrents.

The deluge was of so frightful and continuous a character, that they shrank back again beneath the shelter of the church porch, and there waited until its first fury had passed away.

Such an even-down storm seldom lasts long in our climate, and the consequence was that in about ten minutes the shower had so far subsided that although a continuous rain was falling it bore but a very distant comparison to what had taken place.

'How are we to burn the body on such a night as this?'

'Aye, how indeed?' said another; 'you could not so much as kindle a fire, and if you did, it would not live many minutes.'

'I'll tell you what to do at once,' said one who had as yet borne but a quiet part in the proceedings; 'I'll tell you what to do at once, for I saw it done myself; a vampyre is quite as secure buried in a cross-road with a stake through its body, as if you burned it in all the fires in the world; come on, the rain won't hinder you doing that.'

This was a suggestion highly approved of, and the more so as there was a cross-road close at hand, so that the deed could be done quick, and the parties dispersed to their respective homes, for already the exertion they had taken, and the rain that had fallen, had had a great effect in sobering them.

And even now the perilous and disgusting operation of destroying the body, by fire or any other way, might have been abandoned, had any one of the party suggested such a course – but the dread of a future imputation of cowardice kept all silent.

Once more the coffin was raised by four of the throng, and carried through the churchyard, which was now running in many little rivulets, in consequence of the rain. The cross-road was not above a quarter of a mile from the spot, and while those who were disengaged from carrying the body, were hurrying away to get spades and mattocks, the others walked through the rain, and finally paused at the place they thought suitable for that ancient superstitious rite, which it was thought would make the vampyre rest in peace.

At last a dozen men now arrived well armed with spades and picks, and they commenced the work of digging a deep, rather than a capacious grave, in silence.

A gloomy and apprehensive spirit seemed to come over the whole assemblage, and the probability is that this was chiefly owing to the fact that they now encountered no opposition, and that they were permitted unimpeded to accomplish a purpose which had never yet been attempted within the memory of any of the inhabitants of the place.

The grave was dug, and about two feet depth of soil was thrown in a huge mound upon the surface; the coffin was lowered, and there lay the corpse within that receptacle of poor humanity, unimprisoned by any lid, for that had been left in the vault, and awaiting the doom which they had decreed upon it, but which they now with a shuddering horror shrank from performing.

A hedge stake with a sharp point had been procured, and those who held it looked around them with terrified countenances, while the few links that had not been extinguished by the rain, shed a strange and lurid glare upon all objects.

'It must be done,' said the blacksmith; 'don't let it be said that we got thus far and then were afraid.'

'Do it then yourself,' said the man that held the stake; 'I dare not.'

'Aye, do,' cried several voices; 'you brought us here, why don't you do it – are you afraid after all your boasting?'

'Afraid – afraid of the dead; I'm not afraid of any of you that are alive, and it's not likely I'm going to be afraid of a dead body; you're a pretty set of cowards. I've no animosity against the girl, but I want that we shall all sleep in peace, and that our wives and children should not be disturbed nocturnally in their blessed repose. I'll do it if none of you'll do it, and then you may thank me afterwards for the act, although I suppose if I get into trouble I shall have you all turn tail upon me.'

'No, we won't – no, we won't.'

'Well, well, here goes, whether you do or not. I – I'll do it directly.'

'He shrinks,' cried one.

'No,' said another; 'he'll do it – now for it, stand aside.'

'Stand aside yourself – do you want to fall into the grave.'

The blacksmith shuddered as he held the stake in an attitude to pierce the body, and even up to that moment it seemed to be

a doubtful case, whether he would be able to accomplish his pur
pose or not; at length, when they all thought he was upon the
point of abandoning his design, and casting the stake away, he
thrust it with tremendous force through the body and the back of
the coffin.

The eyes of the corpse opened wide – the hands were clenched, and
a shrill, piercing shriek came from the lips – a shriek that was answered by as many as there were persons present, and then with pallid
fear upon their countenances they rushed headlong from the spot.

[*Epilogue – the final, total destruction of Varney,*
the Vampyre, and conclusion]

We extract from the *Algemeine Zeitung* the following most curious
story, the accuracy of which of course we cannot vouch for, but still
there is a sufficient air of probability about it to induce us to present
it to our readers.

'Late in the evening, about four days since, a tall and mel-
ancholy-looking stranger arrived, and put up at one of the
principal hotels at Naples. He was a most peculiar-looking man,
and considered by the persons of the establishment as about the
ugliest guest they had ever had within the walls of their place.

'In a short time he summoned the landlord, and the following
conversation ensued between him and the strange guest.

'I want,' said the stranger, 'to see all the curiosities of Naples,
and among the rest Mount Vesuvius. Is there any difficulty?'

'None,' replied the landlord, 'with a proper guide.'

A guide was soon secured, who set out with the adventurous
Englishman to make the ascent of the burning mountain.

They went on then until the guide did not think it quite prud-
ent to go any further, as there was a great fissure in the side of
the mountain, out of which a stream of lava was slowly issuing
and spreading itself in rather an alarming manner.

The ugly Englishman, however, pointed to a secure mode of
getting higher still, and they proceeded until they were very near
the edge of the crater itself. The stranger then took his purse
from his pocket and flung it to the guide saying –

'You can keep that for your pains, and for coming into some
danger with me. But the fact was, that I wanted a witness to an
act which I have set my mind upon performing.'

The guide says that these words were spoken with so much
calmness, that he verily believed the act mentioned as about to

be done was some scientific experiment of which he knew that the English were very fond, and he replied –

'Sir, I am only too proud to serve so generous and so distinguished a gentleman. In what way can I be useful?'

'You will make what haste you can,' said the stranger, 'from the mountain, inasmuch as it is covered with sulphurous vapours, inimical to human life, and when you reach the city you will cause to be published an account of my proceedings, and what I say. You will say that you accompanied Varney, the Vampyre to the crater of Mount Vesuvius and that, tired and disgusted with a life of horror, he flung himself in to prevent the possibility of a reanimation of his remains.'

Before, then, the guide could utter anything but a shriek, Varney took one tremendous leap, and disappeared into the burning mouth of the mountain.

The Curse of the Vourdalak

ALEXIS TOLSTOY

Before I start my story, I ask you to forgive me if, during the course of it, I find it necessary to speak about my love affairs more often than might seem appropriate for a man of my advanced age. But I assure you that they must be mentioned if you are to fully understand my story.

Now, having said that, I will begin by telling you that in the year 1759 I was madly in love with the beautiful Duchesse de Gramont. This passion, which I then believed to be deep and lasting, gave me no letup by day or night, and the Duchesse – as young girls often do – enjoyed adding to my torment by teasing me. So much so that in a moment of anger, I decided to ask for a diplomatic mission to the *hospodar* (prince) of Moldavia, who was then involved in negotiations with Versailles over a number of matters. My request was almost instantly granted.

The day before my departure I called on the Duchesse. She received me with less mockery than usual and could not hide her emotions as she said, 'D'Urfé – you are behaving like a madman, but I know you well enough to be sure that you will never go back on a decision, once taken. So I will only ask one thing of you. Accept this little cross as a token of my affection and wear it until you return. It is a family relic which we treasure a great deal.'

With gallantry that was perhaps misplaced at such a moment I kissed not the relic but the delightful hand which proffered it to me, and I fastened the cross around my neck – you can see it now. Since then, I have never been parted from it.

I will not bore you with the details of my journey nor with the observations that I made on the Hungarians and the Serbians, those poor and ignorant people who, enslaved as they were by the Turks, were brave and honest enough not to have forgotten either their dignity or their time-honoured independence. It's enough for me to tell you that having learned to speak a little Polish during my stay in

Warsaw, I soon had a working knowledge of Serbian as well – for these two languages, like Russian and Bohemian are, as you no doubt know very well, only branches of one and the same root, which is known as Slovonian.

Anyway, I knew enough to make myself understood. One day I arrived in a small village. I found those who lived in the house where I intended to stay in a state of confusion, which seemed to me all the more strange because it was a Sunday, a day when the Serbian people customarily devote themselves to different pleasures, such as dancing, shooting, wrestling and so on. I attributed the confusion of my hosts to some very recent misfortune and was about to withdraw when a man of about thirty, tall and impressive to look at, came up to me and shook me by the hand.

'Come in, come in stranger,' he said. 'Don't let yourself be put off by our sadness; you will understand it well enough when you know the cause.'

He then told me about how his old father (whose name was Gorcha), a man of wild and unmanageable temperament, had got up one morning and had taken down his long Turkish rifle from a rack on a wall.

'My children,' he had said to his two sons Georges and Pierre, 'I am going to the mountains to join a band of brave fellows who are hunting that dog Ali Bek.' (That was the name of a Turkish brigand who had been ravaging the countryside for some time.) 'Wait for me patiently for ten days and if I do not return on the tenth, arrange for a funeral mass to be said – for by then I will have been killed. But,' old Gorcha had added, looking very serious indeed, 'if, may God protect you, I should return after the ten days have passed, do not under any circumstances let me come in. I command you, if this should happen, to forget that I was once your father and to pierce me through the heart with an aspen stake, whatever I might say or do, for then I would no longer be human. I would be a cursed *vourdalak*, come to suck your blood.'

It is important at this stage to tell you, that the *vourdalaks* (the name given to vampires by Slavic peoples) are, according to local folklore, dead bodies who rise from their graves to suck the blood of the living. In this respect they behave like all types of vampire, but they have one other characteristic which makes them even more terrifying. The *vourdalaks* prefer to suck the blood of their closest relatives and their most intimate friends; once dead, the victims become vampires themselves. People have claimed that entire villages in Bosnia and Hungary have been transformed into *vourdalaks* in this way. The Abbé Augustin Calmet in his strange book on apparitions cites many horrible examples.

Apparently, commissions have been appointed many times by German emperors to study alleged epidemics of vampirism. These commissions collected many eye-witness accounts. They exhumed bodies, which they found to be sated with blood, and ordered them to be burned in the public square after staking them through the heart. Magistrates who witnessed these executions have stated on oath that they heard blood-curdling shrieks coming from these corpses at the moment the executioner hammered his sharpened stake into their hearts. They have formal depositions to this effect and have corroborated them with signatures and with oaths on the Holy Book.

With this information as background, it should be easier for you to understand the effect that old Gorcha's words had on his sons. Both of them went down on their bended knees and begged him to let them go in his place. But instead of replying he had turned his back on them and had set out for the mountains, singing the refrain of an old ballad. The day I arrived in the village was the very day that Gorcha had fixed for his return, so I had no difficulty understanding why his children were so anxious.

This was a good and honest family. Georges, the older of the two sons, was rugged and weatherbeaten. He seemed to me a serious and decisive man. He was married with two children. His brother Pierre, a handsome youth of about eighteen, looked rather less tough and appeared to be the favourite of a younger sister called Sdenka, who was a genuine Slavic beauty. In addition to the striking beauty of her features, a distant resemblance to the Duchesse de Gramont struck me especially. She had a distinctive line on her forehead which in all my experience I have found only on these two people. This line did not seem particularly attractive at first glance, but became irresistible when you had seen it a few times.

Perhaps I was still very naive. Perhaps this resemblance, combined with a lively and charmingly simple disposition, was really irresistible. I do not know. But I had not been talking with Sdenka for more than two minutes when I already felt for her an affection so tender that it threatened to become something deeper still if I stayed in the village much longer.

We were all sitting together in front of the house, around a table laden with cheeses and dishes of milk. Sdenka was sewing; her sister-in-law was preparing supper for her children, who were playing in the sand; Pierre, who was doing his best to appear at ease, was whistling as he cleaned a *yagatan*, or long Turkish knife. Georges was leaning on the table with his head in his hands and looking for signs of movement on the great highway. He was silent.

For my part, I was profoundly affected by the general atmosphere of sadness and, in a fit of sadness, looked up at the evening clouds which shrouded the dying sun and at the silhouette of a monastery, which was half hidden from my view by a black pine forest.

This monastery, as I subsequently discovered, had been very famous in former times on account of a miraculous icon of the Virgin Mary which, according to legend, had been carried away by the angels and set down on an old oak tree. But at the beginning of the previous century the Turks had invaded this part of the country; they had butchered the monks and pillaged the monastery. Only the walls and a small chapel had survived; an old hermit continued to say mass there. This hermit showed travellers around the ruins and gave hospitality to pilgrims who, as they walked from one place of devotion to another, liked to rest a while at the Monastery of Our Lady of the Oak. As I have said, I didn't learn all this until much later, for on this particular evening my thoughts were very far from the archaeology of Serbia. As often happens when one allows one's imagination free rein, I was musing on past times – on the good old days of my childhood; on the beauties of France that I had left for a wild and faraway country. I was thinking about the Duchesse de Gramont and – why not admit it? – I was also thinking about several other ladies, the memory of whose beauty had quietly entered my thoughts in the train of the beautiful Duchesse. I had soon forgotten all about my hosts and their terrible anxiety.

Suddenly Georges broke the silence. 'Wife,' he said, 'at exactly what time did the old man set out?'

'At eight o'clock. I can clearly remember hearing the monastery bell.'

'Well, that's all right then,' said Georges. 'It cannot be more than half past seven.' And he again looked for signs of movement on the great highway which led to the dark forest.

I have forgotten to tell you that when the Serbians suspect that someone has become a vampire, they avoid mentioning him by name or speaking of him directly, for they think that this would be an invitation for him to leave his tomb. So Georges, when he spoke of his father, now referred to him simply as 'the old man'.

There was a brief silence. Suddenly one of the children started tugging at Sdenka's apron and crying, 'Auntie, when will grandpapa be coming back?'

The only reply he got to this untimely question was a hard slap from Georges. The child began to cry, but his little brother, who by now was surprised and frightened, wanted to know more. 'Father, why are we not allowed to talk about grandpapa?'

Another slap shut him up firmly. Both children now began to howl and the whole family made a sign of the cross. Just at that moment, I heard the sound of the monastery bell. As the first chime of the eight was ringing in our ears, we saw a human figure coming out of the darkness of the forest and approaching us.

'It is he, God be praised,' cried Sdenka, her sister-in-law and Pierre all at once.

'May the good God protect us,' said Georges solemnly. 'How are we to know if the ten days have passed or not?'

Everyone looked at him, terror-struck. But the human form came closer and closer. It was a tall old man with a silver moustache and a pale, stern face; he was dragging himself along with the aid of a stick. The closer he got, the more shocked Georges looked. When the new arrival was a short distance from us, he stopped and stared at his family with eyes that seemed not to see – they were dull, glazed, deep sunk in their sockets.

'Well, well,' he said in a dead voice, 'will no-one get up to welcome me? What is the meaning of this silence, can't you see I am wounded?'

I saw that the old man's left side was dripping with blood.

'Go and help your father,' I said to Georges. 'And you, Sdenka, offer him some refreshment. Look at him – he is almost collapsing from exhaustion!'

'Father,' said Georges, going up to Gorcha, 'show me your wound. I know all about such things and I can take care of it . . .'

He was just about to take off the old man's coat when Gorcha pushed his son aside roughly and clutched at his body with both hands. 'You are too clumsy,' he said, 'leave me alone . . . Now you have hurt me.'

'You must be wounded in the heart,' cried Georges, turning pale. 'Take off your coat, take it off. You must, I insist.'

The old man pulled himself up to his full height. 'Take care,' he said in a sepulchral voice. 'If you so much as touch me, I shall curse you.'

Pierre rushed between Georges and his father. 'Leave him alone,' he said. 'Can't you see that he's suffering?'

'Do not cross him,' George's wife added. 'You know he has never tolerated that.'

At that precise moment we saw a flock of sheep returning from pasture raising a cloud of dust as it made its way towards the house. Whether the dog which was escorting the flock did not recognise its own master, or whether it had some other reason for acting as it did, as soon as it caught sight of Gorcha it stopped dead, hackles raised, and began to howl as if it had seen a ghost.

'What is wrong with that dog?' said the old man, looking more and more furious. 'What is going on here? Have I become a stranger in my own house? Have ten days spent in the mountains changed me so much that even my own dogs do not recognise me?'

'Did you hear that?' said Georges to his wife.

'What of it?'

'He admits that the ten days *have been spent.*'

'Surely not, for he has come back to us within the appointed time.'

'I know what has to be done.'

The dog continued to howl. 'I want that dog destroyed!' cried Gorcha. 'Well, did you hear me?'

Georges made no move, but Pierre got up with tears in his eyes, and grabbing his father's rifle, he aimed at the dog, fired, and the creature rolled over in the dust.

'That was my favourite dog,' he said sulkily. 'I don't know why father wanted it to be destroyed.'

'Because it deserved to be,' bellowed Gorcha. 'Come on now, it's cold and I want to go inside.'

While all this was going on outside, Sdenka had been preparing a cordial for the old man consisting of pears, honey and raisins, laced with *eau de vie*, but her father pushed it aside with disgust. He seemed equally disgusted by the plate of mutton with rice that Georges offered him. Gorcha shuffled over to the fireplace, muttering gibberish from behind clenched teeth.

A pine-log fire crackled in the grate and its flickering light seemed to give life to the pale, emaciated features of the old man. Without the fire's glow, his features could have been taken for those of a corpse.

Sdenka sat down beside him. 'Father,' she said, 'you do not wish to eat anything, you do not wish to rest; perhaps you feel up to telling us about your adventures in the mountains.'

By suggesting that, the young girl knew that she was touching her father's most sensitive spot, for the old man loved to talk of wars and adventures. The trace of a smile creased his colourless lips, although his eyes showed no animation, and as he began to stroke his daughter's beautiful blonde hair, he said: 'Yes, my daughter, yes, Sdenka, I would like to tell you all about my adventures in the mountains – but that must wait for another time, for I am too tired today. I can tell you, though, that Ali Bek is dead and that he perished by my hand. If anyone doubts my word,' continued the old man, looking hard at his two sons, 'here is the proof.'

He undid a kind of sack which was slung behind his back, and pulled out a foul, bloody head which looked about as pale as his own! We all recoiled in horror, but Gorcha gave it to Pierre.

'Take it,' he said, 'and nail it above the door, to show all who pass by that Ali Bek is dead and that the roads are free of brigands – except, of course, for the Sultan's janissaries!'

Pierre was disgusted. But he obeyed. 'Now I understand why that poor dog was howling,' he said. 'He could smell dead flesh!'

'Yes, he could smell dead flesh,' murmured Georges; he had gone out of the room without anyone noticing him and had returned at that moment with something in his hand which he placed carefully against a wall. It looked to me like a sharpened stake.

'Georges,' said his wife, almost in a whisper, 'I hope you do not intend to . . . '

'My brother,' Sdenka added anxiously, 'what do you mean to do? No, no – surely you're not going to . . . '

'Leave me alone,' replied Georges, 'I know what I have to do and I will only do what is absolutely necessary.'

While all this had been going on, night had fallen, and the family went to bed in a part of the house which was separated from my room only by a narrow partition. I must admit that what I had seen that evening had made an impression on my imagination. My candle was out; the moonlight shone through a little window near my bed and cast blurred shadows on the floor and walls. I wanted to go to sleep but I could not. I thought this was because the moonlight was so clear; but when I looked for something to curtain the window, I could find nothing suitable. Then I overheard confused voices from the other side of the partition. I tried to make out what was being said.

'Go to sleep, wife,' said Georges. 'And you Pierre, and you Sdenka. Do not worry, I will watch over you.'

'But Georges,' replied his wife, 'it is I who should keep watch over you – you worked all last night and you must be tired. In any case, I ought to be staying awake to watch over our eldest boy. You know he has not been well since yesterday!'

'Be quiet and go to sleep,' said Georges. 'I will keep watch for both of us.'

'Brother,' put in Sdenka in her sweetest voice, 'there is no need to keep watch at all. Father is already asleep – he seems calm and peaceful enough.'

'Neither of you understands what is going on,' said Georges in a voice which forestalled any argument. 'Go to sleep I tell you, and let me keep watch.'

There followed a long silence. Soon my eyelids grew heavy and sleep began to take possession of my senses.

I thought I saw the door of my room opening slowly, and old Gorcha standing in the doorway. Actually, I did not so much see as *feel* his presence, as there was only darkness behind him. I felt his dead eyes trying to penetrate my deepest thoughts as they watched the movement of my breathing. One step forward, then another. Then, with extreme care, he began to walk towards me, with a wolflike motion. Finally he leaped forward. Now he was right beside my bed. I was absolutely terrified, but somehow managed not to move. The old man leaned over me and his waxen face was so close to mine that I could feel his corpselike breath. Then, with a superhuman effort, I managed to wake up, soaked in perspiration.

There was nobody in my room, but as I looked towards the window I could distinctly see old Gorcha's face pressed against the glass from outside, staring at me with his sunken eyes. By sheer willpower I stopped myself from crying out and I had the presence of mind to stay lying down, just as if I had seen nothing out of the ordinary. Luckily, the old man was only making sure that I was asleep, for he made no attempt to come in, and after staring at me long enough to satisfy himself, he moved away from the window and I could hear his footsteps in the neighbouring room. Georges was sound asleep and snoring loudly enough to wake the dead.

At that moment the child coughed, and I could make out Gorcha's voice. 'You are not asleep, little one?'

'No, grandpapa,' replied the child, 'And I would so like to talk to you.'

'So, you would like to talk to me, would you? And what would we talk about?'

'We would talk about how you fought the Turks. I would love to fight the Turks!'

'I thought you might, child, and I brought back a little present for you. I'll give it to you tomorrow.'

'Grandpapa, grandpapa, give it to me now.'

'But little one, why didn't you talk to me about this when it was daytime?'

'Because papa would not let me.'

'He is careful, your papa . . . So you really would like to have your little present?'

'Oh yes, I would love that, but not here, for papa might wake up.'

'Where then?'

'If we go outside, I promise to be good and not to make any noise at all.'

I thought I could hear Gorcha chuckle as the child got out of bed. I didn't believe in vampires, but the nightmare had preyed on my nerves, and just in case I should have to reproach myself in the morning I got up and banged my fist against the partition. It was enough to wake up the seven sleepers, but there was no sign of life from the family. I threw myself against the door, determined to save the child – but it was locked from the outside and I couldn't shift the bolts. While I was trying to force it open, I saw the old man pass by my window with the little child in his arms.

'Wake up! Wake up!' I cried at the top of my voice, as I shook the partition. Even then only Georges showed any sign of movement.

'Where is the old man?' he murmured blearily.

'Quick,' I yelled, 'he's just taken away your child.'

With one kick, Georges broke down the door of his room – which like mine had been locked from the outside – and he sprinted in the direction of the dark forest. At last I succeeded in waking Pierre, his sister-in-law and Sdenka. We all assembled in front of the house and after a few minutes' anxious waiting we saw Georges return from the dark forest with his son. The child had apparently passed out on the highway, but he was soon revived and didn't seem to be any more ill than before. After questioning him we discovered that his grand-papa had not, in fact, done him any harm; they had apparently gone out together to talk undisturbed, but once outside the child had lost consciousness without remembering why. Gorcha himself had disappeared.

As you can imagine, no-one could sleep for the rest of that night. The next day, I learned that the river Danube, which cut across the highway about a quarter of a league from the village, had begun to freeze over; drift ice now blocked my route. This often happens in these parts, some time between the end of autumn and the beginning of spring. Since the highway was expected to be blocked for some days, I could not think of leaving. In any case, even if I could have left, curiosity – as well as a more powerful emotion – would have held me back. The more I saw Sdenka, the more I felt I was falling in love with her.

I am not among those who believe in love at first sight, but I do believe that there are occasions when love develops more quickly than is usual. Sdenka's strange beauty, her singular resemblance to the Duchesse de Gramont, the fascinating line on her forehead, like that for which I had been prepared to kill myself at least twenty times in France: all this, combined with the incredible, mysterious situation in which I found myself . . . everything helped to nurture in me a passion which, in other circumstances, would perhaps have proved itself to be more vague and passing.

During the course of the day I overheard Sdenka talking to her younger brother. 'What do you think of all this?' she asked. 'Do you also suspect our father?'

'I dare not suspect him,' replied Pierre, 'especially since the child insists that he came to no harm. And as for father's disappearance, you know that he never used to explain his comings and goings.'

'I know,' said Sdenka. 'All the more reason why we must think about saving him, for you know that Georges . . . '

'Yes, yes, I know. It would be useless to talk him out of it. We can at least hide the stake. He certainly won't go out looking for another one, since there is not a single aspen tree this side of the mountains.'

'Yes, let's hide the stake – but don't mention it to the children, for they might chatter about it with Georges listening.'

'We must take care not to let that happen,' said Pierre. And they went their separate ways.

At nightfall we had still discovered nothing about old Gorcha. As on the previous night I was lying on my bed, and the moonlight again stopped me from going to sleep. When at last sleep began to confuse my thoughts, I again felt, as if by instinct, that the old man was coming towards me. I opened my eyes and saw his waxen face pressed against my window.

This time I wanted to get up but could not. All my limbs seemed to be paralysed. After taking a good long look at me, the old man disappeared. I heard him wandering around the house and tapping gently on the window of Georges's room. The child turned over on his bed and moaned as he dreamed. After several minutes' silence the tapping on the window resumed. Then the child groaned once again and woke up.

'Is that you grandpapa?' he asked.

'It is me,' replied a dead voice, 'and I have brought you your little present.'

'But I dare not go outside. Papa has forbidden it.'

'There is no need to go outside; just open the window and embrace me!'

The child got up and I could hear him opening the window. Then somehow finding the strength, I leaped to the foot of my bed and ran over to the partition. I struck it hard with my fist. In a few seconds Georges was on his feet. I heard him mutter an oath. His wife screamed. In no time at all the whole household had gathered around the lifeless child. Just as on the previous occasion, there was no sign of Gorcha. We tried carefully to revive the child, but he was very weak and breathed with difficulty. The poor little chap had no idea why he had passed out. His mother and Sdenka thought it was because of the shock of being caught talking with his grandpapa. I said nothing. However, by now the child seemed to be more calm and everybody except Georges went back to bed.

At daybreak, I overheard Georges waking his wife and whispering to her. Sdenka joined them and I could hear both the women sobbing. The child was dead.

Of the family's despair, the less said the better. Strangely enough no-one blamed the child's death on old Gorcha – at least not openly. Georges sat in silence, but his expression, always gloomy, now became terrible to behold. Two days passed and there was still no sign of the old man. On the night of the third day – the day of the child's burial – I thought I heard footsteps all around the house and an old man's voice which called out the name of the dead child's brother. For a split second I also thought I saw Gorcha's face pressed against my window, but I couldn't be sure if I was imagining it or not, for the moon was veiled by cloud that night. Nevertheless I considered it my duty to mention this apparition to Georges. He questioned the child, who replied that he *had* in fact heard grandpapa calling and had also seen him looking in through the window. Georges strictly charged his son to wake him up if the old man should appear again.

All these happenings did not prevent my passion for Sdenka from developing more and more each day. In the daytime, I couldn't talk to her alone. At night, the mere thought that I would shortly have to leave broke my heart. Sdenka's room was only separated from mine by a kind of corridor which led to the road on one side and a courtyard on the other. When the whole family had gone to bed, I decided to go for a short walk in the fields to ease my mind. As I walked along the corridor I saw that Sdenka's door was slightly open. Instinctively, I stopped and listened. The rustling of her dress, a sound I knew well, made my heart pound against my chest. Then I heard her singing softly. She was singing about a Serbian king who was saying farewell to his lady before going to the war.

'Oh my young Poplar,' said the old king, 'I am going to the war and you will forget me.

'The trees which grow beneath the mountain are slender and pliant, but they are nothing beside your young body!

'The berries of the rowan tree which sway in the wind are red, but your lips are more red than the berries of the rowan tree!

'And I am like an old oak stripped of leaves, and my beard is whiter than the foam of the Danube!

'And you will forget me, oh my soul, and I will die of grief, for the enemy will not dare to kill the old King!'

The beautiful lady replied: 'I swear to be faithful to you and never to forget you. If I should break my oath, come to me after your death and drink all my heart's blood!'

And the old king said: 'So be it!'

And he set off for the war. Soon the beautiful lady forgot him . . . !

At this point Sdenka paused, as if she was frightened to finish the ballad. I could restrain myself no longer. That voice – so sweet, so expressive – was the voice of the Duchesse de Gramont . . . Without pausing to think, I pushed open the door and went in. Sdenka had just taken off her knitted jacket (of a kind often worn by women in those regions). All she was wearing was a nightgown of red silk, embroidered with gold, held tight against her body by a simple, brightly coloured belt. Her fine blonde hair hung loose over her shoulders. She looked more beautiful than ever. She did not seem upset by my sudden entry, but she was confused and blushed slightly.

'Oh,' she said, 'why have you come? What will the family think of me if we are discovered?'

'Sdenka, my soul, do not be frightened! Everyone is asleep. Only the cricket in the grass and the mayfly in the air can hear what I have to say to you.'

'Oh my friend, leave me, leave me! If my brother should discover us I am lost!'

'Sdenka, I will not leave you until you have promised to love me for ever, as the beautiful lady promised the king in your ballad. Soon I will have to leave . . . Who knows when we will see each other again? Sdenka, I love you more than my soul, more than my salvation . . . my life's blood is yours . . . may I not be granted one hour with you in return?'

'Many things can happen in an hour,' said Sdenka calmly. But she did let her hand slip into mine.

'You do not know my brother,' she continued, beginning to tremble. 'I fear he will discover us.'

'Calm yourself, my darling Sdenka. Your brother is exhausted from watching late into the night; he has been lulled to sleep by the wind rustling in the trees; heavy is his sleep, long is the night and I only ask to be granted one hour – then, farewell, perhaps for ever!'

'Oh no, no, not for ever!' cried Sdenka; then she recoiled, as if frightened by the sound of her own voice.

'Oh Sdenka, I see only you, I hear only you; I am no longer master of my own destiny; a superior strength commands my obedience. Forgive me, Sdenka!' Like a madman I clutched her to my heart.

'You are no friend to me,' she cried, tearing herself from my embrace and rushing to another part of the room. I do not know what I said to her then, for I was as alarmed as she was by my own forwardness, not because such boldness had failed me in the past – far from it – but because in spite of my passion, I could not help having a sincere respect for Sdenka's innocence. It is true that I had used the language of gallantry with this girl at first (a language which did not seem to displease the society ladies of the time) but I was now ashamed of these empty phrases and renounced them when I saw that the young girl was too naive to comprehend fully what I meant by them. I stood before her, at a loss as to what to say, when suddenly she began to tremble and look towards the window, terror-struck. I followed her gaze and clearly saw the corpse-like face of Gorcha, staring at us from outside.

At precisely that moment, I felt a heavy hand on my shoulder.

I froze. It was Georges. 'What are you doing here?' he snapped.

Embarrassed by his tone of voice, I simply pointed towards his father, who was still staring at us through the window – but he disappeared the moment Georges turned to look at him.

'I heard the old man and came to warn your sister,' I stammered.

Georges looked me straight in the eye, as if trying to read my innermost thoughts. Then he took me by the arm, led me to my room and left, without a single word.

The next day the family had gathered in front of the house, around a table laden with jugs of milk and cakes.

'Where is the child?' said Georges.

'In the courtyard,' replied his wife. 'He is playing his favourite game, imagining that he is fighting the Turks single-handed.'

No sooner had she said these words, than to our amazement we saw the tall figure of Gorcha walking slowly towards us from out of the dark forest. He sat at the table just as he had done the day I arrived.

'Father, we welcome you,' murmured Georges's wife in a hoarse voice.

'We welcome you, father,' whispered Sdenka and Pierre in unison.

'My father,' said Georges firmly, turning pale, 'we are waiting for you to say Grace!'

The old man glared at him and turned away.

'Yes . . . Grace – say it now!' repeated Georges, crossing himself. 'Say it this instant, or by St George . . . '

Sdenka and her sister-in-law threw themselves at the old man's feet and begged him to say Grace.

'No, no, no,' said the old man. 'He has no right to speak to me in that way, and if he continues, I will curse him!'

Georges got up and rushed into the house. He returned almost immediately, looking furious. 'Where is that stake?' he yelled. 'Where have you hidden it?'

Sdenka and Pierre looked at each other.

'Corpse!' Georges shouted at the old man. 'What have you done with my elder boy? Why have you killed my little child? Give me back my son, you creature of the grave!'

As he said this, he became more and more pale and his eyes began to burn with fury. The old man simply glared at him.

'The stake, the stake,' yelled Georges. 'Whoever has hidden it must answer for all the evils which will befall us!'

At this moment we heard the excited laughter of the younger child. We saw him galloping towards us on a wooden horse, or rather on a long aspen stake, shrieking the Serbian battle cry at the top of his voice. Georges's eyes lit up, as he realised what was happening. He grabbed the stake from the child and threw himself at his father. The old man let out a fearful groan and began to sprint towards the dark forest as if possessed by demons. Georges raced after him across the fields, and soon they were both out of sight.

It was after sunset when Georges returned to the house. He was as pale as death; his hair stood on end. He sat down by the fireside, and I could hear his teeth chattering. No-one could pluck up the courage to question him. By about the time the family normally went to bed he seemed to be more his usual self and, taking me to one side, said to me quite calmly: 'My dear guest, I have been to the river. The ice has gone, the road is clear – nothing now prevents you from leaving. There is no need,' he added, glancing at Sdenka, 'to take your leave of my family. Through me, the family wishes you all the happiness you could desire and I hope that you will have some happy memories of the time you have spent with us. Tomorrow at daybreak, you will find your horse saddled and your guide ready to escort you. Farewell. Think about your host from time to time, and forgive him if your stay has not been as carefree as he would have liked.'

As he said this, even Georges's rough features looked almost friendly. He led me to my room and shook my hand for one last time. Then he began to tremble and his teeth chattered as if he were suffering from the cold.

Now I was alone, I had no thoughts of going to sleep – as you can imagine. Other things were on my mind. I had loved many times in my life, and had experienced the whole range of passions – tenderness, jealousy, fury – but never, not even when I left the Duchesse de Gramont, had I felt anything like the sadness that I felt in my heart at that moment. Before sunrise, I changed into my travelling clothes, hoping to have a few words with Sdenka before I departed. But Georges was waiting for me in the hall. There was no chance of my seeing her again.

I leaped into the saddle and spurred on my horse. I made a resolution to return from Jassy via this village, and although that might be some time hence, the thought made me feel easier in my mind. It was some consolation for me to imagine in advance all the details of my return. But this pleasant reverie was soon shattered. My horse shied away from something and nearly had me out of the saddle. The animal stopped dead, dug in its forelegs and began to snort wildly as if some danger was nearby. I looked around anxiously and saw something moving about a hundred paces away. It was a wolf digging in the ground. Sensing my presence, the wolf ran away; digging my spurs into the horse's flanks, I managed with difficulty to get him to move forward. It was then that I realised that on the spot where the wolf had been standing, there was a freshly dug grave. I seem to remember also that the end of a stake protruded a few inches out of the ground where the wolf had been digging. However, I do not swear to this, for I rode away from that place as fast as I could.

My reasons for going to Jassy kept me there for much longer than I expected – well over six months, in fact. What can I say to justify my conduct during that time? It is a sad fact, but a fact nonetheless, that there are very few emotions in this life which can stand the test of time. The success of my negotiations, which were very well received in Versailles – politics, in a word, vile politics, a subject which has become so boring to us in recent times – preoccupied my thoughts and dimmed the memory of Sdenka. In addition, from the moment I arrived, the wife of the hospodar, a very beautiful lady, did me the honour of receiving my attentions, singling me out from among all the other young foreigners who were staying in Jassy. Like me, she had been brought up to believe in the principles of gallantry; the mere thought that I should rebuff the advances of such a beautiful lady stirred up my blood. So I received her advances with courtesy, and since I was there to represent the interests and rights of France, I made a start by representing those of her husband the hospodar as well.

When I was recalled home, I left by the same road I had ridden to Jassy. I no longer even thought about Sdenka or her family, but one evening when I was riding in the countryside, I heard a bell ringing the eight o'clock chime. I seemed to recognise that sound and my guide told me that it came from a nearby monastery. I asked him the name: it was the monastery of Our Lady of the Oak. I galloped ahead and in no time at all we had reached the monastery gate. The old hermit welcomed us and led us to his hostel.

The number of pilgrims staying there put me off the idea of spending the night at the hostel, and I asked if there was any accommodation available in the village.

'You can stay where you like in the village,' replied the old hermit with a gloomy sigh. 'Thanks to that devil Gorcha, there are plenty of empty houses!'

'What on earth do you mean?' I asked. 'Is old Gorcha still alive?'

'Oh no, he's well and truly buried with a stake through his heart! But he rose from the grave to suck the blood of Georges's little son. The child returned one night and knocked on the door, crying that he was cold and wanted to come home. His foolish mother, although she herself had been present at his burial, did not have the strength of mind to send him back to the cemetery, so she opened the door. He threw himself at her throat and sucked away her life's blood. After she bad been buried, she in turn rose from the grave to suck the blood of her second son, then the blood of her husband, then the blood of her brother-in-law. They all went the same way.'

'And Sdenka?'

'Oh, she went mad with grief; poor, poor child, do not speak to me of her!'

The old hermit had not really answered my question, but I did not have the heart to repeat it. He crossed himself. 'Vampirism is contagious,' he said after a pause. 'Many families in the village have been afflicted by it, many families have been completely destroyed, and if you take my advice you will stay in my hostel tonight; for even if the *vourdalaks* of the village do not attack you, they will terrify you so much that you hair will have turned white before I ring the bells for morning mass.

'I am only a poor and simple monk,' he continued, 'but the generosity of passing travellers gives me enough to provide for their needs. I can offer you fresh country cheese and sweet plums which will make your mouth water; I also have some flagons of Tokay wine which are every bit as good as those which grace the cellars of His Holiness the Patriarch!'

The old hermit seemed to be behaving more like an innkeeper than a poor and simple monk. I decided he had told me some old wives' tales about the village in order to make me feel grateful enough for his hospitality to show my appreciation in the usual way, by giving the holy man enough to provide for the needs of passing travellers. In any case, the word terror has always had the effect on me that a battle-cry has on a war horse. I would have been thoroughly ashamed of myself if I had not set out immediately to see for myself. But my guide, who was less enthusiastic about the idea, asked my permission to stay in the hostel. This I willingly granted.

It took me about half an hour to reach the village. It was deserted. No lights shone through the windows, no songs were being sung. I rode past many houses that I knew, all as silent as the grave. Finally I reached Georges's. Whether I was being sentimental or just rash, I don't know, but it was there I decided to spend the night. I got off my horse, and banged on the gate. Still no sign of life. I pushed the gate and the hinges creaked eerily as it slowly opened. Then I crept into the courtyard. In one of the outhouses I found enough oats to last the night, so I left my horse tethered there, still saddled, and strode towards the main house. Although all the rooms were deserted, no doors were locked. Sdenka's room had been occupied only a few hours before. Some of her clothes were draped carelessly over the bed. A few pieces of jewellery that I had given her, including a small enamel cross from Budapest, lay on her table, sparkling in the moonlight. Even though my love for her was a thing of the past, I must admit that my heart was heavy. Nevertheless, I wrapped myself up in my cloak and stretched out on her bed. Soon I was asleep. I cannot recall everything, but I do remember that I dreamed of Sdenka, as beautiful, as simple and as loving as she had been when first I met her. I remember also feeling ashamed of my selfishness and my inconstancy. How could I have abandoned that poor child who loved me? How could I have forgotten her? Then her image became confused with that of the Duchesse de Gramont and I saw only one person. I threw myself at Sdenka's feet and begged her forgiveness. From the depths of my being, from the depths of my soul came an indescribable feeling of melancholy and of joy.

I lay there dreaming, until I was almost awakened by a gentle musical sound, like the rustling of a cornfield in a light breeze. I heard the sweet rustling of the corn and the music of singing birds, the rushing of a waterfall and the whispering of trees. Then I realised that all these sounds were merely the swishing of a woman's dress and I opened my eyes. There was Sdenka standing beside my bed. The moon was shining so brightly that I could distinguish every single feature which had been so dear to me and which my dream made me love again as if for the first time. Sdenka seemed more beautiful, and somehow more mature. She was dressed as she had been when last I saw her alone: a simple nightgown of red silk, gold embroidered, and a coloured belt, clinging tightly above her hips.

'Sdenka!' I cried, sitting up. 'Is it really you, Sdenka?'

'Yes, it is me,' she replied in a sweet, sad voice. 'It is that same Sdenka you have forgotten. Why did you not return sooner? Everything is finished now; you must leave; a moment longer and you are lost! Farewell my friend, farewell for ever!'

'Sdenka – you have seen so much unhappiness they say! Come, let us talk, let us ease your pain!'

'Oh, my friend, you must not believe everything they say about us; but leave me, leave me now, for if you stay a moment longer you are doomed.'

'Sdenka, what are you afraid of? Can you not grant me an hour, just one hour to talk with you?'

Sdenka began to tremble and her whole being seemed to undergo a strange transformation. 'Yes,' she said, 'one hour, just one hour, the same hour you begged of me when you came into this room and heard me singing the ballad of the old king. Is that what you mean? So be it, I will grant you one hour! But no, no!' she cried, as if fighting her inclinations, 'leave me, go away – leave now, I tell you! Fly, while you still have a chance!'

Her features were possessed with a savage strength. I could not understand why she should be saying these things, but she was so beautiful that I determined to stay, whatever she said. At last she surrendered, sat down beside me, and spoke to me of the past; she blushed as she admitted that she had fallen in love with me the moment she set eyes on me. But little by little I began to notice that Sdenka was not as I had remembered her. Her former timidity had given way to a strange wantonness of manner. She seemed more forward, more knowing. It dawned on me that her behaviour was no longer that of the naive young girl I recalled in my dream. Is it possible, I mused, that Sdenka was never the pure and innocent maiden that I imagined her to be? Did she simply put on an act to please her brother? Was I deceived by an affected virtue? If so, why insist that I leave? Was this perhaps a refinement of teasing? And I thought I knew her! What did it matter? If Sdenka was not a Diana, as I thought, she began to resemble another goddess at least as attractive – perhaps more so. By God! I preferred the role of Adonis to that of Actaeon.

But I abandoned myself passionately to Sdenka, and willingly outdid even her in the provocative game she was playing. Some time passed in sweet intimacy, until, as Sdenka was amusing me by trying on various pieces of jewellery, I thought it would be a good idea to place the little enamel cross around her neck. But as I tried to do this, Sdenka recoiled sharply.

'Enough of these childish games, my dearest,' she said. 'Let us talk about you and what is on your mind!'

This sudden change in Sdenka's behaviour made me pause a moment and think. Looking at her more closely I noticed that she no longer wore around her neck the cluster of tiny icons, holy relics and charms filled with incense which Serbians are usually given as children, to wear for the rest of their lives.

'Sdenka,' I asked, 'where are those things you used to wear around your neck?'

'I have lost them,' she replied impatiently, and hastily changed the subject.

I do not know exactly why, but at that moment I began to feel a strong sense of foreboding. I wanted to leave, but Sdenka held me back. 'What is this?' she said. 'You asked to be granted an hour, and here you are trying to leave after only a few minutes!'

'Sdenka, you were right when you tried to persuade me to leave; I think I hear a noise and I fear we will be discovered!'

'Calm yourself my love, everyone is asleep; only the cricket in the grass and the mayfly in the air can hear what I have to say!'

'No, no, Sdenka, I must leave now . . . !'

'Stay, stay,' she implored, 'I love you more than my soul, more than my salvation. You once told me that your life's blood belonged to me . . . !'

'But your brother – your brother, Sdenka – I have a feeling he will discover us!'

'Calm yourself my soul; my brother has been lulled to sleep by the wind rustling in the trees; heavy is his sleep, long is the night and I only ask to be granted one hour!'

As she said this, Sdenka looked so ravishing that my vague sense of foreboding turned into a strong desire to remain near her. A strange, almost sensual feeling, part fear, part excitement, filled my whole being. As I began to weaken, Sdenka became more tender, and I resolved to surrender, hoping to keep up my guard. However, I have always overestimated my own strength of mind, and when Sdenka, who had noticed that I was holding back, suggested that we chase away the chill of the night by drinking a few glasses of the good hermit's full-blooded wine, I agreed with a readiness which made her smile. The wine had its desired effect. By the second glass, I had forgotten all about the incident of the cross and the holy relics; Sdenka, with her beautiful blonde hair falling loose over her shoulders, with her jewels sparkling in the moonlight, was quite irresistible. Abandoning all restraint, I held her tight in my arms.

Then a strange thing happened. One of those mysterious revelations that I can never hope to explain. If you had asked me then, I would have denied that such things could happen, but now I know better. As I held Sdenka tightly against my body, one of the points of the cross which the Duchesse de Gramont gave me before I left stuck sharply into my chest. The stab of pain that I felt affected me like a ray of light passing through my body. Looking up at Sdenka I saw for the first time that her features, though still beautiful, were those of a corpse; that her eyes did not see; and that her smile was the distorted grimace of a decaying skull. At the same time, I sensed in that room the putrid smell of the charnel-house. The fearful truth was revealed to me in all its ugliness, and I remembered too late what the old hermit had said to me. I realised what a fearsome predicament I was in. Everything depended on my courage and my self-control.

I turned away from Sdenka to hide the horror which was written on my face. It is then that I looked out of the window and saw the satanic figure of Gorcha, leaning on a bloody stake and staring at me with the eyes of a hyena. Pressed against the other window were the waxen features of Georges, who at that moment looked as terrifying as his father. Both were watching my every movement, and I knew that they would pounce on me the moment I tried to escape. So I pretended not to know they were there, and, with incredible self-control, continued passionately to embrace Sdenka, just as I had done before my horrifying discovery. Meanwhile, I desperately racked my brains for some means of escape. I noticed that Gorcha and Georges were exchanging knowing glances with Sdenka and that they were showing signs of losing patience. Then, from somewhere outside, I heard a woman's shriek and the sound of children crying, like the howling of wild cats; these noises set my nerves on edge. Time to make for home, I said to myself, and the sooner the better!

Turning to Sdenka, I raised my voice so that her hideous family would be sure to hear me, 'I am tired, my dear child; I must go to bed and sleep for a few hours. But first I must go and see whether my horse needs feeding. I beg you to stay where you are and wait for me to come back.' I then pressed my mouth against her cold, dead lips and left the room.

I found my horse in a panic, covered with lather and crashing his hooves against the outhouse wall. He had not touched the oats, and the fearful noise he made when he saw me coming gave me goose-flesh, for I feared he would give the game away. But the vampires, who had almost certainly overheard my conversation with Sdenka, did not appear to think that anything suspicious was happening. After making sure that the main gate was open, I vaulted into the saddle and dug my spurs into the horse's flanks.

As I rode out of the gates I just had time to glimpse a whole crowd gathered around the house, many of them with their faces pressed against the windows. I think it was my sudden departure which first confused them, but I cannot be sure: the only sound I could hear at that moment was the regular beat of my horse's hooves which echoed in the night. I was just about to congratulate myself on my cunning, when all of a sudden I heard a fearful noise behind me, like the sound of a hurricane roaring through the mountains. A thousand discordant voices shrieked, moaned and contended with one another. Then complete silence, as if by common assent. And I heard a rhythmic stamping, like a troop of foot soldiers advancing in double-quick time.

I spurred on my horse until I tore into his flanks. A burning terror coursed through my veins. I was making one last effort to preserve my sanity, when I heard a voice behind me which cried out: 'Stop, don't leave me my dearest! I love you more than my soul, I love you more than my salvation! Turn back, turn back, your life's blood is mine!'

A cold breath brushed my ear and I sensed that Sdenka had leaped on to my horse from behind. 'My heart, my soul!' she cried, 'I see only you, hear only you! I am not mistress of my own destiny – a superior force commands my obedience. Forgive me, my dearest, forgive me!'

Twisting her arms around me, she tried to sink her teeth into my neck and to wrench me from my horse. There was a terrible struggle. For some time I had difficulty even defending myself, but eventually I managed to grab hold of Sdenka by curling one arm around her waist and knotting the other hand in her hair. Standing bolt upright in my stirrups, I threw her to the ground!

Then my strength gave out completely and I became delirious. Frenzied shapes pursued me – mad, grimacing faces. Georges and his brother Pierre ran beside the road and tried to block my way. They did not succeed, but just as I was about to give thanks, I looked over my shoulder and caught sight of old Gorcha, who was using his stake to propel himself forward as the Tyrolean mountain men do when they leap over Alpine chasms. But Gorcha did not manage to catch up with me. Then his daughter-in-law, dragging her children behind her, threw one of them to him; he caught the child on the sharpened point of his stake. Using the stake as a catapult he slung the creature towards me with all his might. I fended off the blow, but with the true terrier instinct the little brat sunk his teeth into my horse's neck, and I had some difficulty tearing him away. The other child was propelled towards me in the same way, but he landed beyond the horse and was crushed to pulp. I do not know what happened after that, but when I regained consciousness it was daylight, and I found myself lying near the road next to my dying horse.

So ended a love affair which should perhaps have cured me for ever of the desire to become involved in any others. But though it did not, I still shudder at the thought that if I had given in to Sdenka that terrible night, I should myself have become a vampire!

Carmilla

J. SHERIDAN LE FANU

Prologue

Upon a paper attached to the Narrative which follows, Doctor Hesselius has written a rather elaborate note, which he accompanies with a reference to his Essay on the strange subject which the MS. illuminates.

This mysterious subject he treats, in that Essay, with his usual learning and acumen, and with remarkable directness and condensation. It will form but one volume of the series of that extraordinary man's collected papers.

As I publish the case, in this volume, simply to interest the 'laity', I shall forestall the intelligent lady, who relates it, in nothing; and after due consideration, I have determined, therefore, to abstain from presenting any précis of the learned Doctor's reasoning, or extract from his statement on a subject which he describes as 'involving, not improbably, some of the profoundest arcana of our dual existence, and its intermediates.'

I was anxious on discovering this paper, to reopen the correspondence commenced by Doctor Hesselius, so many years before, with a person so clever and careful as his informant seems to have been. Much to my regret, however, I found that she had died in the interval.

She, probably, could have added little to the Narrative which she communicates in the following pages, with, so far as I can pronounce, such conscientious particularity.

I

An Early Fright

In Styria, we, though by no means magnificent people, inhabit a castle, or schloss. A small income, in that part of the world, goes a great way. Eight or nine hundred a year does wonders. Scantily enough ours would have answered among wealthy people at home. My father is English, and I bear an English name, although I never saw England. But here, in this lonely and primitive place, where everything is so marvellously cheap, I really don't see how ever so much more money would at all materially add to our comforts, or even luxuries.

My father was in the Austrian service, and retired upon a pension and his patrimony, and purchased this feudal residence and the small estate on which it stands, a bargain.

Nothing can be more picturesque or solitary. It stands on a slight eminence in a forest. The road, very old and narrow, passes in front of its drawbridge, never raised in my time, and its moat, stocked with perch, and sailed over by many swans, and floating on its surface white fleets of water lilies.

Over all this the schloss shows its many-windowed front; its towers, and its Gothic chapel.

The forest opens in an irregular and very picturesque glade before its gate, and at the right a steep Gothic bridge carries the road over a stream that winds in deep shadow through the wood. I have said that this is a very lonely place. Judge whether I say truth. Looking from the hall door towards the road, the forest in which our castle stands extends fifteen miles to the right, and twelve to the left. The nearest inhabited village is about seven of your English miles to the left. The nearest inhabited schloss of any historic associations is that of old General Spielsdorf, nearly twenty miles away to the right.

I have said 'the nearest *inhabited* village', because there is, only three miles westward, that is to say in the direction of General Spielsdorf's schloss, a ruined village, with its quaint little church, now roofless, in the aisle of which are the moldering tombs of the proud family of Karnstein, now extinct, who once owned the equally desolate chateau which, in the thick of the forest, overlooks the silent ruins of the town.

Respecting the cause of the desertion of this striking and melancholy spot, there is a legend which I shall relate to you another time.

I must tell you now, how very small is the party who constitute the inhabitants of our castle. I don't include servants, or those dependants who occupy rooms in the buildings attached to the schloss. Listen, and wonder! My father, who is the kindest man on earth, but growing old; and I, at the date of my story, only nineteen. Eight years have passed since then.

I and my father constituted the family at the schloss. My mother, a Styrian lady, died in my infancy, but I had a good-natured governess, who had been with me from, I might almost say, my infancy. I could not remember the time when her fat, benignant face was not a familiar picture in my memory.

This was Madame Perrodon, a native of Berne, whose care and good nature now in part supplied to me the loss of my mother, whom I do not even remember, so early I lost her. She made a third at our little dinner party. There was a fourth, Mademoiselle de Lafontaine, a lady such as you term, I believe, a 'finishing governess'. She spoke French and German, Madame Perrodon French and broken English, to which my father and I added English, which, partly to prevent its becoming a lost language among us, and partly from patriotic motives, we spoke every day. The consequence was a Babel, at which strangers used to laugh, and which I shall make no attempt to reproduce in this narrative. And there were two or three young lady friends besides, pretty nearly of my own age, who were occasional visitors, for longer or shorter terms; and these visits I sometimes returned.

These were our regular social resources; but of course there were chance visits from 'neighbours' of only five or six leagues distance. My life was, notwithstanding, rather a solitary one, I can assure you.

My *gouvernantes* had just so much control over me as you might conjecture such sage persons would have in the case of a rather spoiled girl, whose only parent allowed her pretty nearly her own way in everything.

The first occurrence in my existence which produced a terrible impression upon my mind, which, in fact, never has been effaced, was one of the very earliest incidents of my life which I can recollect. Some people will think it so trifling that it should not be recorded here. You will see, however, by-and-by, why I mention it. The nursery, as it was called, though I had it all to myself, was a large room in the upper storey of the castle, with a steep oak roof. I can't have been more than six years old, when one night I awoke, and looking round the room from my bed, failed to see the nursery-maid. Neither was my nurse there; and I thought myself alone. I was not frightened, for I was one of those happy children who are studiously kept in ignorance of ghost stories, of fairy tales, and of all such lore as makes us cover up our heads when the door cracks suddenly, or the flicker of an expiring candle makes the shadow of a bedpost dance upon the wall, nearer to our faces. I was vexed and insulted at finding myself, as I conceived, neglected, and I began to whimper, preparatory to a hearty bout of roaring; when to my surprise, I saw solemn, but very pretty face looking at me from the side of the bed. I was that of a young lady who was kneeling, with her hands under the coverlet. I looked at her with a kind of pleased wonder, and ceased whimpering. She caressed me with her hands, and lay down beside me on the bed, and drew me towards her, smiling; I felt immediately delightfully soothed, and fell asleep again. I was wakened by a sensation as if two needles ran into my breast very deep at the same moment, and I cried loudly. The lady started back, with her eyes fixed on me, and then slipped down upon the floor, and, as I thought hid herself under the bed.

I was now for the first time frightened, and I yelled with all my might and main. Nurse, nursery-maid, housekeeper, all came running in, and hearing my story, they made light of it, soothing me all they could meanwhile. But, child as I was, I could perceive that their faces were pale with an unwonted look of anxiety, and I saw them look under the bed, and about the room, and peep under tables and pluck open cupboards; and the housekeeper whispered to the nurse: 'Lay your hand along that hollow in the bed; someone *did* lie there, so sure as you did not; the place is still warm.'

I remember the nursery-maid petting me, and all three examining my chest, where I told them I felt the puncture, and pronouncing that there was no sign visible that any such thing had happened to me.

The housekeeper and the two other servants who were in charge of the nursery, remained sitting up all night; and from that time a servant always sat up in the nursery until I was about fourteen.

I was very nervous for a long time after this. A doctor was called in; he was pallid and elderly. How well I remember his long saturnine face, slightly pitted with smallpox, and his chestnut wig. For a good while, every second day, he came and gave me medicine, which of course I hated.

The morning after I saw this apparition I was in a state of terror, and could not bear to be left alone, daylight though it was, for a moment.

I remember my father coming up and standing at the bedside, and talking cheerfully, and asking the nurse a number of questions, and laughing very heartily at one of the answers; and patting me on the shoulder, and kissing me, and telling me not to be frightened, that it was nothing but a dream and could not hurt me.

But I was not comforted, for I knew the visit of the strange woman was *not* a dream; and I was *awfully* frightened.

I was a little consoled by the nursery-maid's assuring me that it was she who had come and looked at me, and lain down beside me in the bed, and that I must have been half-dreaming not to have known her face. But this, though supported by the nurse, did not quite satisfy me.

I remembered, in the course of that day, a venerable old man in a black cassock, coming into the room with the nurse and housekeeper, and talking a little to them, and very kindly to me; his face was very sweet and gentle, and he told me they were going to pray, and joined my hands together, and desired me to say, softly, while they were praying, 'Lord hear all good prayers for us, for Jesus' sake.' I think these were the very words, for I often repeated them to myself, and my nurse used for years to make me say them in my prayers.

I remembered so well the thoughtful sweet face of that white-haired old man, in his black cassock, as he stood in that rude, lofty, brown room, with the clumsy furniture of a fashion three hundred years old about him, and the scanty light entering its shadowy atmosphere through the small lattice. He kneeled, and the three women with him, and he prayed aloud with an earnest quavering voice for what appeared to me a long time. I forget all my life preceding that event, and for some time after it is all obscure also, but the scenes I have just described stand out vivid as the isolated pictures of the phantasmagoria surrounded by darkness.

2

A Guest

I am now going to tell you something so strange that it will require all your faith in my veracity to believe my story. It is not only true, nevertheless, but truth of which I have been an eyewitness.

It was a sweet summer evening, and my father asked me, as he sometimes did, to take a little ramble with him along that beautiful forest vista which I have mentioned as lying in front of the schloss.

'General Spielsdorf cannot come to us so soon as I had hoped,' said my father, as we pursued our walk.

He was to have paid us a visit of some weeks, and we had expected his arrival next day. He was to have brought with him a young lady, his niece and ward, Mademoiselle Rheinfeldt, whom I had never seen, but whom I had heard described as a very charming girl, and in whose society I had promised myself many happy days. I was more disappointed than a young lady living in a town or a bustling neighbourhood can possibly imagine. This visit, and the new acquaintance it promised, had furnished my day dream for many weeks.

'And how soon does he come?' I asked.

'Not till autumn. Not for two months, I dare say,' he answered. 'And I am very glad now, dear, that you never knew Mademoiselle Rheinfeldt.'

'And why?' I asked, both mortified and curious.

'Because the poor young lady is dead,' he replied. 'I quite forgot I had not told you, but you were not in the room when I received the General's letter this evening.'

I was very much shocked. General Spielsdorf had mentioned in his first letter, six or seven weeks before, that she was not so well as he would wish her, but there was nothing to suggest the remotest suspicion of danger.

'Here is the General's letter,' he said, handing it to me. 'I am afraid he is in great affliction; the letter appears to me to have been written very nearly in distraction.'

We sat down on a rude bench, under a group of magnificent lime trees. The sun was setting with all its melancholy splendour behind the sylvan horizon, and the stream that flows beside our home, and passes under the steep old bridge I have mentioned, wound through many a group of noble trees, almost at our feet, reflecting in its current the fading crimson of the sky. General Spielsdorf's letter was so extraordinary, so vehement, and in some places so self-contradictory, that I read it twice over – the second time aloud to my father – and was still unable to account for it, except by supposing that grief had unsettled his mind.

It said:

I have lost my darling daughter, for as such I loved her. During the last days of dear Bertha's illness I was not able to write to you.

Before then I had no idea of her danger. I have lost her, and now learn *all*, too late. She died in the peace of innocence, and in the glorious hope of a blessed futurity. The fiend who betrayed our infatuated hospitality has done it all. I thought I was receiving into my house innocence, gaiety, a charming companion for my lost Bertha. Heavens! what a fool have I been!

I thank God my child died without a suspicion of the cause of her sufferings. She is gone without so much as conjecturing the nature of her illness, and the accursed passion of the agent of all this misery. I devote my remaining days to tracking and extinguishing a monster. I am told I may hope to accomplish my righteous and merciful purpose. At present there is scarcely a gleam of light to guide me. I curse my conceited incredulity, my despicable affectation of superiority, my blindness, my obstinacy – all – too late. I cannot write or talk collectedly now. I am distracted. So soon as I shall have a little recovered, I mean to devote myself for a time to enquiry, which may possibly lead me as far as Vienna. Some time in the autumn, two months hence, or earlier if I live, I will see you – that is, if you permit me; I will then tell you all that I scarce dare put upon paper now. Farewell. Pray for me, dear friend.

In these terms ended this strange letter. Though I had never seen Bertha Rheinfeldt my eyes filled with tears at the sudden intelligence; I was startled, as well as profoundly disappointed.

The sun had now set, and it was twilight by the time I had returned the General's letter to my father.

It was a soft clear evening, and we loitered, speculating upon the possible meanings of the violent and incoherent sentences which I had just been reading. We had nearly a mile to walk before reaching the road that passes the schloss in front, and by that time the moon was shining brilliantly. At the drawbridge we met Madame Perrodon and Mademoiselle de Lafontaine, who had come out, without their bonnets, to enjoy the exquisite moonlight.

We heard their voices gabbling in animated dialogue as we approached. We joined them at the drawbridge, and turned about to admire with them the beautiful scene.

The glade through which we had just walked lay before us. At our left the narrow road wound away under clumps of lordly trees, and was lost to sight amid the thickening forest. At the right the same road crosses the steep and picturesque bridge, near which stands a ruined tower which once guarded that pass; and beyond the bridge an abrupt eminence rises, covered with trees, and showing in the shadows some grey ivy-clustered rocks.

Over the sward and low grounds a thin film of mist was stealing like smoke, marking the distances with a transparent veil; and here and there we could see the river faintly flashing in the moonlight.

No softer, sweeter scene could be imagined. The news I had just heard made it melancholy; but nothing could disturb its character of profound serenity, and the enchanted glory and vagueness of the prospect.

My father, who enjoyed the picturesque, and I, stood looking in silence over the expanse beneath us. The two good governesses, standing a little way behind us, discoursed upon the scene, and were eloquent upon the moon.

Madame Perrodon was fat, middle-aged, and romantic, and talked and sighed poetically. Mademoiselle de Lafontaine – in right of her father who was a German, assumed to be psychological, meta-physical, and something of a mystic – now declared that when the moon shone with a light so intense it was well known that it indicated a special spiritual activity. The effect of the full moon in such a state of brilliancy was manifold. It acted on dreams, it acted on lunacy, it acted on nervous people, it had marvellous physical influences connected with life. Mademoiselle related that her cousin, who was mate of a merchant ship, having taken a nap on deck on such a night, lying on his back, with his face full in the light on the moon, had wakened, after a dream of an old woman clawing him by the cheek, with his features horribly drawn to one side; and his countenance had never quite recovered its equilibrium.

'The moon, this night,' she said, 'is full of idyllic and magnetic influence – and see, when you look behind you at the front of the schloss how all its windows flash and twinkle with that silvery splendour, as if unseen hands had lighted up the rooms to receive fairy guests.'

There are indolent styles of the spirits in which, indisposed to talk ourselves, the talk of others is pleasant to our listless ears; and I gazed on, pleased with the tinkle of the ladies' conversation.

'I have got into one of my moping moods tonight,' said my father, after a silence, and quoting Shakespeare, whom, by way of keeping up our English, he used to read aloud, he said:

> In truth I know not why I am so sad.
> It wearies me: you say it wearies you;
> But how I got it – came by it . . .

'I forget the rest. But I feel as if some great misfortune were hanging over us. I suppose the poor General's afflicted letter has had some-thing to do with it.'

At this moment the unwonted sound of carriage wheels and many hoofs upon the road, arrested our attention.

They seemed to be approaching from the high ground overlooking the bridge, and very soon the equipage emerged from that point. Two horsemen first crossed the bridge, then came a carriage drawn by four horses, and two men rode behind.

It seemed to be the travelling carriage of a person of rank; and we were all immediately absorbed in watching that very unusual spectacle. It became, in a few moments, greatly more interesting, for just as the carriage had passed the summit of the steep bridge, one of the leaders, taking fright, communicated his panic to the rest, and after a plunge or two, the whole team broke into a wild gallop together, and dashing between the horsemen who rode in front, came thundering along the road towards us with the speed of a hurricane.

The excitement of the scene was made more painful by the clear, long-drawn screams of a female voice from the carriage window.

We all advanced in curiosity and horror; me rather in silence, the rest with various ejaculations of terror.

Our suspense did not last long. Just before you reach the castle drawbridge, on the route they were coming, there stands by the roadside a magnificent lime tree, on the other stands an ancient stone cross, at sight of which the horses, now going at a pace that was perfectly frightful, swerved so as to bring the wheel over the projecting roots of the tree.

I knew what was coming. I covered my eyes, unable to see it out, and turned my head away; at the same moment I heard a cry from my lady friends, who had gone on a little.

Curiosity opened my eyes, and I saw a scene of utter confusion. Two of the horses were on the ground, the carriage lay upon its side with two wheels in the air; the men were busy removing the traces, and a lady with a commanding air and figure had got out, and stood with clasped hands, raising the handkerchief that was in them every now and then to her eyes.

Through the carriage door was now lifted a young lady, who appeared to be lifeless. My dear old father was already beside the elder lady, with his hat in his hand, evidently tendering his aid and the resources of his schloss. The lady did not appear to hear him, or to have eyes for anything but the slender girl who was being placed against the slope of the bank.

I approached; the young lady was apparently stunned, but she was certainly not dead. My father, who piqued himself on being something of a physician, had just had his fingers on her wrist and assured

the lady who declared herself her mother, that her pulse, though
faint and irregular, was undoubtedly still distinguishable. The lady
clasped her hands and looked upward, as if in a momentary transport
of gratitude; but immediately she broke out again in that theatrical
way which is, I believe, natural to some people.

She was what is called a fine looking woman for her time of life,
and must have been handsome; she was tall, but not thin, and dressed
in black velvet, and looked rather pale, but with a proud and commanding countenance, though now agitated strangely.

'Who was ever being so born to calamity?' I heard her say, with
clasped hands, as I came up. 'Here am I, on a journey of life and
death, in prosecuting which to lose an hour is possibly to lose all. My
child will not have recovered sufficiently to resume her route for
who can say how long. I must leave her: I cannot, dare not, delay.
How far on, sir, can you tell, is the nearest village? I must leave her
there; and shall not see my darling, or even hear of her till my return,
three months hence.'

I plucked my father by the coat, and whispered earnestly in his ear:
'Oh! papa, pray ask her to let her stay with us – it would be so
delightful. Do, pray.'

'If Madame will entrust her child to the care of my daughter,
and of her good *gouvernante*, Madame Perrodon, and permit her
to remain as our guest, under my charge, until her return, it
will confer a distinction and an obligation upon us, and we shall
treat her with all the care and devotion which so sacred a trust
deserves.'

'I cannot do that, sir, it would be to task your kindness and chivalry
too cruelly,' said the lady, distractedly.

'It would, on the contrary, be to confer on us a very great kindness
at the moment when we most need it. My daughter has just been
disappointed by a cruel misfortune, in a visit from which she had
long anticipated a great deal of happiness. If you confide this young
lady to our care it will be her best consolation. The nearest village on
your route is distant, and affords no such inn as you could think of
placing your daughter at; you cannot allow her to continue her
journey for any considerable distance without danger. If, as you say,
you cannot suspend your journey, you must part with her tonight,
and nowhere could you do so with more honest assurances of care
and tenderness than here.'

There was something in this lady's air and appearance so distinguished and even imposing, and in her manner so engaging, as to

impress one, quite apart from the dignity of her equipage, with a conviction that she was a person of consequence.

By this time the carriage was replaced in its upright position, and the horses, quite tractable, in the traces again.

The lady threw on her daughter a glance which I fancied was not quite so affectionate as one might have anticipated from the beginning of the scene; then she beckoned slightly to my father, and withdrew two or three steps with him out of hearing; and talked to him with a fixed and stern countenance, not at all like that with which she had hitherto spoken.

I was filled with wonder that my father did not seem to perceive the change, and also unspeakably curious to learn what it could be that she was speaking, almost in his ear, with so much earnestness and rapidity.

Two or three minutes at most I think she remained thus employed, then she turned, and a few steps brought her to where her daughter lay, supported by Madame Perrodon. She kneeled beside her for a moment and whispered, as Madame supposed, a little benediction in her ear; then hastily kissing her she stepped into her carriage, the door was closed, the footmen in stately liveries jumped up behind, the outriders spurred on, the postilions cracked their whips, the horses plunged and broke suddenly into a furious canter that threatened soon again to become a gallop, and the carriage whirled away, followed at the same rapid pace by the two horsemen in the rear.

3
We Compare Notes

We followed the *cortège* with our eyes until it was swiftly lost to sight in the misty wood, and the very sound of the hoofs and the wheels died away in the silent night air.

Nothing remained to assure us that the adventure had not been an illusion of a moment but the young lady, who just at that moment opened her eyes. I could not see, for her face was turned from me, but she raised her head, evidently looking about her, and I heard a very sweet voice ask complainingly, 'Where is mamma?'

Our good Madame Perrodon answered tenderly, and added some comfortable assurances.

I then heard her ask: 'Where am I? What is this place?' and after that she said, 'I don't see the carriage; and Matska, where is she?'

Madame answered all her questions in so far as she understood them; and gradually the young lady remembered how the misadventure came about, and was glad to hear that no-one in, or in attendance on, the carriage was hurt; and on learning that her mamma had left her here, till her return in about three months, she wept.

I was going to add my consolations to those of Madame Perrodon, when Mademoiselle de Lafontaine placed her hand upon my arm, saying: 'Don't approach, one at a time is as much as she can at present converse with; a very little excitement would possibly overpower her now.'

As soon as she is comfortably in bed, I thought, I will run up to her room and see her.

My father in the meantime had sent a servant on horseback for the physician, who lived about two leagues away; and a bedroom was being prepared for the young lady's reception.

The stranger now rose, and leaning on Madame's arm, walked slowly over the drawbridge and into the castle gate.

In the hall, servants waited to receive her, and she was conducted forthwith to her room. The room we usually sat in as our drawing room is long, having four windows that looked over the moat and drawbridge, upon the forest scene I have just described.

It is furnished in old carved oak, with large carved cabinets, and the chairs are cushioned with crimson Utrecht velvet. The walls are covered with tapestry, and surrounded with great gold frames, the figures being as large as life, in ancient and very curious costume, and the subjects represented are hunting, hawking, and generally festive. It is not too stately to be extremely comfortable; and here we had our tea, for with his usual patriotic leanings he insisted that the national beverage should make its appearance regularly with our coffee and chocolate.

We sat here this night, and with candles lighted, were talking over the adventure of the evening.

Madame Perrodon and Mademoiselle de Lafontaine were both of our party. The young stranger had hardly lain down in her bed when she sank into a deep sleep; and those ladies had left her in the care of a servant.

'How do you like our guest?' I asked, as soon as Madame entered. 'Tell me all about her?'

'I like her extremely,' answered Madame, 'she is, I almost think, the prettiest creature I ever saw; about your age, and so gentle and nice.'

'She is absolutely beautiful,' threw in Mademoiselle, who had peeped for a moment into the stranger's room.

'And such a sweet voice!' added Madame Perrodon.

'Did you remark a woman in the carriage, after it was set up again, who did not get out,' inquired Mademoiselle, 'but only looked from the window?'

No, we had not seen her.

Then she described a hideous black woman, with a sort of coloured turban on her head, and who was gazing all the time from the carriage window, nodding and grinning derisively towards the ladies, with gleaming eyes and large white eyeballs, and her teeth set as if in fury.

'Did you remark what an ill-looking pack of men the servants were?' asked Madame.

'Yes,' said my father, who had just come in, 'ugly, hang-dog looking fellows as ever I beheld in my life. I hope they mayn't rob the poor lady in the forest. They are clever rogues, however; they got everything to rights in a minute.'

'I dare say they are worn out with too long travelling,' said Madame.

'Besides looking wicked, their faces were so strangely lean, and dark, and sullen. I am very curious, I own; but I dare say the young lady will tell you all about it tomorrow, if she is sufficiently recovered.'

'I don't think she will,' said my father, with a mysterious smile, and a little nod of his head, as if he knew more about it than he cared to tell us.

This made us all the more inquisitive as to what had passed between him and the lady in the black velvet, in the brief but earnest interview that had immediately preceded her departure.

We were scarcely alone, when I entreated him to tell me. He did not need much pressing.

'There is no particular reason why I should not tell you. She expressed a reluctance to trouble us with the care of her daughter, saying she was in delicate health, and nervous, but not subject to any kind of seizure – she volunteered that – nor to any illusion; being, in fact, perfectly sane.'

'How very odd to say all that!' I interpolated. 'It was so unnecessary.'

'At all events it *was* said,' he laughed, 'and as you wish to know all that passed, which was indeed very little, I tell you. She then said, "I am making a long journey of *vital* importance – she emphasised the word – rapid and secret; I shall return for my child in three months; in the meantime, she will be silent as to who we are, whence we come, and whither we are travelling." That is all she said. She spoke very pure French. When she said the word "secret", she paused for a few seconds, looking sternly, her eyes fixed on mine. I fancy she makes a great point of that. You saw how quickly she was gone. I hope I have not done a very foolish thing, in taking charge of the young lady.'

For my part, I was delighted. I was longing to see and talk to her; and only waiting till the doctor should give me leave. You, who live in towns, can have no idea how great an event the introduction of a new friend is, in such a solitude as surrounded us.

The doctor did not arrive till nearly one o'clock; but I could no more have gone to my bed and slept, than I could have overtaken, on foot, the carriage in which the princess in black velvet had driven away.

When the physician came down to the drawing room, it was to report very favourably upon his patient. She was now sitting up, her pulse quite regular, apparently perfectly well. She had sustained no injury, and the little shock to her nerves had passed away quite harmlessly. There could be no harm certainly in my seeing her, if we both wished it; and, with this permission I sent, forthwith, to know whether she would allow me to visit her for a few minutes in her room.

The servant returned immediately to say that she desired nothing more.

You may be sure I was not long in availing myself of this permission.

Our visitor lay in one of the handsomest rooms in the schloss. It was, perhaps, a little stately. There was a sombre piece of tapestry opposite the foot of the bed, representing Cleopatra with the asps to her bosom; and other solemn classic scenes were displayed, a little faded, upon the other walls. But there was gold carving, and rich and varied colour enough in the other decorations of the room, to more than redeem the gloom of the old tapestry.

There were candles at the bedside. She was sitting up, her slender pretty figure enveloped in the soft silk dressing gown, embroidered with flowers, and lined with thick quilted silk, which her mother had thrown over her feet as she lay upon the ground.

What was it that, as I reached the bedside and had just begun my little greeting, struck me dumb in a moment, and made me recoil a step or two from before her? I will tell you.

I saw the very face which had visited me in my childhood at night, which remained so fixed in my memory, and on which I had for so many years so often ruminated with horror, when no-one suspected of what I was thinking.

It was pretty, even beautiful; and when I first beheld it, wore the same melancholy expression.

But this almost instantly lighted into a strange fixed smile of recognition.

There was a silence of fully a minute, and then at length she spoke; I could not.

'How wonderful!' she exclaimed. 'Twelve years ago, I saw your face in a dream, and it has haunted me ever since.'

'Wonderful indeed!' I repeated, overcoming with an effort the horror that had for a time suspended my utterances. 'Twelve years ago, in vision or reality, I certainly saw you. I could not forget your face. It has remained before my eyes ever since.'

Her smile had softened. Whatever I had fancied strange in it, was gone, and it and her dimpling cheeks were now delightfully pretty and intelligent.

I felt reassured, and continued more in the vein which hospitality indicated, to bid her welcome, and to tell her how much pleasure her accidental arrival had given us all, and especially what a happiness it was to me.

I took her hand as I spoke. I was a little shy, as lonely people are, but the situation made me eloquent, and even bold. She pressed my hand, she laid hers upon it, and her eyes glowed, as, looking hastily into mine, she smiled again, and blushed.

She answered my welcome very prettily. I sat down beside her, still wondering; and she said: 'I must tell you my vision about you; it is so very strange that you and I should have had, each of the other, so vivid a dream, that each should have seen, I you and you me, looking as we do now, when of course we both were mere children. I was a child, about six years old, and I awoke from a confused and troubled dream, and found myself in a room, unlike my nursery, wainscoted clumsily in some dark wood, and with cupboards and bedsteads, and chairs, and benches placed about it. The beds were, I thought, all empty, and the room itself without anyone but myself in it; and I, after looking about me for some time, and admiring especially an iron candlestick with two branches, which I should certainly know again, crept under one of the beds to reach the window; but as I got from under the bed,

I heard someone crying; and looking up, while I was still upon my knees, I saw you – most assuredly you – as I see you now; a beautiful young lady, with golden hair and large blue eyes, and lips – your lips – you as you are here.

'Your looks won me; I climbed on the bed and put my arms about you, and I think we both fell asleep. I was aroused by a scream; you were sitting up screaming. I was frightened, and slipped down upon the ground, and, it seemed to me, lost consciousness for a moment; and when I came to myself, I was again in my nursery at home. Your face I have never forgotten since. I could not be misled by mere resemblance. *You are* the lady whom I saw then.'

It was now my turn to relate my corresponding vision, which I did, to the undisguised wonder of my new acquaintance.

'I don't know which should be most afraid of the other,' she said, again smiling – 'If you were less pretty I think I should be very much afraid of you, but being as you are, and you and I both so young, I feel only that I have made your acquaintance twelve years ago, and have already a right to your intimacy; at all events it does seem as if we were destined, from our earliest childhood, to be friends. I wonder whether you feel as strangely drawn towards me as I do to you; I have never had a friend – shall I find one now?' She sighed, and her fine dark eyes gazed passionately on me.

Now the truth is, I felt rather unaccountably towards the beautiful stranger. I did feel, as she said, 'drawn towards her', but there was also something of repulsion. In this ambiguous feeling, however, the sense of attraction immensely prevailed. She interested and won me; she was so beautiful and so indescribably engaging.

I perceived now something of languor and exhaustion stealing over her, and hastened to bid her good night.

'The doctor thinks,' I added, 'that you ought to have a maid to sit up with you tonight; one of ours is waiting, and you will find her a very useful and quiet creature.'

'How kind of you, but I could not sleep, I never could with an attendant in the room. I shan't require any assistance – and, shall I confess my weakness, I am haunted with a terror of robbers. Our house was robbed once, and two servants murdered, so I always lock my door. It has become a habit – and you look so kind I know you will forgive me. I see there is a key in the lock.'

She held me close in her pretty arms for a moment and whispered in my ear, 'Good night, darling, it is very hard to part with you, but good night; tomorrow, but not early, I shall see you again.'

She sank back on the pillow with a sigh, and her fine eyes followed me with a fond and melancholy gaze, and she murmured again 'Good night, dear friend.'

Young people like, and even love, on impulse. I was flattered by the evident, though as yet undeserved, fondness she showed me. I liked the confidence with which she at once received me. She was determined that we should be very near friends.

Next day came and we met again. I was delighted with my companion; that is to say, in many respects.

Her looks lost nothing in daylight – she was certainly the most beautiful creature I had ever seen, and the unpleasant remembrance of the face presented in my early dream, had lost the effect of the first unexpected recognition.

She confessed that she had experienced a similar shock on seeing me, and precisely the same faint antipathy that had mingled with my admiration of her. We now laughed together over our momentary horrors.

4

Her Habits – a Saunter

I told you that I was charmed with her in most particulars.

There were some that did not please me so well.

She was above the middle height of women. I shall begin by describing her.

She was slender, and wonderfully graceful. Except that her movements were languid – very languid – indeed, there was nothing in her appearance to indicate an invalid. Her complexion was rich and brilliant; her features were small and beautifully formed; her eyes large, dark, and lustrous; her hair was quite wonderful, I never saw hair so magnificently thick and long when it was down about her shoulders; I have often placed my hands under it, and laughed with wonder at its weight. It was exquisitely fine and soft, and in colour a rich very dark brown, with something of gold. I loved to let it down, tumbling with its own weight, as, in her room, she lay back in her chair talking in her sweet low voice; I used to fold and braid it, and spread it out and play with it. Heavens! if I had but known all!

I said there were particulars which did not please me. I have told you that her confidence won me the first night I saw her; but I found that she exercised with respect to herself, her mother, her history, everything in fact connected with her life, plans, and people, an ever wakeful reserve. I dare say I was unreasonable, perhaps I was wrong; I dare say I ought to have respected the solemn injunction laid upon my father by the stately lady in black velvet. But curiosity is a restless and unscrupulous passion, and no one girl can endure, with patience, that hers should be baffled by another. What harm could it do anyone to tell me what I so ardently desired to know? Had she no trust in my good sense or honour? Why would she not believe me when I assured her, so solemnly, that I would not divulge one syllable of what she told me to any mortal breathing.

There was a coldness, it seemed to me, beyond her years, in her smiling melancholy persistent refusal to afford me the least ray of light.

I cannot say we quarrelled upon this point, for she would not quarrel upon any. It was, of course, very unfair of me to press her, very ill-bred, but I really could not help it; and I might just as well have let it alone.

What she did tell me amounted, in my unconscionable estimation – to nothing.

It was all summed up in three very vague disclosures:

First – her name was Carmilla.

Second – her family was very ancient and noble.

Third – her home lay in the direction of the west.

She would not tell me the name of her family, nor their armorial bearings, nor the name of their estate, nor even that of the country they lived in.

You are not to suppose that I worried her incessantly on these subjects. I watched opportunity, and rather insinuated than urged my inquiries. Once or twice, indeed, I did attack her more directly. But no matter what my tactics, utter failure was invariably the result. Reproaches and caresses were all lost upon her. But I must add this, that her evasion was conducted with so pretty a melancholy and deprecation, with so many, and even passionate declarations of her liking for me, and trust in my honour, and with so many promises that I should at last know all, that I could not find it in my heart long to be offended with her.

She used to place her pretty arms about my neck, draw me to her, and laying her cheek to mine, murmur with her lips near my ear, 'Dearest, your little heart is wounded; think me not cruel because I obey the irresistible law of my strength and weakness; if your dear heart is wounded, my wild heart bleeds with yours. In the rapture of my enormous humiliation I live in your warm life, and you shall die –

die, sweetly die – into mine. I cannot help it; as I draw near to you, you, in your turn, will draw near to others, and learn the rapture of that cruelty, which yet is love; so, for a while, seek to know no more of me and mine, but trust me with all your loving spirit.'

And when she had spoken such a rhapsody, she would press me more closely in her trembling embrace, and her lips in soft kisses gently glow upon my cheek.

Her agitations and her language were unintelligible to me.

From these foolish embraces, which were not of very frequent occurrence, I must allow, I used to wish to extricate myself; but my energies seemed to fail me. Her murmured words sounded like a lullaby in my ear, and soothed my resistance into a trance, from which I only seemed to recover myself when she withdrew her arms.

In these mysterious moods I did not like her. I experienced a strange tumultuous excitement that was pleasurable, ever and anon, mingled with a vague sense of fear and disgust. I had no distinct thoughts about her while such scenes lasted, but I was conscious of a love growing into adoration, and also of abhorrence. This I know is paradox, but I can make no other attempt to explain the feeling.

I now write, after an interval of more than ten years, with a trembling hand, with a confused and horrible recollection of certain occurrences and situations, in the ordeal through which I was unconsciously passing; though with a vivid and very sharp remembrance of the main current of my story.

But, I suspect, in all lives there are certain emotional scenes, those in which our passions have been most wildly and terribly roused, that are of all others the most vaguely and dimly remembered.

Sometimes after an hour of apathy, my strange and beautiful companion would take my hand and hold it with a fond pressure, renewed again and again; blushing softly, gazing in my face with languid and burning eyes, and breathing so fast that her dress rose and fell with the tumultuous respiration. It was like the ardour of a lover; it embarrassed me; it was hateful and yet overpowering; and with gloating eyes she drew me to her, and her hot lips travelled along my cheek in kisses; and she would whisper, almost in sobs, 'You are mine, you *shall* be mine, you and I are one for ever.' Then she had thrown herself back in her chair, with her small hands over her eyes, leaving me trembling.

'Are we related,' I used to ask; 'what can you mean by all this? I remind you perhaps of someone whom you love; but you must

not, I hate it; I don't know you – I don't know myself when you
look so and talk so.'

She used to sigh at my vehemence, then turn away and drop my
hand.

Respecting these very extraordinary manifestations I strove in vain
to form any satisfactory theory – I could not refer them to affectation
or trick. It was unmistakably the momentary breaking out of sup-
pressed instinct and emotion. Was she, notwithstanding her mother's
volunteered denial, subject to brief visitations of insanity; or was there
here a disguise and a romance? I had read in old storybooks of such
things. What if a boyish lover had found his way into the house,
and sought to prosecute his suit in masquerade, with the assistance
of a clever old adventuress. But there were many things against this
hypothesis, highly interesting as it was to my vanity.

I could boast of no little attentions such as masculine gallantry
delights to offer. Between these passionate moments there were long
intervals of commonplace, of gaiety, of brooding melancholy, during
which, except that I detected her eyes so full of melancholy fire,
following me, at times I might have been as nothing to her. Except in
these brief periods of mysterious excitement her ways were girlish;
and there was always a languor about her, quite incompatible with a
masculine system in a state of health.

In some respects her habits were odd. Perhaps not so singular in
the opinion of a town lady like you, as they appeared to us rustic
people. She used to come down very late, generally not till one
o'clock, she would then take a cup of chocolate, but eat nothing; we
then went out for a walk, which was a mere saunter, and she seemed,
almost immediately, exhausted, and either returned to the schloss or
sat on one of the benches that were placed, here and there, among
the trees. This was a bodily languor in which her mind did not
sympathise. She was always an animated talker, and very intelligent.

She sometimes alluded for a moment to her own home, or mentioned an adventure or situation, or an early recollection, which
indicated a people of strange manners, and described customs of
which we knew nothing. I gathered from these chance hints that her
native country was much more remote than I had at first fancied.

As we sat thus one afternoon under the trees a funeral passed us by.
It was that of a pretty young girl, whom I had often seen, the
daughter of one of the rangers of the forest. The poor man was
walking behind the coffin of his darling; she was his only child, and
he looked quite heartbroken.

Peasants walking two-and-two came behind, they were singing a
funeral hymn.

I rose to mark my respect as they passed, and joined in the hymn
they were very sweetly singing.

My companion shook me a little roughly, and I turned surprised.

She said brusquely, 'Don't you perceive how discordant that is?'

'I think it very sweet, on the contrary,' I answered, vexed at the
interruption, and very uncomfortable, lest the people who composed
the little procession should observe and resent what was passing.

I resumed, therefore, instantly, and was again interrupted. 'You
pierce my ears,' said Carmilla, almost angrily, and stopping her ears
with her tiny fingers. 'Besides, how can you tell that your religion
and mine are the same; your forms wound me, and I hate funerals.
What a fuss! Why you must die – *everyone* must die; and all are
happier when they do. Come home.'

'My father has gone on with the clergyman to the churchyard. I
thought you knew she was to be buried today.'

'She? I don't trouble my head about peasants. I don't know who
she is,' answered Carmilla, with a flash from her fine eyes.

'She is the poor girl who fancied she saw a ghost a fortnight ago,
and has been dying ever since, till yesterday, when she expired.'

'Tell me nothing about ghosts. I shan't sleep tonight if you do.'

'I hope there is no plague or fever coming; all this looks very like
it,' I continued. 'The swineherd's young wife died only a week ago,
and she thought something seized her by the throat as she lay in her
bed, and nearly strangled her. Papa says such horrible fancies do
accompany some forms of fever. She was quite well the day before.
She sank afterwards, and died before a week.'

'Well, *her* funeral is over, I hope, and *her* hymn sung; and our ears
shan't be tortured with that discord and jargon. It has made me
nervous. Sit down here, beside me; sit close; hold my hand; press it
hard – hard – harder.'

We had moved a little back, and had come to another seat.

She sat down. Her face underwent a change that alarmed and
even terrified me for a moment. It darkened, and became horribly
livid; her teeth and hands were clenched, and she frowned and
compressed her lips, while she stared down upon the ground at her
feet, and trembled all over with a continued shudder as irrepressible
as ague. All her energies seemed strained to suppress a fit, with
which she was then breathlessly tugging; and at length a low convulsive cry of suffering broke from her, and gradually the hysteria

subsided. 'There! That comes of strangling people with hymns' she said at last. 'Hold me, hold me still. It is passing away.'

And so gradually it did; and perhaps to dissipate the sombre im pression which the spectacle had left upon me, she became unusuall' animated and chatty; and so we got home.

This was the first time I had seen her exhibit any definable symp toms of that delicacy of health which her mother had spoken of. I was the first time, also, I had seen her exhibit anything like temper.

Both passed away like a summer cloud; and never but once after wards did I witness on her part a momentary sign of anger. I will tel you how it happened.

She and I were looking out of one of the long drawing room windows, when there entered the courtyard, over the drawbridge, a figure of a wanderer whom I knew very well. He used to visit the schloss generally twice a year.

It was the figure of a hunchback, with the sharp lean features that generally accompany deformity. He wore a pointed black beard, and he was smiling from ear to ear, showing his white fangs. He was dressed in buff, black, and scarlet, and crossed with more straps and belts than I could count, from which hung all manner of things. Behind, he carried a magic lantern, and two boxes, which I well knew, in one of which was a salamander, and in the other a man drake. These monsters used to make my father laugh. They were compounded of parts of monkeys, parrots, squirrels, fish, and hedge hogs, dried and stitched together with great neatness and startling effect. He had a fiddle, a box of conjuring apparatus, a pair of foils and masks attached to his belt, several other mysterious cases dang ling about him, and a black staff with copper ferrules in his hand. His companion was a rough spare dog, that followed at his heels, but stopped short, suspiciously, at the drawbridge, and in a little while began to howl dismally.

In the meantime the mountebank, standing in the midst of the courtyard, raised his grotesque hat, and made us a very ceremonious bow, paying his compliments very volubly in execrable French, and German not much better.

Then, disengaging his fiddle, he began to scrape a lively air to which he sang with a merry discord, dancing with ludicrous airs and activity, that made me laugh, in spite of the dog's howling.

Then he advanced to the window with many smiles and salut ations, and his hat in his left hand, his fiddle under his arm, and with a fluency that never took breath, he gabbled a long advertisement of

ll his accomplishments, and the resources of the various arts which
e placed at our service, and the curiosities and entertainments
which it was in his power, at our bidding, to display.

'Will your ladyships be pleased to buy an amulet against the oupire,
which is going like the wolf, I hear, through these woods,' he said
dropping his hat on the pavement. 'They are dying of it right and left
and here is a charm that never fails; only pinned to the pillow, and
you may laugh in his face.'

These charms consisted of oblong slips of vellum, with cabalistic
ciphers and diagrams upon them.

Carmilla instantly purchased one, and so did I.

He was looking up, and we were smiling down upon him, amused;
at least, I can answer for myself. His piercing black eye, as he looked
up in our faces, seemed to detect something that fixed for a moment
his curiosity. In an instant he unrolled a leather case, full of all
manner of odd little steel instruments.

'See here, my lady,' he said, displaying it, and addressing me, 'I
profess, among other things less useful, the art of dentistry. Plague
take the dog!' he interpolated. 'Silence, beast! He howls so that your
ladyships can scarcely hear a word. Your noble friend, the young lady
at your right, has the sharpest tooth – long, thin, pointed, like an
awl, like a needle; ha, ha! With my sharp and long sight, as I look up,
I have seen it distinctly; now if it happens to hurt the young lady, and
I think it must, here am I, here are my file, my punch, my nippers; I
will make it round and blunt, if her ladyship pleases; no longer the
tooth of a fish, but of a beautiful young lady as she is. Hey? Is the
young lady displeased? Have I been too bold? Have I offended her?'

The young lady, indeed, looked very angry as she drew back from
the window.

'How dares that mountebank insult us so? Where is your father? I
shall demand redress from him. My father would have had the wretch
tied up to the pump, and flogged with a cart whip, and burnt to the
bones with the cattle brand!'

She retired from the window a step or two, and sat down, and
had hardly lost sight of the offender, when her wrath subsided as
suddenly as it had risen, and she gradually recovered her usual tone,
and seemed to forget the little hunchback and his follies.

My father was out of spirits that evening. On coming in he told
us that there had been another case very similar to the two fatal
ones which had lately occurred. The sister of a young peasant on
his estate, only a mile away, was very ill, had been, as she described

it, attacked very nearly in the same way, and was now slowly bu steadily sinking.

'All this,' said my father, 'is strictly referable to natural causes These poor people infect one another with their superstitions, an so repeat in imagination the images of terror that have infested thei neighbouurs.'

'But that very circumstance frightens one horribly,' said Carmilla

'How so?' inquired my father.

'I am so afraid of fancying I see such things; I think it would be as bad as reality.'

'We are in God's hands: nothing can happen without his per mission, and all will end well for those who love him. He is ou faithful creator; He has made us all, and will take care of us.'

'Creator! *Nature*!' said the young lady in answer to my gentle father. 'And this disease that invades the country is natural. Nature All things proceed from Nature – don't they? All things in the heaven, in the earth, and under the earth, act and live as Nature ordains? I think so.'

'The doctor said he would come here today,' said my father, after a silence. 'I want to know what he thinks about it, and what he thinks we had better do.'

'Doctors never did me any good,' said Carmilla.

'Then you have been ill?' I asked.

'More ill than ever you were,' she answered.

'Long ago?'

'Yes, a long time. I suffered from this very illness; but I forget all but my pain and weakness, and they were not so bad as are suffered in other diseases.'

'You were very young then?'

'I dare say; let us talk no more of it. You would not wound a friend?'

She looked languidly in my eyes, and passed her arm round my waist lovingly, and led me out of the room. My father was busy over some papers near the window.

'Why does your papa like to frighten us?' said the pretty girl with a sigh and a little shudder.

'He doesn't, dear Carmilla, it is the very furthest thing from his mind.'

'Are you afraid, dearest?'

'I should be, very much, if I fancied there was any real danger of my being attacked as those poor people were.'

'You are afraid to die?'

'Yes, everyone is.'

'But to die as lovers may – to die together, so that they may live together. Girls are caterpillars while they live in the world, to be finally butterflies when the summer comes; but in the meantime there are grubs and larvae, don't you see – each with their peculiar propensities, necessities and structure. So says Monsieur Buffon, in his big book, in the next room.'

Later in the day the doctor came, and was closeted with papa for some time.

He was a skilful man, of sixty and upwards; he wore powder, and shaved his pale face as smooth as a pumpkin. He and papa emerged from the room together, and I heard papa laugh, and say as they came out: 'Well, I do wonder at a wise man like you. What do you say to hippogriffs and dragons?'

The doctor was smiling, and made answer, shaking his head –

'Nevertheless life and death are mysterious states, and we know little of the resources of either.'

And so they walked on, and I heard no more. I did not then know what the doctor had been broaching, but I think I guess it now.

5

A Wonderful Likeness

This evening there arrived from Gratz the grave, dark-faced son of the picture cleaner, with a horse and cart laden with two large packing cases, having many pictures in each. It was a journey of ten leagues, and whenever a messenger arrived at the schloss from our little capital of Gratz, we used to crowd about him in the hall, to hear the news.

This arrival created in our secluded quarters quite a sensation. The cases remained in the hall, and the messenger was taken charge of by the servants till he had eaten his supper. Then with assistants, and armed with hammer, ripping chisel, and turnscrew, he met us in the hall, where we had assembled to witness the unpacking of the cases.

Carmilla sat looking listlessly on, while one after the other the old pictures, nearly all portraits, which had undergone the process of renovation, were brought to light. My mother was of an old Hungarian family, and most of these pictures, which were about to be restored to their places, had come to us through her.

My father had a list in his hand, from which he read, as the artist rummaged out the corresponding numbers. I don't know that the pictures were very good, but they were, undoubtedly, very old, and some of them very curious also. They had, for the most part, the merit of being now seen by me, I may say, for the first time; for the smoke and dust of time had all but obliterated them.

'There is a picture that I have not seen yet,' said my father. 'In one corner, at the top of it, is the name, as well as I could read, "Marcia Karnstein", and the date "1698"; and I am curious to see how it has turned out.'

I remembered it; it was a small picture, about a foot and a half high, and nearly square, without a frame; but it was so blackened by age that I could not make it out.

The artist now produced it, with evident pride. It was quite beautiful; it was startling; it seemed to live. It was the effigy of Carmilla!

'Carmilla, dear, here is an absolute miracle. Here you are, living, smiling, ready to speak, in this picture. Isn't it beautiful, Papa? And see, even the little mole on her throat.'

My father laughed, and said 'Certainly it is a wonderful likeness,' but he looked away, and to my surprise seemed but little struck by it, and went on talking to the picture cleaner, who was also something of an artist, and discoursed with intelligence about the portraits or other works, which his art had just brought into light and colour, while I was more and more lost in wonder the more I looked at the picture.

'Will you let me hang this picture in my room, papa?' I asked.

'Certainly, dear,' said he, smiling, 'I'm very glad you think it so like. It must be prettier even than I thought it, if it is.'

The young lady did not acknowledge this pretty speech, did not seem to hear it. She was leaning back in her seat, her fine eyes under their long lashes gazing on me in contemplation, and she smiled in a kind of rapture.

'And now you can read quite plainly the name that is written in the corner. It is not Marcia; it looks as if it was done in gold. The name is Mircalla, Countess Karnstein, and this is a little coronet over and underneath A.D.1698. I am descended from the Karnsteins; that is, mamma was.'

'Ah!' said the lady, languidly, 'so am I, I think, a very long descent, very ancient. Are there any Karnsteins living now?'

'None who bear the name, I believe. The family were ruined, I believe, in some civil wars, long ago, but the ruins of the castle are only about three miles away.'

'How interesting!' she said, languidly. 'But see what beautiful moonlight!' She glanced through the hall door, which stood a little open. 'Suppose you take a little ramble round the court, and look down at the road and river.'

'It is so like the night you came to us,' I said.

She sighed, smiling.

She rose, and each with her arm about the other's waist, we walked out upon the pavement.

In silence, slowly we walked down to the drawbridge, where the beautiful landscape opened before us.

'And so you were thinking of the night I came here?' she almost whispered. 'Are you glad I came?'

'Delighted, dear Carmilla,' I answered.

'And you asked for the picture you think like me, to hang in your room,' she murmured with a sigh, as she drew her arm closer about my waist, and let her pretty head sink upon my shoulder. 'How romantic you are, Carmilla,' I said. 'Whenever you tell me your story, it will be made up chiefly of some one great romance.'

She kissed me silently.

'I am sure, Carmilla, you have been in love; that there is, at this moment, an affair of the heart going on.'

'I have been in love with no-one, and never shall,' she whispered, 'unless it should be with you.'

How beautiful she looked in the moonlight!

Shy and strange was the look with which she quickly hid her face in my neck and hair, with tumultuous sighs, that seemed almost to sob, and pressed in mine a hand that trembled.

Her soft cheek was glowing against mine. 'Darling, darling,' she murmured, 'I live in you; and you would die for me, I love you so.'

I started from her.

She was gazing on me with eyes from which all fire, all meaning had flown, and a face colourless and apathetic.

'Is there a chill in the air, dear?' she said drowsily. 'I almost shiver; have I been dreaming? Let us come in. Come; come; come in.'

'You look ill, Carmilla; a little faint. You certainly must take some wine,' I said.

'Yes. I will. I'm better now. I shall be quite well in a few minutes. Yes, do give me a little wine,' answered Carmilla, as we approached the door. 'Let us look again for a moment; it is the last time, perhaps, I shall see the moonlight with you.'

'How do you feel now, dear Carmilla? Are you really better?' asked.

I was beginning to take alarm, lest she should have been stricken with the strange epidemic that they said had invaded the country about us.

'Papa would be grieved beyond measure,' I added, 'if he thought you were ever so little ill, without immediately letting us know. We have a very skilful doctor near us, the physician who was with papa today.'

'I'm sure he is. I know how kind you all are; but, dear child, I am quite well again. There is nothing ever wrong with me, but a little weakness.

'People say I am languid; I am incapable of exertion; I can scarcely walk as far as a child of three years old: and every now and then the little strength I have falters, and I become as you have just seen me. But after all I am very easily set up again; in a moment I am perfectly myself. See how I have recovered.'

So, indeed, she had; and she and I talked a great deal, and very animated she was; and the remainder of that evening passed without any recurrence of what I called her infatuations. I mean her crazy talk and looks, which embarrassed and even frightened me.

But there occurred that night an event which gave my thoughts quite a new turn, and seemed to startle even Carmilla's languid nature into momentary energy.

6

A Very Strange Agony

When we got into the drawing room, and had sat down to our coffee and chocolate, although Carmilla did not take any, she seemed quite herself again, and Madame, and Mademoiselle de Lafontaine, joined us, and made a little card party, in the course of which papa came in for what he called his 'dish of tea'.

When the game was over he sat down beside Carmilla on the sofa, and asked her, a little anxiously, whether she had heard from her mother since her arrival.

She answered 'No'.

He then asked whether she knew where a letter would reach her at present.

'I cannot tell,' she answered ambiguously, 'but I have been thinking of leaving you; you have been already too hospitable and too kind o me. I have given you an infinity of trouble, and I should wish to take a carriage tomorrow, and post in pursuit of her; I know where I shall ultimately find her, although I dare not yet tell you.'

'But you must not dream of any such thing,' exclaimed my father, to my great relief. 'We can't afford to lose you so, and I won't consent to your leaving us, except under the care of your mother, who was so good as to consent to your remaining with us till she should herself return. I should be quite happy if I knew that you heard from her: but this evening the accounts of the progress of the mysterious disease that has invaded our neighbourhood, grow even more alarming; and my beautiful guest, I do feel the responsibility, unaided by advice from your mother, very much. But I shall do my best; and one thing is certain, that you must not think of leaving us without her distinct direction to that effect. We should suffer too much in parting from you to consent to it easily.'

'Thank you, sir, a thousand times for your hospitality,' she answered, smiling bashfully. 'You have all been too kind to me; I have seldom been so happy in all my life before, as in your beautiful chateau, under your care, and in the society of your dear daughter.'

So he gallantly, in his old-fashioned way, kissed her hand, smiling and pleased at her little speech.

I accompanied Carmilla as usual to her room, and sat and chatted with her while she was preparing for bed.

'Do you think,' I said at length, 'that you will ever confide fully in me?'

She turned round smiling, but made no answer, only continued to smile on me.

'You won't answer that?' I said. 'You can't answer pleasantly; I ought not to have asked you.'

'You were quite right to ask me that, or anything. You do not know how dear you are to me, or you could not think any confidence too great to look for. But I am under vows, no nun half so awfully, and I dare not tell my story yet, even to you. The time is very near when you shall know everything. You will think me cruel, very selfish, but love is always selfish; the more ardent, the more selfish. How jealous I am you cannot know. You must come with me, loving me, to death; or else hate me and still come with me, and *hating* me through death and after. There is no such word as indifference in my apathetic nature.'

'Now, Carmilla, you are going to talk your wild nonsense again,' I said hastily.

'Not I, silly little fool as I am, and full of whims and fancies; for your sake I'll talk like a sage. Were you ever at a ball?'

'No; how you do run on. What is it like? How charming it must be.'

'I almost forget, it is years ago.'

I laughed.

'You are not so old. Your first ball can hardly be forgotten yet.'

'I remember everything about it – with an effort. I see it all, as divers see what is going on above them, through a medium, dense, rippling, but transparent. There occurred that night what has confused the picture, and made its colours faint. I was all but assassinated in my bed, wounded here,' she touched her breast, 'and never was the same since.'

'Were you near dying?'

'Yes, very – a cruel love – strange love, that would have taken my life. Love will have its sacrifices. No sacrifice without blood. Let us go to sleep now; I feel so lazy. How can I get up just now and lock my door?'

She was lying with her tiny hands buried in her rich wavy hair, under her cheek, her little head upon the pillow, and her glittering eyes followed me wherever I moved, with a kind of shy smile that I could not decipher.

I bid her good night, and crept from the room with an uncomfortable sensation.

I often wondered whether our pretty guest ever said her prayers. I certainly had never seen her upon her knees. In the morning she never came down until long after our family prayers were over, and at night she never left the drawing room to attend our brief evening prayers in the hall.

If it had not been that it had casually come out in one of our careless talks that she had been baptised, I should have doubted her being a Christian. Religion was a subject on which I had never heard her speak a word. If I had known the world better, this particular neglect or antipathy would not have so much surprised me.

The precautions of nervous people are infectious, and persons of a like temperament are pretty sure, after a time, to imitate them. I had adopted Carmilla's habit of locking her bedroom door, having taken into my head all her whimsical alarms about midnight invaders and prowling assassins. I had also adopted her precaution of making a brief search through her room, to satisfy herself that no lurking assassin or robber was 'ensconced'.

These wise measures taken, I got into my bed and fell asleep. A light was burning in my room. This was an old habit, of very early date, and which nothing could have tempted me to dispense with.

Thus fortified I might take my rest in peace. But dreams come through stone walls, light up dark rooms, or darken light ones, and their persons make their exits and their entrances as they please, and laugh at locksmiths.

I had a dream that night that was the beginning of a very strange agony.

I cannot call it a nightmare, for I was quite conscious of being asleep.

But I was equally conscious of being in my room, and lying in bed, precisely as I actually was. I saw, or fancied I saw, the room and its furniture just as I had seen it last, except that it was very dark, and I saw something moving round the foot of the bed, which at first I could not accurately distinguish. But I soon saw that it was a sooty-black animal that resembled a monstrous cat. It appeared to me about four or five feet long, for it measured fully the length of the hearthrug as it passed over it; and it continued to-ing and fro-ing with the lithe, sinister restlessness of a beast in a cage. I could not cry out, although as you may suppose, I was terrified. Its pace was growing faster, and the room rapidly darker and darker, and at length so dark that I could no longer see anything of it but its eyes. I felt it spring lightly on the bed. The two broad eyes approached my face, and suddenly I felt a stinging pain as if two large needles darted, an inch or two apart, deep into my breast. I waked with a scream. The room was lighted by the candle that burnt there all through the night, and I saw a female figure standing at the foot of the bed, a little at the right side. It was in a dark loose dress, and its hair was down and covered its shoulders. A block of stone could not have been more still. There was not the slightest stir of respiration. As I stared at it, the figure appeared to have changed its place, and was now nearer the door; then, close to it, the door opened, and it passed out.

I was now relieved, and able to breathe and move. My first thought was that Carmilla had been playing me a trick, and that I had forgotten to secure my door. I hastened to it, and found it locked as usual on the inside. I was afraid to open it – I was horrified. I sprang into my bed and covered my head up in the bedclothes, and lay there more dead than alive till morning.

7

Descending

It would be vain my attempting to tell you the horror with which even now, I recall the occurrence of that night. It was no such transitory terror as a dream leaves behind it. It seemed to deepen by time, and communicated itself to the room and the very furniture that had encompassed the apparition.

I could not bear next day to be alone for a moment. I should have told papa, but for two opposite reasons. At one time I thought he would laugh at my story, and I could not bear its being treated as a jest; and at another I thought he might fancy that I had been attacked by the mysterious complaint which had invaded our neighbourhood. I had myself no misgiving of the kind, and as he had been rather an invalid for some time, I was afraid of alarming him.

I was comfortable enough with my good-natured companions, Madame Perrodon, and the vivacious Mademoiselle Lafontaine. They both perceived that I was out of spirits and nervous, and at length I told them what lay so heavy at my heart.

Mademoiselle laughed, but I fancied that Madame Perrodon looked anxious.

'By-the-by,' said Mademoiselle, laughing, 'the long lime tree walk, behind Carmilla's bedroom window, is haunted!'

'Nonsense!' exclaimed Madame, who probably thought the theme rather inopportune, 'and who tells that story, my dear?'

'Martin says that he came up twice, when the old yard gate was being repaired, before sunrise, and twice saw the same female figure walking down the lime tree avenue.'

'So he well might, as long as there are cows to milk in the river fields,' said Madame.

'I dare say; but Martin chooses to be frightened, and never did I see fool more frightened.'

'You must not say a word about it to Carmilla, because she can see down that walk from her room window,' I interposed, 'and she is, if possible, a greater coward than I.'

Carmilla came down rather later than usual that day.

'I was so frightened last night,' she said, so soon as were together, 'and I am sure I should have seen something dreadful if it had not been for that charm I bought from the poor little hunchback whom I called such hard names. I had a dream of something black coming round my bed, and I awoke in a perfect horror, and I really thought, for some seconds, I saw a dark figure near the chimney-piece, but I felt under my pillow for my charm, and the moment my fingers touched it, the figure disappeared, and I felt quite certain, only that I had it by me, that something frightful would have made its appearance, and, perhaps, throttled me, as it did those poor people we heard of.

'Well, listen to me,' I began, and recounted my adventure, at the recital of which she appeared horrified.

'And had you the charm near you?' she asked, earnestly.

'No, I had dropped it into a china vase in the drawing room, but I shall certainly take it with me tonight, as you have so much faith in it.'

At this distance of time I cannot tell you, or even understand, how I overcame my horror so effectually as to lie alone in my room that night. I remember distinctly that I pinned the charm to my pillow. I fell asleep almost immediately, and slept even more soundly than usual all night.

Next night I passed as well. My sleep was delightfully deep and dreamless.

But I wakened with a sense of lassitude and melancholy, which, however, did not exceed a degree that was almost luxurious.

'Well, I told you so,' said Carmilla, when I described my quiet sleep, 'I had such delightful sleep myself last night; I pinned the charm to the breast of my nightdress. It was too far away the night before. I am quite sure it was all fancy, except the dreams. I used to think that evil spirits made dreams, but our doctor told me it is no such thing. Only a fever passing by, or some other malady, as they often do, he said, knocks at the door, and not being able to get in, passes on, with that alarm.'

'And what do you think the charm is?' said I.

'It has been fumigated or immersed in some drug, and is an antidote against the malaria,' she answered.

'Then it acts only on the body?'

'Certainly; you don't suppose that evil spirits are frightened by bits of ribbon, or the perfumes of a druggist's shop? No, these complaints, wandering in the air, begin by trying the nerves, and so infect the brain, but before they can seize upon you, the antidote repels them. That I am sure is what the charm has done for us. It is nothing magical, it is simply natural.'

I should have been happier if I could have quite agreed with Carmilla, but I did my best, and the impression was a little losing its force.

For some nights I slept profoundly; but still every morning I felt the same lassitude, and a languor weighed upon me all day. I felt myself a changed girl. A strange melancholy was stealing over me, a melancholy that I would not have interrupted. Dim thoughts of death began to open, and an idea that I was slowly sinking took gentle, and somehow not unwelcome, possession of me. If it was sad, the tone of mind which this induced was also sweet.

Whatever it might be, my soul acquiesced in it.

I would not admit that I was ill, I would not consent to tell my papa, or to have the doctor sent for.

Carmilla became more devoted to me than ever, and her strange paroxysms of languid adoration more frequent. She used to gloat on me with increasing ardour the more my strength and spirits waned. This always shocked me like a momentary glare of insanity.

Without knowing it, I was now in a pretty advanced stage of the strangest illness under which mortal ever suffered. There was an unaccountable fascination in its earlier symptoms that more than reconciled me to the incapacitating effect of that stage of the malady. This fascination increased for a time, until it reached a certain point, when gradually a sense of the horrible mingled itself with it, deepening, as you shall hear, until it discoloured and perverted the whole state of my life.

The first change I experienced was rather agreeable. It was very near the turning-point from which began the descent of Avernus.

Certain vague and strange sensations visited me in my sleep. The prevailing one was of that pleasant, peculiar cold thrill which we feel in bathing, when we move against the current of a river. This was soon accompanied by dreams that seemed interminable, and were so vague that I could never recollect their scenery and persons, or any one connected portion of their action. But they left an awful impression, and a sense of exhaustion, as if I had passed through a long period of great mental exertion and danger.

After all these dreams there remained on waking a remembrance of having been in a place very nearly dark, and of having spoken to people whom I could not see; and especially of one clear voice, of a female's, very deep, that spoke as if at a distance, slowly, and producing always the same sensation of indescribable solemnity and fear. Sometimes there came a sensation as if a hand was drawn softly along my cheek and neck. Sometimes it was as if warm lips kissed me, and longer and longer and more lovingly as they reached my throat, but there the caress fixed itself. My heart beat aster, my breathing rose and fell rapidly and full drawn; a sobbing, that rose into a sense of strangulation, supervened, and turned into a dreadful convulsion, in which my senses left me and I became unconscious.

It was now three weeks since the commencement of this unaccountable state.

My sufferings had, during the last week, told upon my appearance. I had grown pale, my eyes were dilated and darkened underneath, and the languor which I had long felt began to display itself in my countenance.

My father asked me often whether I was ill; but, with an obstinacy which now seems to me unaccountable, I persisted in assuring him that I was quite well.

In a sense this was true. I had no pain, I could complain of no bodily derangement. My complaint seemed to be one of the imagination, or the nerves, and, horrible as my sufferings were, I kept them, with a morbid reserve, very nearly to myself.

It could not be that terrible complaint which the peasants called the oupire, for I had now been suffering for three weeks, and they were seldom ill for much more than three days, when death put an end to their miseries.

Carmilla complained of dreams and feverish sensations, but by no means of so alarming a kind as mine. I say that mine were extremely alarming. Had I been capable of comprehending my condition, I would have invoked aid and advice on my knees. The narcotic of an unsuspected influence was acting upon me, and my perceptions were benumbed.

I am going to tell you now of a dream that led immediately to an odd discovery.

One night, instead of the voice I was accustomed to hear in the dark, I heard one, sweet and tender, and at the same time terrible, which said, 'Your mother warns you to beware of the assassin.' At the same time a light unexpectedly sprang up, and I saw Carmilla, standing, near the foot of my bed, in her white nightdress, bathed, from her chin to her feet, in one great stain of blood.

I wakened with a shriek, possessed with the one idea that Carmilla was being murdered. I remember springing from my bed, and my next recollection is that of standing on the lobby, crying for help.

Madame and Mademoiselle came scurrying out of their rooms in alarm; a lamp burned always on the lobby, and seeing me, they soon learned the cause of my terror.

I insisted on our knocking at Carmilla's door. Our knocking wa
unanswered.

It soon became a pounding and an uproar. We shrieked her name
but all was vain.

We all grew frightened, for the door was locked. We hurried back
in panic, to my room. There we rang the bell long and furiously
If my father's room had been at that side of the house, we would
have called him up at once to our aid. But, alas! he was quite out of
hearing, and to reach him involved an excursion for which we none
of us had courage.

Servants, however, soon came running up the stairs; I had got on
my dressing gown and slippers meanwhile, and my companions were
already similarly furnished. Recognising the voices of the servants on
the lobby, we sallied out together; and having renewed, as fruitlessly,
our summons at Carmilla's door, I ordered the men to force the lock.
They did so, and we stood, holding our lights aloft, in the doorway,
and so stared into the room.

We called her by name, but there was still no reply. We looked
round the room. Everything was undisturbed. It was exactly in the
state in which I had left it on bidding her good night. But Carmilla
was gone.

8
Search

At sight of the room, perfectly undisturbed except for our violent
entrance, we began to cool a little, and soon recovered our senses
sufficiently to dismiss the men. It had struck Mademoiselle that
possibly Carmilla had been wakened by the uproar at her door, and
in her first panic had jumped from her bed, and hid herself in a press,
or behind a curtain, from which she could not, of course, emerge
until the majordomo and his myrmidons had withdrawn. We now
recommenced our search, and began to call her name again.

It was all to no purpose. Our perplexity and agitation increased.
We examined the windows, but they were secured. I implored of
Carmilla, if she had concealed herself, to play this cruel trick no
longer – to come out and to end our anxieties. It was all useless. I was
by this time convinced that she was not in the room, nor in the
dressing room, the door of which was still locked on this side. She
could not have passed it. I was utterly puzzled. Had Carmilla discovered one of those secret passages which the old housekeeper said

were known to exist in the schloss, although the tradition of their exact situation had been lost? A little time would, no doubt, explain all – utterly perplexed as, for the present, we were.

It was past four o'clock, and I preferred passing the remaining hours of darkness in Madame's room. Daylight brought no solution of the difficulty.

The whole household, with my father at its head, was in a state of agitation next morning. Every part of the chateau was searched. The grounds were explored. No trace of the missing lady could be discovered. The stream was about to be dragged; my father was in distraction; what a tale to have to tell the poor girl's mother on her return. I, too, was almost beside myself, though my grief was quite of a different kind.

The morning was passed in alarm and excitement. It was now one o'clock, and still no tidings. I ran up to Carmilla's room, and found her standing at her dressing-table. I was astounded. I could not believe my eyes. She beckoned me to her with her pretty finger, in silence. Her face expressed extreme fear.

I ran to her in an ecstasy of joy; I kissed and embraced her again and again. I ran to the bell and rang it vehemently, to bring others to the spot who might at once relieve my father's anxiety.

'Dear Carmilla, what has become of you all this time? We have been in agonies of anxiety about you,' I exclaimed. 'Where have you been? How did you come back?'

'Last night has been a night of wonders,' she said.

'For mercy's sake, explain all you can.'

'It was past two last night,' she said, 'when I went to sleep as usual in my bed, with my doors locked, that of the dressing room, and that opening upon the gallery. My sleep was uninterrupted, and, so far as I know, dreamless; but I woke just now on the sofa in the dressing room there, and I found the door between the rooms open, and the other door forced. How could all this have happened without my being wakened? It must have been accompanied with a great deal of noise, and I am particularly easily wakened; and how could I have been carried out of my bed without my sleep having been interrupted, I whom the slightest stir startles?'

By this time, Madame, Mademoiselle, my father, and a number of the servants were in the room. Carmilla was, of course, overwhelmed with inquiries, congratulations, and welcomes. She had but one story to tell, and seemed the least able of all the party to suggest any way of accounting for what had happened.

My father took a turn up and down the room, thinking. I saw Carmilla's eye follow him for a moment with a sly, dark glance.

When my father had sent the servants away, Mademoiselle having gone in search of a little bottle of valerian and salvolatile, and there being no-one now in the room with Carmilla, except my father, Madame, and myself, he came to her thoughtfully, took her hand very kindly, led her to the sofa, and sat down beside her.

'Will you forgive me, my dear, if I risk a conjecture, and ask a question?'

'Who can have a better right?' she said. 'Ask what you please, and I will tell you everything. But my story is simply one of bewilderment and darkness. I know absolutely nothing. Put any question you please, but you know, of course, the limitations mamma has placed me under.'

'Perfectly, my dear child. I need not approach the topics on which she desires our silence. Now, the marvel of last night consists in your having been removed from your bed and your room, without being wakened, and this removal having occurred apparently while the windows were still secured, and the two doors locked upon the inside. I will tell you my theory and ask you a question.'

Carmilla was leaning on her hand dejectedly; Madame and I were listening breathlessly.

'Now, my question is this. Have you ever been suspected of walking in your sleep?'

'Never, since I was very young indeed.'

'But you did walk in your sleep when you were young?'

'Yes; I know I did. I have been told so often by my old nurse.'

My father smiled and nodded.

'Well, what has happened is this. You got up in your sleep, unlocked the door, not leaving the key, as usual, in the lock, but taking it out and locking it on the outside; you again took the key out, and carried it away with you to some one of the five-and-twenty rooms on this floor, or perhaps upstairs or downstairs. There are so many rooms and closets, so much heavy furniture, and such accumulations of lumber, that it would require a week to search this old house thoroughly. Do you see, now, what I mean?'

'I do, but not all,' she answered.

'And how, papa, do you account for her finding herself on the sofa in the dressing room, which we had searched so carefully?'

'She came there after you had searched it, still in her sleep, and at last awoke spontaneously, and was as much surprised to find herself where she was as anyone else. I wish all mysteries were as easily and

nnocently explained as yours, Carmilla,' he said, laughing. 'And so
we may congratulate ourselves on the certainty that the most natural
explanation of the occurrence is one that involves no drugging, no
tampering with locks, no burglars, or poisoners, or witches – nothing
that need alarm Carmilla, or anyone else, for our safety.'

Carmilla was looking charmingly. Nothing could be more beautiful than her tints. Her beauty was, I think, enhanced by that graceful
languor that was peculiar to her. I think my father was silently
contrasting her looks with mine, for he said: 'I wish my poor Laura
was looking more like herself'; and he sighed.

So our alarms were happily ended, and Carmilla restored to her
friends.

9

The Doctor

As Carmilla would not hear of an attendant sleeping in her room,
my father arranged that a servant should sleep outside her door, so
that she would not attempt to make another such excursion without
being arrested at her own door.

That night passed quietly; and next morning early, the doctor,
whom my father had sent for without telling me a word about it,
arrived to see me.

Madame accompanied me to the library; and there the grave little
doctor with white hair and spectacles, whom I mentioned before,
was waiting to receive me.

I told him my story, and as I proceeded he grew graver and graver.

We were standing, he and I, in the recess of one of the windows,
facing one another. When my statement was over, he leaned with his
shoulders against the wall, and with his eyes fixed on me earnestly,
with an interest in which was a dash of horror.

After a minute's reflection, he asked Madame if he could see my
father.

He was sent for accordingly, and as he entered, smiling, he said: 'I
dare say, doctor, you are going to tell me that I am an old fool for
having brought you here; I hope I am.'

But his smile faded into shadow as the doctor, with a very grave
face, beckoned him to him.

He and the doctor talked for some time in the same recess where
I had just conferred with the physician. It seemed an earnest and
argumentative conversation. The room is very large, and I and

Madame stood together, burning with curiosity, at the farther end. Not a word could we hear, however, for they spoke in a very low tone, and the deep recess of the window quite concealed the doctor from view, and very nearly my father, whose foot, arm, and shoulder only could we see; and the voices were, I suppose, all the less audible for the sort of closet which the thick wall and window formed.

After a time my father's face looked into the room; it was pale, thoughtful, and, I fancied, agitated.

'Laura, dear, come here for a moment. Madame, we shan't trouble you, the doctor says, at present.'

Accordingly I approached, for the first time a little alarmed; for, although I felt very weak, I did not feel ill; and strength, one always fancies, is a thing that may be picked up when we please.

My father held out his hand to me, as I drew near, but he was looking at the doctor, and he said: 'It certainly is very odd; I don't understand it quite. Laura, come here, dear; now attend to Doctor Spielsberg, and recollect yourself.'

'You mentioned a sensation like that of two needles piercing the skin, somewhere about your neck, on the night when you experienced your first horrible dream. Is there still any soreness?'

'None at all,' I answered.

'Can you indicate with your finger about the point at which you think this occurred?'

'Very little below my throat – here,' I answered.

I wore a morning dress, which covered the place I pointed to.

'Now you can satisfy yourself,' said the doctor. 'You won't mind your papa's lowering your dress a very little. It is necessary, to detect a symptom of the complaint under which you have been suffering.'

I acquiesced. It was only an inch or two below the edge of my collar.

'God bless me! – So it is,' exclaimed my father, growing pale.

'You see it now with your own eyes,' said the doctor, with a gloomy triumph.

'What is it?' I exclaimed, beginning to be frightened.

'Nothing, my dear young lady, but a small blue spot, about the size of the tip of your little finger; and now,' he continued, turning to papa, 'the question is what is best to be done?'

'Is there any danger?' I urged, in great trepidation.

'I trust not, my dear,' answered the doctor. 'I don't see why you should not recover. I don't see why you should not begin immediately to get better. That is the point at which the sense of strangulation begins?'

'Yes,' I answered.

'And – recollect as well as you can – the same point was a kind of centre of that thrill which you described just now, like the current of a cold stream running against you?'

'It may have been; I think it was.'

'Ay, you see?' he added, turning to my father. 'Shall I say a word to Madame?'

'Certainly,' said my father.

He called Madame to him, and said: 'I find my young friend here far from well. It won't be of any great consequence, I hope; but it will be necessary that some steps be taken, which I will explain by-and-by; but in the meantime, Madame, you will be so good as not to let Miss Laura be alone for one moment. That is the only direction I need give for the present. It is indispensable.'

'We may rely upon your kindness, Madame, I know,' added my father.

Madame satisfied him eagerly.

'And you, dear Laura, I know you will observe the doctor's direction.'

'I shall have to ask your opinion upon another patient, whose symptoms slightly resemble those of my daughter, that have just been detailed to you – very much milder in degree, but I believe quite of the same sort. She is a young lady – our guest; but as you say you will be passing this way again this evening, you can't do better than take your supper here, and you can then see her. She does not come down till the afternoon.'

'I thank you,' said the doctor. 'I shall be with you, then, at about seven this evening.'

And then they repeated their directions to me and to Madame, and with this parting charge my father left us, and walked out with the doctor; and I saw them pacing together up and down between the road and the moat, on the grassy platform in front of the castle, evidently absorbed in earnest conversation.

The doctor did not return. I saw him mount his horse there, take his leave, and ride away eastward through the forest.

Nearly at the same time I saw the man arrive from Dranfield with the letters, and dismount and hand the bag to my father.

In the meantime, Madame and I were both busy, lost in conjecture as to the reasons of the singular and earnest direction which the doctor and my father had concurred in imposing. Madame, as she afterwards told me, was afraid the doctor apprehended a sudden seizure, and that, without prompt assistance, I might either lose my life in a fit, or at least be seriously hurt.

The interpretation did not strike me; and I fancied, perhaps luckily for my nerves, that the arrangement was prescribed simply to secure a companion who would prevent my taking too much exercise, or eating unripe fruit, or doing any of the fifty foolish things to which young people are supposed to be prone.

About half an hour after, my father came in – he had a letter in his hand – and said: 'This letter had been delayed; it is from General Spielsdorf. He might have been here yesterday, he may not come till tomorrow or he may be here today.'

He put the open letter into my hand; but he did not look pleased, as he used when a guest, especially one so much loved as the General, was coming.

On the contrary, he looked as if he wished him at the bottom of the Red Sea. There was plainly something on his mind which he did not choose to divulge.

'Papa, darling, will you tell me this?' said I, suddenly laying my hand on his arm, and looking, I am sure, imploringly in his face.

'Perhaps,' he answered, smoothing my hair caressingly over my eyes.

'Does the doctor think me very ill?'

'No, dear; he thinks, if right steps are taken, you will be quite well again; at least, on the high road to a complete recovery, in a day or two,' he answered, a little dryly. 'I wish our good friend, the General, had chosen any other time; that is, I wish you had been perfectly well to receive him.'

'But do tell me, papa,' I insisted, 'what does he think is the matter with me?'

'Nothing; you must not plague me with questions,' he answered, with more irritation than I ever remember him to have displayed before; and seeing that I looked wounded, I suppose, he kissed me, and added, 'You shall know all about it in a day or two; that is, all that I know. In the meantime you are not to trouble your head about it.'

He turned and left the room, but came back before I had done wondering and puzzling over the oddity of all this; it was merely to say that he was going to Karnstein, and had ordered the carriage to be ready at twelve, and that I and Madame should accompany him; he was going to see the priest who lived near those picturesque grounds, upon business, and as Carmilla had never seen them, she could follow, when she came down, with Mademoiselle, who would bring materials for what you call a picnic, which might be laid for us in the ruined castle.

At twelve o'clock, accordingly, I was ready, and not long after, my father, Madame and I set out upon our projected drive.

Passing the drawbridge we turn to the right, and follow the road over the steep Gothic bridge, westward, to reach the deserted village and ruined castle of Karnstein.

No sylvan drive can be fancied prettier. The ground breaks into gentle hills and hollows, all clothed with beautiful wood, totally destitute of the comparative formality which artificial planting and early culture and pruning impart.

The irregularities of the ground often lead the road out of its course, and cause it to wind beautifully round the sides of broken hollows and the steeper sides of the hills, among varieties of ground almost inexhaustible.

Turning one of these points, we suddenly encountered our old friend the General, riding towards us, attended by a mounted servant. His portmanteaus were following in a hired wagon, such as we term a cart.

The General dismounted as we pulled up, and, after the usual greetings, was easily persuaded to accept the vacant seat in the carriage and send his horse on with his servant to the schloss.

10
Bereaved

It was about ten months since we had last seen him: but that time had sufficed to make an alteration of years in his appearance. He had grown thinner; something of gloom and anxiety had taken the place of that cordial serenity which used to characterise his features. His dark blue eyes, always penetrating, now gleamed with a sterner light from under his shaggy grey eyebrows. It was not such a change as grief alone usually induces, and angrier passions seemed to have had their share in bringing it about.

We had not long resumed our drive, when the General began to talk, with his usual soldierly directness, of the bereavement, as he termed it, which he had sustained in the death of his beloved niece and ward; and he then broke out in a tone of intense bitterness and fury, inveighing against the 'hellish arts' to which she had fallen a victim, and expressing, with more exasperation than piety, his wonder that Heaven should tolerate so monstrous an indulgence of the lusts and malignity of hell.

My father, who saw at once that something very extraordinary had befallen, asked him, if not too painful to him, to detail the circumstances which he thought justified the strong terms in which he expressed himself.

'I should tell you all with pleasure,' said the General, 'but you would not believe me.'

'Why should I not?' he asked.

'Because,' he answered testily, 'you belicve in nothing but what consorts with your own prejudices and illusions. I remember when I was like you, but I have learned better.'

'Try me,' said my father; 'I am not such a dogmatist as you suppose. Besides which, I very well know that you generally require proof for what you believe, and am, therefore, very strongly predisposed to respect your conclusions.'

'You are right in supposing that I have not been led lightly into a belief in the marvellous – for what I have experienced *is* marvellous – and I have been forced by extraordinary evidence to credit that which ran counter, diametrically, to all my theories. I have been made the dupe of a preternatural conspiracy.'

Notwithstanding his professions of confidence in the General's penetration, I saw my father, at this point, glance at the General, with, as I thought, a marked suspicion of his sanity.

The General did not see it, luckily. He was looking gloomily and curiously into the glades and vistas of the woods that were opening before us.

'You are going to the Ruins of Karnstein?' he said. 'Yes, it is a lucky coincidence; do you know I was going to ask you to bring me there to inspect them. I have a special object in exploring. There is a ruined chapel, ain't there, with a great many tombs of that extinct family?'

'So there are – highly interesting,' said my father. 'I hope you are thinking of claiming the title and estates?'

My father said this gaily, but the General did not recollect the laugh, or even the smile, which courtesy exacts for a friend's joke; on the contrary, he looked grave and even fierce, ruminating on a matter that stirred his anger and horror.

'Something very different,' he said, gruffly. 'I mean to unearth some of those fine people. I hope, by God's blessing, to accomplish a pious sacrilege here, which will relieve our earth of certain monsters, and enable honest people to sleep in their beds without being assailed by murderers. I have strange things to tell you, my dear friend, such as I myself would have scouted as incredible a few months since.'

My father looked at him again, but this time not with a glance of suspicion – with an eye, rather, of keen intelligence and alarm.

'The house of Karnstein,' he said, 'has been long extinct: a hundred years at least. My dear wife was maternally descended from the Karnsteins. But the name and title have long ceased to exist. The castle is a ruin; the very village is deserted; it is fifty years since the smoke of a chimney was seen there; not a roof left.'

'Quite true. I have heard a great deal about that since I last saw you; a great deal that will astonish you. But I had better relate everything in the order in which it occurred,' said the General. 'You saw my dear ward – my child, I may call her. No creature could have been more beautiful, and only three months ago none more blooming.'

'Yes, poor thing! when I saw her last she certainly was quite lovely,' said my father. 'I was grieved and shocked more than I can tell you, my dear friend; I knew what a blow it was to you.'

He took the General's hand, and they exchanged a kind pressure. Tears gathered in the old soldier's eyes. He did not seek to conceal them. He said: 'We have been very old friends; I knew you would feel for me, childless as I am. She had become an object of very near interest to me, and repaid my care by an affection that cheered my home and made my life happy. That is all gone. The years that remain to me on earth may not be very long; but by God's mercy I hope to accomplish a service to mankind before I die, and to subserve the vengeance of Heaven upon the fiends who have murdered my poor child in the spring of her hopes and beauty!'

'You said, just now, that you intended relating everything as it occurred,' said my father. 'Pray do; I assure you that it is not mere curiosity that prompts me.'

By this time we had reached the point at which the Drunstall road, by which the General had come, diverges from the road which we were travelling to Karnstein.

'How far is it to the ruins?' inquired the General, looking anxiously forward.

'About half a league,' answered my father. 'Pray let us hear the story you were so good as to promise.'

11
The Story

'With all my heart,' said the General, with an effort; and after a short pause in which to arrange his subject, he commenced one of the strangest narratives I ever heard.

'My dear child was looking forward with great pleasure to the visit you had been so good as to arrange for her to your charming daughter.' Here he made me a gallant but melancholy bow. 'In the meantime we had an invitation to my old friend the Count Carlsfeld, whose schloss is about six leagues to the other side of Karnstein. It was to attend the series of fêtes which, you remember, were given by him in honour of his illustrious visitor, the Grand Duke Charles.'

'Yes; and very splendid, I believe, they were,' said my father.

'Princely! But then his hospitalities are quite regal. He has Aladdin's lamp. The night from which my sorrow dates was devoted to a magnificent masquerade. The grounds were thrown open, the trees hung with coloured lamps. There was such a display of fireworks as Paris itself had never witnessed. And such music – music, you know, is my weakness – such ravishing music! The finest instrumental band, perhaps, in the world, and the finest singers who could be collected from all the great operas in Europe. As you wandered through these fantastically illuminated grounds, the moon-lighted chateau throwing a rosy light from its long rows of windows, you would suddenly hear these ravishing voices stealing from the silence of some grove, or rising from boats upon the lake. I felt myself, as I looked and listened, carried back into the romance and poetry of my early youth.

'When the fireworks were ended, and the ball beginning, we returned to the noble suite of rooms that were thrown open to the dancers. A masked ball, you know, is a beautiful sight; but so brilliant a spectacle of the kind I never saw before.

'It was a very aristocratic assembly. I was myself almost the only "nobody" present.

'My dear child was looking quite beautiful. She wore no mask. Her excitement and delight added an unspeakable charm to her features, always lovely. I remarked a young lady, dressed magnificently, but wearing a mask, who appeared to me to be observing my ward with extraordinary interest. I had seen her, earlier in the evening, in the great hall, and again, for a few minutes, walking near us, on the terrace under the castle windows, similarly employed. A lady, also

masked, richly and gravely dressed, and with a stately air, like a
person of rank, accompanied her as a chaperon.

'Had the young lady not worn a mask, I could, of course, have
been much more certain upon the question whether she was really
watching my poor darling.

'I am now well assured that she was.

'We were now in one of the salons. My poor dear child had been
dancing, and was resting a little in one of the chairs near the door; I
was standing near. The two ladies I have mentioned had approached
and the younger took the chair next my ward, while her companion
stood beside me, and for a little time addressed herself, in a low tone,
to her charge.

'Availing herself of the privilege of her mask, she turned to me, and
in the tone of an old friend, and calling me by my name, opened a
conversation with me, which piqued my curiosity a good deal. She
referred to many scenes where she had met me – at Court, and at
distinguished houses. She alluded to little incidents which I had long
ceased to think of, but which, I found, had only lain in abeyance in
my memory, for they instantly started into life at her touch.

'I became more and more curious to ascertain who she was, every
moment. She parried my attempts to discover very adroitly and
pleasantly. The knowledge she showed of many passages in my life
seemed to me all but unaccountable; and she appeared to take a not
unnatural pleasure in foiling my curiosity, and in seeing me flounder
in my eager perplexity, from one conjecture to another.

'In the meantime the young lady, whom her mother called by the
odd name of Millarca, when she once or twice addressed her, had,
with the same ease and grace, got into conversation with my ward.

'She introduced herself by saying that her mother was a very old
acquaintance of mine. She spoke of the agreeable audacity which a
mask rendered practicable; she talked like a friend; she admired her
dress, and insinuated very prettily her admiration of her beauty.
She amused her with laughing criticisms upon the people who
crowded the ballroom, and laughed at my poor child's fun. She
was very witty and lively when she pleased, and after a time they
had grown very good friends, and the young stranger lowered
her mask, displaying a remarkably beautiful face. I had never seen
it before, neither had my dear child. But though it was new to us,
the features were so engaging, as well as lovely, that it was impossible not to feel the attraction powerfully. My poor girl did so. I
never saw anyone more taken with another at first sight, unless,

indeed, it was the stranger herself, who seemed quite to have los
her heart to her.

'In the meantime, availing myself of the licence of a masquerade,
put not a few questions to the elder lady.

'"You have puzzled me utterly," I said, laughing. "Is that no
enough? Won't you, now, consent to stand on equal terms, and dc
me the kindness to remove your mask?"

'"Can any request be more unreasonable?" she replied. "Ask a lady
to yield an advantage! Beside, how do you know you should recognise me? Years make changes."

'"As you see," I said, with a bow, and, I suppose, a rather melancholy little laugh.

'"As philosophers tell us," she said; "and how do you know that a
sight of my face would help you?"

'"I should take chance for that," I answered. "It is vain trying to
make yourself out an old woman; your figure betrays you."

'"Years, nevertheless, have passed since I saw you, rather since you
saw me, for that is what I am considering. Millarca, there, is my
daughter; I cannot then be young, even in the opinion of people
whom time has taught to be indulgent, and I may not like to be compared with what you remember me. You have no mask to remove.
You can offer me nothing in exchange."

'"My petition is to your pity, to remove it."

'"And mine to yours, to let it stay where it is," she replied.

'"Well, then, at least you will tell me whether you are French or
German; you speak both languages so perfectly."

'"I don't think I shall tell you that, General; you intend a surprise,
and are meditating the particular point of attack."

'"At all events, you won't deny this," I said, "that being honoured
by your permission to converse, I ought to know how to address
you. Shall I say Madame la Comtesse?"

'She laughed, and she would, no doubt, have met me with another
evasion – if, indeed, I can treat any occurrence in an interview every
circumstance of which was prearranged, as I now believe, with the
profoundest cunning, as liable to be modified by accident.

'"As to that," she began; but she was interrupted, almost as she
opened her lips, by a gentleman, dressed in black, who looked particularly elegant and distinguished, with this drawback, that his face was
the most deadly pale I ever saw, except in death. He was in no
masquerade – in the plain evening dress of a gentleman; and he said,
without a smile, but with a courtly and unusually low bow –

'"Will Madame la Comtesse permit me to say a very few words which may interest her?"

'The lady turned quickly to him, and touched her lip in token of silence; she then said to me, "Keep my place for me, General; I shall return when I have said a few words."

'And with this injunction, playfully given, she walked a little aside with the gentleman in black, and talked for some minutes, apparently very earnestly. They then walked away slowly together in the crowd, and I lost them for some minutes.

'I spent the interval in cudgelling my brains for a conjecture as to the identity of the lady who seemed to remember me so kindly, and I was thinking of turning about and joining in the conversation between my pretty ward and the Countess's daughter, and trying whether, by the time she returned, I might not have a surprise in store for her, by having her name, title, chateau, and estates at my fingers' ends. But at this moment she returned, accompanied by the pale man in black, who said: "I shall return and inform Madame la Comtesse when her carriage is at the door."

'He withdrew with a bow.'

12

A Petition

'"Then we are to lose Madame la Comtesse, but I hope only for a few hours," I said, with a low bow.

'"It may be that only, or it may be a few weeks. It was very unlucky his speaking to me just now as he did. Do you now know me?"

'I assured her I did not.

'"You shall know me," she said, "but not at present. We are older and better friends than, perhaps, you suspect. I cannot yet declare myself. I shall in three weeks pass your beautiful schloss, about which I have been making enquiries. I shall then look in upon you for an hour or two, and renew a friendship which I never think of without a thousand pleasant recollections. This moment a piece of news has reached me like a thunderbolt. I must set out now, and travel by a devious route, nearly a hundred miles, with all the dispatch I can possibly make. My perplexities multiply. I am only deterred by the compulsory reserve I practise as to my name from making a very singular request of you. My poor child has not quite recovered her strength. Her horse fell with her, at a hunt which she had ridden out to witness, her nerves have not yet recovered the shock, and our physician says that she must on no account exert herself for some time to come. We came here, in consequence, by very easy stages – hardly six leagues a day. I must now travel day and night, on a mission of life and death – a mission the critical and momentous nature of which I shall be able to explain to you when we meet, as I hope we shall, in a few weeks, without the necessity of any concealment."

'She went on to make her petition, and it was in the tone of a person from whom such a request amounted to conferring, rather than seeking, a favour.

'This was only in manner, and, as it seemed, quite unconsciously. Than the terms in which it was expressed, nothing could be more deprecatory. It was simply that I would consent to take charge of her daughter during her absence.

'This was, all things considered, a strange, not to say, an audacious request. She in some sort disarmed me, by stating and admitting everything that could be urged against it, and throwing herself entirely upon my chivalry. At the same moment, by a fatality that seems to have predetermined all that happened, my poor child came to my side, and, in an undertone, besought me to invite her new friend, Millarca, to pay us a visit. She had just been sounding her, and thought, if her mamma would allow her, she would like it extremely.

'At another time I should have told her to wait a little, until, at least, we knew who they were. But I had not a moment to think in. The two ladies assailed me together, and I must confess the refined and beautiful face of the young lady, about which there was something extremely engaging, as well as the elegance and fire of high birth, determined me; and, quite overpowered, I submitted and undertook, too easily, the care of the young lady, whom her mother called Millarca.

'The Countess beckoned to her daughter, who listened with grave attention while she told her, in general terms, how suddenly and peremptorily she had been summoned, and also of the arrangement she had made for her under my care, adding that I was one of her earliest and most valued friends.

'I made, of course, such speeches as the case seemed to call for, and found myself, on reflection, in a position which I did not half like.

'The gentleman in black returned, and very ceremoniously conducted the lady from the room.

'The demeanour of this gentleman was such as to impress me with the conviction that the Countess was a lady of very much more importance than her modest title alone might have led me to assume.

'Her last charge to me was that no attempt was to be made to learn more about her than I might have already guessed, until her return. Our distinguished host, whose guest she was, knew her reasons.

' "But here," she said, "neither I nor my daughter could safely remain for more than a day. I removed my mask imprudently for a moment, about an hour ago, and, too late, I fancied you saw me. So I resolved to seek an opportunity of talking a little to you. Had I found that you had seen me, I would have thrown myself on your high sense of honour to keep my secret some weeks. As it is, I am satisfied that you did not see me; but if you now suspect, or, on reflection, should suspect, who I am, I commit myself, in like manner, entirely to your honour. My daughter will observe the same secrecy, and I well know that you will, from time to time, remind her, lest she should thoughtlessly disclose it."

'She whispered a few words to her daughter, kissed her hurriedly twice, and went away, accompanied by the pale gentleman in black, and disappeared in the crowd.

' "In the next room," said Millarca, "there is a window that looks upon the hall door. I should like to see the last of mamma, and to kiss my hand to her."

'We assented, of course, and accompanied her to the window. We looked out, and saw a handsome old-fashioned carriage, with a troop of couriers and footmen. We saw the slim figure of the pale gentleman in black, as he held a thick velvet cloak, and placed it about her shoulders and threw the hood over her head. She nodded to him, and just touched his hand with hers. He bowed low repeatedly as the door closed, and the carriage began to move.

' "She is gone," said Millarca, with a sigh.

' "She is gone," I repeated to myself, for the first time – in the hurried moments that had elapsed since my consent – reflecting upon the folly of my act.

' "She did not look up," said the young lady, plaintively.

' "The Countess had taken off her mask, perhaps, and did not care to show her face," I said; "and she could not know that you were in the window."

'She sighed, and looked in my face. She was so beautiful that I relented. I was sorry I had for a moment repented of my hospitality, and I determined to make her amends for the unavowed churlishness of my reception.

'The young lady, replacing her mask, joined my ward in persuading me to return to the grounds, where the concert was soon to be renewed. We did so, and walked up and down the terrace that lies under the castle windows.

'Millarca became very intimate with us, and amused us with lively descriptions and stories of most of the great people whom we saw upon the terrace. I liked her more and more every minute. Her gossip, without being ill-natured, was extremely diverting to me who had been so long out of the great world. I thought what life she would give to our sometimes lonely evenings at home.

'This ball was not over until the morning sun had almost reached the horizon. It pleased the Grand Duke to dance till then, so loyal people could not go away, or think of bed.

'We had just got through a crowded saloon, when my ward asked me what had become of Millarca. I thought she had been by her side, and she fancied she was by mine. The fact was, we had lost her.

'All my efforts to find her were vain. I feared that she had mistaken, in the confusion of a momentary separation from us, other people for her new friends, and had, possibly, pursued and lost them in the extensive grounds which were thrown open to us.

'Now, in its full force, I recognised a new folly in my having undertaken the charge of a young lady without so much as knowing her name; and fettered as I was by promises, of the reasons for imposing which I knew nothing, I could not even point my inquiries by saying that the missing young lady was the daughter of the Countess who had taken her departure a few hours before.

'Morning broke. It was clear daylight before I gave up my search. It was not till near two o'clock next day that we heard anything of my missing charge.

'At about that time a servant knocked at my niece's door, to say that he had been earnestly requested by a young lady, who appeared to be in great distress, to make out where she could find the General Baron Spielsdorf and the young lady his daughter, in whose charge she had been left by her mother.

'There could be no doubt, notwithstanding the slight inaccuracy, that our young friend had turned up; and so she had. Would to heaven we *had* lost her!

'She told my poor child a story to account for her having failed to recover us for so long. Very late, she said, she had got to the housekeeper's bedroom in despair of finding us, and had then fallen into a deep sleep which, long as it was, had hardly sufficed to recruit her strength after the fatigues of the ball.

'That day Millarca came home with us. I was only too happy, after all, to have secured so charming a companion for my dear girl.'

13
The Woodman

'There soon, however, appeared some drawbacks. In the first place, Millarca complained of extreme languor – the weakness that remained after her late illness – and she never emerged from her room till the afternoon was pretty far advanced. In the next place, it was accidentally discovered, although she always locked her door on the inside, and never disturbed the key from its place till she admitted the maid to assist at her toilet, that she was undoubtedly sometimes absent from her room in the very early morning, and at various times later in the day, before she wished it to be understood that she was stirring. She was repeatedly seen from the windows of the schloss, in the first faint grey of the morning, walking through the trees, in an easterly direction, and looking like a person in a trance. This convinced me that she walked in her sleep. But this hypothesis did not solve the puzzle. How did she pass out from her room, leaving the door locked on the inside? How did she escape from the house without unbarring door or window?

'In the midst of my perplexities, an anxiety of a far more urgent kind presented itself.

'My dear child began to lose her looks and health, and that in a manner so mysterious, and even horrible, that I became thoroughly frightened.

'She was at first visited by appalling dreams; then, as she fancied, by a spectre, sometimes resembling Millarca, sometimes in the shape of a beast, indistinctly seen, walking round the foot of her bed, from side to side.

'Lastly came sensations. One, not unpleasant, but very peculiar, she said, resembled the flow of an icy stream against her breast. At a later time, she felt something like a pair of large needles pierce her, a little below the throat, with a very sharp pain. A few nights after, followed a gradual and convulsive sense of strangulation; then came unconsciousness.'

I could hear distinctly every word the kind old General was saying, because by this time we were driving upon the short grass that spreads on either side of the road as you approach the roofless village which had not shown the smoke of a chimney for more than half a century.

You may guess how strangely I felt as I heard my own symptoms so exactly described in those which had been experienced by the poor girl who, but for the catastrophe which followed, would have been at that moment a visitor at my father's chateau. You may suppose, also, how I felt as I heard him detail habits and mysterious peculiarities which were, in fact, those of our beautiful guest, Carmilla!

A vista opened in the forest; we were on a sudden under the chimneys and gables of the ruined village, and the towers and battlements of the dismantled castle, round which gigantic trees are grouped, overhung us from a slight eminence.

In a frightened dream I got down from the carriage, and in silence, for we had each abundant matter for thinking; we soon mounted the ascent, and were among the spacious chambers, winding stairs, and dark corridors of the castle.

'And this was once the palatial residence of the Karnsteins!' said the old General at length, as from a great window he looked out across the village, and saw the wide, undulating expanse of forest. 'It was a bad family, and here its bloodstained annals were written,' he continued. 'It is hard that they should, after death, continue to plague the human race with their atrocious lusts. That is the chapel of the Karnsteins, down there.'

He pointed down to the grey walls of the Gothic building partly visible through the foliage, a little way down the steep. 'And I hear the axe of a woodman,' he added, 'busy among the trees that surround it; he possibly may give us the information of which I am in search, and point out the grave of Mircalla, Countess of Karnstein. These rustics preserve the local traditions of great families, whose stories die out among the rich and titled so soon as the families themselves become extinct.'

'We have a portrait, at home, of Mircalla, the Countess Karnstein; should you like to see it?' asked my father.

'Time enough, dear friend,' replied the General. 'I believe that I have seen the original; and one motive which has led me to you earlier than I at first intended, was to explore the chapel which we are now approaching.'

'What! see the Countess Mircalla,' exclaimed my father; 'why, she has been dead more than a century!'

'Not so dead as you fancy, I am told,' answered the General.

'I confess, General, you puzzle me utterly,' replied my father, looking at him, I fancied, for a moment with a return of the suspicion

I detected before. But although there was anger and detestation, at times, in the old General's manner, there was nothing flighty.

'There remains to me,' he said, as we passed under the heavy arch of the Gothic church – for its dimensions would have justified its being so styled – 'but one object which can interest me during the few years that remain to me on earth, and that is to wreak on her the vengeance which, I thank God, may still be accomplished by a mortal arm.'

'What vengeance can you mean?' asked my father, in increasing amazement.

'I mean, to decapitate the monster,' he answered, with a fierce flush, and a stamp that echoed mournfully through the hollow ruin, and his clenched hand was at the same moment raised, as if it grasped the handle of an axe, while he shook it ferociously in the air.

'What?' exclaimed my father, more than ever bewildered.

'To strike her head off.'

'Cut her head off!'

'Aye, with a hatchet, with a spade, or with anything that can cleave through her murderous throat. You shall hear,' he answered, trembling with rage. And hurrying forward he said: 'That beam will answer for a seat; your dear child is fatigued; let her be seated, and I will, in a few sentences, close my dreadful story.'

The squared block of wood, which lay on the grass-grown pavement of the chapel, formed a bench on which I was very glad to seat myself, and in the meantime the General called to the woodman, who had been removing some boughs which leaned upon the old walls; and, axe in hand, the hardy old fellow stood before us.

He could not tell us anything of these monuments; but there was an old man, he said, a ranger of this forest, at present sojourning in the house of the priest, about two miles away, who could point out every monument of the old Karnstein family; and, for a trifle, he undertook to bring him back with him, if we would lend him one of our horses, in little more than half an hour.

'Have you been long employed about this forest?' asked my father of the old man.

'I have been a woodman here,' he answered in his patois, 'under the forester, all my days; so has my father before me, and so on, as many generations as I can count up. I could show you the very house in the village here, in which my ancestors lived.'

'How came the village to be deserted?' asked the General.

'It was troubled by revenants, sir; several were tracked to their graves, there detected by the usual tests, and extinguished in the usual way, by decapitation, by the stake, and by burning; but not until many of the villagers were killed.

'But after all these proceedings according to law,' he continued – 'so many graves opened, and so many vampires deprived of their horrible animation – the village was not relieved. But a Moravian nobleman, who happened to be travelling this way, heard how matters were, and being skilled – as many people are in his country – in such affairs, he offered to deliver the village from its tormentor. He did so thus: there being a bright moon that night, he ascended, shortly after sunset, the towers of the chapel here, from whence he could distinctly see the churchyard beneath him; you can see it from that window. From this point he watched until he saw the vampire come out of his grave, and place near it the linen clothes in which he had been folded, and then glide away towards the village to plague its inhabitants.

'The stranger, having seen all this, came down from the steeple, took the linen wrappings of the vampire, and carried them up to the top of the tower, which he again mounted. When the vampire returned from his prowlings and missed his clothes, he cried furiously to the Moravian, whom he saw at the summit of the tower, and who, in reply, beckoned him to ascend and take them. Whereupon the vampire, accepting his invitation, began to climb the steeple, and so soon as he had reached the battlements, the Moravian, with a stroke of his sword, clove his skull in twain, hurling him down to the churchyard, whither, descending by the winding stairs, the stranger followed and cut his head off, and next day delivered it and the body to the villagers, who duly impaled and burnt them.

'This Moravian nobleman had authority from the then head of the family to remove the tomb of Mircalla, Countess Karnstein, which he did effectually, so that in a little while its site was quite forgotten.'

'Can you point out where it stood?' asked the General, eagerly.

The forester shook his head, and smiled.

'Not a soul living could tell you that now,' he said; 'besides, they say her body was removed; but no-one is sure of that either.'

Having thus spoken, as time pressed, he dropped his axe and departed, leaving us to hear the remainder of the General's strange story.

14
The Meeting

My beloved child,' he resumed, 'was now growing rapidly worse. The physician who attended her had failed to produce the slightest impression on her disease, for such I then supposed it to be. He saw my alarm, and suggested a consultation. I called in an abler physician, from Gratz.

'Several days elapsed before he arrived. He was a good and pious, as well as a learned man. Having seen my poor ward together, they withdrew to my library to confer and discuss. I, from the adjoining room, where I awaited their summons, heard these two gentlemen's voices raised in something sharper than a strictly philosophical discussion. I knocked at the door and entered. I found the old physician from Gratz maintaining his theory. His rival was combating it with undisguised ridicule, accompanied with bursts of laughter. This unseemly manifestation subsided and the altercation ended on my entrance.

' "Sir," said my first physician, "my learned brother seems to think that you want a conjuror, and not a doctor."

' "Pardon me," said the old physician from Gratz, looking displeased, "I shall state my own view of the case in my own way another time. I grieve, Monsieur le General, that by my skill and science I can be of no use. Before I go I shall do myself the honour to suggest something to you."

'He seemed thoughtful, and sat down at a table and began to write.

'Profoundly disappointed, I made my bow, and as I turned to go, the other doctor pointed over his shoulder to his companion who was writing, and then, with a shrug, significantly touched his forehead.

'This consultation, then, left me precisely where I was. I walked out into the grounds, all but distracted. The doctor from Gratz, in ten or fifteen minutes, overtook me. He apologised for having followed me, but said that he could not conscientiously take his leave without a few words more. He told me that he could not be mistaken; no natural disease exhibited the same symptoms; and that death was already very near. There remained, however, a day, or possibly two, of life. If the fatal seizure were at once arrested, with great care and skill her strength might possibly return. But all hung now upon the confines of the irrevocable. One more assault might extinguish the last spark of vitality which is, every moment, ready to die.

'"And what is the nature of the seizure you speak of?" I entreated

'"I have stated all fully in this note, which I place in your hands upon the distinct condition that you send for the nearest clergyman, and open my letter in his presence, and on no account read it till he is with you; you would despise it else, and it is a matter of life and death. Should the priest fail you, then, indeed, you may read it."

'He asked me, before taking his leave finally, whether I would wish to see a man curiously learned upon the very subject, which, after I had read his letter, would probably interest me above all others, and he urged me earnestly to invite him to visit him there; and so took his leave.

'The ecclesiastic was absent, and I read the letter by myself. At another time, or in another case, it might have excited my ridicule. But into what quackeries will not people rush for a last chance, where all accustomed means have failed, and the life of a beloved object is at stake?

'Nothing, you will say, could be more absurd than the learned man's letter.

'It was monstrous enough to have consigned him to a madhouse. He said that the patient was suffering from the visits of a vampire! The punctures which she described as having occurred near the throat, were, he insisted, the insertion of those two long, thin, and sharp teeth which, it is well known, are peculiar to vampires; and there could be no doubt, he added, as to the well-defined presence of the small livid mark which all concurred in describing as that induced by the demon's lips, and every symptom described by the sufferer was in exact conformity with those recorded in every case of a similar visitation.

'Being myself wholly sceptical as to the existence of any such portent as the vampire, the supernatural theory of the good doctor furnished, in my opinion, but another instance of learning and intelligence oddly associated with some one hallucination. I was so miserable, however, that, rather than try nothing, I acted upon the instructions of the letter.

'I concealed myself in the dark dressing room that opened upon the poor patient's room, in which a candle was burning, and watched there till she was fast asleep. I stood at the door, peeping through the small crevice, my sword laid on the table beside me, as my directions prescribed, until, a little after one, I saw a large black object, very ill-defined, crawl, as it seemed to me, over the foot of the bed, and swiftly spread itself up to the poor girl's throat, where it swelled, in a moment, into a great, palpitating mass.

'For a few moments I had stood petrified. I now sprang forward, with my sword in my hand. The black creature suddenly contracted towards the foot of the bed, glided over it, and, standing on the floor about a yard below the foot of the bed, with a glare of skulking ferocity and horror fixed on me, I saw Millarca. Speculating I know not what, I struck at her instantly with my sword; but I saw her standing near the door, unscathed. Horrified, I pursued, and struck again. She was gone; and my sword flew to shivers against the door.

'I can't describe to you all that passed on that horrible night. The whole house was up and stirring. The spectre Millarca was gone. But her victim was sinking fast, and before the morning dawned, she died.'

The old General was agitated. We did not speak to him. My father walked to some little distance, and began reading the inscriptions on the tombstones; and thus occupied, he strolled into the door of a side chapel to prosecute his researches. The General leaned against the wall, dried his eyes, and sighed heavily. I was relieved on hearing the voices of Carmilla and Madame, who were at that moment approaching. The voices died away.

In this solitude, having just listened to so strange a story, connected, as it was, with the great and titled dead, whose monuments were mouldering among the dust and ivy round us, and every incident of which bore so awfully upon my own mysterious case – in this haunted spot, darkened by the towering foliage that rose on every side, dense and high above its noiseless walls – a horror began to steal over me, and my heart sank as I thought that my friends were, after all, not about to enter and disturb this triste and ominous scene.

The old General's eyes were fixed on the ground, as he leaned with his hand upon the basement of a shattered monument.

Under a narrow, arched doorway, surmounted by one of those demoniacal grotesques in which the cynical and ghastly fancy of old Gothic carving delights, I saw very gladly the beautiful face and figure of Carmilla enter the shadowy chapel.

I was just about to rise and speak, and nodded smiling in answer to her peculiarly engaging smile; when with a cry, the old man by my side caught up the woodman's hatchet, and started forward. On seeing him a brutalised change came over her features. It was an instantaneous and horrible transformation, as she made a crouching step backwards. Before I could utter a scream, he struck at her with all his force, but she dived under his blow, and unscathed, caught him in her tiny grasp by the wrist. He struggled for a moment to release his arm, but his hand opened, the axe fell to the ground, and the girl was gone.

He staggered against the wall. His grey hair stood upon his head, and a moisture shone over his face, as if he were at the point of death.

The frightful scene had passed in a moment. The first thing I recollect after, is Madame standing before me, and impatiently repeating again and again, the question, 'Where is Mademoiselle Carmilla?'

I answered at length, 'I don't know – I can't tell – she went there,' and I pointed to the door through which Madame had just entered; 'only a minute or two since.'

'But I have been standing there, in the passage, ever since Mademoiselle Carmilla entered; and she did not return.'

She then began to call 'Carmilla', through every door and passage and from the windows, but no answer came.

'She called herself Carmilla?' asked the General, still agitated.

'Carmilla, yes,' I answered.

'Aye,' he said; 'that is Millarca. That is the same person who long ago was called Mircalla, Countess Karnstein. Depart from this accursed ground, my poor child, as quickly as you can. Drive to the clergyman's house, and stay there till we come. Begone! May you never behold Carmilla more; you will not find her here.'

15
Ordeal and Execution

As he spoke one of the strangest-looking men I ever beheld entered the chapel at the door through which Carmilla had made her entrance and her exit. He was tall, narrow-chested, stooping, with high shoulders, and dressed in black. His face was brown and dried in with deep furrows; he wore an oddly-shaped hat with a broad leaf. His hair, long and grizzled, hung on his shoulders. He wore a pair of gold spectacles, and walked slowly, with an odd shambling gait, with his face sometimes turned up to the sky, and sometimes bowed down towards the ground, and seemed to wear a perpetual smile; his long thin arms were swinging, and his lank hands, in old black gloves ever so much too wide for them, waving and gesticulating in utter abstraction.

'The very man!' exclaimed the General, advancing with manifest delight. 'My dear Baron, how happy I am to see you, I had no hope of meeting you so soon.' He signed to my father, who had by this time returned, and led the fantastic old gentleman, whom he called the Baron, to meet him. He introduced him formally, and they at once entered into earnest conversation. The stranger took a roll of paper from his pocket, and spread it on the worn surface of a tomb that stood by. He had a pencil-case in his fingers, with which he traced imaginary lines from point to point on the paper, which from their often glancing from it, together, at certain points of the building, I concluded to be a plan of the chapel. He accompanied what I may term his lecture, with occasional readings from a dirty little book, whose yellow leaves were closely written over.

They sauntered together down the side aisle, opposite to the spot where I was standing, conversing as they went; then they began measuring distances by paces, and finally they all stood together, facing a piece of the side wall, which they began to examine with great minuteness; pulling off the ivy that clung over it, and rapping the plaster with the ends of their sticks, scraping here, and knocking there. At length they ascertained the existence of a broad marble tablet, with letters carved in relief upon it.

With the assistance of the woodman, who soon returned, a monumental inscription, and carved escutcheon, were disclosed. They proved to be those of the long lost monument of Mircalla, Countess Karnstein.

The old General, though not I fear given to the praying mood, raised his hands and eyes to heaven in mute thanksgiving, for some moments.

'Tomorrow,' I heard him say; 'the commissioner will be here, and the Inquisition will be held according to law.'

Then turning to the old man with the gold spectacles, whom I have described, he shook him warmly by both hands and said: 'Baron, how can I thank you? How can we all thank you? You will have delivered this region from a plague that has scourged its inhabitants for more than a century. The horrible enemy, thank God, is at last tracked.'

My father led the stranger aside, and the General followed. I know that he had led them out of hearing, that he might relate my case, and I saw them glance often quickly at me, as the discussion proceeded.

My father came to me, kissed me again and again, and leading me from the chapel, said: 'It is time to return, but before we go home, we must add to our party the good priest, who lives but a little way from this; and persuade him to accompany us to the schloss.'

In this quest we were successful: and I was glad, being unspeakabl
fatigued when we reached home. But my satisfaction was changed t
dismay, on discovering that there were no tidings of Carmilla. Of th
scene that had occurred in the ruined chapel, no explanation wa
offered to me, and it was clear that it was a secret which my father fo
the present determined to keep from me.

The sinister absence of Carmilla made the remembrance of th
scene more horrible to me. The arrangements for the night wer
singular. Two servants and Madame were to sit up in my room tha
night; and the ecclesiastic with my father kept watch in the adjoining
dressing room.

The priest had performed certain solemn rites that night, the
purport of which I did not understand any more than I compre-
hended the reason of this extraordinary precaution taken for my
safety during sleep.

I saw all clearly a few days later.

The disappearance of Carmilla was followed by the discontinuance
of my nightly sufferings.

You have heard, no doubt, of the appalling superstition that prevails in Upper and Lower Styria, in Moravia, Silesia, in Turkish
Serbia, in Poland, even in Russia; the superstition, so we must call it,
of the Vampire.

If human testimony, taken with every care and solemnity, jud-
icially, before commissions innumerable, each consisting of many
members all chosen for integrity and intelligence, and constituting
reports more voluminous perhaps than exist upon any one other
class of cases, is worth anything, it is difficult to deny, or even to
doubt, the existence of such a phenomenon as the Vampire.

For my part I have heard no theory by which to explain what I
myself have witnessed and experienced, other than that supplied by
the ancient and well-attested belief of the country.

The next day the formal proceedings took place in the Chapel of
Karnstein.

The grave of the Countess Mircalla was opened; and the General
and my father recognised each his perfidious and beautiful guest, in
the face now disclosed to view. The features, though a hundred and
fifty years had passed since her funeral, were tinted with the warmth
of life. Her eyes were open; no cadaverous smell exhaled from the
coffin. The two medical men, one officially present, the other on the
part of the promoter of the inquiry, attested the marvellous fact that
there was a faint but appreciable respiration, and a corresponding

action of the heart. The limbs were perfectly flexible, the flesh elastic; and the leaden coffin floated with blood, in which to a depth of seven inches, the body lay immersed.

Here then, were all the admitted signs and proofs of vampirism. The body, therefore, in accordance with the ancient practice, was raised, and a sharp stake driven through the heart of the vampire, who uttered a piercing shriek at the moment, in all respects such as might escape from a living person in the last agony. Then the head was struck off, and a torrent of blood flowed from the severed neck. The body and head was next placed on a pile of wood, and reduced to ashes, which were thrown upon the river and borne away, and that territory has never since been plagued by the visits of a vampire.

My father has a copy of the report of the Imperial Commission, with the signatures of all who were present at these proceedings, attached in verification of the statement. It is from this official paper that I have summarised my account of this last shocking scene.

16
Conclusion

I write all this you suppose with composure. But far from it; I cannot think of it without agitation. Nothing but your earnest desire so repeatedly expressed, could have induced me to sit down to a task that has unstrung my nerves for months to come, and reinduced a shadow of the unspeakable horror which years after my deliverance continued to make my days and nights dreadful, and solitude insupportably terrific.

Let me add a word or two about that quaint Baron Vordenburg, to whose curious lore we were indebted for the discovery of the Countess Mircalla's grave.

He had taken up his abode in Gratz, where, living upon a mere pittance, which was all that remained to him of the once princely estates of his family in Upper Styria, he devoted himself to the minute and laborious investigation of the marvellously authenticated tradition of Vampirism. He had at his fingers' ends all the great and little works upon the subject.

Magia Posthuma, *Phlegon de Mirabilibus*, *Augustinus de Cura pro Mortuis*, *Philosophicae et Christianae Cogitationes de Vampiris*, by John Christofer Herenberg; and a thousand others, among which I remember only a few of those which he lent to my father. He had a voluminous digest of all the judicial cases, from which he had extracted a system of principles that appear to govern – some always, and others occasionally only – the condition of the vampire. I may mention, in passing, that the deadly pallor attributed to that sort of revenants, is a mere melodramatic fiction. They present, in the grave, and when they show themselves in human society, the appearance of healthy life. When disclosed to light in their coffins, they exhibit all the symptoms that are enumerated as those which proved the vampire-life of the long-dead Countess Karnstein.

How they escape from their graves and return to them for certain hours every day, without displacing the clay or leaving any trace of disturbance in the state of the coffin or the cerements, has always been admitted to be utterly inexplicable. The amphibious existence of the vampire is sustained by daily renewed slumber in the grave. Its horrible lust for living blood supplies the vigour of its waking existence. The vampire is prone to be fascinated with an engrossing vehemence, resembling the passion of love, by particular persons. In pursuit of these it will exercise inexhaustible patience and stratagem, for access to a particular object may be obstructed in a hundred ways. It will never desist until it has satiated its passion, and drained the very life of its coveted victim. But it will, in these cases, husband and protract its murderous enjoyment with the refinement of an epicure, and heighten it by the gradual approaches of an artful courtship. In these cases it seems to yearn for something like sympathy and consent. In ordinary ones it goes direct to its object, overpowers with violence, and strangles and exhausts often at a single feast.

The vampire is apparently subject, in certain situations, to special conditions. In the particular instance of which I have given you a relation, Mircalla seemed to be limited to a name which, if not her real one, should at least reproduce, without the omission or addition of a single letter, those, as we say anagrammatically, which compose it.

Carmilla did this; so did Millarca.

My father related to the Baron Vordenburg, who remained with us for two or three weeks after the expulsion of Carmilla, the story about the Moravian nobleman and the vampire at Karnstein church-yard, and then he asked the Baron how he had discovered the exact position of the long-concealed tomb of the Countess Mircalla? The Baron's grotesque features puckered up into a mysterious smile; he looked down, still smiling, on his worn spectacle case and fumbled with it. Then looking up, he said: 'I have many journals, and other papers, written by that remarkable man; the most curious among

hem is one treating of the visit of which you speak, to Karnstein. The
radition, of course, discolours and distorts a little. He might have
)een termed a Moravian nobleman, for he had changed his abode to
hat territory, and was, beside, a noble. But he was, in truth, a native of
Jpper Styria. It is enough to say that in very early youth he had been
a passionate and favoured lover of the beautiful Mircalla, Countess
Karnstein. Her early death plunged him into inconsolable grief. It is
the nature of vampires to increase and multiply, but according to an
ascertained and ghostly law.

'Assume, at starting, a territory perfectly free from that pest.
How does it begin, and how does it multiply itself? I will tell you.
A person, more or less wicked, puts an end to himself. A suicide,
under certain circumstances, becomes a vampire. That spectre visits
living people in their slumbers; they die, and almost invariably, in
the grave, develop into vampires. This happened in the case of the
beautiful Mircalla, who was haunted by one of those demons. My
ancestor, Vordenburg, whose title I still bear, soon discovered this,
and in the course of the studies to which he devoted himself,
learned a great deal more.

'Among other things, he concluded that suspicion of vampirism
would probably fall, sooner or later, upon the dead Countess, who in
life had been his idol. He conceived a horror, be she what she might,
of her remains being profaned by the outrage of a posthumous
execution. He has left a curious paper to prove that the vampire, on
its expulsion from its amphibious existence, is projected into a far
more horrible life; and he resolved to save his once beloved Mircalla
from this.

'He adopted the stratagem of a journey here, a pretended removal
of her remains, and a real obliteration of her monument. When age
had stolen upon him, and from the vale of years he looked back on
the scenes he was leaving, he considered, in a different spirit, what he
had done, and a horror took possession of him. He made the tracings
and notes which have guided me to the very spot, and drew up a
confession of the deception that he had practised. If he had intended
any further action in this matter, death prevented him; and the hand
of a remote descendant has, too late for many, directed the pursuit to
the lair of the beast.'

We talked a little more, and among other things he said was this:
'One sign of the vampire is the power of the hand. The slender hand
of Mircalla closed like a vice of steel on the General's wrist when he
raised the hatchet to strike. But its power is not confined to its grasp;

it leaves a numbness in the limb it seizes, which is slowly, if ever recovered from.'

The following Spring my father took me a tour through Italy. We remained away for more than a year. It was long before the terror of recent events subsided; and to this hour the image of Carmilla returns to memory with ambiguous alternations – sometimes the playful, languid, beautiful girl; sometimes the writhing fiend I saw in the ruined church; and often from a reverie I have started, fancying I heard the light step of Carmilla at the drawing room door.

Dracula and the Three Brides

BRAM STOKER

[JONATHAN HARKER'S JOURNAL]

5 May

I must have been asleep, for certainly if I had been fully awake I must have noticed the approach to such a remarkable place. In the gloom the courtyard looked of considerable size, and as several dark ways led from it under great round arches it perhaps seemed bigger than it really is. I have not yet been able to see it by daylight.

When the *calèche* stopped the driver jumped down, and held out his hand to assist me to alight. Again I could not but notice his prodigious strength. His hand actually seemed like a steel vice that could have crushed mine if he had chosen. Then he took out my traps, and placed them on the ground beside me as I stood close to a great door, old and studded with large iron nails, and set in a projecting doorway of massive stone. I could see even in the dim light that the stone was massively carved, but that the carving had been much worn by time and weather. As I stood, the driver jumped again into his seat and shook the reins; the horses started forward, and trap and all disappeared down one of the dark openings.

I stood in silence where I was, for I did not know what to do. Of bell or knocker there was no sign; through these frowning walls and dark window openings it was not likely that my voice could penetrate. The time I waited seemed endless, and I felt doubts and fears crowding upon me. What sort of place had I come to, and among what kind of people? What sort of grim adventure was it on which I had embarked? Was this a customary incident in the life of a solicitor's clerk sent out to explain the purchase of a London estate to a foreigner? Solicitor's clerk! Mina would not like that. Solicitor – for just before leaving London I got word that my examination was successful; and I am now a full-blown solicitor! I began to rub my eyes and pinch myself to see if I were awake. It all seemed like a horrible nightmare to me, and I expected that I should suddenly awake, and find myself at home, with the dawn struggling in through the windows, as I had now and again felt in the morning after a day of overwork. But my flesh answered the pinching test, and my eyes were not to be deceived. I was indeed awake and among the Carpathians. All I could do now was to be patient, and to wait the coming of the morning.

Just as I had come to this conclusion I heard a heavy step approaching behind the great door, and saw through the chinks the gleam of a coming light. Then there was the sound of rattling chains and the clanking of massive bolts drawn back. A key was turned with the loud grating noise of long disuse, and the great door swung back.

Within stood a tall old man, clean-shaven save for a long white moustache, and clad in black from head to foot, without a single speck of colour about him anywhere. He held in his hand an antique silver lamp, in which the flame burned without chimney or globe of any kind, throwing long, quivering shadows as it flickered in the draught of the open door.

The old man motioned me in with his right hand with a courtly gesture, saying in excellent English, but with a strange intonation: 'Welcome to my house! Enter freely and of your own will!' He made no motion of stepping to meet me, but stood like a statue, as though his gesture of welcome had fixed him into stone. The instant, however, that I had stepped over the threshold, he moved impulsively forward, and holding out his hand grasped mine with a strength which made me wince, an effect which was not lessened by the fact that it seemed as cold as ice – more like the hand of a dead than a living man.

Again he said: 'Welcome to my house. Come freely. Go safely. And leave something of the happiness you bring!' The strength of the handshake was so much akin to that which I had noticed in the driver, whose face I had not seen, that for a moment I doubted if it were not the same person to whom I was speaking; so, to make sure, I said interrogatively: 'Count Dracula?'

He bowed in a courtly way as he replied: 'I am Dracula. And I bid you welcome, Mr Harker, to my house. Come in; the night air is chill, and you must need to eat and rest.' As he was speaking he put the lamp on a bracket on the wall, and stepping out, took my luggage; he had carried it in before I could forestall him.

I protested, but he insisted: 'Nay, sir, you are my guest. It is late, and my people are not available. Let me see to your comfort myself.'

He insisted on carrying my traps along the passage, and then up a great winding stair, and along another great passage, on whose stone floor our steps rang heavily. At the end of this he threw open a heavy door, and I rejoiced to see within a well-lit room in which a table was spread for supper, and on whose mighty hearth a great fire of logs flamed and flared.

The count halted, putting down my bags, closed the door, and crossing the room, opened another door, which led into a small octagonal room lit by a single lamp, and seemingly without a window of any sort. Passing through this, he opened another door, and motioned me to enter. It was a welcome sight; for here was a great bedroom well lighted and warmed with another log fire, which sent a hollow roar up the wide chimney.

The count himself left my luggage inside and withdrew, saying, before he closed the door: 'You will need, after your journey, to refresh yourself by making your toilet. I trust you will find all you wish. When you are ready come into the other room, where you will find your supper prepared.'

The light and warmth and the count's courteous welcome seemed to have dissipated all my doubts and fears. Having then reached my normal state, I discovered that I was half-famished with hunger; so making a hasty toilet, I went into the other room.

I found supper already laid out. My host, who stood on one side of the great fireplace, leaning against the stonework, made a graceful wave of his hand to the table, and said: 'I pray you, be seated and sup how you please. You will, I trust, excuse me that I do not join you; but I have dined already, and I do not sup.'

I handed to him the sealed letter which Mr Hawkins had entrusted to me. He opened it and read it gravely; then, with a charming smile, he handed it to me to read.

One passage of it, at least, gave me a thrill of pleasure:

I much regret that an attack of gout, from which malady I am a constant sufferer, forbids absolutely any travelling on my part for some time to come; but I am happy to say I can send a sufficient substitute, one in whom I have every possible confidence. He is a young man, full of energy and talent in his own way, and of a very faithful disposition. He is discreet and silent, and has grown into manhood in my service. He shall be ready to attend on you when you will during his stay, and shall take your instructions in all matters.

The count himself came forward and took off the cover of a dish, and I fell to at once on an excellent roast chicken. This, with some cheese and a salad and a bottle of old Tokay, of which I had two glasses, was my supper. During the time I was eating it the count asked me many questions as to my journey, and I told him by degrees all I had experienced.

By this time I had finished my supper, and by my host's desire had drawn up a chair by the fire and begun to smoke a cigar which he offered me, at the same time excusing himself that he did not smoke. I had now an opportunity of observing him, and found him of a very marked physiognomy.

His face was a strong – a very strong – aquiline, with high bridge of the thin nose and peculiarly arched nostrils; with lofty domed fore-head, and hair growing scantily round the temples, but profusely elsewhere. His eyebrows were very massive, almost meeting over the nose, and with bushy hair that seemed to curl in its own profusion. The mouth, so far as I could see it under the heavy moustache, was fixed and rather cruel-looking, with peculiarly sharp white teeth; these protruded over the lips, whose remarkable ruddiness showed astonishing vitality in a man of his years. For the rest, his ears were pale and at the tops extremely pointed; the chin was broad and strong, and the cheeks firm though thin. The general effect was one of extraordinary pallor.

Hitherto I had noticed the backs of his hands as they lay on his knees in the firelight, and they had seemed rather white and fine; but seeing them now close to me, I could not but notice that they were rather coarse – broad, with squat fingers. Strange to say, there were hairs in the centre of the palm. The nails were long and fine, and cut to a sharp point. As the count leaned over me and his hands touched me, I could not repress a shudder. It may have been that his breath was rank, but a horrible feeling of nausea came over me, which, do what I would, I could not conceal. The count, evidently noticing it, drew back; and with a grim sort of smile, which showed more than he had yet done his protuberant teeth, sat himself down again on his own side of the fireplace. We were both silent for a while; and as I looked towards the window I saw the first dim streak of the coming dawn. There seemed a strange stillness over everything; but as I listened I heard, as if from down below in the valley, the howling of many wolves.

The count's eyes gleamed, and he said: 'Listen to them – the children of the night. What music they make!' Seeing, I suppose, ome expression in my face strange to him, he added: 'Ah, sir, you dwellers in the city cannot enter into the feelings of the hunter.' Then he rose and said: 'But you must be tired. Your bedroom is all ready, and tomorrow you shall sleep as late as you will. I have to be away till the afternoon; so sleep well and dream well!' and, with a courteous bow, he opened for me himself the door to the octagonal room, and I entered my bedroom . . .

I am all in a sea of wonders. I doubt; I fear; I think strange things which I dare not confess to my own soul. God keep me, if only for the sake of those dear to me!

7 May

It is again early morning, but I have rested and enjoyed the last twenty-four hours. I slept till late in the day, and awoke of my own accord. When I had dressed myself I went into the room where we had supped, and found a cold breakfast laid out, with coffee kept hot by the pot being placed on the hearth.

There was a card on the table, on which was written: 'I have to be absent for a while. Do not wait for me. – D.' So I set to and enjoyed a hearty meal. When I had done, I looked for a bell, so that I might let the servants know I had finished; but I could not find one. There are certainly odd deficiencies in the house, considering the extra-ordinary evidences of wealth which are round me. The table service is of gold, and so beautifully wrought that it must be of immense value. The curtains and upholstery of the chairs and sofas and the hangings of my bed are of the costliest and most beautiful fabrics, and must have been of fabulous value when they were made, for they are centuries old, though in excellent order. I saw something like them in Hampton Court, but there they were worn and frayed and moth-eaten. But still in none of the rooms is there a mirror. There is not even a toilet glass on my table, and I had to get the little shaving-glass from my bag before I could either shave or brush my hair. I have not yet seen a servant anywhere, or heard a sound near the castle except the howling of wolves. When I had finished my meal – I do not know whether to call it breakfast or dinner, for it was between five and six o'clock when I had it – I looked about for something to read, for I did not like to go about the castle until I had asked the count's permission. There was absolutely nothing in the room, book, newspaper, or even writing materials; so I opened another door in the room and found a sort of library. The door opposite mine I tried, but found it locked.

In the library I found, to my great delight, a vast number of English books, whole shelves full of them, and bound volumes of magazines and newspapers. A table in the centre was littered with English magazines and newspapers, though none of them were of very recent date. The books were of the most varied kind – history, geography, politics, political economy, botany, geology, law – all relating to England and English life and customs and manners. There were even such books of reference as the *London Directory*, *Red-books* and *Blue-books*, *Whitaker's Almanack*, the *Army and Navy Lists*, and – it somehow gladdened my heart to see it – the *Law List*.

Whilst I was looking at the books, the door opened, and the count entered. He saluted me in a hearty way, and hoped that I had had a good night's rest.

Then he went on: 'I am glad you found your way in here, for I am sure there is much that will interest you. These friends' – and he laid his hand on some of the books – 'have been good friends to me, and for some years past, ever since I had the idea of going to London, have given me many, many hours of pleasure. Through them I have come to know your great England; and to know her is to love her. I long to go through the crowded streets of your mighty London, to be in the midst of the whirl and rush of humanity, to share its life, its change, its death, and all that makes it what it is. But alas! as yet I only know your tongue through books. To you, my friend, I look that I know it to speak.'

'But, count,' I said, 'you know and speak English thoroughly!' He bowed gravely.

'I thank you, my friend, for your all-too-flattering estimate, but yet I fear that I am but a little way on the road I would travel. True, I know the grammar and the words, but yet I know not how to speak them.'

'Indeed,' I said, 'you speak excellently.'

'Not so,' he answered. 'Well I know that, did I move and speak in your London, none there are who would not know me for a stranger. That is not enough for me. Here I am noble; I am *boyar*; the common people know me, and I am master. But a stranger in a strange land, he is no-one; men know him not – and to know not is to care not for. I am content if I am like the rest, so that no man stops if he sees me, or pause in his speaking if he hear my words, to say, "Ha, ha! a stranger!" I have been so long master that I would be master still – or at least that none other should be master of me. You come to me not alone as agent of my friend Peter Hawkins, of Exeter, to tell me all about my new estate in London. You shall, I trust, rest here with me a while, so that by our talking I may learn the English intonation; and I would that you tell me when I make error, even of the smallest, in my speaking. I am sorry that I had to be away so long today; but you will, I know, forgive one who has so many important affairs in hand.'

Of course I said all I could about being willing, and asked if I might come into that room when I chose.

He answered, 'Yes, certainly,' and added: 'You may go anywhere you wish in the castle, except where the doors are locked, where of course you will not wish to go. There is reason that all things are as they are, and did you see with my eyes and know with my knowledge, you would perhaps better understand.'

I said I was sure of this, and then he went on: 'We are in Transylvania; and Transylvania is not England. Our ways are not your ways, and there shall be to you many strange things. Nay, from what you have told me of your experiences already, you know something of what strange things here may be.'

This led to much conversation. And as it was evident that he wanted to talk, if only for talking's sake, I asked him many questions regarding things that had already happened to me or come within my notice. Sometimes he sheered off the subject, or turned the conversation by pretending not to understand; but generally he answered all I asked most frankly. Then as time went on, and I had got somewhat bolder, I asked him of some of the strange things of the preceding night; as, for instance, why the coachman went to the places where we had seen the blue flames. Was it indeed true that they showed where gold was hidden? He then explained to me that it was commonly believed that on a certain night of the year – last night, in fact, when all evil spirits are supposed to have unchecked sway – a blue flame is seen over any place where treasure has been concealed. 'That treasure *has* been hidden,' he went on, 'in the region through which you came last night, there can be but little doubt; for it was the ground fought over for centuries by the Wallachian, the Saxon, and the Turk. Why, there is hardly a foot of soil in all this region that has not been enriched by the blood of men, patriots or invaders. In old days there were stirring times, when the Austrian and the Hungarian came up in hordes, and the patriots went out to meet them – men and women, the aged and the children too – and waited their coming on the rocks above the passes, that they might sweep destruction on them with their artificial avalanches. When the invader was triumphant he found but little, for whatever there was had been sheltered in the friendly soil.'

'But how,' said I, 'can it have remained so long undiscovered, when there is a sure index to it if men will but take the trouble to look?'

The count smiled, and as his lips ran back over his gums, the long, sharp, canine teeth showed out strangely; he answered: 'Because your peasant is at heart a coward and a fool! Those flames only appear on one night. And on that night no man of this land will, if he can help it, stir without his doors. And, dear sir, even if he did he would not know what to do. Why, even the peasant that you tell me of who marked the place of the flame would not know where to look in daylight even for his own work. You would not, I dare be sworn, be able to find these places again?'

'There you are right,' I said. 'I know no more than the dead where even to look for them.' Then we drifted into other matters.

'Come,' he said at last, 'tell me of London and of the house which you have procured for me.' With an apology for my remissness, I went into my own room to get the papers from my bag. Whilst I was placing them in order I heard a rattling of china and silver in the next room, and as I passed through, noticed that the table had been cleared and the lamp lit, for it was by this time deep into the dark. The lamps were also lit in the study or library, and I found the count lying on the sofa, reading, of all things in the world, an English *Bradshaw's Guide*. When I came in he cleared the books and papers from the table; and with him I went into plans and deeds and figures of all sorts. He was interested in everything, and asked me a myriad questions about the place and its surroundings. He clearly had studied beforehand all he could get on the subject of the neighbourhood, for he evidently at the end knew very much more than I did.

When I remarked this, he answered: 'Well, but, my friend, is it not needful that I should? When I go there I shall be all alone, and my friend Harker Jonathan – nay, pardon me, I fall into my country's habit of putting your patronymic first – my friend Jonathan Harker will not be by my side to correct and aid me. He will be in Exeter, miles away, probably working at papers of the law with my other friend, Peter Hawkins. So!'

We went thoroughly into the business of the purchase of the estate at Purfleet. When I had told him the facts and got his signature to the necessary papers, and had written a letter with them ready to post to Mr Hawkins, he began to ask me how I had come across so suitable a place.

I read to him the notes which I had made at the time, and which I inscribe here: 'At Purfleet, on a by-road, I came across just such a place as seemed to be required, and where was displayed a dilapidated notice that the place was for sale. It is surrounded by a high wall, of ancient structure, built of heavy stones, and has not been repaired for a large number of years. The closed gates were of heavy old oak and iron, all eaten with rust.

'The estate is called Carfax, no doubt a corruption of the old *Quatre Face*, as the house is four-sided, agreeing with the cardinal points of the compass. It contains in all some twenty acres, quite surrounded by the solid stone wall above mentioned. There are many trees on it, which make it in places gloomy, and there is a deep, dark-looking pond or small lake, evidently fed by some springs, as the water is clear and flows away in a fair-sized stream. The house is very large and of all periods back, I should say, to mediaeval times, for one part is of stone immensely thick, with only a few windows high up and heavily barred with iron. It looks like part of a keep, and is close to an old chapel or church. I could not enter it, as I had not the key of the door leading to it from the house, but I have taken with my Kodak views of it from various points. The house has been added to, but in a very straggling way, and I can only guess at the amount of ground it covers, which must be very great. There are but few houses close at hand, one being a very large house only recently added to and formed into a private lunatic asylum. It is not, however, visible from the grounds.'

When I had finished, he said: 'I am glad that it is old and big. I myself am of an old family, and to live in a new house would kill me. A house cannot be made habitable in a day; and, after all, how few days go to make up a century. I rejoice also that there is a chapel of old times. We Transylvanian nobles love not to think that our bones may be amongst the common dead. I seek not gaiety nor mirth, not the bright voluptuousness of much sunshine and sparkling waters which please the young and gay. I am no longer young. And my heart, through weary years of mourning over the dead, is not attuned to mirth. Moreover, the walls of my castle are broken; the shadows are many, and the wind breathes cold through the broken battlements and casements. I love the shade and the shadow, and would be alone with my thoughts when I may.'

Somehow his words and his look did not seem to accord, or else it was that his cast of face made his smile look malignant and saturnine.

Presently, with an excuse, he left me, asking me to put all my papers together. He was some little time away, and I began to look at some of the books around me. One was an atlas, which I found opened naturally at England, as if that map had been much used. On looking at it I found in certain places little rings marked, and on examining these I noticed that one was near London on the east side, manifestly where his new estate was situated; the other two were Exeter, and Whitby on the Yorkshire coast.

It was the better part of an hour when the count returned. 'Aha!' he said, 'still at your books? Good! But you must not work always. Come; I am informed that your supper is ready.' He took my arm, and we went into the next room, where I found an excellent supper ready on the table. The count again excused himself, as he had dined out on his being away from home. But he sat as on the previous night, and chatted whilst I ate. After supper I smoked, as on the last evening, and the count stayed with me, chatting and asking questions on every conceivable subject, hour after hour. I felt that it was getting very late indeed, but I did not say anything, for I felt under obligation to meet my host's wishes in every way. I was not sleepy, as the long sleep yesterday had fortified me; but I could not help experiencing that chill which comes over one at the coming of the dawn, which is like, in its way, the turn of the tide. They say that people who are near death die generally at the change to the dawn or at the turn of the tide; anyone who has, when tired, and tied as it were to his post, experienced this change in the atmosphere can well believe it.

All at once we heard the crow of a cock coming up with preternatural shrillness through the clear morning air; Count Dracula, jumping to his feet, said: 'Why, there is the morning again! How remiss I am to let you stay up so long! You must make your conversation regarding my dear new country of England less interesting, so that I may not forget how time flies by us,' and, with a courtly bow, he left me.

I went into my own room and drew the curtains, but there was little to notice; my window opened into the courtyard; all I could see was the warm grey of quickening sky. So I pulled the curtains again, and have written of this day.

8 May

I began to fear as I wrote in this book that I was getting too diffuse; but now I am glad that I went into detail from the first, for there is something so strange about this place and all in it that I cannot but feel uneasy. I wish I were safe out of it, or that I had never come. It may be that this strange night-existence is telling on me; but would that that were all! If there were anyone to talk to I could bear it, but there is no-one. I have only the count to speak with, and he! – I fear I am myself the only living soul within the place. Let me be prosaic so far as facts can be; it will help me to bear up, and imagination must not run riot with me. If it does I am lost. Let me say at once how I stand – or seem to.

I only slept a few hours when I went to bed, and feeling that I could not sleep any more, got up. I had hung my shaving-glass by the window, and was just beginning to shave. Suddenly I felt a hand on my shoulder, and heard the count's voice saying to me, 'Good morning'. I started, for it amazed me that I had not seen him, since the reflection of the glass covered the whole room behind me. In starting I had cut myself slightly, but did not notice it at the moment. Having answered the count's salutation, I turned to the glass again to see how I had been mistaken. This time there could be no error, for the man was close to me, and I could see him over my shoulder. But there was no reflection of him in the mirror! The whole room behind me was displayed; but there was no sign of a man in it, except myself. This was startling, and, coming on the top of so many strange things, was beginning to increase that vague feeling of uneasiness which I always have when the count is near; but at that instant I saw that the cut had bled a little, and the blood was trickling over my chin. I laid down the razor, turning as I did so half-round to look for some sticking-plaster. When the count saw my face, his eyes blazed with a sort of demoniac fury, and he suddenly made a grab at my throat. I drew away, and his hand touched the string of beads which held the crucifix. It made an instant change in him, for the fury passed so quickly that I could hardly believe that it was ever there.

'Take care,' he said, 'take care how you cut yourself. It is more dangerous than you think in this country.' Then seizing the shaving-glass, he went on: 'And this is the wretched thing that has done the mischief. It is a foul bauble of man's vanity. Away with it!' and opening the heavy window with one wrench of his terrible hand, he flung out the glass, which was shattered into a thousand pieces on the stones of the courtyard far below. Then he withdrew without a word. It is very annoying, for I do not see how I am to shave, unless in my watchcase or the bottom of the shaving-pot, which is, fortunately, of metal.

When I went into the dining-room, breakfast was prepared; but I could not find the count anywhere. So I breakfasted alone. It is strange that as yet I have not seen the count eat or drink. He must be a very peculiar man! After breakfast I did a little exploring in the castle. I went out on the stairs and found a room looking towards the south. The view was magnificent, and from where I stood there was every opportunity of seeing it. The castle is on the very edge of a terrible precipice. A stone falling from the window would fall a thousand feet without touching anything! As far as the eye can reach is a sea of green treetops, with occasionally a deep rift where there is a chasm. Here and there are silver threads where the rivers wind in deep gorges through the forests.

But I am not in heart to describe beauty, for when I had seen the view I explored further; doors, doors, doors everywhere, and all locked and bolted. In no place save from the windows in the castle walls is there an available exit.

The castle is a veritable prison, and I am a prisoner!

[JONATHAN HARKER'S JOURNAL, CONTINUED]

When I found that I was a prisoner a sort of wild feeling came over me. I rushed up and down the stairs, trying every door and peering out of every window I could find; but after a little the conviction of my helplessness overpowered all other things. When I look back after a few hours I think I must have been mad for the time, for I behaved much as a rat does in a trap. When, however, the conviction had come to me that I was helpless I sat down quietly – as quietly as I have ever done anything in my life – and began to think over what was best to be done. I am thinking still, and as yet have come to no definite conclusion. Of one thing only am I certain: that it is no use making my ideas known to the count. He knows well that I am imprisoned; and as he has done it himself, and has doubtless his own motives for it, he would only deceive me if I trusted him fully with the facts. So far as I can see, my only plan will be to keep my knowledge and my fears to myself, and my eyes open. I am, I know, either being deceived, like a baby, by my own fears, or else I am in desperate straits; and if the latter be so, I need, and shall need, all my brains to get through. I had hardly come to this conclusion when I heard the great door below shut, and knew that the count had returned. He did not come at once into the library, so I went cautiously to my own room and found him making the bed. This was odd, but only confirmed what I had all along thought – that there were no servants in the house. When later I saw him through the chink of the hinges of the door laying the table in the dining-room, I was assured of it; for if he does himself all these menial offices, surely it is proof that there is no-one else to do them. This gave me a fright, for if there is no-one else in the castle, it must have been the count himself who was the driver of the coach that brought me here. This is a terrible thought; for if so, what does it mean that he could control the wolves, as he did, by only holding up his hand in silence? How was it that all the people at Bistritz and on the coach had some terrible fear for me? What meant the giving of the cruci-fix, of the garlic, of the wild rose, of the mountain ash? Bless that good, good woman who hung the crucifix round my neck! for it is a comfort and a strength to me whenever I touch it. It is odd that a thing which I have been taught to regard with disfavour and as idolatrous should in a time of loneliness and trouble be of help. Is it that there is something in the essence of the thing itself, or that it is a medium, a tangible help, in conveying memories of sympathy and comfort? Some time, if it may be, I must examine this matter and try to make up my mind about it. In the meantime I must find out all I can about Count Dracula, as it may help me to understand. Tonight he may talk of himself, if I turn the conversation that way. I must be very careful, however, not to awake his suspicion.

Midnight

I have had a long talk with the count. I asked him a few questions on Transylvanian history, and he warmed up to the subject wonderfully. In his speaking of things and people, and especially of battles, he spoke as if he had been present at them all. This he afterwards explained by saying that to a *boyar* the pride of his house and name is his own pride, that their glory is his glory, that their fate is his fate. Whenever he spoke of his house he always said 'we', and spoke almost in the plural, like a king speaking. I wish I could put down all he said exactly as he said it, for to me it was most fascinating. It seemed to have in it a whole history of the country. He grew excited as he spoke, and walked about the room pulling his great white moustache and grasping anything on which he laid his hands as though he would crush it by main strength.

One thing he said which I shall put down as nearly as I can; for it tells in its way the story of his race: 'We Szekelys have a right to be proud, for in our veins flows the blood of many brave races who fought as the lion fights, for lordship. Here, in the whirlpool of European races, the Ugric tribe bore down from Iceland the fighting spirit which Thor and Wodin gave them, which their Berserkers displayed to such fell intent on the seaboards of Europe, aye, and of Asia and Africa, too, till the peoples thought that the werewolves themselves had come. Here, too, when they came, they found the Huns, whose warlike fury had swept the earth like a living flame, till the dying peoples held that in their veins ran the blood of those old witches who, expelled from Scythia, had mated with the devils in the desert. Fools, fools! What devil or what witch was ever so great as Attila, whose blood is in these veins?' He held up his arms. 'Is it a wonder that we were a conquering race; that we were proud; that when the Magyar, the Lombard, the Avar, the Bulgar, or the Turk poured his thousands on our frontiers, we drove them back? Is it strange that when Arpad and his legions swept through the Hungarian fatherland he found us here when he reached the frontier; that the Honfoglalas was completed there? And when the Hungarian flood swept eastward, the Szekelys were claimed as kindred by the victorious Magyars, and to us for centuries was trusted the guarding of the frontier of Turkeyland; aye, and more than that, endless duty of the frontier guard, for, as the Turks say, "water sleeps, and enemy is sleepless". Who more gladly than we throughout the Four Nations received the "bloody sword", or at its warlike call flocked quicker to the standard of the King? When was redeemed that great shame of my nation, the shame of Cassova, when the flags of the Wallach and the Magyar went down beneath the Crescent; who was it but one of my own race who as Voivode crossed the Danube and beat the Turk on his own ground! This was a Dracula indeed. Who was it that his own unworthy brother, when he had fallen, sold his people to the Turk and brought the shame of slavery on them! Was it not this Dracula, indeed, who inspired that other of his race who in a later age again and again brought his forces over the great river into Turkeyland; who, when he was beaten back, came again, and again, and again, though he had to come alone from the bloody field where his troops were being slaughtered, since he knew that he alone could ultimately triumph? They said that he thought only of himself. Bah! what good are peasants without a leader? Where ends the war without a brain and heart to conduct it? Again, when, after the battle of Mohacs, we threw off the Hungarian yoke, we of the Dracula blood were amongst their leaders, for our spirit would not brook that we were not free. Ah, young sir, the Szekelys – and the Dracula as their heart's blood, their brains, and their swords – can boast a record that mushroom growths like the Hapsburgs and the Romanoffs can never reach. The warlike days are over. Blood is too precious a thing in these days of dishonourable peace; and the glories of the great races are as a tale that is told.'

It was by this time close on morning, and we went to bed. (*Mem.*, this diary seems horribly like the beginning of the *Arabian Nights*, for everything has to break off at cockcrow – or like the ghost of Hamlet's father.)

12 May

Let me begin with facts – bare, meagre facts, verified by books and figures, and of which there can be no doubt. I must not confuse them with experiences which will have to rest on my own observation or my memory of them. Last evening when the count came from his room he began by asking me questions on legal matters and on the doing of certain kinds of business. I had spent the day wearily over books, and, simply to keep my mind occupied, went over some of the matters I had been examined in at Lincoln's Inn. There was a certain method in the count's enquiries, so I shall try to put them down in sequence; the knowledge may somehow or sometime be useful to me.

First, he asked if a man in England might have two solicitors, or more. I told him he might have a dozen if he wished, but that it would not be wise to have more than one solicitor engaged in one transaction, as only one could act at a time, and that to change would be certain to militate against his interest. He seemed thoroughly to understand, and went on to ask if there would be any practical difficulty in having one man to attend, say, to banking, and another to look after shipping, in case local help were needed in a place far from the home of the banking solicitor.

I asked him to explain more fully, so that I might not by any chance mislead him, so he said: 'I shall illustrate. Your friend and mine, Mr Peter Hawkins, from under the shadow of your beautiful cathedral at Exeter, which is far from London, buys for me through your good self my place at London. Good! Now here let me say frankly, lest you should think it strange that I have sought the services of one so far off from London instead of someone resident there, that my motive was that no local interest might be served save my wish only; and as one of London resident might, perhaps, have some purpose of himself or friend to serve I went thus afield to seek my agent, whose labours should be only to my interest. Now, suppose I, who have much of affairs, wish to ship goods, say, to Newcastle, or Durham, or Harwich, or Dover, might it not be that it could with more ease be done by consigning to one in these ports?' I answered that certainly it would be most easy, but that we solicitors had a system of agency one for the other, so that local work could be done locally on instruction from any solicitor, so that the client, simply placing himself in the hands of one man, could have his wishes carried out by him without further trouble.

'But,' said he, 'I could be at liberty to direct myself. Is it not so?'

'Of course,' I replied; 'and such is often done by men of business, who do not like the whole of their affairs to be known by any one person.'

'Good!' he said, and then went on to ask about the means of making consignments and the forms to be gone through, and of all sorts of difficulties which might arise, but by forethought could be guarded against. I explained all these things to him to the best of my ability, and he certainly left me under the impression that he would have made a wonderful solicitor, for there was nothing that he did not think of or foresee. For a man who was never in the country, and who did not evidently do much in the way of business, his knowledge and acumen were wonderful.

When he had satisfied himself on these points of which he had spoken, and I had verified all as well as I could by the books available, he suddenly stood up and said: 'Have you written since your first letter to our friend Mr Peter Hawkins, or to any other?' It was with some bitterness in my heart that I answered that I had not, that as yet I had not seen any opportunity of sending letters to anybody.

'Then write now, my young friend,' he said, laying a heavy hand on my shoulder; 'write to our friend and to any other; and say, if it will please you, that you shall stay with me until a month from now.'

'Do you wish me to stay so long?' I asked, for my heart grew cold at the thought.

'I desire it much; nay, I will take no refusal. When your master, employer, what you will, engaged that someone should come on his behalf, it was understood that my needs only were to be consulted. I have not stinted. Is it not so?'

What could I do but bow acceptance? It was Mr Hawkins's interest, not mine, and I had to think of him, not myself; and besides, while Count Dracula was speaking, there was that in his eyes and in his bearing which made me remember that I was a prisoner, and that if I wished it I could have no choice.

The count saw his victory in my bow, and his mastery in the trouble of my face, for he began at once to use them, but in his own smooth, resistless way: 'I pray you, my good young friend, that you will not discourse of things other than business in your letters. It will doubtless please your friends to know that you are well, and that you look forward to getting home to them. Is it not so?' As he spoke he handed me three sheets of notepaper and three envelopes. They were all of the thinnest foreign post, and looking at them, then at him, and noticing his quiet smile, with the sharp, canine teeth lying over the red under-lip, I understood as well as if he had spoken that I should be careful what I wrote, for he would be able to read it. So I determined to write only formal notes now, but to write fully to Mr Hawkins in secret, and also to Mina, for to her I could write in shorthand, which would puzzle the count, if he did see it. When I had written my two letters I sat quiet, reading a book whilst the count wrote several notes, referring as he wrote them to some books on his table. Then he took up my two and placed them with his own, and put by his writing materials, after which, the instant the door had closed behind him, I leaned over and looked at the letters, which were face down on the table. I felt no compunction in doing so, for under the circumstances I felt that I should protect myself in every way I could.

One of the letters was directed to Samuel F. Billington, 7 The Crescent, Whitby; another to Herr Leutner, Varna; the third was to Coutts & Co., London, and the fourth to Herren Klopstock & Billreuth, bankers, Buda-Pesth. The second and fourth were unsealed. I was just about to look at them when I saw the door-handle move. I sank back in my seat, having just had time to replace the letters as they had been and to resume my book before the count, holding still another letter in his hand, entered the room.

He took up the letters on the table and stamped them carefully, and then, turning to me, said: 'I trust you will forgive me, but I have much work to do in private this evening. You will, I hope, find all things as you wish.'

At the door he turned, and after a moment's pause said: 'Let me advise you, my dear young friend – nay, let me warn you with all seriousness, that should you leave these rooms you will not by any chance go to sleep in any other part of the castle. It is old, and has many memories, and there are bad dreams for those who sleep unwisely. Be warned! Should sleep now or ever overcome you, or be like to do, then haste to your own chamber or to these rooms, for your rest will then be safe. But if you be not careful in this respect, then – ' He finished his speech in a gruesome way, for he motioned with his hands as if he were washing them. I quite understood; my only doubt was as to whether any dream could be more terrible than the unnatural, horrible net of gloom and mystery which seemed closing round me.

Later

I endorse the last words written, but this time there is no doubt in question. I shall not fear to sleep in any place where he is not. I have placed the crucifix over the head of my bed – I imagine that my rest is thus freer from dreams; and there it shall remain.

When he left me I went to my room. After a little while, not hearing any sound, I came out and went up the stone stair to where I could look out towards the south. There was some sense of freedom in the vast expanse, inaccessible though it was to me, as compared with the narrow darkness of the courtyard. Looking out on this, I felt that I was indeed in prison, and I seemed to want a breath of fresh air, though it were of the night. I am beginning to feel this nocturnal existence tell on me. It is destroying my nerve. I start at my own shadow, and am full of all sorts of horrible imaginings. God knows that there is ground for any terrible fear in this accursed place! I looked out over the beautiful expanse, bathed in soft yellow moon-light till it was almost as light as day. In the soft light the distant hills became melted, and the shadows in the valleys and gorges of velvety blackness. The mere beauty seemed to cheer me; there was peace and comfort in every breath I drew. As I leaned from the window my eye was caught by something moving a storey below me, and some-what to my left, where I imagined, from the lie of the rooms, that the windows of the count's own room would look out. The window at which I stood was tall and deep, stone-mullioned, and though weather-worn, was still complete; but it was evidently many a day since the case had been there. I drew back behind the stonework, and looked carefully out.

What I saw was the count's head coming out from the window. I did not see the face, but I knew the man by the neck and the movement of his back and arms. In any case, I could not mistake the hands which I had had so many opportunities of studying. I was at first interested and somewhat amused, for it is wonderful how small a matter will interest and amuse a man when he is a prisoner. But my very feelings changed to repulsion and terror when I saw the whole man slowly emerge from the window and begin to crawl down the castle wall over that dreadful abyss, *face down*, with his cloak spreading out around him like great wings. At first I could not believe my eyes. I thought it was some trick of the moonlight, some weird effect of shadow; but I kept looking, and it could be no delusion. I saw the fingers and toes grasp the corners of the stones, worn clear of the mortar by the stress of years, and by thus using every projection and inequality move downwards with considerable speed, just as a lizard moves along a wall.

What manner of man is this, or what manner of creature is it in the semblance of man? I feel the dread of this horrible place overpowering me; I am in fear – in awful fear – and there is no escape for me; I am encompassed about with terrors that I dare not think of . . .

15 May

Once more have I seen the count go out in his lizard fashion. He moved downwards in a sidelong way, some hundred feet down, and a good deal to the left. He vanished into some hole or window. When his head had disappeared I leaned out to try and see more, but without avail – the distance was too great to allow a proper angle of sight. I knew he had left the castle now, and thought to use the opportunity to explore more than I had dared to do as yet. I went back to the room, and taking a lamp, tried all the doors. They were all locked as I had expected, and the locks were comparatively new; but I went down the stone stairs to the hall where I had entered originally. I found I could pull back the bolts easily enough and unhook the great chains; but the door was locked, and the key was gone! That key must be in the count's room; I must watch should his door be unlocked, so that I may get it and escape. I went on to make a thorough examination of the various stairs and passages, and to try the doors that opened from them. One or two small rooms near the hall were open, but there was nothing to see in them except old furniture, dusty with age and moth-eaten. At last, however, I found one door at the top of a stairway which, though it seemed to be locked, gave a little under pressure. I tried it harder, and found that it was not really locked, but that the resistance came from the fact that the hinges had fallen somewhat, and the heavy door rested on the floor. Here was an opportunity which I might not have again, so I exerted myself, and with many efforts forced it back so that I could enter. I was now in a wing of the castle further to the right than the rooms I knew and a storey lower down. From the windows I could see that the suite of rooms lay along to the south of the castle, the windows of the end room looking out both west and south. On the latter side, as well as to the former, there was a great precipice. The castle was built on the corner of a great rock, so that on three sides it was quite impregnable, and great windows were placed here where sling, or bow, or culverin could not reach, and consequently light and comfort, impossible to a position which had to be guarded, were secured. To the west was a great valley, and then, rising far away, great jagged mountain fastnesses, rising peak on peak, the sheer rock studded with mountain ash and thorn, whose roots clung in cracks and crevices and crannies of the stone. This was evidently the portion of the castle occupied in bygone days, for the furniture had more air of comfort than any I had seen. The windows were curtainless, and the yellow moonlight, flooding in through the diamond panes, enabled one to see even colours, whilst it softened the wealth of dust which lay over all and disguised in some measure the ravages of time and the moth. My lamp seemed to be of little effect in the brilliant moonlight, but I was glad to have it with me, for there was a dread loneliness in the place which chilled my heart and made my nerves tremble. Still, it was better than living alone in the rooms which I had come to hate from the presence of the count, and after trying a little to school my nerves, I found a soft quietude come over me. Here I am, sitting at a little oak table where in old times possibly some fair lady sat to pen, with much thought and many blushes, her ill-spelt love-letter, and writing in my diary in shorthand all that has happened since I closed it last. It is nineteenth century up-to-date with a vengeance. And yet, unless my senses deceive me, the old centuries had, and have, powers of their own which mere 'modernity' cannot kill.

Later: the morning of 16 May

God preserve my sanity, for to this I am reduced. Safety and the assurance of safety are things of the past. Whilst I live on here there is but one thing to hope for: that I may not go mad, if, indeed, I be not mad already. If I be sane, then surely it is maddening to think that of all the foul things that lurk in this hateful place the count is the least dreadful to me; that to him alone I can look for safety, even though this be only whilst I can serve his purpose. Great God! merciful God! Let me be calm, for out of that way lies madness indeed. I begin to get new lights on certain things which have puzzled me. Up to now I never quite knew what Shakespeare meant when he made Hamlet say –

> My tablets! Quick, my tablets!
> 'Tis meet that I put it down, etc.,

for now, feeling as though my own brain were unhinged or as if the shock had come which must end in its undoing, I turn to my diary for repose. The habit of entering accurately must help to soothe me.

The count's mysterious warning frightened me at the time; it frightens me more now when I think of it, for in future he has a fearful hold upon me. I shall fear to doubt what he may say!

When I had written in my diary and had fortunately replaced the book and pen in my pocket, I felt sleepy. The count's warning came into my mind, but I took a pleasure in disobeying it. The sense of sleep was upon me, and with it the obstinacy which sleep brings as outrider. The soft moonlight soothed, and the wide expanse without gave a sense of freedom which refreshed me. I determined not to return tonight to the gloom-haunted rooms, but to sleep here, where of old ladies had sat and sung and lived sweet lives whilst their gentle breasts were sad for their menfolk away in the midst of remorseless wars. I drew a great couch out of its place near the corner, so that, as I lay, I could look at the lovely view to east and south, and unthinking of and uncaring for the dust, composed myself for sleep.

I suppose I must have fallen asleep; I hope so, but I fear, for all that followed was startlingly real – so real that now, sitting here in the broad, full sunlight of the morning, I cannot in the least believe that it was all sleep.

I was not alone. The room was the same, unchanged in any way since I came into it; I could see along the floor, in the brilliant moonlight, my own footsteps marked where I had disturbed the long accumulation of dust. In the moonlight opposite me were three young women, ladies by their dress and manner. I thought at the time that I must be dreaming when I saw them, for, though the moonlight was behind them, they threw no shadow on the floor. They came close to me and looked at me for some time and then whispered together. Two were dark, and had high aquiline noses, like the count's, and great dark, piercing eyes, that seemed to be almost red when contrasted with the pale yellow moon. The other was fair, as fair as can be, with great, wavy masses of golden hair and eyes like pale sapphires. I seemed somehow to know her face, and to know it in connection with some dreamy fear, but I could not recollect at the moment how or where. All three had brilliant white teeth that shone like pearls against the ruby of their voluptuous lips. There was something about them that made me uneasy, some longing and at the same time some deadly fear. I felt in my heart a wicked, burning desire that they would kiss me with those red lips. It is not good to note this down, lest some day it should meet Mina's eyes and cause her pain; but it is the truth. They whispered together, and then they all three laughed – such a silvery, musical laugh, but as hard as though the sound never could have come through the softness of human lips. It was like the intolerable, tingling sweetness of water-glasses when played on by a cunning hand. The fair girl shook her head coquettishly, and the other two urged her on.

One said: 'Go on! You are first, and we shall follow; yours is the right to begin.'

The other added: 'He is young and strong; there are kisses for us all.' I lay quiet, looking out under my eyelashes in an agony of delightful anticipation. The fair girl advanced and bent over me till I could feel the movement of her breath upon me. Sweet it was in one sense, honey-sweet, and sent the same tingling through the nerves as her voice, but with a bitter underlying the sweet, a bitter offensiveness, as one smells in blood.

I was afraid to raise my eyelids, but looked out and saw perfectly under the lashes. The fair girl went on her knees and bent over me, fairly gloating. There was a deliberate voluptuousness which was both thrilling and repulsive, and as she arched her neck she actually licked her lips like an animal, till I could see in the moonlight the moisture shining on the scarlet lips and on the red tongue as it lapped the white sharp teeth. Lower and lower went her head as the lips went below the range of my mouth and chin and seemed about to fasten on my throat. Then she paused, and I could hear the churning sound of her tongue as it licked her teeth and lips, and could feel the hot breath on my neck. Then the skin of my throat began to tingle as one's flesh does when the hand that is to tickle it approaches nearer – nearer. I could feel the soft, shivering touch of the lips on the supersensitive skin of my throat, and the hard dents of two sharp teeth, just touching and pausing there. I closed my eyes in a languorous ecstasy and waited – waited with beating heart.

But at that instant another sensation swept though me as quick as lightning. I was conscious of the presence of the count, and of his being as if lapped in a storm of fury. As my eyes opened involuntarily I saw his strong hand grasp the slender neck of the fair woman and with giant's power draw it back, the blue eyes transformed with fury, the white teeth champing with rage, and the fair cheeks blazing red with passion. But the count! Never did I imagine such wrath and fury, even in the demons of the pit. His eyes were positively blazing. The red light in them was lurid, as if the flames of hell-fire blazed behind them. His face was deathly pale, and the lines of it were hard like drawn wires; the thick eyebrows that met over the nose now seemed like a heaving bar of white-hot metal. With a fierce sweep of his arm, he hurled the woman from him, and then motioned to the others, as though he were beating them back; it was the same imperious gesture that I had seen used to the wolves. In a voice which, though low and almost a whisper, seemed to cut through the air and then ring round the room, he exclaimed: 'How dare you touch him, any of you? How dare you cast eyes on him when I had forbidden it? Back, I tell you all! This man belongs to me! Beware how you meddle with him, or you'll have to deal with me.'

The fair girl, with a laugh of ribald coquetry, turned to answer him: 'You yourself never loved; you never love!' On this the other women joined, and such a mirthless, hard, soulless laughter rang through the room that it almost made me faint to hear; it seemed like the pleasure of fiends.

Then the count turned, after looking at my face attentively, and said in a soft whisper: 'Yes, I too can love; you yourselves can tell it from the past. Is it not so? Well, now I promise you that when I am done with him, you shall kiss him at your will. Now go! Go! I must awaken him, for there is work to be done.'

'Are we to have nothing tonight?' said one of them, with a low laugh, as she pointed to the bag which he had thrown upon the floor, and which moved as though there were some living thing within it. For answer he nodded his head. One of the women jumped forward and opened it. If my ears did not deceive me there was a gasp and a low wail, as of a half-smothered child. The women closed round, whilst I was aghast with horror; but as I looked they disappeared, and with them the dreadful bag. There was no door near them, and they could not have passed me without my noticing. They simply seemed to fade into the rays of the moonlight and pass out through the window, for I could see outside the dim, shadowy forms for a moment before they entirely faded away.

Then the horror overcame me, and I sank down unconscious.

For the Blood is the Life

F. MARION CRAWFORD

We had dined at sunset on the broad roof of the old tower, because it was cooler there during the great heat of summer. Besides, the little kitchen was built at one corner of the great square platform, which made it more convenient than if the dishes had to be carried down the steep stone steps, broken in places and everywhere worn with age. The tower was one of those built all down the west coast of Calabria by the Emperor Charles V early in the sixteenth century, to keep off the Barbary pirates, when the unbelievers were allied with Francis I against the Emperor and the Church. They have gone to ruin, a few still stand intact, and mine is one of the largest. How it came into my possession ten years ago, and why I spend a part of each year in it, are matters which do not concern this tale. The tower stands in one of the loneliest spots in southern Italy, at the extremity of a curving rocky promontory, which forms a small but safe natural harbour at the southern extremity of the Gulf of Policastro, and just north of Cape Scalea, the birthplace of Judas Iscariot, according to the old local legend. The tower stands alone on this hooked spur of the rock, and there is not a house to be seen within three miles of it. When I go there I take a couple of sailors, one of whom is a fair cook, and when I am away it is in charge of a gnomelike little being who was once a miner and who attached himself to me long ago.

My friend, who sometimes visits me in my summer solitude, is an artist by profession, a Scandinavian by birth, and a cosmopolitan by force of circumstances. We had dined at sunset; the sunset glow had reddened and faded again, and the evening purple steeped the vast chain of the mountains that embrace the deep gulf to eastward and rear themselves higher and higher toward the south. It was hot, and we sat at the landward corner of the platform, waiting for the night breeze to come down from the lower hills. The colour sank out of the air, there was a little interval of deep-grey twilight, and a lamp sent a yellow streak from the open door of the kitchen, where the men were getting their supper.

Then the moon rose suddenly above the crest of the promontory, flooding the platform and lighting up every little spur of rock and knoll of grass below us, down to the edge of the motionless water. My friend lighted his pipe and sat looking at a spot on the hillside. I knew that he was looking at it, and for a long time past I had wondered whether he would ever see anything there that would fix his attention. I knew that spot well. It was clear that he was interested at last, though it was a long time before he spoke. Like most painters, he trusts to his own eyesight, as a lion trusts his strength and a stag his speed, and he is always disturbed when he cannot reconcile what he sees with what he believes that he ought to see.

'It's strange,' he said. 'Do you see that little mound just on this side of the boulder?'

'Yes,' I said, and I guessed what was coming.

'It looks like a grave,' observed Holger.

'Very true. It does look like a grave.'

'Yes,' continued my friend, his eyes still fixed on the spot. 'But the strange thing is that I see the body lying on the top of it. Of course,' continued Holger, turning his head on one side as artists do, 'it must be an effect of light. In the first place, it is not a grave at all. Secondly, if it were, the body would be inside and not outside. Therefore, it's an effect of the moonlight. Don't you see it?'

'Perfectly; I always see it on moonlight nights.'

'It doesn't seem to interest you much,' said Holger.

'On the contrary, it does interest me, though I am used to it. You're not so far wrong, either. The mound is really a grave.'

'Nonsense!' cried Holger, incredulously. 'I suppose you'll tell me what I see lying on it is really a corpse!'

'No,' I answered, 'it's not. I know, because I have taken the trouble to go down and see.'

'Then what is it?' asked Holger.

'It's nothing.'

'You mean that it's an effect of light, I suppose?'

'Perhaps it is. But the inexplicable part of the matter is that it makes no difference whether the moon is rising or setting, or waxing or waning. If there's any moonlight at all, from east or west or overhead, so long as it shines on the grave you can see the outline of the body on top.'

Holger stirred up his pipe with the point of his knife, and then used his finger for a stopper. When the tobacco burned well he rose from his chair.

'If you don't mind,' he said, 'I'll go down and take a look at it.'

He left me, crossed the roof, and disappeared down the dark steps. I did not move, but sat looking down until he came out of the tower below. I heard him humming an old Danish song as he crossed the open space in the bright moonlight, going straight to the mysterious mound. When he was ten paces from it, Holger stopped short, made two steps forward, and then three or four backward, and then stopped again. I knew what that meant. He had reached the spot where the Thing ceased to be visible – where, as he would have said, the effect of light changed.

Then he went on till he reached the mound and stood upon it. I could see the Thing still, but it was no longer lying down; it was on its knees now, winding its white arms round Holger's body and looking up into his face. A cool breeze stirred my hair at that moment, as the night wind began to come down from the hills, but it felt like a breath from another world.

The Thing seemed to be trying to climb to its feet, helping itself up by Holger's body while he stood upright, quite unconscious of it and apparently looking toward the tower, which is very picturesque when the moonlight falls upon it on that side.

'Come along!' I shouted. 'Don't stay there all night!'

It seemed to me that he moved reluctantly as he stepped from the mound, or else with difficulty. That was it. The Thing's arms were still round his waist, but its feet could not leave the grave. As he came slowly forward it was drawn and lengthened like a wreath of mist, thin and white, till I saw distinctly that Holger shook himself, as a man does who feels a chill. At the same instant a little wail of pain came to me on the breeze – it might have been the cry of the small owl that lives among the rocks – and the misty presence floated swiftly back from Holger's advancing figure and lay once more at its length upon the mound.

Again I felt the cool breeze in my hair, and this time an icy thrill of dread ran down my spine. I remembered very well that I had once gone down there alone in the moonlight; that presently, being near, I had seen nothing; that, like Holger, I had gone and had stood upon the mound; and I remembered how, when I came back, sure that there was nothing there, I had felt the sudden conviction that there was something after all if I would only look behind me. I remembered the strong temptation to look back, a temptation I had resisted as unworthy of a man of sense, until, to get rid of it, I had shaken myself just as Holger did.

And now I knew that those white, misty arms had been round me too; I knew it in a flash, and I shuddered as I remembered that I had heard the night owl then too. But it had not been the night owl. It was the cry of the Thing.

I refilled my pipe and poured out a cup of strong southern wine; in less than a minute Holger was seated beside me again.

'Of course there's nothing there,' he said, 'but it's creepy, all the same. Do you know, when I was coming back I was so sure that there was something behind me that I wanted to turn round and look? It was an effort not to.'

He laughed a little, knocked the ashes out of his pipe, and poured himself out some wine. For a while neither of us spoke, and the moon rose higher, and we both looked at the Thing that lay on the mound.

'You might make a story about that,' said Holger after a long time. 'There is one,' I answered. 'If you're not sleepy, I'll tell it to you.' 'Go ahead,' said Holger, who likes stories.

Old Alario was dying up there in the village behind the hill. You remember him, I have no doubt. They say that he made his money by selling sham jewellery in South America, and escaped with his gains when he was found out. Like all those fellows, if they bring anything back with them, he at once set to work to enlarge his house; and, as there are no masons here, he sent all the way to Paola for two workmen. They were a rough-looking pair of scoundrels – a Neapolitan who had lost one eye and a Sicilian with an old scar half an inch deep across his left cheek. I often saw them, for on Sundays they used to come down here and fish off the rocks. When Alario caught the fever that killed him the masons were still at work. As he had agreed that part of their pay should be their board and lodging, he made them sleep in the house. His wife was dead, and he had an only son called Angelo, who was a much better sort than himself. Angelo was to marry the daughter of the richest man in the village, and, strange to say, though the marriage was arranged by their parents, the young people were said to be in love with each other.

For that matter, the whole village was in love with Angelo, and among the rest a wild, good-looking creature called Cristina, who was more like a gipsy than any girl I ever saw about here. She had very red lips and very black eyes, she was built like a greyhound, and had the tongue of the devil. But Angelo did not care a straw for her. He was rather a simple-minded fellow, quite different from his old scoundrel of a father, and under what I should call normal circumstances I really believe that he would never have looked at any girl except the nice plump little creature, with a fat dowry, whom his father meant him to marry. But things turned up which were neither normal nor natural.

On the other hand, a very handsome young shepherd from the hills above Maratea was in love with Cristina, who seems to have been quite indifferent to him. Cristina had no regular means of subsistence, but she was a good girl and willing to do any work or go on errands to any distance for the sake of a loaf of bread or a mess of beans, and permission to sleep under cover. She was especially glad when she could get something to do about the house of Angelo's father. There is no doctor in the village, and when the neighbours saw that old Alario was dying they sent Cristina to Scalea to fetch one. That was late in the afternoon, and if they had waited so long, it was because the dying miser refused to allow any such extravagance while he was able to speak. But while Cristina was gone, matters grew rapidly worse, the priest was brought to the bedside, and when he had done what he could he gave it as his opinion to the bystanders that the old man was dead, and left the house.

You know these people. They have a physical horror of death. Until the priest spoke, the room had been full of people. The words were hardly out of his mouth before it was empty. It was night now. They hurried down the dark steps and out into the street.

Angelo was away, Cristina had not come back – the simple woman servant who had nursed the sick man fled with the rest, and the body was left alone in the flickering light of the earthen oil lamp.

Five minutes later two men looked in cautiously and crept forward toward the bed. They were the one-eyed Neapolitan mason and his Sicilian companion. They knew what they wanted. In a moment they had dragged from under the bed a small but heavy iron-bound box, and long before anyone thought of coming back to the dead man they had left the house and the village under cover of the darkness. It was easy enough, for Alario's house is the last toward the gorge which leads down here, and the thieves merely went out by the back door, got over the stone wall, and had nothing to risk after that except the possibility of meeting some belated countryman, which was very small indeed, since few of the people use that path. They had a mattock and shovel, and they made their way here without accident.

I am telling you this story as it must have happened, for, of course, there were no witnesses to this part of it. The men brought the box down by the gorge, intending to bury it until they should be able to come back and take it away in a boat. They must have been clever enough to guess that some of the money would be in paper notes, for they would otherwise have buried it on the beach in the wet sand, where it would have been much safer. But the paper would have rotted if they had been obliged to leave it there long, so they dug their hole down there, close to that boulder. Yes, just where the mound is now.

Cristina did not find the doctor in Scalea, for he had been sent for from a place up the valley, halfway to San Domenico. If she had found him, he would have come on his mule by the upper road, which is smoother but much longer. But Cristina took the short cut by the rocks, which passes about fifty feet above the mound, and goes round that corner. The men were digging when she passed, and she heard them at work. It would not have been like her to go by without finding out what the noise was, for she was never afraid of anything in her life, and, besides, the fishermen sometimes came ashore here at night to get a stone for an anchor or to gather sticks to make a little fire. The night was dark, and Cristina probably came close to the two men before she could see what they were doing. She knew them, of course, and they knew her, and understood instantly that they were in her power. There was only one thing to be done for their safety, and they did it. They knocked her on the head, they dug the hole deep, and they buried her quickly with the iron-bound chest. They must have understood that their only chance of escaping suspicion lay in getting back to the village before their absence was noticed, for they returned immediately, and were found half an hour later gossiping quietly with the man who was making Alario's coffin. He was a crony of theirs, and had been working at the repairs in the old man's house. So far as I have been able to make out, the only persons who were supposed to know where Alario kept his treasure were Angelo and the one woman servant I have mentioned. Angelo was away; it was the woman who discovered the theft.

It is easy enough to understand why no-one else knew where the money was. The old man kept his door locked and the key in

his pocket when he was out, and did not let the woman enter
to clean the place unless he was there himself. The whole village
knew that he had money somewhere, however, and the masons
had probably discovered the whereabouts of the chest by climbing
in at the window in his absence. If the old man had not been
delirious until he lost consciousness, he would have been in frightful agony of mind for his riches. The faithful woman servant
forgot their existence only for a few moments when she fled with
the rest, overcome by the horror of death. Twenty minutes had
not passed before she returned with the two hideous old hags
who are always called in to prepare the dead for burial. Even then
she had not at first the courage to go near the bed with them, but
she made a pretence of dropping something, went down on her
knees as if to find it, and looked under the bedstead. The walls of
the room were newly whitewashed down to the floor, and she saw
at a glance that the chest was gone. It had been there in the afternoon, it had therefore been stolen in the short interval since she
had left the room.

There are no carabineers stationed in the village; there is not
so much as a municipal watchman, for there is no municipality.
There never was such a place, I believe. Scalea is supposed to look
after it in some mysterious way, and it takes a couple of hours to
get anybody from there. As the old woman had lived in the village
all her life, it did not even occur to her to apply to any civil
authority for help. She simply set up a howl and ran through the
village in the dark, screaming out that her dead master's house had
been robbed. Many of the people looked out, but at first no-one
seemed inclined to help her. Most of them, judging her by themselves, whispered to each other that she had probably stolen the
money herself. The first man to move was the father of the girl
whom Angelo was to marry; having collected his household, all of
whom felt a personal interest in the wealth which was to have
come into the family, he declared it to be his opinion that the chest
had been stolen by the two journeyman masons who lodged in the
house. He headed a search for them, which naturally began in
Alario's house and ended in the carpenter's workshop, where the
thieves were found discussing a measure of wine with the carpenter
over the half-finished coffin, by the light of one earthen lamp filled
with oil and tallow. The search party at once accused the delin-
quents of the crime, and threatened to lock them up in the cellar
till the carabineers could be fetched from Scalea. The two men

looked at each other for one moment, and then without the slightest hesitation they put out the single light, seized the unfinished coffin between them, and using it as a sort of battering ram, dashed upon their assailants in the dark. In a few moments they were beyond pursuit.

That is the end of the first part of the story. The treasure had disappeared, and as no trace of it could be found the people naturally supposed that the thieves had succeeded in carrying it off. The old man was buried, and when Angelo came back at last he had to borrow money to pay for the miserable funeral, and had some difficulty in doing so. He hardly needed to be told that in losing his inheritance he had lost his bride. In this part of the world marriages are made on strictly business principles, and if the promised cash is not forthcoming on the appointed day the bride or the bridegroom whose parents have failed to produce it may as well take themselves off, for there will be no wedding. Poor Angelo knew that well enough. His father had been possessed of hardly any land, and now that the hard cash which he had brought from South America was gone, there was nothing left but debts for the building materials that were to have been used for enlarging and improving the old house. Angelo was beggared, and the nice plump little creature who was to have been his turned up her nose at him in the most approved fashion. As for Cristina, it was several days before she was missed, for no-one remembered that she had been sent to Scalea for the doctor, who had never come. She often disappeared in the same way for days together, when she could find a little work here and there at the distant farms among the hills. But when she did not come back at all, people began to wonder, and at last made up their minds that she had connived with the masons and had escaped with them.

I paused and emptied my glass.

'That sort of thing could not happen anywhere else,' observed Holger, filling his everlasting pipe again. 'It is wonderful what a natural charm there is about murder and sudden death in a romantic country like this. Deeds that would be simply brutal and disgusting anywhere else become dramatic and mysterious because this is Italy and we are living in a genuine tower of Charles V built against genuine Barbary pirates.'

'There's something in that,' I admitted. Holger is the most romantic man in the world inside of himself, but he always thinks it necessary to explain why he feels anything.

'I suppose they found the poor girl's body with the box,' he said presently.

'As it seems to interest you,' I answered, 'I'll tell you the rest of the story.'

The moon had risen high by this time; the outline of the Thing on the mound was clearer to our eyes than before.

The village very soon settled down to its small, dull life. No-one missed old Alario, who had been away so much on his voyages to South America that he had never been a familiar figure in his native place. Angelo lived in the half-finished house, and because he had no money to pay the old woman servant she would not stay with him, but once in a long time she would come and wash a shirt for him for old acquaintance' sake. Besides the house, he had inherited a small patch of ground at some distance from the village; he tried to cultivate it, but he had no heart in the work, for he knew he could never pay the taxes on it and on the house, which would certainly be confiscated by the Government, or seized for the debt of the building material, which the man who had supplied it refused to take back.

Angelo was very unhappy. So long as his father had been alive and rich, every girl in the village had been in love with him; but that was all changed now. It had been pleasant to be admired and courted, and invited to drink wine by fathers who had girls to marry. It was hard to be stared at coldly, and sometimes laughed at because he had been robbed of his inheritance. He cooked his miserable meals for himself, and from being sad became melancholy and morose.

At twilight, when the day's work was done, instead of hanging about in the open space before the church with young fellows of his own age, he took to wandering in lonely places on the outskirts of the village till it was quite dark. Then he slunk home and went to bed to save the expense of a light. But in those lonely twilight hours he began to have strange waking dreams. He was not always alone, for often when he sat on the stump of a tree, where the narrow path turns down the gorge, he was sure that a woman came up noiselessly over the rough stones, as if her feet were bare; and she stood under a clump of chestnut trees only half a dozen yards down the path, and beckoned to him without speaking. Though she was in the shadow he knew that her lips were red, and that when they parted a little and smiled at him she showed two small sharp teeth. He knew this at first rather than saw it, and he knew that it was Cristina, and that she was dead. Yet he was not afraid; he only wondered whether it was a dream, for he thought that if he had been awake he should have been frightened.

Besides, the dead woman had red lips, and that could only happen in a dream. Whenever he went near the gorge after sunset she was already there waiting for him, or else she very soon appeared, and he began to be sure that she came a little nearer to him every day. At first he had only been sure of her blood-red mouth, but now each feature grew distinct, and the pale face looked at him with deep and hungry eyes.

It was the eyes that grew dim. Little by little he came to know that some day the dream would not end when he turned away to go home, but would lead him down the gorge out of which the vision rose. She was nearer now when she beckoned to him. Her cheeks were not livid like those of the dead, but pale with starvation, with the furious and unappeased physical hunger of her eyes that devoured him. They feasted on his soul and cast a spell over him, and at last they were close to his own and held them. He could not tell whether her breath was as hot as fire or as cold as ice; he could not tell whether her red lips burned his or froze them, or whether her five fingers on his wrists seared scorching scars or bit his flesh like frost; he could not tell whether he was awake or asleep, whether she was alive or dead, but he knew that she loved him, she alone of all creatures, earthly or unearthly, and her spell had power over him.

When the moon rose high that night the shadow of that Thing was not alone down there upon the mound.

Angelo awoke in the cool dawn, drenched with dew and chilled through flesh, and blood, and bone. He opened his eyes to the faint grey light, and saw the stars still shining overhead. He was very weak, and his heart was beating so slowly that he was almost like a man fainting. Slowly he turned his head on the mound, as on a pillow, but the other face was not there. Fear seized him suddenly, a fear unspeakable and unknown; he sprang to his feet and fled up the gorge, and he never looked behind him until he reached the door of the house on the outskirts of the village. Drearily he went to his work that day, and wearily the hours dragged themselves after the sun, till at last he touched the sea and sank, and the great sharp hills above Maratea turned purple against the dove-coloured eastern sky.

Angelo shouldered his heavy hoe and left the field. He felt less tired now than in the morning when he had begun to work, but he promised himself that he would go home without lingering by the gorge, and eat the best supper he could get himself, and sleep all night in his bed like a Christian man. Not again would he be tempted down the narrow way by a shadow with red lips and icy breath; not again would he dream that dream of terror and delight. He was near the village now; it was half an hour since the sun had set, and the cracked church bell sent little discordant echoes across the rocks and ravines to tell all good people that the day was done. Angelo stood still a moment where the path forked, where it led toward the village on the left, and down to the gorge on the right, where a clump of chestnut trees overhung the narrow way. He stood still a minute, lifting his battered hat from his head and gazing at the fast-fading sea westward, and his lips moved as he silently repeated the familiar evening prayer. His lips moved, but the words that followed them in his brain lost their meaning and turned into others, and ended in a name that he spoke aloud – 'Cristina!' With the name, the tension of his will relaxed suddenly, reality went out and the dream took him again and bore him on swiftly and surely like a man walking in his sleep, down, down, by the steep path in the gathering darkness. And as she glided beside him, Cristina whispered strange sweet things in his ear, which somehow, if he had been awake, he knew that he could not quite have understood; but now they were the most wonderful words he had ever heard in his life. And she kissed him also, but not upon his mouth. He felt her sharp kisses upon his white throat, and he knew that her lips were red. So the wild dream sped on through twilight and darkness and moonrise, and all the glory of the summer's night. But in the chilly dawn he lay as one half dead upon the mound down there, recalling and not recalling, drained of his blood, yet strangely longing to give those red lips more. Then came the fear, the awful nameless panic, the mortal horror that guards the confines of the world we see not, neither know of as we know of other things, but which we feel when its icy chill freezes our bones and stirs our hair with the touch of a ghostly hand. Once more Angelo sprang from the mound and fled up the gorge in the breaking day, but his step was less sure this time, and he panted for breath as he ran; and when he came to the bright spring of water that rises halfway up the hillside, he dropped upon his knees and hands and plunged his whole face in and drank as he had never drunk before – for it was the thirst of the wounded man who has lain bleeding all night long upon the battlefield.

She had him fast now, and he could not escape her, but would come to her every evening at dusk until she had drained him of his last drop of blood. It was in vain that when the day was done he tried to take another turning and to go home by a path that did not lead near the gorge. It was in vain that he made promises to himself each morning at dawn when he climbed the lonely way up from the shore to the village. It was all in vain, for when the sun sank burning into the sea, and the coolness of the evening stole out as from a hiding-place to delight the weary world, his feet turned toward the old way, and she was waiting for him in the shadow under the chestnut trees; and then all happened as before, and she fell to kissing his white throat even as she flitted lightly down the way, winding one arm about him. And as his blood failed, she grew more hungry and more thirsty every day, and every day when he awoke in the early dawn it was harder to rouse himself to the effort of climbing the steep path to the village; and when he went to his work his feet dragged painfully, and there was hardly strength in his arms to wield the heavy hoe. He scarcely spoke to anyone now, but the people said he was 'consuming himself' for love of the girl he was to have married when he lost his inheritance; and they laughed heartily at the thought, for this is not a very romantic country. At this time, Antonio, the man who stays here to look after the tower, returned from a visit to his people, who live near Salerno. He had been away all the time since before Alario's death and knew nothing of what had happened. He has told me that he came back late in the afternoon and shut himself up in the tower to eat and sleep, for he was very tired. It was past midnight when he awoke, and when he looked out the waning moon was rising over the shoulder of the hill. He looked out toward the mound, and he saw something, and he did not sleep again that night. When he went out again in the morning it was broad daylight, and there was nothing to be seen on the mound but loose stones and driven sand. Yet he did not go very near it; he went straight up the path to the village and directly to the house of the old priest.

'I have seen an evil thing this night,' he said; 'I have seen how the dead drink the blood of the living. And the blood is the life.'

'Tell me what you have seen,' said the priest in reply.

Antonio told him everything he had seen.

'You must bring your book and your holy water tonight,' he added. 'I will be here before sunset to go down with you, and if it pleases your reverence to sup with me while we wait, I will make ready.'

'I will come,' the priest answered, 'for I have read in old books of these strange beings which are neither quick nor dead, and which lie ever fresh in their graves, stealing out in the dusk to taste life and blood.'

Antonio cannot read, but he was glad to see that the priest understood the business; for, of course, the books must have instructed him as to the best means of quieting the half-living Thing forever.

So Antonio went away to his work, which consists largely in sitting on the shady side of the tower, when he is not perched upon a rock with a fishing line catching nothing. But on that day he went twice to look at the mound in the bright sunlight, and he searched round and round it for some hole through which the being might get in and out; but he found none. When the sun began to sink and the air was cooler in the shadows, he went up to fetch the old priest, carrying a little wicker basket with him; and in this they placed a bottle of holy water, and the basin, and sprinkler, and the stole which the priest would need; and they came down and waited in the door of the tower till it should be dark. But while the light still lingered very grey and faint, they saw something moving, just there, two figures, a man's that walked, and a woman's that flitted beside him, and while her head lay on his shoulder she kissed his throat. The priest has told me that, too, and that his teeth chattered and he grasped Antonio's arm. The vision passed and disappeared into the shadow. Then Antonio got the leathern flask of strong liquor, which he kept for great occasions, and poured such a draught as made the old man feel almost young again; and he got the lantern, and his pick and shovel, and gave the priest his stole to put on and the holy water to carry, and they went out together toward the spot where the work was to be done. Antonio says that in spite of the rum his own knees shook together, and the priest stumbled over his Latin. For when they were yet a few yards from the mound the flickering light of the lantern fell upon Angelo's white face, unconscious as if in sleep, and on his upturned throat, over which a very thin red line of blood trickled down into his collar; and the flickering light of the lantern played upon another face that looked up from the feast – upon two deep, dead eyes that saw in spite of death – upon parted lips redder than life itself – upon two gleaming teeth on which glistened a rosy drop. Then the priest, good old man, shut his eyes tight and showered holy water before him, and his cracked voice rose almost to a scream; and then Antonio, who is no coward after all, raised his pick in one hand and the lantern in the other, as he sprang forward, not knowing what the end should be; and then he swears that he heard a woman's cry, and the Thing was gone, and Angelo lay alone on the mound unconscious, with the red line on his throat and the beads of deathly sweat on his cold forehead. They lifted him, half-dead as he was, and laid him on the ground close by; then Antonio went to work, and the priest helped him, though he was old and could not do much; and they dug deep, and at last Antonio, standing in the grave, stooped down with his lantern to see what he might see.

His hair used to be dark brown, with grizzled streaks about the temples; in less than a month from that day he was as grey as a badger. He was a miner when he was young, and most of these fellows have seen ugly sights now and then, when accidents have happened, but he had never seen what he saw that night – that Thing which is neither alive nor dead, that Thing that will abide neither above ground nor in the grave. Antonio had brought something with him which the priest had not noticed. He had made it that afternoon – a sharp stake shaped from a piece of tough old driftwood. He had it with him now, and he had his heavy pick, and he had taken the lantern down into the grave. I don't think any power on earth could make him speak of what happened then, and the old priest was too frightened to look in. He says he heard Antonio breathing like a wild beast, and moving as if he were fighting with something almost as strong as himself; and he heard an evil sound also, with blows, as of something violently driven through flesh and bone: and then the most awful sound of all – a woman's shriek, the unearthly scream of a woman neither dead nor alive, but buried deep for many days. And he, the poor old priest, could only rock himself as he knelt there in the sand, crying aloud his prayers and exorcisms to drown these dreadful sounds. Then suddenly a small ironbound chest was thrown up and rolled over against the old man's knee, and in a moment more Antonio was beside him, his face as white as tallow in the flickering light of the lantern, shovelling the sand and pebbles into the grave with furious haste, and looking over the edge till the pit was half full; and the priest had said that there was much fresh blood on Antonio's hands and on his clothes.

I had come to the end of my story. Holger finished his wine and leaned back in his chair.

'So Angelo got his own again,' he said. 'Did he marry the prim and plump young person to whom he had been betrothed?'

'No; he had been badly frightened. He went to South America, and has not been heard of since.'

'And that poor thing's body is there still, I suppose,' said Holger. Is it quite dead yet, I wonder?'

I wonder, too. But whether it is dead or alive, I should hardly care to see it, even in broad daylight.

Antonio is as grey as a badger, and he has never been quite the same man since that night.

Good Lady Ducayne

MARY ELIZABETH BRADDON

I

Bella Rolleston had made up her mind that her only chance of earning her bread and helping her mother to an occasional crust was by going out into the great unknown world as companion to a lady. She was willing to go to any lady rich enough to pay her a salary and so eccentric as to wish for a hired companion. Five shillings told off reluctantly from one of those sovereigns which were so rare with the mother and daughter, and which melted away so quickly, five solid shillings, had been handed to a smartly-dressed lady in an office in Harbeck Street, London, W., in the hope that this very Superior Person would find a situation and a salary for Miss Rolleston. The Superior Person glanced at the two half-crowns as they lay on the table where Bella's hand had placed them, to make sure they were neither of them florins, before she wrote a description of Bella's qualifications and requirements in a formidable-looking ledger.

'Age?' she asked, curtly.

'Eighteen, last July.'

'Any accomplishments?'

'No; I am not at all accomplished. If I were I should want to be a governess – a companion seems the lowest stage.'

'We have some highly accomplished ladies on our books as companions, or chaperon companions.'

'Oh, I know!' babbled Bella, loquacious in her youthful candour. 'But that is quite a different thing. Mother hasn't been able to afford a piano since I was twelve years old, so I'm afraid I've forgotten how to play. And I have had to help mother with her needlework, so there hasn't been much time to study.'

'Please don't waste time upon explaining what you can't do, but kindly tell me anything you can do,' said the Superior Person, crushingly, with her pen poised between delicate fingers waiting to write.

'Can you read aloud for two or three hours at a stretch? Are you active and handy, an early riser, a good walker, sweet-tempered, and obliging?'

'I can say yes to all those questions except about the sweetness. I think I have a pretty good temper, and I should be anxious to oblige anybody who paid for my services. I should want them to feel that I was really earning my salary.'

'The kind of ladies who come to me would not care for a talkative companion,' said the Person, severely, having finished writing in her book. 'My connection lies chiefly among the aristocracy, and in that class considerable deference is expected.'

'Oh, of course,' said Bella; 'but it's quite different when I'm talking to you. I want to tell you all about myself once and forever.'

'I am glad it is to be only once!' said the Person, with the edges of her lips.

The Person was of uncertain age, tightly laced in a black silk gown. She had a powdery complexion and a handsome clump of somebody else's hair on the top of her head. It may be that Bella's girlish freshness and vivacity had an irritating effect upon nerves weakened by an eight-hour day in that overheated second floor in Harbeck Street. To Bella the official apartment, with its Brussels carpet, velvet curtains and velvet chairs, and French clock, ticking loud on the marble chimney-piece, suggested the luxury of a palace, as compared with another second floor in Walworth where Mrs Rolleston and her daughter had managed to exist for the last six years.

'Do you think you have anything on your books that would suit me?' faltered Bella, after a pause.

'Oh, dear no; I have nothing in view at present,' answered the Person, who had swept Bella's half-crowns into a drawer, absent-mindedly, with the tips of her fingers. 'You see, you are so very unformed – so much too young to be companion to a lady of position. It is a pity you have not enough education for a nursery governess; that would be more in your line.'

'And do you think it will be very long before you can get me a situation?' asked Bella, doubtfully.

'I really cannot say. Have you any particular reason for being so impatient – not a love affair, I hope?'

'A love affair!' cried Bella, with flaming cheeks. 'What utter nonsense. I want a situation because mother is poor, and I hate being a burden to her. I want a salary that I can share with her.'

'There won't be much margin for sharing in the salary you are likely to get at your age – and with your – very – unformed manners,' said the Person, who found Bella's peony cheeks, bright eyes, and unbridled vivacity more and more oppressive.

'Perhaps if you'd be kind enough to give me back the fee I could take it to an agency where the connection isn't quite so aristocratic,' said Bella, who – as she told her mother in her recital of the interview – was determined not to be sat upon.

'You will find no agency that can do more for you than mine,' replied the Person, whose harpy fingers never relinquished coin. 'You will have to wait for your opportunity. Yours is an exceptional case: but I will bear you in mind, and if anything suitable offers I will write to you. I cannot say more than that.'

The half-contemptuous bend of the stately head, weighted with borrowed hair, indicated the end of the interview. Bella went back to Walworth – tramped sturdily every inch of the way in the September afternoon – and 'took off' the Superior Person for the amusement of her mother and the landlady, who lingered in the shabby little sitting-room after bringing in the tea-tray, to applaud Miss Rolleston's 'taking off'.

'Dear, dear, what a mimic she is!' said the landlady. 'You ought to have let her go on the stage, mum. She might have made her fortune as an actress.

2

Bella waited and hoped, and listened for the postman's knocks which brought such store of letters for the parlours and the first floor, and so few for that humble second floor, where mother and daughter sat sewing with hand and with wheel and treadle, for the greater part of the day. Mrs Rolleston was a lady by birth and education; but it had been her bad fortune to marry a scoundrel; for the last half-dozen years she had been that worst of widows, a wife whose husband had deserted her. Happily, she was courageous, industrious, and a clever needlewoman; and she had been able just to earn a living for herself and her only child, by making mantles and cloaks for a West-end house. It was not a luxurious living. Cheap lodgings in a shabby street off the Walworth Road, scanty dinners, homely food, well-worn raiment, had been the portion of mother and daughter; but they loved each other so dearly, and Nature had made them both so light-hearted, that they had contrived somehow to be happy.

But now this idea of going out into the world as companion to some fine lady had rooted itself into Bella's mind, and although she idolised her mother, and although the parting of mother and daughter must needs tear two loving hearts into shreds, the girl longed for enterprise and change and excitement, as the pages of old longed to be knights, and to start for the Holy Land to break a lance with the infidel.

She grew tired of racing downstairs every time the postman knocked, only to be told 'nothing for you, miss', by the smudgy-faced drudge who picked up the letters from the passage floor. 'Nothing for you, miss,' grinned the lodging-house drudge, till at last Bella took heart of grace and walked up to Harbeck Street, and asked the Superior Person how it was that no situation had been found for her.

'You are too young,' said the Person, 'and you want a salary.'

'Of course I do,' answered Bella; 'don't other people want salaries?'

'Young ladies of your age generally want a comfortable home.'

'I don't,' snapped Bella: 'I want to help mother.'

'You can call again this day week,' said the Person; 'or, if I hear of anything in the meantime, I will write to you.'

No letter came from the Person, and in exactly a week Bella put on her neatest hat, the one that had been seldomest caught in the rain, and trudged off to Harbeck Street.

It was a dull October afternoon, and there was a greyness in the air which might turn to fog before night. The Walworth Road shops gleamed brightly through that grey atmosphere, and though to a young lady reared in Mayfair or Belgravia such shop-windows would have been unworthy of a glance, they were a snare and temptation for Bella. There were so many things that she longed for, and would never be able to buy.

Harbeck Street is apt to be empty at this dead season of the year, a long, long street, an endless perspective of eminently respectable houses. The Person's office was at the further end, and Bella looked down that long, grey vista almost despairingly, more tired than usual with the trudge from Walworth. As she looked, a carriage passed her, an old-fashioned, yellow chariot, on cee springs, drawn by a pair of high grey horses, with the stateliest of coachmen driving them, and a tall footman sitting by his side.

'It looks like the fairy godmother's coach,' thought Bella. 'I shouldn't wonder if it began by being a pumpkin.'

It was a surprise when she reached the Person's door to find the yellow chariot standing before it, and the tall footman waiting near the doorstep. She was almost afraid to go in and meet the owner of that splendid carriage. She had caught only a glimpse of its occupant as the chariot rolled by, a plumed bonnet, a patch of ermine.

The Person's smart page ushered her upstairs and knocked at the official door. 'Miss Rolleston,' he announced, apologetically, while Bella waited outside.

'Show her in,' said the Person, quickly; and then Bella heard her murmuring something in a low voice to her client.

Bella went in fresh, blooming, a living image of youth and hope, and before she looked at the Person her gaze was riveted by the owner of the chariot.

Never had she seen anyone as old as the old lady sitting by the Person's fire: a little old figure, wrapped from chin to feet in an ermine mantle; a withered, old face under a plumed bonnet – a face so wasted by age that it seemed only a pair of eyes and a peaked chin. The nose was peaked, too, but between the sharply pointed chin and the great, shining eyes, the small, aquiline nose was hardly visible.

'This is Miss Rolleston, Lady Ducayne.'

Claw-like fingers, flashing with jewels, lifted a double eyeglass to Lady Ducayne's shining black eyes, and through the glasses Bella saw those unnaturally bright eyes magnified to a gigantic size, and glaring at her awfully.

'Miss Torpinter has told me all about you,' said the old voice that belonged to the eyes. 'Have you good health? Are you strong and active, able to eat well, sleep well, walk well, able to enjoy all that there is good in life?'

'I have never known what it is to be ill, or idle,' answered Bella.

'Then I think you will do for me.'

'Of course, in the event of references being perfectly satisfactory,' put in the Person.

'I don't want references. The young woman looks frank and innocent. I'll take her on trust.'

'So like you, dear Lady Ducayne,' murmured Miss Torpinter.

'I want a strong young woman whose health will give me no trouble.'

'You have been so unfortunate in that respect,' cooed the Person, whose voice and manner were subdued to a melting sweetness by the old woman's presence.

'Yes, I've been rather unlucky,' grunted Lady Ducayne.

'But I am sure Miss Rolleston will not disappoint you, though certainly after your unpleasant experience with Miss Tomson, who looked the picture of health – and Miss Blandy, who said she had never seen a doctor since she was vaccinated – '

'Lies, no doubt,' muttered Lady Ducayne, and then turning to Bella, she asked, curtly, 'You don't mind spending the winter in Italy, I suppose?'

In Italy! The very word was magical. Bella's fair young face flushed crimson.

'It has been the dream of my life to see Italy,' she gasped.

From Walworth to Italy! How far, how impossible such a journey had seemed to that romantic dreamer.

'Well, your dream will be realised. Get yourself ready to leave Charing Cross by the train deluxe this day week at eleven. Be sure you are at the station a quarter before the hour. My people will look after you and your luggage.'

Lady Ducayne rose from her chair, assisted by her crutch-stick, and Miss Torpinter escorted her to the door.

'And with regard to salary?' questioned the Person on the way.

'Salary, oh, the same as usual – and if the young woman wants a quarter's pay in advance you can write to me for a check,' Lady Ducayne answered, carelessly.

Miss Torpinter went all the way downstairs with her client, and waited to see her seated in the yellow chariot. When she came upstairs again she was slightly out of breath, and she had resumed that superior manner which Bella had found so crushing.

'You may think yourself uncommonly lucky, Miss Rolleston,' she said. 'I have dozens of young ladies on my books whom I might have recommended for this situation – but I remembered having told you to call this afternoon – and I thought I would give you a chance. Old Lady Ducayne is one of the best people on my books. She gives her companion a hundred a year, and pays all travelling expenses. You will live in the lap of luxury.'

'A hundred a year! How too lovely! Shall I have to dress very grandly? Does Lady Ducayne keep much company?'

'At her age! No, she lives in seclusion – in her own apartments – her French maid, her footman, her medical attendant, her courier.'

'Why did those other companions leave her?' asked Bella.

'Their health broke down!'

'Poor things, and so they had to leave?'

'Yes, they had to leave. I suppose you would like a quarter's salary n advance?'

'Oh, yes, please. I shall have things to buy.'

'Very well, I will write for Lady Ducayne's check, and I will send you the balance after deducting my commission for the year.'

'To be sure, I had forgotten the commission.'

'You don't suppose I keep this office for pleasure.'

'Of course not,' murmured Bella, remembering the five shillings entrance fee; but nobody could expect a hundred a year and a winter in Italy for five shillings.

3

From Miss Rolleston, at Cap Ferrino, to Mrs Rolleston, in Beresford Street, Walworth, London.

How I wish you could see this place, dearest; the blue sky, the olive woods, the orange and lemon orchards between the cliffs and the sea – sheltering in the hollow of the great hills – and with summer waves dancing up to the narrow ridge of pebbles and weeds which is the Italian idea of a beach! Oh, how I wish you could see it all, mother dear, and bask in this sunshine, that makes it so difficult to believe the date at the head of this paper. November! The air is like an English June – the sun is so hot that I can't walk a few yards without an umbrella. And to think of you at Walworth while I am here! I could cry at the thought that perhaps you will never see this lovely coast, this wonderful sea, these summer flowers that bloom in winter. There is a hedge of pink geraniums under my window, mother – a thick rank hedge, as if the flowers grew wild – and there are Dijon roses climbing over arches and palisades all along the terrace – a rose garden full of bloom in November! Just picture it all! You could never imagine the luxury of this hotel. It is nearly new, and has been built and decorated regardless of expense. Our rooms are upholstered in pale blue satin, which shows up Lady Ducayne's parchment complexion; but as she sits all day in a corner of the balcony basking in the sun, except when she is in her carriage, and all the evening in her armchair close to the fire, and never sees anyone but her own people, her complexion matters very little.

She has the handsomest suite of rooms in the hotel. My bedroom is inside hers, the sweetest room – all blue satin and white lace – white enamelled furniture, looking-glasses on every wall, till I know my pert little profile as I never knew it before. The room was really meant for Lady Ducayne's dressing-room, but she ordered one of the blue satin couches to be arranged as a bed for me – the prettiest little bed, which I can wheel near the window on sunny mornings, as it is on castors and easily moved about. I feel as if Lady Ducayne were a funny old grandmother who had suddenly appeared in my life, very, very rich, and very, very kind.

She is not at all exacting. I read aloud to her a good deal, and she dozes and nods while I read. Sometimes I hear her moaning in her sleep – as if she had troublesome dreams. When she is tired of my reading she orders Francine, her maid, to read a French novel to her, and I hear her chuckle and groan now and then, as if she were more interested in those books than in Dickens or Scott. My French is not good enough to follow Francine, who reads very quickly. I have a great deal of liberty, for Lady Ducayne often tells me to run away and amuse myself; I roam about the hills for hours. Everything is so lovely. I lose myself in olive woods, always climbing up and up towards the pine woods above – and above the pines there are the snow mountains that just show their white peaks above the dark hills. Oh, you poor dear, how can I ever make you understand what this place is like – you, whose poor, tired eyes have only the opposite side of Beresford Street? Sometimes I go no farther than the terrace in front of the hotel, which is a favourite lounging-place with everybody. The gardens lie below, and the tennis courts where I sometimes play with a very nice girl, the only person in the hotel with whom I have made friends. She is a year older than I, and has come to Cap Ferrino with her brother, a doctor – or a medical student who is going to be a doctor. He passed his M.B. exam, at Edinburgh just before they left home, Lotta told me. He came to Italy entirely on his sister's account. She had a troublesome chest attack last summer and was ordered to winter abroad. They are orphans, quite alone in the world, and so fond of each other. It is very nice for me to have such a friend as Lotta. She is so thoroughly respectable. I can't help using that word, for some of the girls in this hotel go on in a way that I know you would shudder at. Lotta was brought up by an aunt, deep down in the country, and knows hardly anything about life. Her brother won't allow her to read a novel, French or English, that he has not read and approved.

'He treats me like a child,' she told me, 'but I don't mind, for it's nice to know somebody loves me, and cares about what I do, and even about my thoughts.'

Perhaps this is what makes some girls so eager to marry – the want of someone strong and brave and honest and true to care for them and order them about. I want no-one, mother darling, for I have you, and you are all the world to me. No husband could ever come between us two. If I ever were to marry he would have only the second place in my heart. But I don't suppose I ever shall marry, or even know what it is like to have an offer of marriage. No young man can afford to marry a penniless girl nowadays. Life is too expensive.

Mr Stafford. Lotta's brother, is very clever, and very kind. He thinks it is rather hard for me to have to live with such an old woman as Lady Ducayne, but then he does not know how poor we are – you and I – and what a wonderful life this seems to me in this lovely place. I feel a selfish wretch for enjoying all my luxuries, while you, who want them so much more than I, have none of them – hardly know what they are like, do you, dearest? – for my scamp of a father began to go to the dogs soon after you were married, and since then life has been all trouble and care and struggle for you.

This letter was written when Bella had been less than a month at Cap Ferrino, before the novelty had worn off the landscape, and before the pleasure of luxurious surroundings had begun to cloy. She wrote to her mother every week, such long letters as girls who have lived in closest companionship with a mother alone can write; letters that are like a diary of heart and mind. She wrote gaily always; but when the new year began Mrs Rolleston thought she detected a note of melancholy under all those lively details about the place and the people.

'My poor girl is getting homesick,' she thought. 'Her heart is in Beresford Street.'

It might be that she missed her new friend and companion, Lotta Stafford, who had gone with her brother for a little tour to Genoa and Spezia, and as far as Pisa. They were to return before February; but in the meantime Bella might naturally feel very solitary among all those strangers, whose manners and doings she described so well.

The mother's instinct had been true. Bella was not so happy as she had been in that first flush of wonder and delight which followed the change from Walworth to the Riviera. Somehow, she knew not how, lassitude had crept upon her. She no longer loved to climb the hills, no longer flourished her orange stick in sheer gladness of heart as her light feet skipped over the rough ground and the coarse grass on the mountain side. The odour of rosemary and thyme, the fresh breath of the sea, no longer filled her with rapture. She thought of Beresford Street and her mother's face with a sick longing. They were so far – so far away! And then she thought of Lady Ducayne, sitting by the heaped-up olive logs in the overheated salon – thought of that wizened-nutcracker profile, and those gleaming eyes, with an invincible horror.

Visitors at the hotel had told her that the air of Cap Ferrino was relaxing – better suited to age than to youth, to sickness than to health. No doubt it was so. She was not so well as she had been at Walworth; but she told herself that she was suffering only from the pain of separation from the dear companion of her girlhood, the mother who had been nurse, sister, friend, flatterer, all things in this world to her. She had shed many tears over that parting, had spent many a melancholy hour on the marble terrace with yearning eyes looking westward, and with her heart's desire a thousand miles away.

She was sitting in her favourite spot, an angle at the eastern end of the terrace, a quiet little nook sheltered by orange trees, when she heard a couple of Riviera habitués talking in the garden below. They were sitting on a bench against the terrace wall.

She had no idea of listening to their talk, till the sound of Lady Ducayne's name attracted her, and then she listened without any thought of wrongdoing. They were talking no secrets – just casually discussing a hotel acquaintance.

They were two elderly people whom Bella only knew by sight. An English clergyman who had wintered abroad for half his lifetime; a stout, comfortable, well-to-do spinster, whose chronic bronchitis obliged her to migrate annually.

'I have met her about Italy for the last ten years,' said the lady; 'but have never found out her real age.'

'I put her down at a hundred – not a year less,' replied the parson. 'Her reminiscences all go back to the Regency. She was evidently then in her zenith; and I have heard her say things that showed she was in Parisian society when the First Empire was at its best – before Josephine was divorced.'

'She doesn't talk much now.'

'No; there's not much life left in her. She is wise in keeping herself secluded. I only wonder that wicked old quack, her Italian doctor, didn't finish her off years ago.'

'I should think it must be the other way, and that he keeps her alive.'

'My dear Miss Manders, do you think foreign quackery ever kept anybody alive?'

'Well, there she is – and she never goes anywhere without him. He certainly has an unpleasant countenance.'

'Unpleasant,' echoed the parson, 'I don't believe the foul fiend himself can beat him in ugliness. I pity that poor young woman who has to live between old Lady Ducayne and Dr Parravicini.'

'But the old lady is very good to her companions.'

'No doubt. She is very free with her cash; the servants call her good Lady Ducayne. She is a withered old female Croesus, and knows she'll never be able to get through her money, and doesn't relish the idea of other people enjoying it when she's in her coffin. People who live to be as old as she is become slavishly attached to life. I dare say she's generous to those poor girls – but she can't make them happy. They die in her service.'

'Don't say they, Mr Carton; I know that one poor girl died at Mentone last spring.'

'Yes, and another poor girl died in Rome three years ago. I was there at the time. Good Lady Ducayne left her there in an English family. The girl had every comfort. The old woman was very liberal to her – but she died. I tell you, Miss Manders, it is not good for any young woman to live with two such horrors as Lady Ducayne and Parravicini.'

They talked of other things – but Bella hardly heard them. She sat motionless, and a cold wind seemed to come down upon her from the mountains and to creep up to her from the sea, till she shivered as she sat there in the sunshine, in the shelter of the orange trees in the midst of all that beauty and brightness.

Yes, they were uncanny, certainly, the pair of them – she so like an aristocratic witch in her withered old age; he of no particular age, with a face that was more like a waxen mask than any human countenance Bella had ever seen. What did it matter? Old age is venerable, and worthy of all reverence; and Lady Ducayne had been very kind to her. Dr Parravicini was a harmless, inoffensive student, who seldom looked up from the book he was reading. He had his private sitting-room, where he made experiments in chemistry and natural science – perhaps in alchemy. What could it matter to Bella? He had always been polite to her, in his far-off way. She could not be more happily placed than she was – in this palatial hotel, with this rich old lady.

No doubt she missed the young English girl who had been so friendly, and it might be that she missed the girl's brother, for Mr Stafford had talked to her a good deal – had interested himself in the books she was reading, and her manner of amusing herself when she was not on duty.

'You must come to our little salon when you are "off", as the hospital nurses call it, and we can have some music. No doubt you play and sing?' Upon which Bella had to own with a blush of shame that she had forgotten how to play the piano ages ago.

'Mother and I used to sing duets sometimes between the lights, without accompaniment,' she said, and the tears came into her eyes as she thought of the humble room, the half-hour's respite from work, the sewing machine standing where a piano ought to have been, and her mother's plaintive voice, so sweet, so true, so dear.

Sometimes she found herself wondering whether she would ever see that beloved mother again. Strange forebodings came into her mind. She was angry with herself for giving way to melancholy thoughts.

One day she questioned Lady Ducayne's French maid about those two companions who had died within three years.

'They were poor, feeble creatures,' Francine told her. 'They looked fresh and bright enough when they came to Miladi; but they ate too much, and they were lazy. They died of luxury and idleness. Miladi was too kind to them. They had nothing to do, and so they took to fancying things; fancying the air didn't suit them, that they couldn't sleep.'

'I sleep well enough, but I have had a strange dream several times since I have been in Italy.'

'Ah, you had better not begin to think about dreams, or you will be like those other girls. They were dreamers – and they dreamt themselves into the cemetery.'

The dream troubled her a little, not because it was a ghastly or frightening dream, but on account of sensations which she had never felt before in sleep – a whirring of wheels that went round in her brain, a great noise like a whirlwind, but rhythmical like the ticking of a gigantic clock: and then in the midst of this uproar as of winds and waves she seemed to sink into a gulf of unconsciousness, out of sleep into far deeper sleep – total extinction. And then, after that black interval, there had come the sound of voices, and then again the whirr of wheels, louder and louder – and again the black – and then she awoke, feeling languid and oppressed.

She told Dr Parravicini of her dream one day, on the only occasion when she wanted his professional advice. She had suffered rather severely from the mosquitoes before Christmas – and had been almost frightened at finding a wound upon her arm which she could only attribute to the venomous sting of one of these torturers. Parravicini put on his glasses, and scrutinised the angry mark on the round, white arm as Bella stood before him and Lady Ducayne with her sleeve rolled up above her elbow.

'Yes, that's rather more than a joke,' he said; 'he has caught you on the top of a vein. What a vampire! But there's no harm done, signorina, nothing that a little dressing of mine won't heal. You must always show me any bite of this nature. It might be dangerous if neglected. These creatures feed on poison and disseminate it.'

'And to think that such tiny creatures can bite like this,' said Bella; 'my arm looks as if it had been cut by a knife.'

'If I were to show you a mosquito's sting under my microscope you wouldn't be surprised at that,' replied Parravicini.

Bella had to put up with the mosquito bites, even when they came on the top of a vein, and produced that ugly wound. The wound recurred now and then at longish intervals, and Bella found Dr Parravicini's dressing a speedy cure. If he were the quack his enemies called him, he had at least a light hand and a delicate touch in performing this small operation.

Bella Rolleston to Mrs Rolleston – April 14th

EVER DEAREST

Behold the cheque for my second quarter's salary – five and twenty pounds. There is no-one to pinch off a whole tenner for a year's commission as there was last time, so it is all for you, mother, dear. I have plenty of pocket-money in hand from the cash I brought away with me, when you insisted on my keeping more than I wanted. It isn't possible to spend money here – except on occasional tips to servants, or sous to beggars and children – unless one had lots to spend, for everything one would like to buy – tortoise-shell, coral, lace – is so ridiculously dear that only a millionaire ought to look at it. Italy is a dream of beauty: but for shopping, give me Newington Causeway.

You ask me so earnestly if I am quite well that I fear my letters must have been very dull lately. Yes, dear, I am well – but I am not quite so strong as I was when I used to trudge to the West-end to buy half a pound of tea – just for a constitutional walk – or to Dulwich to look at the pictures. Italy is relaxing; and I feel what the people here call "slack". But I fancy I can see your dear face looking worried as you read this. Indeed, and indeed, I am not ill. I am only a little tired of this lovely scene – as I suppose one might get tired of looking at one of Turner's pictures if it hung on a wall that was always opposite one. I think of you every hour in every day – think of you and our homely little room – our dear little shabby parlour, with the armchairs from the wreck of your old home, and Dick singing in his cage over the sewing machine. Dear, shrill, maddening Dick, who, we flattered our-selves, was so passionately fond of us. Do tell me in your next letter that he is well.

My friend Lotta and her brother never came back after all. They went from Pisa to Rome. Happy mortals! And they are to be on the Italian lakes in May; which lake was not decided when Lotta last wrote to me. She has been a charming correspondent, and has confided all her little flirtations to me. We are all to go to Bellaggio next week – by Genoa and Milan. Isn't that lovely? Lady Ducayne travels by the easiest stages – except when she is bottled up in the train deluxe. We shall stop two days at Genoa and one at Milan. What a bore I shall be to you with my talk about Italy when I come home.

Love and love – and ever more love from your adoring,

BELLA

4

Herbert Stafford and his sister had often talked of the pretty English girl with her fresh complexion, which made such a pleasant touch of rosy colour among all those sallow faces at the Grand Hotel. The young doctor thought of her with a compassionate tenderness – her utter loneliness in that great hotel where there were so many people, her bondage to that old, old woman, where everybody else was free to think of nothing but enjoying life. It was a hard fate; and the poor child was evidently devoted to her mother, and felt the pain of separation – 'only two of them, and very poor, and all the world to each other', he thought.

Lotta told him one morning that they were to meet again at Bellaggio. 'The old thing and her court are to be there before we are,' she said. 'I shall be charmed to have Bella again. She is so bright and gay – in spite of an occasional touch of homesickness. I never took to a girl on a short acquaintance as I did to her.'

'I like her best when she is homesick,' said Herbert; 'for then I am sure she has a heart.'

'What have you to do with hearts, except for dissection? Don't forget that Bella is an absolute pauper. She told me in confidence that her mother makes mantles for a West-end shop. You can hardly have a lower depth than that.'

'I shouldn't think any less of her if her mother made match-boxes.'

'Not in the abstract – of course not. Matchboxes are honest labour. But you couldn't marry a girl whose mother makes mantles.'

'We haven't come to the consideration of that question yet,' answered Herbert, who liked to provoke his sister.

In two years' hospital practice he had seen too much of the grim realities of life to retain any prejudices about rank. Cancer, phthisis, gangrene, leave a man with little respect for humanity. The kernel is always the same – fearfully and wonderfully made – a subject for pity and terror.

Mr Stafford and his sister arrived at Bellaggio in a fair May evening. The sun was going down as the steamer approached the pier; and all that glory of purple bloom which curtains every wall at this season of the year flushed and deepened in the glowing light. A group of ladies were standing on the pier watching the arrivals, and among them Herbert saw a pale face that startled him out of his wonted composure.

'There she is,' murmured Lotta, at his elbow, 'but how dreadfully changed. She looks a wreck.'

They were shaking hands with her a few minutes later, and a flush had lighted up her poor pinched face in the pleasure of meeting.

'I thought you might come this evening,' she said. 'We have been here a week.'

She did not add that she had been there every evening to watch the boat in, and a good many times during the day. The Grand Bretagne was close by, and it had been easy for her to creep to the pier when the boat bell rang. She felt a joy in meeting these people again; a sense of being with friends; a confidence which Lady Ducayne's goodness had never inspired in her.

'Oh, you poor darling, how awfully ill you must have been,' exclaimed Lotta, as the two girls embraced.

Bella tried to answer, but her voice was choked with tears.

'What has been the matter, dear? That horrid influenza, I suppose?'

'No, no, I have not been ill – I have only felt a little weaker than I used to be. I don't think the air of Cap Ferrino quite agreed with me.'

'It must have disagreed with you abominably. I never saw such a change in anyone. Do let Herbert doctor you. He is fully qualified, you know. He prescribed for ever so many influenza patients at the Londres. They were glad to get advice from an English doctor in a friendly way.'

'I am sure he must be very clever!' faltered Bella, 'but there is really nothing the matter. I am not ill, and if I were ill, Lady Ducayne's physician – '

'That dreadful man with the yellow face? I would as soon one of the Borgias prescribed for me. I hope you haven't been taking any of his medicines.'

'No, dear, I have taken nothing. I have never complained of being ill.'

This was said while they were all three walking to the hotel. The Staffords' rooms had been secured in advance, pretty ground-floor rooms, opening into the garden. Lady Ducayne's statelier apartments were on the floor above.

'I believe these rooms are just under ours,' said Bella.

'Then it will be all the easier for you to run down to us,' replied Lotta, which was not really the case, as the grand staircase was in the centre of the hotel.

'Oh, I shall find it easy enough,' said Bella. 'I'm afraid you'll have too much of my society. Lady Ducayne sleeps away half the day in this warm weather, so I have a good deal of idle time; and I get awfully moped thinking of mother and home.'

Her voice broke upon the last word. She could not have thought of that poor lodging which went by the name of home more tenderly had it been the most beautiful that art and wealth ever created. She moped and pined in this lovely garden, with the sunlit lake and the romantic hills spreading out their beauty before her. She was homesick and she had dreams; or, rather, an occasional recurrence of that one bad dream with all its strange sensations – it was more like a hallucination than dreaming – the whirring of wheels, the sinking into an abyss, the struggling back to consciousness. She had the dream shortly before she left Cap Ferrino, but not since she had come to Bellaggio, and she began to hope the air in this lake district suited her better, and that those strange sensations would never return.

Mr Stafford wrote a prescription and had it made up at the chemist's near the hotel. It was a powerful tonic, and after two bottles, and a row or two on the lake, and some rambling over the hills and in the meadows where the spring flowers made earth seem paradise, Bella's spirits and looks improved as if by magic.

'It is a wonderful tonic,' she said, but perhaps in her heart of hearts she knew that the doctor's kind voice, and the friendly hand that helped her in and out of the boat, and the lake, had something to do with her cure.

'I hope you don't forget that her mother makes mantles,' Lotta said warningly.

'Or matchboxes; it is just the same thing, so far as I am concerned.'

'You mean that in no circumstances could you think of marrying her?'

'I mean that if ever I love a woman well enough to think of marrying her, riches or rank will count for nothing with me. But I fear – I fear your poor friend may not live to be any man's wife.'

'Do you think her so very ill?'

He sighed, and left the question unanswered.

One day, while they were gathering wild hyacinths in an upland meadow, Bella told Mr Stafford about her bad dream.

'It is curious only because it is hardly like a dream,' she said. 'I dare say you could find some commonsense reason for it. The position of my head on my pillow, or the atmosphere, or something.'

And then she described her sensations; how in the midst of sleep there came a sudden sense of suffocation; and then those whirring wheels, so loud, so terrible; and then a blank, and then a coming back to waking consciousness.

'Have you ever had chloroform given you – by a dentist, for instance?'

'Never – Dr Parravicini asked me that question one day.'

'Lately?'

'No, long ago, when we were in the train de luxe.'

'Has Dr Parravicini prescribed for you since you began to feel weak and ill?'

'Oh, he has given me a tonic from time to time, but I hate medicine, and took very little of the stuff. And then I am not ill, only weaker than I used to be. I was ridiculously strong and well when I lived at

Walworth, and used to take long walks every day. Mother made me take those tramps to Dulwich or Norwood, for fear I should suffer from too much sewing machine; sometimes – but very seldom – she went with me. She was generally toiling at home while I was enjoying fresh air and exercise. And she was very careful about our food – that, however plain it was, it should be always nourishing and ample. I owe it to her care that I grew up such a great, strong creature.'

'You don't look great or strong now, you poor dear,' said Lotta.

'I'm afraid Italy doesn't agree with me.'

'Perhaps it is not Italy, but being cooped up with Lady Ducayne that has made you ill.'

'But I am never cooped up. Lady Ducayne is absurdly kind, and lets me roam about or sit in the balcony all day if I like. I have read more novels since I have been with her than in all the rest of my life.'

'Then she is very different from the average old lady, who is usually a slave driver,' said Stafford. 'I wonder why she carries a companion about with her if she has so little need of society.'

'Oh, I am only part of her state. She is inordinately rich – and the salary she gives me doesn't count. Apropos of Dr Parravicini, I know he is a clever doctor, for he cures my horrid mosquito bites.'

'A little ammonia would do that, in the early stage of the mischief. But there are no mosquitoes to trouble you now.'

'Oh, yes, there are; I had a bite just before we left Cap Ferrino.' She pushed up her loose lawn sleeve, and exhibited a scar, which he scrutinised intently, with a surprised and puzzled look.

'This is no mosquito bite,' he said.

'Oh, yes it is – unless there are snakes or adders at Cap Ferrino.'

'It is not a bite at all. You are trifling with me. Miss Rolleston – you have allowed that wretched Italian quack to bleed you. They killed the greatest man in modern Europe that way, remember. How very foolish of you.'

'I was never bled in my life, Mr Stafford.'

'Nonsense! Let me look at your other arm. Are there any more mosquito bites?'

'Yes; Dr Parravicini says I have a bad skin for healing, and that the poison acts more virulently with me than with most people.'

Stafford examined both her arms in the broad sunlight, scars new and old.

'You have been very badly bitten, Miss Rolleston,' he said, 'and if ever I find the mosquito I shall make him smart. But, now tell me, my dear girl, on your word of honour, tell me as you would tell a friend who is sincerely anxious for your health and happiness – as you would tell your mother if she were here to question you – have you no knowledge of any cause for these scars except mosquito bites – no suspicion even?'

'No, indeed! No, upon my honour! I have never seen a mosquito biting my arm. One never does see the horrid little fiends. But I have heard them trumpeting under the curtains and I know that I have often had one of the pestilent wretches buzzing about me.'

Later in the day Bella and her friends were sitting at tea in the garden, while Lady Ducayne took her afternoon drive with her doctor.

'How long do you mean to stop with Lady Ducayne, Miss Rolleston?' Herbert Stafford asked, after a thoughtful silence, breaking suddenly upon the trivial talk of the two girls.

'As long as she will go on paying me twenty-five pounds a quarter.'

'Even if you feel your health breaking down in her service?'

'It is not the service that has injured my health. You can see that I have really nothing to do – to read aloud for an hour or so once or twice a week; to write a letter once in a while to a London tradesman. I shall never have such an easy time with anybody. And nobody else would give me a hundred a year.'

'Then you mean to go on till you break down; to die at your post?'

'Like the other two companions? No! If ever I feel seriously ill – really ill – I shall put myself in a train and go back to Walworth without stopping.'

'What about the other two companions?'

'They both died. It was very unlucky for Lady Ducayne. That's why she engaged me; she chose me because I was ruddy and robust. She must feel rather disgusted at my having grown white and weak. By-the-bye, when I told her about the good your tonic had done me, she said she would like to see you and have a little talk with you about her own case.'

'And I should like to see Lady Ducayne. When did she say this?'

'The day before yesterday.'

'Will you ask her if she will see me this evening?'

'With pleasure! I wonder what you will think of her? She looks rather terrible to a stranger; but Dr Parravicini says she was once a famous beauty.'

It was nearly ten o'clock when Mr Stafford was summoned by message from Lady Ducayne, whose courier came to conduct him to her ladyship's salon. Bella was reading aloud when the visitor was admitted; and he noticed the languor in the low, sweet tones, the evident effort.

'Shut up the book,' said the querulous old voice. 'You are beginning to drawl like Miss Blandy.'

Stafford saw a small, bent figure crouching over the piled up olive logs; a shrunken old figure in a gorgeous garment of black and crimson brocade, a skinny throat emerging from a mass of old Venetian lace, clasped with diamonds that flashed like fireflies as the trembling old head turned towards him.

The eyes that looked at him out of the face were almost as bright as the diamonds – the only living feature in that narrow parchment mask. He had seen terrible faces in the hospital – faces on which disease had set dreadful marks – but he had never seen a face that impressed him so painfully as this withered countenance, with its indescribable horror of death outlived, a face that should have been hidden under a coffin-lid years and years ago.

The Italian physician was standing on the other side of the fireplace, smoking a cigarette, and looking down at the little old woman brooding over the hearth as if he were proud of her.

'Good evening, Mr Stafford; you can go to your room, Bella, and write your everlasting letter to your mother at Walworth,' said Lady Ducayne. 'I believe she writes a page about every wild flower she discovers in the woods and meadows. I don't know what else she can find to write about,' she added, as Bella quietly withdrew to the pretty little bedroom opening out of Lady Ducayne's spacious apartment. Here, as at Cap Ferrino, she slept in a room adjoining the old lady's.

'You are a medical man, I understand, Mr Stafford.'

'I am a qualified practitioner, but I have not begun to practise.'

'You have begun upon my companion, she tells me.'

'I have prescribed for her, certainly, and I am happy to find my prescription has done her good; but I look upon that improvement as temporary. Her case will require more drastic treatment.'

'Never mind her case. There is nothing the matter with the girl – absolutely nothing – except girlish nonsense; too much liberty and not enough work.'

'I understand that two of your ladyship's previous companions died of the same disease,' said Stafford, looking first at Lady Ducayne, who gave her tremulous old head an impatient jerk, and then at Parravicini, whose yellow complexion had paled a little under Stafford's scrutiny.

'Don't bother me about my companions, sir,' said Lady Ducayne. 'I sent for you to consult you about myself – not about a parcel of anaemic girls. You are young, and medicine is a progressive science, the newspapers tell me. Where have you studied?'

'In Edinburgh – and in Paris.'

'Two good schools. And know all the new-fangled theories, the modern discoveries – that remind one of the medieval witchcraft, of Albertus Magnus, and George Ripley; you have studied hypnotism – electricity?'

'And the transfusion of blood,' said Stafford, very slowly, looking at Parravicini.

'Have you made any discovery that teaches you to prolong human life – any elixir – any mode of treatment? I want my life prolonged, young man. That man there has been my physician for thirty years. He does all he can to keep me alive – after his lights. He studies all the new theories of all the scientists – but he is old; he gets older every day – his brain-power is going – he is bigoted – prejudiced – can't receive new ideas – can't grapple with new systems. He will let me die if I am not on my guard against him.'

'You are of an unbelievable ingratitude, Ecclenza,' said Parravicini.

'Oh, you needn't complain. I have paid you thousands to keep me alive. Every year of my life has swollen your hoards; you know there is nothing to come to you when I am gone. My whole fortune is left to endow a home for indigent women of quality who have reached their ninetieth year. Come, Mr Stafford, I am a rich woman. Give me a few years more in the sunshine, a few years more above ground, and I will give you the price of a fashionable London practice – I will set you up at the West-end.'

'How old are you, Lady Ducayne?'

'I was born the day Louis XVI was guillotined.'

'Then I think you have had your share of the sunshine and the pleasures of the earth, and that you should spend your few remaining days in repenting your sins and trying to make atonement for the young lives that have been sacrificed to your love of life.'

'What do you mean by that, sir?'

'Oh, Lady Ducayne, need I put your wickedness and your physician's still greater wickedness in plain words? The poor girl who is now in your employment has been reduced from robust health to a condition of absolute danger by Dr Parravicini's experimental surgery; and I have no doubt those other two young women who broke down in your service were treated by him in the same manner. I could take upon myself to demonstrate – by most convincing evidence, to a jury of medical men – that Dr Parravicini has been bleeding Miss Rolleston after putting her under chloroform, at intervals, ever since she has been in your service. The deterioration in the girl's health speaks for itself; the lancet marks upon the girl's arms are unmistakable; and her description of a series of sensations, which she calls a dream, points unmistakably to the administration of chloroform while she was sleeping. A practice so nefarious, so murderous, must, if exposed, result in a sentence only less severe than the punishment of murder.'

'I laugh,' said Parravicini, with an airy motion of his skinny fingers; 'I laugh at once at your theories and at your threats. I, Parravicini Leopold, have no fear that the law can question anything I have done.'

'Take the girl away, and let me hear no more of her,' cried Lady Ducayne, in the thin, old voice, which so poorly matched the energy and fire of the wicked old brain that guided its utterances. 'Let her go back to her mother – I want no more girls to die in my service. There are girls enough and to spare in the world, God knows.'

'If you ever engage another companion – or take another English girl into your service, Lady Ducayne, I will make all England ring with the story of your wickedness.'

'I want no more girls. I don't believe in his experiments. They have been full of danger for me as well as for the girl – an air bubble, and I should be gone. I'll have no more of his dangerous quackery. I'll find some new man – a better man than you, sir, a discoverer like Pasteur, or Virchow, a genius – to keep me alive. Take your girl away, young man. Marry her if you like. I'll write a cheque for a thousand pounds, and let her go and live on beef and beer, and get strong and plump again. I'll have no more such experiments. Do you hear, Parravicini?' she screamed, vindictively, the yellow, wrinkled face distorted with fury, the eyes glaring at him.

The Staffords carried Bella Rolleston off to Varese next day, she very loath to leave Lady Ducayne, whose liberal salary afforded such help for the dear mother. Herbert Stafford insisted, however, treating Bella as coolly as if he had been the family physician, and she had been given over wholly to his care.

'Do you suppose your mother would let you stop here to die?' he asked. 'If Mrs Rolleston knew how ill you are, she would come post haste to fetch you.'

'I shall never be well again till I get back to Walworth,' answered Bella, who was low-spirited and inclined to tears this morning, a reaction after her good spirits of yesterday.

'We'll try a week or two at Varese first,' said Stafford. 'When you can walk halfway up Monte Generoso without palpitation of the heart, you shall go back to Walworth.'

'Poor mother, how glad she will be to see me, and how sorry that I've lost such a good place.'

This conversation took place on the boat when they were leaving Bellaggio. Lotta had gone to her friend's room at seven o'clock that morning, long before Lady Ducayne's withered eyelids had opened to the daylight, before even Francine, the French maid, was astir, and had helped to pack a Gladstone bag with essentials, and hustled Bella downstairs and out of doors before she could make any strenuous resistance.

'It's all right,' Lotta assured her. 'Herbert had a good talk with Lady Ducayne last night, and it was settled for you to leave this morning. She doesn't like invalids, you see.'

'No,' sighed Bella, 'she doesn't like invalids. It was very unlucky that I should break down, just like Miss Tomson and Miss Blandy.'

'At any rate, you are not dead, like them,' answered Lotta, 'and my brother says you are not going to die.'

It seemed rather a dreadful thing to be dismissed in that offhand way, without a word of farewell from her employer.

'I wonder what Miss Torpinter will say when I go to her for another situation,' Bella speculated, ruefully, while she and her friends were breakfasting on board the steamer.

'Perhaps you may never want another situation,' said Stafford.

'You mean that I may never be well enough to be useful to anybody?'

'No, I don't mean anything of the kind.'

It was after dinner at Varese, when Bella had been induced to take a whole glass of Chianti, and quite sparkled after that unaccustomed stimulant, that Mr Stafford produced a letter from his pocket.

'I forgot to give you Lady Ducayne's letter of adieu!' he said.

'What, did she write to me? I am so glad – I hated to leave her in such a cool way; for after all she was very kind to me, and if I didn't like her it was only because she was too dreadfully old.'

She tore open the envelope. The letter was short and to the point –

Goodbye, child. Go and marry your doctor. I enclose a farewell gift for your trousseau.

ADELINE DUCAYNE

'A hundred pounds, a whole year's salary – no – why, it's for a – a cheque for a thousand!' cried Bella. 'What a generous old soul! She really is the dearest old thing.'

'She just missed being very dear to you, Bella,' said Stafford.

He had dropped into the use of her Christian name while they were on board the boat. It seemed natural now that she was to be in his charge till they all three went back to England.

'I shall take upon myself the privileges of an elder brother till we land at Dover,' he said; 'after that – well, it must be as you please.'

The question of their future relations must have been satisfactorily settled before they crossed the Channel, for Bella's next letter to her mother communicated three startling facts.

First, that the enclosed check for £1,000 was to be invested in debenture stock in Mrs Rolleston's name, and was to be her very own, income and principal, for the rest of her life.

Next, that Bella was going home to Walworth immediately.

And last, that she was going to be married to Mr Herbert Stafford in the following autumn.

'And I am sure you will adore him, mother, as much as I do,' wrote Bella.

'It is all good Lady Ducayne's doing. I never could have married if I had not secured that little nest-egg for you. Herbert says we shall be able to add to it as the years go by, and that wherever we live there shall be always a room in our house for you. The word "mother-in-law" has no terrors for him.'

An Episode of Cathedral History

M. R. JAMES

There was once a learned gentleman who was deputed to examine and report upon the archives of the Cathedral of Southminster. The examination of these records demanded a very considerable expenditure of time: hence it became advisable for him to engage lodgings in the city: for though the Cathedral body were profuse in their offers of hospitality, Mr Lake felt that he would prefer to be master of his day. This was recognised as reasonable. The Dean eventually wrote advising Mr Lake, if he were not already suited, to communicate with Mr Worby, the principal Verger, who occupied a house convenient to the church and was prepared to take in a quiet lodger for three or four weeks. Such an arrangement was precisely what Mr Lake desired. Terms were easily agreed upon, and early in December, like another Mr Datchery (as he remarked to himself), the investigator found himself in the occupation of a very comfortable room in an ancient and 'cathedraly' house.

One so familiar with the customs of Cathedral churches, and treated with such obvious consideration by the Dean and Chapter of this Cathedral in particular, could not fail to command the respect of the Head Verger. Mr Worby even acquiesced in certain modifications of statements he had been accustomed to offer for years to parties of visitors. Mr Lake, on his part, found the Verger a very cheery companion, and took advantage of any occasion that presented itself for enjoying his conversation when the day's work was over.

One evening, about nine o'clock, Mr Worby knocked at his lodger's door. 'I've occasion,' he said, 'to go across to the Cathedral, Mr Lake, and I think I made you a promise when I did so next I would give you the opportunity to see what it looks like at night time. It is quite fine and dry outside, if you care to come.'

'To be sure I will; very much obliged to you, Mr Worby, for thinking of it, but let me get my coat.'

'Here it is, sir, and I've another lantern here that you'll find advisable for the steps, as there's no moon.'

'Anyone might think we were Jasper and Durdles, over again, mightn't they,' said Lake, as they crossed the close, for he had ascertained that the Verger had read *Edwin Drood*.

'Well, so they might,' said Mr Worby, with a short laugh, 'though I don't know whether we ought to take it as a compliment. Odd ways, I often think, they had at that Cathedral, don't it seem so to you, sir? Full choral matins at seven o'clock in the morning all the year round. Wouldn't suit our boys' voices nowadays, and I think there's one or two of the men would be applying for a rise if the Chapter was to bring it in – particular the alltoes.'

They were now at the south-west door. As Mr Worby was un-locking it, Lake said, 'Did you ever find anybody locked in here by accident?'

'Twice I did. One was a drunk sailor; however he got in I don't know. I s'pose he went to sleep in the service, but by the time I got to him he was praying fit to bring the roof in. Lor'! what a noise that man did make! Said it was the first time he'd been inside a church for ten years, and blest if ever he'd try it again. The other was an old sheep: them boys it was, up to their games. That was the last time they tried it on, though. There, sir, now you see what we look like; our late Dean used now and again to bring parties in, but he preferred a moonlight night, and there was a piece of verse he'd coat to 'em, relating to a Scotch cathedral, I understand; but I don't know, I almost think the effect's better when it's all dark-like. Seems to add to the size and heighth. Now if you won't mind stopping somewhere in the nave while I go up into the choir where my business lays, you'll see what I mean.'

Accordingly Lake waited, leaning against a pillar, and watched the light wavering along the length of the church, and up the steps into the choir, until it was intercepted by some screen or other furniture, which only allowed the reflection to be seen on the piers and roof. Not many minutes had passed before Worby reappeared at the door of the choir and by waving his lantern signalled to Lake to rejoin him.

'I suppose it *is* Worby, and not a substitute,' thought Lake to himself, as he walked up the nave. There was, in fact, nothing untoward. Worby showed him the papers which he had come to fetch out of the Dean's stall, and asked him what he thought of the spectacle: Lake agreed that it was well worth seeing. 'I suppose,' he said, as they walked towards the altar-steps together, 'that you're too much used to going about here at night to feel nervous – but you must get a start every now and then, don't you, when a book falls down or a door swings to.'

'No, Mr Lake, I can't say I think much about noises, not nowadays: I'm much more afraid of finding an escape of gas or a burst in the stove pipes than anything else. Still there have been times, years ago. Did you notice that plain altar-tomb there – fifteenth century we say it is, I don't know if you agree to that? Well, if you didn't look at it, just come back and give it a glance, if you'd be so good.' It was on the north side of the choir, and rather awkwardly placed: only about three feet from the enclosing stone screen. Quite plain, as the Verger had said, but for some ordinary stone panelling. A metal cross of some size on the northern side (that next to the screen) was the solitary feature of any interest.

Lake agreed that it was not earlier than the Perpendicular period: 'but,' he said, 'unless it's the tomb of some remarkable person, you'll forgive me for saying that I don't think it's particularly noteworthy.'

'Well, I can't say as it is the tomb of anybody noted in 'istory,' said Worby, who had a dry smile on his face, 'for we don't own any record whatsoever of who it was put up to. For all that, if you've half an hour to spare, sir, when we get back to the house, Mr Lake, I could tell you a tale about that tomb. I won't begin on it now; it strikes cold here, and we don't want to be dawdling about all night.'

'Of course I should like to hear it immensely.'

'Very well, sir, you shall. Now if I might put a question to you,' he went on, as they passed down the choir aisle, 'in our little local guide – and not only there, but in the little book on our Cathedral in the series – you'll find it stated that this portion of the building was erected previous to the twelfth century. Now of course I should be glad enough to take that view, but – mind the step, sir – but, I put it to you – does the lay of the stone 'ere in this portion of the wall (which he tapped with his key) does it to your eye carry the flavour of what you might call Saxon masonry? No? I thought not; no more it does to me: now, if you'll believe me, I've said as much to those men – one's the librarian of our Free Libry here, and the other came down from London on purpose – fifty times, if I have once, but I might just as well have talked to that bit of stonework. But there it is, I suppose everyone's got their opinions.'

The discussion of this peculiar trait of human nature occupied Mr Worby almost up to the moment when he and Lake re-entered the former's house. The condition of the fire in Lake's sitting-room led to a suggestion from Mr Worby that they should finish the evening in his own parlour. We find them accordingly settled there some short time afterwards.

Mr Worby made his story a long one, and I will not undertake to tell it wholly in his own words, or in his own order. Lake committed the substance of it to paper immediately after hearing it, together with some few passages of the narrative which had fixed themselves *verbatim* in his mind; I shall probably find it expedient to condense Lake's record to some extent.

Mr Worby was born, it appeared, about the year 1828. His father before him had been connected with the Cathedral, and likewise his grandfather. One or both had been choristers, and in later life both had done work as mason and carpenter respectively about the fabric. Worby himself, though possessed, as he frankly acknowledged, of an indifferent voice, had been drafted into the choir at about ten years of age.

It was in 1840 that the wave of the Gothic revival smote the Cathedral of Southminster. 'There was a lot of lovely stuff went then, sir,' said Worby, with a sigh. 'My father couldn't hardly believe it when he got his orders to clear out the choir. There was a new dean just come in – Dean Burscough it was – and my father had been 'prenticed to a good firm of joiners in the city, and knew what good work was when he saw it. Crool it was, he used to say: all that beautiful wainscot oak, as good as the day it was put up, and garlands-like of foliage and fruit, and lovely old gilding work on the coats of arms and the organ pipes. All went to the timber yard – every bit except some little pieces worked up in the Lady Chapel, and 'ere in this overmantel. Well – I may be mistook, but I say our choir never looked as well since. Still there was a lot found out about the history of the church, and no doubt but what it did stand in need of repair. There were very few winters passed but what we'd lose a pinnicle.' Mr Lake expressed his concurrence with Worby's views of restoration, but owns to a fear about this point lest the story proper should never be reached. Possibly this was perceptible in his manner.

Worby hastened to reassure him, 'Not but what I could carry on about that topic for hours at a time, and do do when I see my opportunity. But Dean Burscough he was very set on the Gothic period, and nothing would serve him but everything must be made agreeable to that. And one morning after service he appointed for my father to meet him in the choir, and he came back after he'd taken off his robes in the vestry, and he'd got a roll of paper with him, and the verger that was then brought in a table, and they begun spreading it out on the table with prayer books to keep it down, and my father helped 'em, and he saw it was a picture of the inside of a choir in a Cathedral; and the Dean – he was a quick-spoken gentleman – he says, "Well, Worby, what do you think of that?" "Why," says my father, "I don't think I 'ave the pleasure of knowing that view. Would that be Hereford Cathedral, Mr Dean?" "No, Worby," says the Dean, "that's Southminster Cathedral as we hope to see it before many years." "In-deed, sir,' says my father, and that was all he did say – leastways to the Dean – but he used to tell me he felt really faint in himself when he looked round our choir as I can remember it, all comfortable and furnished-like, and then see this nasty little dry picter, as he called it, drawn out by some London architect. Well, there I am again. But you'll see what I mean if you look at this old view.'

Worby reached down a framed print from the wall. 'Well, the long and the short of it was that the Dean he handed over to my father a copy of an order of the Chapter that he was to clear out every bit of the choir – make a clean sweep – ready for the new work that was being designed up in town, and he was to put it in hand as soon as ever he could get the breakers together. Now then, sir, if you look at that view, you'll see where the pulpit used to stand: that's what I want you to notice, if you please.' It was, indeed, easily seen; an unusually large structure of timber with a domed sounding-board, standing at the east end of the stalls on the north side of the choir, facing the bishop's throne. Worby proceeded to explain that during the alterations, services were held in the nave, the members of the choir being thereby disappointed of an anticipated holiday, and the organist in particular incurring the suspicion of having wilfully damaged the mechanism of the temporary organ that was hired at considerable expense from London.

The work of demolition began with the choir screen and organ loft, and proceeded gradually eastwards, disclosing, as Worby said, many interesting features of older work. While this was going on, the members of the Chapter were, naturally, in and about the choir a great deal, and it soon became apparent to the elder Worby – who could not help overhearing some of their talk – that, on the part of the senior Canons especially, there must have been a good deal of disagreement before the policy now being carried out had been adopted. Some were of opinion that they should catch their deaths of cold in the return-stalls, unprotected by a screen from the draughts in the nave: others objected to being exposed to the view of persons in the choir aisles, especially, they said, during the sermons, when they found it helpful to listen in a posture which was liable to misconstruction. The strongest opposition, however, came from the oldest of the body, who up to the last moment objected to the removal of the pulpit. 'You ought not to touch it, Mr Dean,' he said with great emphasis one morning, when the two were standing before it: 'you don't know what mischief you may do.' 'Mischief? It's not a work of any particular merit, Canon.' 'Don't call me Canon,' said the old man with great asperity, 'that is, for thirty years I've been known as Dr Ayloff, and I shall be obliged, Mr Dean, if you would kindly humour me in that matter. And as to the pulpit (which I've preached from for thirty years, though I don't insist on that) all I'll say is, I *know* you're doing wrong in moving it.' 'But what sense could there be, my dear Doctor, in leaving it where it is, when we're fitting up the rest of the choir in a totally different *style*? What reason could be given – apart from the look of the thing?' 'Reason! reason!' said old Dr Ayloff; 'if you young men – if I may say so without any disrespect, Mr Dean – if you'd only listen to reason a little, and not be always asking for it, we should get on better. But there, I've said my say.' The old gentleman hobbled off, and as it proved, never entered the Cathedral again. The season – it was a hot summer – turned sickly on a sudden. Dr Ayloff was one of the first to go, with some affection of the muscles of the thorax, which took him painfully at night. And at many services the number of choirmen and boys was very thin.

Meanwhile the pulpit had been done away with. In fact, the sounding-board (part of which still exists as a table in a summer-house in the palace garden) was taken down within an hour or two of Dr Ayloff's protest. The removal of the base – not effected without considerable trouble – disclosed to view, greatly to the exultation of the restoring party, an altar-tomb – the tomb, of course, to which Worby had attracted Lake's attention that same evening. Much fruitless research was expended in attempts to identify the occupant; from that day to this he has never had a name put to him. The structure had been most carefully boxed in under the pulpit-base, so that such slight ornament as it possessed was not defaced; only on the north side of it there was what looked like an injury; a gap between two of the slabs composing the side. It might be two or three inches across. Palmer, the mason, was directed to fill it up in a week's time, when he came to do some other small jobs near that part of the choir.

The season was undoubtedly a very trying one. Whether the church was built on a site that had once been a marsh, as was suggested, or for whatever reason, the residents in its immediate neighbourhood had, many of them, but little enjoyment of the exquisite sunny days and the calm nights of August and September. To several of the older people – Dr Ayloff, among others, as we have seen – the summer proved downright fatal, but even among the younger, few escaped either a sojourn in bed for a matter of weeks, or at the least, a brooding sense of oppression, accompanied by hateful nightmares. Gradually there formulated itself a suspicion – which grew into a conviction – that the alterations in the Cathedral had something to say in the matter. The widow of a former old verger, a pensioner of the Chapter of Southminster, was visited by dreams, which she retailed to her friends, of a shape that slipped out of the little door of the south transept as the dark fell in, and flitted – taking a fresh direction every night – about the close, disappearing for a while in house after house, and finally emerging again when the night sky was paling. She could see nothing of it, she said, but that it was a moving form: only she had an impression that when it returned to the church, as it seemed to do in the end of the dream, it turned its head: and then, she could not tell why, but she thought it had red eyes. Worby remembered hearing the old lady tell this dream at a tea-party in the house of the chapter clerk. Its recurrence might, perhaps, he said, be taken as a symptom of approaching illness; at any rate before the end of September the old lady was in her grave.

The interest excited by the restoration of this great church was not confined to its own county. One day that summer an F.S.A., of some celebrity, visited the place. His business was to write an account of the discoveries that had been made, for the Society of Antiquaries, and his wife, who accompanied him, was to make a series of illustrative drawings for his report. In the morning she employed herself in making a general sketch of the choir; in the afternoon she devoted herself to details. She first drew the newly exposed altar-tomb, and when that was finished, she called her husband's attention to a beautiful piece of diaper-ornament on the screen just behind it, which had, like the tomb itself, been completely concealed by the pulpit. Of course, he said, an illustration of that must be made; so she seated herself on the tomb and began a careful drawing which occupied her till dusk.

Her husband had by this time finished his work of measuring and description, and they agreed that it was time to be getting back to their hotel. 'You may as well brush my skirt, Frank,' said the lady, 'it must have got covered with dust, I'm sure.' He obeyed dutifully; but, after a moment, he said, 'I don't know whether you value this dress particularly, my dear, but I'm inclined to think it's seen its best days. There's a great bit of it gone.' 'Gone? Where?' said she. 'I don't know where it's gone, but it's off at the bottom edge behind here.' She pulled it hastily into sight, and was horrified to find a jagged tear extending some way into the substance of the stuff; very much, she said, as if a dog had rent it away. The dress was, in any case, hopelessly spoilt, to her great vexation, and though they looked everywhere, the missing piece could not be found. There were many ways, they concluded, in which the injury might have come about, for the choir was full of old bits of woodwork with nails sticking out of them. Finally, they could only suppose that one of these had caused the mischief, and that the workmen, who had been about all day, had carried off the particular piece with the fragment of dress still attached to it.

It was about this time, Worby thought, that his little dog began to wear an anxious expression when the hour for it to be put into the shed in the back yard approached. (For his mother had ordained that it must not sleep in the house.) One evening, he said, when he was just going to pick it up and carry it out, it looked at him 'like a Christian, and waved its.'an' I was going to say – well, you know 'ow they do carry on sometimes, and the end of it was I put it under my coat, and 'uddled it upstairs – and I'm afraid I as good as deceived my poor mother on the subject. After that the dog acted very artful with 'iding itself under the bed for half-an-hour or more before bed-time came, and we worked it so as my mother never found out what we'd done.' Of course Worby was glad of its company anyhow, but more particularly when the nuisance that is still remembered in South-minster as 'the crying' set in.

'Night after night,' said Worby, 'that dog seemed to know it was coming; he'd creep out, he would, and snuggle into the bed and cuddle right up to me shivering, and when the crying come he'd be like a wild thing, shoving his head under my arm, and I was fully near as bad. Six or seven times we'd hear it, not more, and when he'd dror out his 'ed again I'd know it was over for that night. What was it like, sir? Well, I never heard but one thing that seemed to hit it off. I happened to be playing about in the Close, and there was two of the Canons met and said "Good morning" one to another. "Sleep well last night?" says one – it was Mr Henslow that one, and Mr Lyall was the other – "Can't say I did," says Mr Lyall, "rather too much of Isaiah 34. 14 for me." "34. 14," says Mr Henslow, "what's that?" "You call yourself a Bible reader!" says Mr Lyall. (Mr Henslow, you must know, he was one of what used to be termed Simeon's lot – pretty much what we should call the Evangelical party.) "You go and look it up." I wanted to know what he was getting at myself, and so off I ran home and got out my own Bible, and there it was: "the satyr shall cry to his fellow." Well, I thought, is that what we've been listening to these past nights? And I tell you it made me look over my shoulder a time or two. Of course I'd asked my father and mother about what it could be before that, but they both said it was most likely cats: but they spoke very short, and I could see they was troubled. My word! that was a noise – 'ungry-like, as if it was calling after someone that wouldn't come. If ever you felt you wanted company, it would be when you was waiting for it to begin again. I believe two or three nights there was men put on to watch in different parts of the Close; but they all used to get together in one corner, the nearest they could to the High Street, and nothing came of it.

'Well, the next thing was this. Me and another of the boys – he's in business in the city now as a grocer, like his father before him – we'd gone up in the Close after morning service was over, and we heard old Palmer the mason bellowing to some of his men. So we went up nearer, because we knew he was a rusty old chap and there might be some fun going. It appears Palmer'd told this man to stop up the chink in that old tomb. Well, there was this man keeping on saying he'd done it the best he could, and there was Palmer carrying on like all possessed about it. "Call that making a job of it?" he says. "If you had your rights you'd get the sack for this. What do you suppose I pay you your wages for? What do you suppose I'm going to say to the Dean and Chapter when they come round, as come they may do any time, and see where you've been bungling about covering the 'ole place with mess and plaster and Lord knows what?" "Well, master, I done the best I could," says the man; "I don't know no more than what you do 'ow it come to fall out this way. I tamped it right in the 'ole," he says, "and now it's fell out," he says, "I never see."

' "Fell out?" says old Palmer, "why it's nowhere near the place. Blowed out, you mean," and he picked up a bit of plaster, and so did I, that was laying up against the screen, three or four feet off, and not dry yet; and old Palmer he looked at it curious-like, and then he turned round on me and he says, "Now then, you boys, have you been up to some of your games here?" "No," I says, "I haven't, Mr

Palmer; there's none of us been about here till just this minute," and while I was talking the other boy, Evans, he got looking in through the chink, and I heard him draw in his breath, and he came away sharp and up to us, and says he, "I believe there's something in there. I saw something shiny." "What! I dare say," says old Palmer; "Well, I ain't got time to stop about there. You, William, you go off and get some more stuff and make a job of it this time; if not, there'll be trouble in my yard," he says.

'So the man he went off, and Palmer too, and us boys stopped behind, and I says to Evans, "Did you really see anything in there?" "Yes," he says, "I did indeed." So then I says, "Let's shove something in and stir it up." And we tried several of the bits of wood that was laying about, but they were all too big. Then Evans he had a sheet of music he'd brought with him, an anthem or a service, I forget which it was now, and he rolled it up small and shoved it in the chink; two or three times he did it, and nothing happened. "Give it me, boy," I said, and I had a try. No, nothing happened. Then, I don't know why I thought of it, I'm sure, but I stooped down just opposite the chink and put my two fingers in my mouth and whistled – you know the way – and at that I seemed to think I heard something stirring, and I says to Evans, "Come away," I says; "I don't like this." "Oh, rot," he says, "Give me that roll," and he took it and shoved it in. And I don't think ever I see anyone go so pale as he did. "I say, Worby," he says, 'it's caught, or else someone's got hold of it." "Pull it out or leave it," I says, "Come and let's get off." So he gave a good pull, and it came away. Leastways most of it did, but the end was gone. Torn off it was, and Evans looked at it for a second and then he gave a sort of a croak and let it drop, and we both made off out of there as quick as ever we could. When we got outside Evans says to me, "Did you see the end of that paper." "No," I says, "only it was torn." "Yes, it was," he says, "but it was wet too, and black!" Well, partly because of the fright we had, and partly because that music was wanted in a day or two, and we knew there'd be a set-out about it with the organist, we didn't say nothing to anyone else, and I suppose the workmen they swept up the bit that was left along with the rest of the rubbish. But Evans, if you were to ask him this very day about it, he'd stick to it he saw that paper wet and black at the end where it was torn.'

After that the boys gave the choir a wide berth, so that Worby was not sure what was the result of the mason's renewed mending of the tomb. Only he made out from fragments of conversation dropped by the workmen passing through the choir that some difficulty had been met with, and that the governor – Mr Palmer to wit – had tried his own hand at the job. A little later, he happened to see Mr Palmer himself knocking at the door of the Deanery and being admitted by the butler. A day or so after that, he gathered from a remark his father let fall at breakfast that something a little out of the common was to be done in the Cathedral after morning service on the morrow. "And I'd just as soon it was today," his father added, "I don't see the use of running risks." "Father," I says, "what are you going to do in the Cathedral tomorrow?" and he turned on me as savage as I ever see him – he was a wonderful good-tempered man as a general thing, my poor father was. "My lad," he says, "I'll trouble you not to go picking up your elders' and betters' talk: it's not manners and it's not straight. What I'm going to do or not going to do in the Cathedral tomorrow is none of your business: and if I catch sight of you hanging about the place tomorrow after your work's done, I'll send you home with a flea in your ear. Now you mind that." Of course I said I was very sorry and that, and equally of course I went off and laid my plans with Evans. We knew there was a stair up in the corner of the transept which you can get up to the triforium, and in them days the door to it was pretty well always open, and even if it wasn't we knew the key usually laid under a bit of matting hard by. So we made up our minds we'd be putting away music and that, next morning while the rest of the boys was clearing off, and then slip up the stairs and watch from the triforium if there was any signs of work going on.

'Well, that same night I dropped off asleep as sound as a boy does, and all of a sudden the dog woke me up, coming into the bed, and thought I, now we're going to get it sharp, for he seemed more frightened than usual. After about five minutes sure enough came this cry. I can't give you no idea what it was like; and so near too – nearer than I'd heard it yet – and a funny thing, Mr Lake, you know what a place this Close is for an echo, and particular if you stand this side of it. Well, this crying never made no sign of an echo at all. But, as I said, it was dreadful near this night; and on the top of the start I got with hearing it, I got another fright; for I heard something rustling outside in the passage. Now to be sure I thought I was done; but I noticed the dog seemed to perk up a bit, and next there was someone whispered outside the door, and I very near laughed out loud, for I knew it was my father and mother that had got out of bed with the noise. "Whatever is it?" says my mother. "Hush! I don't know," says my father, excited-like, "'don't disturb the boy. I hope he didn't hear nothing."

'So, me knowing they were just outside, it made me bolder, and I slipped out of bed across to my little window – giving on the Close – but the dog he bored right down to the bottom of the bed – and I looked out. First go off I couldn't see anything. Then right down in the shadow under a buttress I made out what I shall always say was two spots of red – a dull red it was – nothing like a lamp or a fire, but just so as you could pick 'em out of the black shadow. I hadn't but just sighted 'em when it seemed we wasn't the only people that had been disturbed, because I see a window in a house on the left-hand side become lighted up, and the light moving. I just turned my head to make sure of it, and then looked back into the shadow for those two red things, and they were gone, and for all I peered about and stared, there was not a sign more of them. Then come my last fright that night – something come against my bare leg – but that was all right: that was my little dog had come out of bed, and prancing about, making a great to-do, only holding his tongue, and me seeing he was quite in spirits again, I took him back to bed and we slept the night out!

'Next morning I made out to tell my mother I'd had the dog in my room, and I was surprised, after all she'd said about it before, how quiet she took it. "Did you?" she says. "Well, by good rights you ought to go without your breakfast for doing such a thing behind my back: but I don't know as there's any great harm done, only another time you ask my permission, do you hear?" A bit after that I said something to my father about having heard the cats again. "*Cats*," he says, and he looked over at my poor mother, and she coughed and he says, "Oh! ah! yes, cats. I believe I heard 'em myself."

'That was a funny morning altogether: nothing seemed to go right. The organist he stopped in bed, and the minor Canon he forgot it was the 19th day and waited for the *Venite*; and after a bit the deputy he set off playing the chant for evensong, which was a minor; and then the Decani boys were laughing so much they couldn't sing, and when it came to the anthem the solo boy he got took with the giggles, and made out his nose was bleeding, and shoved the book at me what hadn't practised the verse and wasn't much of a singer if I *had* known it. Well, things was rougher, you see, fifty years ago, and I got a nip from the counter-tenor behind me that I remembered.

'So we got through somehow, and neither the men nor the boys weren't by way of waiting to see whether the Canon in residence – Mr Henslow it was – would come to the vestries and fine 'em, but I

lon't believe he did: for one thing I fancy he'd read the wrong lesson
or the first time in his life, and knew it. Anyhow Evans and me didn't
ind no difficulty in slipping up the stairs as I told you, and when we
got up we laid ourselves down flat on our stomachs where we could
ust stretch our heads out over the old tomb, and we hadn't but just
done so when we heard the verger that was then, first shutting the
iron porch-gates and locking the south-west door, and then the
transept door, so we knew there was something up, and they meant
to keep the public out for a bit.

'Next thing was, the Dean and the Canon come in by their door on
the north, and then I see my father, and old Palmer, and a couple of
their best men, and Palmer stood a-talking for a bit with the Dean in
the middle of the choir. He had a coil of rope and the men had crows.
All of 'em looked a bit nervous. So there they stood talking, and at
last I heard the Dean say, "Well, I've no time to waste, Palmer. If you
think this'll satisfy Southminster people, I'll permit it to be done; but
I must say this, that never in the whole course of my life have I heard
such arrant nonsense from a practical man as I have from you. Don't
you agree with me, Henslow?" As far as I could hear Mr Henslow
said something like "Oh! well we're told, aren't we, Mr Dean, not to
judge others?" and the Dean he gave a kind of sniff, and walked
straight up to the tomb, and took his stand behind it with his back
to the screen, and the others they come edging up rather gingerly.
Henslow, he stopped on the south side and scratched on his chin, he
did. Then the Dean spoke up: "Palmer," he says, "which can you do
easiest, get the slab off the top, or shift one of the side slabs?"

'Old Palmer and his men they pottered about a bit looking round
the edge of the top slab and sounding the sides on the south and east
and west and everywhere but the north. Henslow said something
about it being better to have a try at the south side, because there was
more light and more room to move about in. Then my father, who'd
been watching of them, went round to the north side, and knelt
down and felt of the slab by the chink, and he got up and dusted his
knees and says to the Dean: "Beg pardon, Mr Dean, but I think if Mr
Palmer'll try this here slab he'll find it'll come out easy enough.
Seems to me one of the men could prise it out with his crow by
means of this chink." "Ah! thank you, Worby," says the Dean; "that's
a good suggestion. Palmer, let one of your men do that, will you?"

'So the man come round, and put his bar in and bore on it, and just
that minute when they were all bending over, and we boys got our
heads well out over the edge of the triforium, there come a most

fearful crash down at the west end of the choir, as if a whole stack of big timber had fallen down a flight of stairs. Well, you can't expect me to tell you everything that happened all in a minute. Of course there was a terrible commotion. I heard the slab fall out, and the crowbar on the floor, and I heard the Dean say 'Good God!'

'When I looked down again I saw the Dean tumbled over on the floor, the men was making off down the choir, Henslow was just going to help the Dean up, Palmer was going to stop the men, as he said afterwards, and my father was sitting on the altar step with his face in his hands. The Dean he was very cross. "I wish to goodness you'd look where you're coming to, Henslow," he says. "Why you should all take to your heels when a stick of wood tumbles down I cannot imagine," and all Henslow could do, explaining he was right away on the other side of the tomb, would not satisfy him.

'Then Palmer came back and reported there was nothing to account for this noise and nothing seemingly fallen down, and when the Dean finished feeling of himself they gathered round – except my father, he sat where he was – and someone lighted up a bit of candle and they looked into the tomb. "Nothing there," says the Dean, "what did I tell you? Stay! here's something. What's this: a bit of music paper, and a piece of torn stuff – part of a dress it looks like. Both quite modern – no interest whatever. Another time perhaps you'll take the advice of an educated man" – or something like that, and off he went, limping a bit, and out through the north door, only as he went he called back angry to Palmer for leaving the door standing open. Palmer called out "Very sorry, sir," but he shrugged his shoulders, and Henslow says, "I fancy Mr Dean's mistaken. I closed the door behind me, but he's a little upset." Then Palmer says, "Why, where's Worby?" and they saw him sitting on the step and went up to him. He was recovering himself, it seemed, and wiping his forehead, and Palmer helped him up on to his legs, as I was glad to see.

'They were too far off for me to hear what they said, but my father pointed to the north door in the aisle, and Palmer and Henslow both of them looked very surprised and scared. After a bit, my father and Henslow went out of the church, and the others made what haste they could to put the slab back and plaster it in. And about as the clock struck twelve the Cathedral was opened again and us boys made the best of our way home.

'I was in a great taking to know what it was had given my poor father such a turn, and when I got in and found him sitting in his

hair taking a glass of spirits, and my mother standing looking
anxious at him, I couldn't keep from bursting out and making
confession where I'd been. But he didn't seem to take on, not in the
way of losing his temper. "You was there, was you? Well did you
see it?" "I see everything, father," I said, "except when the noise
came." "Did you see what it was knocked the Dean over?" he says,
"that what come out of the monument? You didn't? Well, that's a
mercy." "Why, what was it, father?" I said. "Come, you must have
seen it," he says. "*Didn't* you see? A thing like a man, all over hair,
and two great eyes to it?"

'Well, that was all I could get out of him that time, and later on he
seemed as if he was ashamed of being so frightened, and he used to
put me off when I asked him about it. But years after, when I was got
to be a grown man, we had more talk now and again on the matter,
and he always said the same thing. "Black it was," he'd say, "and a
mass of hair, and two legs, and the light caught on its eyes."

'Well, that's the tale of that tomb, Mr Lake; it's one we don't tell
to our visitors, and I should be obliged to you not to make any use of
it till I'm out of the way. I doubt Mr Evans'll feel the same as I do, if
you ask him.'

This proved to be the case. But over twenty years have passed by,
and the grass is growing over both Worby and Evans; so Mr Lake felt
no difficulty about communicating his notes – taken in 1890 – to me.
He accompanied them with a sketch of the tomb and a copy of the
short inscription on the metal cross which was affixed at the expense
of Dr Lyall to the centre of the northern side. It was from the Vulgate
of Isaiah xxxiv., and consisted merely of the three words –

IBI CUBAVIT LAMIA

The Horla

GUY DE MAUPASSANT

May 8. What a lovely day! I have spent all the morning lying in the grass in front of my house, under the enormous plane tree that shades the whole of it. I like this part of the country and I like to live here because I am attached to it by old associations, by those deep and delicate roots which attach man to the soil on which his ancestors were born and died, which attach him to the ideas and usages of the place as well as to the food, to local expressions, to the peculiar twang of the peasants, to the smell of the soil, of the villages and of the atmosphere itself.

I love my house in which I grew up. From my windows I can see the Seine which flows alongside my garden, on the other side of the high road, almost through my grounds, the great and wide Seine, which goes to Rouen and Havre, and is covered with boats passing to and fro.

On the left, down yonder, lies Rouen, that large town, with its blue roofs under its pointed Gothic towers. These are innumerable, slender or broad, dominated by the spire of the cathedral, and full of bells which sound through the blue air on fine mornings, sending their sweet and distant iron clang even as far as my home: that song of the metal, which the breeze wafts in my direction, now stronger and now weaker, according as the wind is stronger or lighter.

What a delicious morning it was!

About eleven o'clock, a long line of boats drawn by a steam tug as big as a fly, and which scarcely puffed while emitting its thick smoke, passed my gate.

After two English schooners, whose red flag fluttered in space, there came a magnificent Brazilian three-master; it was perfectly white, and wonderfully clean and shining. I saluted it, I hardly knew why, except that the sight of the vessel gave me great pleasure.

May 12. I have had a slight feverish attack for the last few days, and I feel ill, or rather I feel low-spirited.

Whence come those mysterious influences which change our happiness into discouragement, and our self-confidence into diffidence? One might almost say that the air, the invisible air, is full of unknowable Powers whose mysterious presence we have to endure. I wake up in the best spirits, with an inclination to sing. Why? I go down to the edge of the water, and suddenly, after walking a short distance, I return home wretched, as if some misfortune were awaiting me there. Why? Is it a cold shiver which, passing over my skin, has upset my nerves and given me low spirits? Is it the form of the clouds, the colour of the sky, or the colour of the surrounding objects which is so changeable, that has troubled my thoughts as they passed before my eyes? Who can tell? Everything that we touch without knowing it, everything that we handle without feeling it, all that we meet without clearly distinguishing it, has a rapid, surprising and inexplicable effect upon us and upon our senses, and, through them, on our ideas and on our heart itself.

How profound that mystery of the Invisible is! We cannot fathom it with our miserable senses, with our eyes which are unable to perceive what is either too small or too great, too near to us or too far from us – neither the inhabitants of a star nor of a drop of water; nor with our ears that deceive us, for they transmit to us the vibrations of the air in sonorous notes. They are fairies who work the miracle of changing these vibrations into sounds, and by that metamorphosis give birth to music, which makes the silent motion of nature musical . . . with our sense of smell which is less keen than that of a dog . . . with our sense of taste which can scarcely distinguish the age of wine!

Oh! if we only had other organs which would work other miracles in our favour, what a number of fresh things we might discover around us!

May 16. I am ill, decidedly! I was so well last month! I am feverish, horribly feverish, or rather I am in a state of feverish enervation, which makes my mind suffer as much as my body. I have, continually, that horrible sensation of some impending danger, that apprehension of some coming misfortune, or of approaching death – that presentiment which is, no doubt, an attack of some illness which is still unknown, which germinates in the flesh and in the blood.

May 17. I have just come from consulting my physician, for I could no longer get any sleep. He said my pulse was rapid, my eyes dilated, my nerves highly strung, but there were no alarming symptoms. I must take a course of shower baths and of bromide of potassium.

May 25. No change! My condition is really very peculiar. As the evening comes on, an incomprehensible feeling of disquietude seizes me, just as if night concealed some threatening disaster. I dine hurriedly, and then try to read, but I do not understand the words, and can scarcely distinguish the letters. Then I walk up and down my drawing-room, oppressed by a feeling of confused and irresistible fear, the fear of sleep and fear of my bed.

About ten o'clock I go up to my room. As soon as I enter it I double-lock and bolt the door; I am afraid . . . of what? Up to the present time I have been afraid of nothing . . . I open my cupboards, and look under my bed; I listen . . . to what? How strange it is that a simple feeling of discomfort, impeded or heightened circulation, perhaps the irritation of a nerve filament, a slight congestion, a small disturbance in the imperfect delicate functioning of our living machinery, may turn the most light-hearted of men into a melancholy one, and make a coward of the bravest? Then, I go to bed, and wait for sleep as a man might wait for the executioner. I wait for its coming with dread, and my heart beats and my legs tremble, while my whole body shivers beneath the warmth of the bed-clothes, until all at once I fall asleep, as though one should plunge into a pool of stagnant water in order to drown. I do not feel it coming on as I did formerly, this perfidious sleep which is close to me and watching me, which is going to seize me by the head, to close my eyes and annihilate me.

I sleep – a long time – two or three hours perhaps – then a dream – no – a nightmare lays hold on me. I feel that I am in bed and asleep . . . I feel it and I know it . . . and I feel also that somebody is coming close to me, is looking at me, touching me, is getting on to my bed, is kneeling on my chest, is taking my neck between his hands and squeezing it . . . squeezing it with all his might in order to strangle me.

I struggle, bound by that terrible sense of powerlessness which paralyses us in our dreams; I try to cry out – but I cannot; I want to move – I cannot do so; I try, with the most violent efforts and breathing hard, to turn over and throw off this being who is crushing and suffocating me – I cannot!

And then, suddenly, I wake up, trembling and bathed in perspiration; I light a candle and find that I am alone, and after that crisis, which occurs every night, I at length fall asleep and slumber tranquilly till morning.

June 2. My condition has grown worse. What is the matter with me? The bromide does me no good, and the shower baths have no effect. Sometimes, in order to tire myself thoroughly, though I am fatigued enough already, I go for a walk in the forest of Roumare. I used to think first that the fresh light and soft air, impregnated with the odour of herbs and leaves, would instil new blood into my veins and impart fresh energy to my heart. I turned into a broad hunting road, and then turned toward La Bouille, through a narrow path, between two rows of exceedingly tall trees, which placed a thick green, almost black, roof between the sky and me.

A sudden shiver ran through me, not a cold shiver, but a strange shiver of agony, and I hastened my steps, uneasy at being alone in the forest, afraid, stupidly and without reason, of the profound solitude. Suddenly it seemed to me as if I were being followed, that somebody was walking at my heels, close, quite close to me, near enough to touch me.

I turned round suddenly, but I was alone. I saw nothing behind me except the straight, broad path, empty and bordered by high trees, horribly empty; before me it also extended until it was lost in the distance, and looked just the same, terrible.

I closed my eyes. Why? And then I began to turn round on one heel very quickly, just like a top. I nearly fell down, and opened my eyes; the trees were dancing round me and the earth heaved; I was obliged to sit down. Then ah! I no longer remembered how I had come! What a strange idea! What a strange, strange idea! I did not in the least know. I started off to the right, and got back into the avenue which had led me into the middle of the forest.

June 3. I have had a terrible night. I shall go away for a few weeks, for no doubt a journey will set me up again.

July 2. I have come back, quite cured, and have had a most delightful trip into the bargain. I have been to Mont Saint-Michel, which I had not seen before.

What a sight, when one arrives, as I did, at Avranches, toward the end of the day! The town stands on a hill, and I was taken into the public garden at the extremity of the town. I uttered a cry of astonishment. An extraordinarily large bay lay extended before me, as far as my eyes could reach, between two hills which were lost to sight in the mist; and in the middle of this immense yellow bay, under a clear, golden sky, a peculiar hill rose up, sombre and pointed in the midst of the sand. The sun had just disappeared, and under the still flaming sky appeared the outline of that fantastic rock which bears on its summit a fantastic monument.

At daybreak I went out to it. The tide was low, as it had been the night before, and I saw that wonderful abbey rise up before me as I approached it. After several hours' walking, I reached the enormous mass of rocks which supports the little town, dominated by the great church. Having climbed the steep and narrow street, I entered the most wonderful Gothic building that has ever been built to God on earth, as large as a town, full of low rooms which seem buried beneath vaulted roofs, and lofty galleries supported by delicate columns.

I entered this gigantic granite gem, which is as light as a bit of lace, covered with towers, with slender belfries with spiral stair-cases, which raise their strange heads that bristle with chimeras, with devils, with fantastic animals, with monstrous flowers, to the blue sky by day, and to the black sky by night, and are connected by finely carved arches.

When I had reached the summit I said to the monk who accom-panied me: 'Father, how happy you must be here!' And he replied: 'It is very windy here, monsieur', and so we began to talk while watch-ing the rising tide, which ran over the sand and covered it as with a steel cuirass.

And then the monk told me stories, all the old stories belonging to the place, legends, nothing but legends.

One of them struck me forcibly. The country people, those be-longing to the Mount, declare that at night one can hear voices talking on the sands, and then that one hears two goats bleating, one with a strong, the other with a weak voice. Incredulous people declare that it is nothing but the cry of the sea birds, which occas-ionally resembles bleatings, and occasionally, human lamentations; but belated fishermen swear that they have met an old shepherd wandering between tides on the sands around the little town. His head is completely concealed by his cloak and he is followed by a billy goat with a man's face, and a nanny goat with a woman's face, both having long, white hair and talking incessantly and quarrelling in an unknown tongue. Then suddenly they cease and begin to bleat with all their might.

'Do you believe it?' I asked the monk. 'I scarcely know,' he replied, and I continued: 'If there are other beings beside ourselves on this earth, how comes it that we have not known it long since, or why have *you* not seen them? How is that *I* have not seen them?' He replied: 'Do we see the hundred-thousandth part of what exists? Look here; there is the wind, which is the strongest force in nature, which knocks down men, and blows down buildings, destroys cliffs and casts great ships on the rocks; the wind which kills, which whistles, which sighs, which roars – have you ever seen it, and can you see it? It exists for all that, however.'

I was silent before this simple reasoning. That man was a philosopher, or perhaps a fool; I could not say which exactly, so I held my tongue. What he had said had often been in my own thoughts.

July 3. I have slept badly; certainly there is some feverish influence here, for my coachman is suffering in the same way as I am. When I went back home yesterday, I noticed his singular paleness, and I asked him: 'What is the matter with you, Jean?' 'The matter is that I never get any rest, and my nights devour my days. Since your departure, monsieur, there has been a spell over me.'

However, the other servants are all well, but I am very much afraid of having another attack myself.

July 4. I am decidedly ill again; for my old nightmares have returned. Last night I felt somebody leaning on me and sucking my life from between my lips. Yes, he was sucking it out of my throat, like a leech. Then he got up, satiated, and I woke up, so exhausted, crushed and weak that I could not move. If this continues for a few days, I shall certainly go away again.

July 5. Have I lost my reason? What happened last night is so strange that my head wanders when I think of it!

I had locked my door, as I do now every evening, and then, being thirsty, I drank half a glass of water, and accidentally noticed that the water bottle was full up to the cut-glass stopper.

Then I went to bed and fell into one of my terrible sleeps, from which I was aroused in about two hours by a still more frightful shock.

Picture to yourself a sleeping man who is being murdered and who wakes up with a knife in his lung, and whose breath rattles, who is covered with blood, and who can no longer breathe and is about to die, and does not understand – there you have it.

Having recovered my senses, I was thirsty again, so I lit a candle and went to the table on which stood my water bottle. I lifted it up and tilted it over my glass, but nothing came out. It was empty! It was completely empty! At first I could not understand it at all, and then suddenly I was seized by such a terrible feeling that I had to sit down, or rather I fell into a chair! Then I sprang up suddenly to look about me; then I sat down again, overcome by astonishment and fear, in front of the transparent glass bottle! I looked at it with fixed eyes, trying to conjecture, and my hands trembled! Somebody had drunk he water, but who? I? I without any doubt. It could surely only be I. In that case I was a somnambulist; I lived, without knowing it, that mysterious double life which makes us doubt whether there are not two beings in us, or whether a strange, unknowable and invisible being does not at such moments, when our soul is in a state of torpor, animate our captive body, which obeys this other being as it obeys us, and more than it obeys ourselves.

Oh! who will understand my horrible agony? Who will understand the emotion of a man who is sound in mind, wide awake, full of common sense, who looks in horror through the glass of a water bottle for a little water that disappeared while he was asleep? I remained thus until it was daylight, without venturing to go to bed again.

July 6. I am going mad. Again all the contents of my water bottle have been drunk during the night – or rather, I have drunk it!

But is it I? Is it I? Who could it be? Who? Oh! God! am I going mad? Who will save me?

July 10. I have just been through some surprising ordeals. Decidedly I am mad! And yet! . . .

On July 6, before going to bed, I put some wine, milk, water, bread and strawberries on my table. Somebody drank – I drank – all the water and a little of the milk, but neither the wine, bread nor the strawberries were touched.

On the seventh of July I renewed the same experiment, with the same results, and on July 8, I left out the water and the milk, and nothing was touched.

Lastly, on July 9, I put only water and milk on my table, taking care to wrap up the bottles in white muslin and to tie down the stoppers. Then I rubbed my lips, my beard and my hands with pencil lead, and went to bed.

Irresistible sleep seized me, which was soon followed by a terrible awakening. I had not moved, and there was no mark of lead on the sheets. I rushed to the table. The muslin round the bottles remained intact; I undid the string, trembling with fear. All the water had been drunk, and so had the milk! Ah! great God! . . .

I must start for Paris immediately.

July 12. Paris. I must have lost my head during the last few days! I must be the plaything of my enervated imagination, unless I am really a somnambulist, or that I have been under the power of one of those hitherto unexplained influences which are called suggestions. In any case, my mental state bordered on madness, and twenty-four hours of Paris sufficed to restore my equilibrium.

Yesterday, after doing some business and paying some visits which instilled fresh and invigorating air into my soul, I wound up the evening at the *Théâtre-Français*. A play by Alexandre Dumas the younger was being acted, and his active and powerful imagination completed my cure. Certainly solitude is dangerous for active minds. We require around us men who can think and talk. When we are alone for a long time, we people space with phantoms.

I returned along the boulevards to my hotel in excellent spirits. Amid the jostling of the crowd I thought, not without irony, of my terrors and surmises of the previous week, because I had believed – yes, I had believed – that an invisible being lived beneath my roof. How weak our brains are, and how quickly they are terrified and led into error by a small incomprehensible fact.

Instead of saying simply: 'I do not understand because I do not know the cause', we immediately imagine terrible mysteries and supernatural powers.

July 14. Fête of the Republic. I walked through the streets, amused as a child at the firecrackers and flags. Still it is very foolish to be merry on a fixed date, by Government decree. The populace is an imbecile flock of sheep, now stupidly patient, and now in ferocious revolt. Say to it: 'Amuse yourself', and it amuses itself. Say to it: 'Vote for the Emperor', and it votes for the Emperor, and then say to it: 'Vote for the Republic', and it votes for the Republic.

Those who direct it are also stupid; only, instead of obeying men, they obey principles which can only be stupid, sterile and false, for the very reason that they *are* principles, that is to say, ideas which are considered as certain and unchangeable, in this world where one is certain of nothing, since light is an illusion and noise is an illusion.

July 16. I saw some things yesterday that troubled me very much.

I was dining at the house of my cousin, Madame Sable, whose husband is colonel of the 76th Chasseurs at Limoges. There were two young women there, one of whom had married a medical man, Dr Parent, who devotes much attention to nervous diseases and to the remarkable manifestations taking place at this moment under the influence of hypnotism and suggestion.

He related to us at some length the wonderful results obtained by English scientists and by the doctors of the Nancy school; and the facts which he adduced appeared to me so strange that I declared that I was altogether incredulous.

'We are,' he declared, 'on the point of discovering one of the most important secrets of nature; I mean to say, one of its most

mportant secrets on this earth, for there are certainly others of
a different kind of importance up in the stars, yonder. Ever since
man has thought, ever since he has been able to express and write
down his thoughts, he has felt himself close to a mystery which is
impenetrable to his gross and imperfect senses, and he endeavours
to supplement through his intellect the inefficiency of his senses. As
long as that intellect remained in its elementary stage, these apparitions of invisible spirits assumed forms that were commonplace,
though terrifying. Thence sprang the popular belief in the supernatural, the legends of wandering spirits, of fairies, of gnomes,
ghosts, I might even say the legend of God; for our conceptions of
the workman-creator, from whatever religion they may have come
down to us, are certainly the most mediocre, the most stupid and
the most incredible inventions that ever sprang from the terrified
brain of any human beings. Nothing is truer than what Voltaire
says: "God made man in His own image, but man has certainly paid
Him back in his own coin."

'However, for rather more than a century men seem to have had a
presentiment of something new. Mesmer and some others have put
us on an unexpected track, and, especially within the last two or three
years, we have arrived at really surprising results.'

My cousin, who is also very incredulous, smiled, and Dr Parent said
to her: 'Would you like me to try and send you to sleep, madame?'
'Yes, certainly.'

She sat down in an easy chair, and he began to look at her fixedly,
so as to fascinate her. I suddenly felt myself growing uncomfortable,
my heart beating rapidly and a choking sensation in my throat. I saw
Madame Sable's eyes becoming heavy, her mouth twitching and her
bosom heaving, and at the end of ten minutes she was asleep.

'Go behind her,' the doctor said to me, and I took a seat behind
her. He put a visiting card into her hands, and said to her: 'This is
a looking-glass; what do you see in it?' And she replied: 'I see my
cousin.' 'What is he doing?' 'He is twisting his moustache.' 'And
now?' 'He is taking a photograph out of his pocket.' 'Whose photograph is it?' 'His own.'

That was true, and the photograph had been given me that same
evening at the hotel.

'What is his attitude in this portrait?' 'He is standing up with his
hat in his hand.'

She saw, therefore, on that card, on that piece of white pasteboard,
as if she had seen it in a mirror.

The young women were frightened, and exclaimed: 'That is enough! Quite, quite enough!'

But the doctor said to Madame Sable authoritatively: 'You will rise at eight o'clock tomorrow morning; then you will go and call on your cousin at his hotel and ask him to lend you five thousand francs which your husband demands of you, and which he will ask for when he sets out on his coming journey.'

Then he woke her up.

On returning to my hotel, I thought over this curious séance, and I was assailed by doubts, not as to my cousin's absolute and undoubted good faith, for I had known her as well as if she were my own sister ever since she was a child, but as to a possible trick on the doctor's part. Had he not, perhaps, kept a glass hidden in his hand, which he showed to the young woman in her sleep, at the same time as he did the card? Professional conjurors do things that are just as singular.

So I went home and to bed, and this morning, at about half-past eight, I was awakened by my valet, who said to me: 'Madame Sable has asked to see you immediately, monsieur.' I dressed hastily and went to her.

She sat down in some agitation, with her eyes on the floor, and without raising her veil she said to me: 'My dear cousin, I am going to ask a great favour of you.' 'What is it, cousin?' 'I do not like to tell you, and yet I must. I am in absolute need of five thousand francs.' 'What, you?' 'Yes, I, or rather my husband, who has asked me to procure them for him.'

I was so thunderstruck that I stammered out my answers. I asked myself whether she had not really been making fun of me with Dr Parent, if it was not merely a very well-acted farce which had been rehearsed beforehand. On looking at her attentively, however, all my doubts disappeared. She was trembling with grief, so painful was this step to her, and I was convinced that her throat was full of sobs.

I knew that she was very rich and I continued: 'What! has not your husband five thousand francs at his disposal? Come, think. Are you sure that he commissioned you to ask me for them?'

She hesitated for a few seconds, as if she were making a great effort to search her memory, and then she replied: 'Yes . . . yes, I am quite sure of it.' 'He has written to you?'

She hesitated again and reflected, and I guessed the torture of her thoughts. She did not know. She only knew that she was to borrow five thousand francs of me for her husband. So she told a lie. 'Yes, he has written to me.' 'When, pray? You did not mention it to me

esterday.' 'I received his letter this morning.' 'Can you show it me?'
No; no . . . no . . . it contained private matters . . . things too personal
o ourselves . . . I burned it.' 'So your husband runs into debt?'

She hesitated again, and then murmured: 'I do not know.' There-
upon I said bluntly: 'I have not five thousand francs at my disposal at
this moment, my dear cousin.'

She uttered a kind of cry as if she were in pain and said: 'Oh! oh! I
beseech you, I beseech you to get them for me . . . '

She got excited and clasped her hands as if she were praying to me!
I heard her voice change its tone; she wept and stammered, harassed
and dominated by the irresistible order that she had received.

'Oh! oh! I beg you to . . . if you knew what I am suffering . . . I want
them today.'

I had pity on her: 'You shall have them by and by, I swear to you.'
'Oh! thank you! Thank you! How kind you are.'

I continued: 'Do you remember what took place at your house
last night?' 'Yes.' 'Do you remember that Dr Parent sent you to
sleep?' 'Yes.' 'Oh! very well, then; he ordered you to come to me
this morning to borrow five thousand francs, and at this moment
you are obeying that suggestion.'

She considered for a few moments, and then replied: 'But as it is
my husband who wants them – '

For a whole hour I tried to convince her, but could not succeed,
and when she had gone I went to the doctor. He was just going out,
and he listened to me with a smile, and said: 'Do you believe now?'
'Yes, I cannot help it.' 'Let us go to your cousin's.'

She was already half asleep on a reclining chair, overcome with
fatigue. The doctor felt her pulse, looked at her for some time with
one hand raised toward her eyes, which she closed by degrees under
the irresistible power of this magnetic influence, and when she was
asleep, he said: 'Your husband does not require the five thousand
francs any longer! You must, therefore, forget that you asked your
cousin to lend them to you, and, if he speaks to you about it, you will
not understand him.'

Then he woke her up, and I took out a pocket-book and said: 'Here
is what you asked me for this morning, my dear cousin.' But she was
so surprised that I did not venture to persist; nevertheless, I tried to
recall the circumstance to her, but she denied it vigorously, thought I
was making fun of her, and, in the end, very nearly lost her temper.

There! I have just come back, and I have not been able to eat any
lunch, for this experiment has altogether upset me.

July 19. Many people to whom I told the adventure laughed at me
I no longer know what to think. The wise man says: 'It may be!'

July 21. I dined at Bougival, and then I spent the evening at a
boatmen's ball. Decidedly everything depends on place and surroundings. It would be the height of folly to believe in the supernatural on
the Ile de la Grenouillière . . . but on top of Mont Saint-Michel? . .
and in India? We are terribly influenced by our surroundings. I shall
return home next week.

July 30. I came back to my own house yesterday. Everything is
going on well.

August 2. Nothing new; it is splendid weather, and I spend my days
in watching the Seine flowing past.

August 4. Quarrels among my servants. They declare that the
glasses are broken in the cupboards at night. The footman accuses
the cook, who accuses the seamstress, who accuses the other two.
Who is the culprit? It is a clever person who can tell.

August 6. This time I am not mad. I have seen . . . I have seen . . .
I have seen! . . . I can doubt no longer . . . I have seen it! . . .

I was walking at two o'clock among my rose trees, in the full sunlight . . . in the walk bordered by autumn roses which are beginning
to fall. As I stopped to look at a Géant de Bataille, which had three
splendid blossoms, I distinctly saw the stalk of one of the roses near
me bend, as if an invisible hand had bent it, and then break, as if that
hand had picked it! Then the flower raised itself, following the curve
which a hand would have described in carrying it toward a mouth,
and it remained suspended in the transparent air, all alone and
motionless, a terrible red spot, three yards from my eyes. In desperation I rushed at it to take it! I found nothing; it had disappeared.
Then I was seized with furious rage against myself, for a reasonable
and serious man should not have such hallucinations.

But was it an hallucination? I turned round to look for the stalk,
and I found it at once, on the bush, freshly broken, between two
other roses which remained on the branch. I returned home then,
my mind greatly disturbed; for I am certain now, as certain as I am of
the alternation of day and night, that there exists close to me an
invisible being that lives on milk and water, that can touch objects,
take them and change their places; that is, consequently, endowed
with a material nature, although it is imperceptible to our senses, and
that lives as I do, under my roof –

August 7. I slept tranquilly. He drank the water out of my decanter,
but did not disturb my sleep.

I wonder if I am mad. As I was walking just now in the sun by the river side, doubts as to my sanity arose in me; not vague doubts such as I have had hitherto, but definite, absolute doubts. I have seen mad people, and I have known some who have been quite intelligent, lucid, even clear-sighted in every concern of life, except on one point. They spoke readily, clearly, profoundly on everything, when suddenly their mind struck upon the shoals of their madness and broke to pieces there, and scattered and floundered in that furious and terrible sea, full of rolling waves, fogs and squalls, which is called *madness.*

I certainly should think that I was mad, absolutely mad, if I were not conscious, did not perfectly know my condition, did not fathom it by analysing it with the most complete lucidity. I should, in fact, be only a rational man who was labouring under an hallucination. Some unknown disturbance must have arisen in my brain, one of those disturbances which physiologists of the present day try to note and to verify; and that disturbance must have caused a deep gap in my mind and in the sequence and logic of my ideas. Similar phenomena occur in dreams which lead us among the most unlikely phantasmagoria, without causing us any surprise, because our verifying apparatus and our organ of control are asleep, while our imaginative faculty is awake and active. Is it not possible that one of the imperceptible notes of the cerebral keyboard had been paralysed in me? Some men lose the recollection of proper names, of verbs, or of numbers, or merely of dates, in consequence of an accident. The localisation of all the variations of thought has been established nowadays; why, then, should it be surprising if my faculty of controlling the unreality of certain hallucinations were dormant in me for the time being?

I thought of all this as I walked by the side of the water. The sun shone brightly on the river and made earth delightful, while it filled me with a love for life, for the swallows, whose agility always delights my eye, for the plants by the riverside, the rustle of whose leaves is a pleasure to my ears.

By degrees, however, an inexplicable feeling of discomfort seized me. It seemed as if some unknown force were numbing and stopping me, were preventing me from going further, and were calling me back. I felt that painful wish to return which oppresses you when you have left a beloved invalid at home, and when you are seized with a presentiment that he is worse.

I therefore returned in spite of myself, feeling certain that I should find some bad news awaiting me, a letter or a telegram. There was nothing, however, and I was more surprised and uneasy than if I had had another fantastic vision.

August 8. I spent a terrible evening yesterday. He does not show himself any more, but I feel that he is near me, watching me, looking at me, penetrating me, dominating me, and more redoubtable when he hides himself thus than if he were to manifest his constant and invisible presence by supernatural phenomena. However, I slept.

August 9. Nothing, but I am afraid.

August 10. Nothing; what will happen tomorrow?

August 11. Still nothing; I cannot stop at home with this fear hanging over me and these thoughts in my mind; I shall go away.

August 12. Ten o'clock at night. All day long I have been trying to get away, and have not been able. I wish to accomplish this simple and easy act of freedom – to go out – to get into my carriage in order to go to Rouen – and I have not been able to do it. What is the reason?

August 13. When one is attacked by certain maladies, all the springs of our physical being appear to be broken, all our energies destroyed, all our muscles relaxed; our bones, too, have become as soft as flesh, and our blood as liquid as water. I am experiencing these sensations in my moral being in a strange and distressing manner. I have no longer any strength, any courage, any self-control, not even any power to set my own will in motion. I have no power left to will anything; but someone does it for me and I obey.

August 14. I am lost. Somebody possesses my soul and dominates it. Somebody orders all my acts, all my movements, all my thoughts. I am no longer anything in myself, nothing except an enslaved and terrified spectator of all the things I do. I wish to go out; I cannot. He does not wish to, and so I remain, trembling and distracted, in the armchair in which he keeps me sitting. I merely wish to get up and to rouse myself; I cannot! I am riveted to my chair, and my chair adheres to the ground in such a manner that no power could move us.

Then, suddenly, I must, I must go to the bottom of my garden to pick some strawberries and eat them, and I go there. I pick the strawberries and eat them! Oh, my God! my God! Is there a God? If there be one, deliver me! Save me! Succour me! Pardon! Pity! Mercy! Save me! Oh, what sufferings! What torture! What horror!

August 15. This is certainly the way in which my poor cousin was possessed and controlled when she came to borrow five thousand francs of me. She was under the power of a strange will which had entered into her, like another soul, like another parasitic and dominating soul. Is the world coming to an end?

But who is he, this invisible being that rules me? This unknowable being, this rover of a supernatural race?

Invisible beings exist, then! How is it, then, that since the beginning of the world they have never manifested themselves precisely as they do to me? I have never read of anything that resembles what goes on in my house. Oh, if I could only leave it, if I could only go away, escape, and never return! I should be saved, but I cannot.

August 16. I managed to escape today for two hours, like a prisoner who finds the door of his dungeon accidentally open. I suddenly felt that I was free and that he was far away, and so I gave orders to harness the horses as quickly as possible, and I drove to Rouen. Oh, how delightful to be able to say to a man who obeys you: 'Go to Rouen!'

I made him pull up before the library, and I begged them to lend me Dr Herrmann Herestauss' treatise on the unknown inhabitants of the ancient and modern world.

Then, as I was getting into my carriage, I intended to say: 'To the railway station!' but instead of this I shouted – I did not say, I shouted – in such a loud voice that all the passers-by turned round: 'Home!' and I fell back on the cushion of my carriage, overcome by mental agony. He had found me again and regained possession of me.

August 17. Oh, what a night! What a night! And yet it seems to me that I ought to rejoice. I read until one o'clock in the morning! Herestauss, doctor of philosophy and theogony, wrote the history of the manifestation of all those invisible beings which hover round man, or of whom he dreams. He describes their origin, their domain, their power; but none of them resembles the one which haunts me. One might say that man, ever since he began to think, has had a foreboding fear of a new being, stronger than himself, his successor in this new world, and that, feeling his presence, and not being able to foresee the nature of that master, he has, in his terror, created the whole race of occult beings, of vague phantoms born of fear.

Having, therefore, read until one o'clock in the morning, I went and sat down at the open window, in order to cool my forehead and my thoughts, in the calm night air. It was very pleasant and warm! How I should have enjoyed such a night formerly!

There was no moon, but the stars darted out their rays in the dark heavens. Who inhabits those worlds? What forms, what living beings, what animals are there yonder? What can they do more than we can? What do they see which we do not know? Will not one of them, some day or other, traversing space, appear on our earth to conquer it, just as the Norsemen formerly crossed the sea in order to sub-jugate nations more feeble than themselves?

We are so weak, so defenceless, so ignorant, so small, we who live on this particle of mud which revolves in a drop of water.

I fell asleep, dreaming thus in the cool night air, and when I had slept for about three-quarters of an hour, I opened my eyes without moving, awakened by I know not what confused and strange sens-ation. At first I saw nothing, and then suddenly it appeared to me as if a page of a book which had remained open on my table turned over of its own accord. Not a breath of air had come in at my window, and I was surprised, and waited. In about four minutes, I saw, I saw, yes, I saw with my own eyes, another page lift itself up and fall down on the others, as if a finger had turned it over. My armchair was empty, appeared empty, but I knew that he was there, he, and sitting in my place, and that he was reading. With a furious bound, the bound of an enraged wild beast that springs at its tamer, I crossed my room to seize him, to strangle him, to kill him! But before I could reach it, the chair fell over as if somebody had run away from me – my table rocked, my lamp fell and went out, and my window closed as if some thief had been surprised and had fled out into the night, shutting it behind him.

So he had run away; he had been afraid; he, afraid of me!

But – but – tomorrow – or later – some day or other – I should be able to hold him in my clutches and crush him against the ground! Do not dogs occasionally bite and strangle their masters?

August 18. I have been thinking the whole day long. Oh, yes, I will obey him, follow his impulses, fulfil all his wishes, show myself humble, submissive, a coward. He is the stronger; but the hour will come –

August 19. I know – I know – I know all! I have just read the following in the *Revue du Monde Scientifique*:

A curious piece of news comes to us from Rio de Janeiro. Madness, an epidemic of madness, which may be compared to that contagious madness which attacked the people of Europe in the Middle Ages, is at this moment raging in the Province of San-Paolo. The terrified inhabitants are leaving their houses, saying that they are pursued, possessed, dominated like human cattle by invisible, though tangible beings, a species of vampire, which feed on their life while they are asleep, and who, besides, drink water and milk without appearing to touch any other nourishment.

Professor Don Pedro Henriquez, accompanied by several medical savants, has gone to the Province of San-Paolo, in order to study the origin and the manifestations of this surprising madness on the spot, and to propose such measures to the Emperor as may appear to him to be most fitted to restore the mad population to reason.

Ah! Ah! I remember now that fine Brazilian three-master which passed in front of my windows as it was going up the Seine, on the 8th day of last May! I thought it looked so pretty, so white and bright! That Being was on board of her, coming from there, where its race originated. And it saw me! It saw my house which was also white, and it sprang from the ship onto the land. Oh, merciful heaven!

Now I know, I can divine. The reign of man is over, and he has come. He who was feared by primitive man; whom disquieted priests exorcised; whom sorcerers evoked on dark nights, without having seen him appear, to whom the imagination of the transient masters of the world lent all the monstrous or graceful forms of gnomes, spirits, genii, fairies and familiar spirits. After the coarse conceptions of primitive fear, more clear-sighted men foresaw it more clearly. Mesmer divined it, and ten years ago physicians accurately discovered the nature of his power, even before he exercised it himself. They played with this new weapon of the Lord, the sway of a mysterious will over the human soul, which had become a slave. They called it magnetism, hypnotism, suggestion – what do I know? I have seen them amusing themselves like rash children with this horrible power! Woe to us! Woe to man! He has come, the – the – what does he call himself – the – I fancy that he is shouting out his name to me and I do not hear him – the – yes – he is shouting it out – I am listening – I cannot – he repeats it – the – Horla – I hear – the Horla – it is he – the Horla – he has come!

Ah! the vulture has eaten the pigeon; the wolf has eaten the lamb; the lion has devoured the sharp-horned buffalo; man has killed the lion with an arrow, with sword, with gunpowder; but the Horla will make of man what we have made of the horse and of the ox; his chattel, his slave and his food, by the mere power of his will. Woe to us!

But, nevertheless, the animal sometimes revolts and kills the man who has subjugated it. I should also like – I shall be able to – but I must know him, touch him, see him! Scientists say that animals' eyes, being different from ours, do not distinguish objects as ours do. And my eye cannot distinguish this newcomer who is oppressing me.

Why? Oh, now I remember the words of the monk at Mont Saint-Michel: 'Can we see the hundred-thousandth part of what exists? See here; there is the wind, which is the strongest force in nature, which knocks down men, and bowls down buildings, uproots trees, raises the sea into mountains of water, destroys cliffs and casts great ships on the breakers; the wind which kills, which whistles, which sighs, which roars – have you ever seen it, and can you see it? It exists for all that, however!'

And I went on thinking: my eyes are so weak, so imperfect, that they do not even distinguish hard bodies, if they are as transparent as glass! If a glass without tinfoil behind it were to bar my way, I should run into it, just as a bird which has flown into a room breaks its head against the window-panes. A thousand things, moreover, deceive man and lead astray. Why should it then be surprising that he cannot perceive an unknown body through which the light passes?

A new being! Why not? It was assuredly bound to come! Why should we be the last? We do not distinguish it any more than all the others created before us! The reason is, that its nature is more perfect, its body finer and more finished than ours, that ours is so weak, so awkwardly constructed, encumbered with organs that are always tired, always on the strain like machinery that is too complicated, which lives like a plant and like a beast, nourishing itself on air, herbs and flesh, an animal machine which is a prey to maladies, to malformations, to decay; broken-winded, badly regulated, simple and eccentric, ingeniously badly made, at once a coarse and a delicate piece of workmanship, the rough sketch of a being that might become intelligent and grand.

We are only a few, so few in this world, from the oyster up to man. Why should there not be one more, once that period is passed which separates the successive apparitions from all the different species?

Why not one more? Why not, also, other trees with immense, splendid flowers, perfuming whole regions? Why not other elements besides fire, air, earth, and water? There are four, only four, those nursing fathers of various beings! What a pity! Why are there not forty, four hundred, four thousand? How poor everything is, how mean and wretched! grudgingly produced, roughly constructed, clumsily made! Ah, the elephant and the hippopotamus, what grace! And the camel, what elegance!

But the butterfly, you will say, a flying flower? I dream of one that should be as large as a hundred worlds, with wings whose shape, beauty, colours and motion I cannot even express. But I see it – it flutters from star to star, refreshing them and perfuming them with the light and harmonious breath of its flight! And the people up there look at it as it passes in an ecstasy of delight!

What is the matter with me? It is he, the Horla, who haunts me, and who makes me think of these foolish things! He is within me, he is becoming my soul; I shall kill him!

August 19. I shall kill him. I have seen him! Yesterday I sat down at my table and pretended to write very assiduously. I knew quite well that he would come prowling round me, quite close to me, so close that I might perhaps be able to touch him, to seize him. And then – then I should have the strength of desperation; I should have my hands, my knees, my chest, my forehead, my teeth to strangle him, to crush him, to bite him, to tear him to pieces. And I watched for him with all my over-excited senses.

I had lighted my two lamps and the eight wax candles on my mantelpiece, as if with this light I could discover him.

My bedstead, my old oak post bedstead, stood opposite to me; on my right was the fireplace; on my left, the door which was carefully closed, after I had left it open for some time in order to attract him; behind me was a very high wardrobe with a looking-glass in it, before which I stood to shave and dress every day, and in which I was in the habit of glancing at myself from head to foot every time I passed it.

I pretended to be writing in order to deceive him, for he also was watching me, and suddenly I felt – I was certain that he was reading over my shoulder, that he was there, touching my ear.

I got up, my hands extended, and turned round so quickly that I almost fell. Eh! well? It was as bright as at midday, but I did not see my reflection in the mirror! It was empty, clear, profound, full of light! But my figure was not reflected in it – and I, I was opposite to it! I saw the large, clear glass from top to bottom, and I looked at it with unsteady eyes; and I did not dare to advance; I did not venture to make a movement, feeling that he was there, but that he would escape me again, he whose imperceptible body had absorbed my reflection.

How frightened I was! And then, suddenly, I began to see myself in a mist in the depths of the looking-glass, in a mist as it were a sheet of water; and it seemed to me as if this water were flowing clearer every moment. It was like the end of an eclipse. Whatever it was that hid me did not appear to possess any clearly defined outlines, but a sort of opaque transparency which gradually grew clearer.

At last I was able to distinguish myself completely, as I do every day when I look at myself.

I had seen it! And the horror of it remained with me, and makes me shudder even now.

August 20. How could I kill it, as I could not get hold of it? Poison? But it would see me mix it with the water; and then, would our poisons have any effect on its impalpable body? No – no – no doubt about the matter – Then – then? –

August 21. I sent for a blacksmith from Rouen, and ordered iron shutters for my room, such as some private hotels in Paris have on the ground floor, for fear of burglars, and he is going to make me an iron door as well. I have made myself out a coward, but I do not care about that!

September 10. Rouen, Hôtel Continental. It is done – it is done – but is he dead? My mind is thoroughly upset by what I have seen.

Well then, yesterday, the locksmith having put on the iron shutters and door, I left everything until midnight, although it was getting cold.

Suddenly I felt that he was there, and joy, mad joy, took possession of me. I got up softly, and walked up and down for some time, so that he might not suspect anything; then I took off my boots and put on my slippers carelessly; then I fastened the iron shutters, and, going back to the door, quickly double-locked it with a padlock, putting the key into my pocket.

Suddenly I noticed that he was moving restlessly round me, that in his turn he was frightened and was ordering me to let him out. I nearly yielded; I did not, however, but putting my back to the door, I half opened it, just enough to allow me to go out backward, and as I am very tall my head touched the casing. I was sure that he had not been able to escape, and I shut him up alone, quite alone. What happiness! I had him fast. Then I ran downstairs; in the drawing-room, which was under my bedroom, I took the two lamps and I poured all the oil on the carpet, the furniture, everywhere; then I set fire to it and made my escape, after having carefully double-locked the door.

I went and hid myself at the bottom of the garden, in a clump of laurel bushes. How long it seemed! How long it seemed! Everything was dark, silent, motionless, not a breath of air and not a star, but heavy banks of clouds which one could not see, but which weighed, oh, so heavily on my soul.

I looked at my house and waited. How long it was! I already began to think that the fire had gone out of its own accord, or that he had extinguished it, when one of the lower windows gave way under the violence of the flames, and a long, soft, caressing sheet of red flame mounted up the white wall, and enveloped it as far as the roof. The light fell on the trees, the branches, and the leaves, and a shiver of fear pervaded them also! The birds awoke, a dog began to howl, and it seemed to me as if the day were breaking! Almost immediately two other windows flew into fragments, and I saw that the whole of the lower part of my house was nothing but a terrible furnace. But a cry, a horrible, shrill, heartrending cry, a woman's cry, sounded through the night, and two garret windows were opened! I had forgotten the servants! I saw their terror-stricken faces, and their arms waving frantically.

Then overwhelmed with horror, I set off to run to the village, shouting: 'Help! help! Fire! fire!' I met some people who were already coming to the scene, and I returned with them.

By this time the house was nothing but a horrible and magnificent funeral pile, a monstrous funeral pile which lit up the whole country, a funeral pile where men were burning, and where he was burning also, He, He, my prisoner, that new Being, the new master, the Horla!

Suddenly the whole roof fell in between the walls, and a volcano of flames darted up to the sky. Through all the windows which opened on that furnace, I saw the flames darting, and I thought that he was there, in that kiln, dead.

Dead? Perhaps? – His body? Was not his body, which was transparent, indestructible by such means as would kill ours?

If he were not dead? – Perhaps time alone has power over that Invisible and Redoubtable Being. Why this transparent, unrecognisable body, this body belonging to a spirit, if it also has to fear ills, infirmities and premature destruction?

Premature destruction? All human terror springs from that! After man, the Horla. After him who can die every day, at any hour, at any moment, by any accident, came the one who would die only at his own proper hour, day, and minute, because he had touched the limits of his existence!

No – no – without any doubt – he is not dead – Then – then – I suppose I must kill myself! . . .

Bewitched

EDITH WHARTON

The snow was still falling thickly when Orrin Bosworth, who farmed the land south of Lonetop, drove up in his cutter to Saul Rutledge's gate. He was surprised to see two other cutters ahead of him. From them descended two muffled figures. Bosworth, with increasing surprise, recognised Deacon Hibben, from North Ashmore, and Sylvester Brand, the widower, from the old Bearcliff farm on the way to Lonetop.

It was not often that anybody in Hemlock County entered Saul Rutledge's gate; least of all in the dead of winter, and summoned (as Bosworth, at any rate, had been) by Mrs Rutledge, who passed, even in that unsocial region, for a woman of cold manners and solitary character. The situation was enough to excite the curiosity of a less imaginative man than Orrin Bosworth.

As he drove in between the broken-down white gate-posts topped by fluted urns the two men ahead of him were leading their horses to the adjoining shed. Bosworth followed, and hitched his horse to a post. Then the three tossed off the snow from their shoulders, clapped their numb hands together, and greeted each other.

'Hallo, Deacon.'

'Well, well, Orrin – ' They shook hands.

' 'Day, Bosworth,' said Sylvester Brand, with a brief nod. He seldom put any cordiality into his manner, and on this occasion he was still busy about his horse's bridle and blanket.

Orrin Bosworth, the youngest and most communicative of the three, turned back to Deacon Hibben, whose long face, queerly blotched and mouldy-looking, with blinking peering eyes, was yet less forbidding than Brand's heavily-hewn countenance.

'Queer, our all meeting here this way. Mrs Rutledge sent me a message to come,' Bosworth volunteered.

The Deacon nodded. 'I got a word from her too – Andy Pond come with it yesterday noon. I hope there's no trouble here – '

He glanced through the thickening fall of snow at the desolate front of the Rutledge house, the more melancholy in its present neglected state because, like the gate-posts, it kept traces of former elegance. Bosworth had often wondered how such a house had come to be built in that lonely stretch between North Ashmore and Cold Corners. People said there had once been other houses like it, forming a little township called Ashmore, a sort of mountain colony created by the caprice of an English Royalist officer, one Colonel Ashmore, who had been murdered by the Indians, with all his family, long before the Revolution. This tale was confirmed by the fact that the ruined cellars of several smaller houses were still to be discovered under the wild growth of the adjoining slopes, and that the Communion plate of the moribund Episcopal church of Cold Corners was engraved with the name of Colonel Ashmore, who had given it to the church of Ashmore in the year 1723. Of the church itself no traces remained. Doubtless it had been a modest wooden edifice, built on piles, and the conflagration which had burnt the other houses to the ground's edge had reduced it utterly to ashes. The whole place, even in summer, wore a mournful solitary air, and people wondered why Saul Rutledge's father had gone there to settle.

'I never knew a place,' Deacon Hibben said, 'as seemed as far away from humanity. And yet it ain't so in miles.'

'Miles ain't the only distance,' Orrin Bosworth answered; and the two men, followed by Sylvester Brand, walked across the drive to the front door. People in Hemlock County did not usually come and go by their front doors, but all three men seemed to feel that, on an occasion which appeared to be so exceptional, the usual and more familiar approach by the kitchen would not be suitable.

They had judged rightly; the Deacon had hardly lifted the knocker when the door opened and Mrs Rutledge stood before them.

'Walk right in,' she said in her usual dead-level tone; and Bosworth, as he followed the others, thought to himself: 'Whatever's happened, she's not going to let it show in her face.'

It was doubtful, indeed, if anything unwonted would be made to show in Prudence Rutledge's face, so limited was its scope, so fixed were its features. She was dressed for the occasion in a black calico with white spots, a collar of crochet-lace fastened by a gold brooch, and a grey woollen shawl, crossed under her arms and tied at the back. In her small narrow head the only marked prominence was that of the brow projecting roundly over pale spectacled eyes. Her dark

hair, parted above this prominence, passed tight and flat over the tips
of her ears into a small braided coil at the nape; and her contracted
head looked still narrower from being perched on a long hollow neck
with cord-like throat muscles. Her eyes were of a pale cold grey, her
complexion was an even white. Her age might have been anywhere
from thirty-five to sixty.

The room into which she led the three men had probably been
the dining-room of the Ashmore house. It was now used as a front
parlour, and a black stove planted on a sheet of zinc stuck out from
the delicately fluted panels of an old wooden mantel. A newly-lit
fire smouldered reluctantly, and the room was at once close and
bitterly cold.

'Andy Pond,' Mrs Rutledge cried to someone at the back of the
house, 'step out and call Mr Rutledge. You'll likely find him in the
wool-shed, or round the barn somewheres.' She rejoined her visitors.
'Please suit yourselves to seats,' she said.

The three men, with an increasing air of constraint, took the chairs
she pointed out, and Mrs Rutledge sat stiffly down upon a fourth,
behind a rickety bead-work table. She glanced from one to the other
of her visitors.

'I presume you folks are wondering what it is I asked you to come
here for,' she said in her dead-level voice. Orrin Bosworth and
Deacon Hibben murmured an assent; Sylvester Brand sat silent, his
eyes, under their great thicket of eyebrows, fixed on the huge boot-
tip swinging before him.

'Well, I allow you didn't expect it was for a party,' continued Mrs
Rutledge.

No-one ventured to respond to this chill pleasantry, and she
continued: 'We're in trouble here, and that's a fact. And we need
advice – Mr Rutledge and myself do.' She cleared her throat, and
added in a lower tone, her pitilessly clear eyes looking straight
before her: 'There's a spell been cast over Mr Rutledge.'

The Deacon looked up sharply, an incredulous smile pinching his
thin lips. 'A spell?'

'That's what I said: he's bewitched.'

Again the three visitors were silent; then Bosworth, more at ease or
less tongue-tied than the others, asked with an attempt at humour:
'Do you use the word in the strict Scripture sense, Mrs Rutledge?'

She glanced at him before replying: 'That's how *he* uses it.'

The Deacon coughed and cleared his long rattling throat. 'Do you
care to give us more particulars before your husband joins us?'

Mrs Rutledge looked down at her clasped hands, as if considering the question. Bosworth noticed that the inner fold of her lids was the same uniform white as the rest of her skin, so that when she dropped them her rather prominent eyes looked like the sightless orbs of a marble statue. The impression was unpleasing, and he glanced away at the text over the mantelpiece, which read: *The Soul That Sinneth It Shall Die.*

'No,' she said at length, 'I'll wait.'

At this moment Sylvester Brand suddenly stood up and pushed back his chair. 'I don't know,' he said, in his rough bass voice, 'as I've got any particular lights on Bible mysteries; and this happens to be the day I was to go down to Starkfield to close a deal with a man.'

Mrs Rutledge lifted one of her long thin hands. Withered and wrinkled by hard work and cold, it was nevertheless of the same leaden white as her face. 'You won't be kept long,' she said. 'Won't you be seated?'

Farmer Brand stood irresolute, his purplish underlip twitching. 'The Deacon here – such things is more in his line . . . '

'I want you should stay,' said Mrs Rutledge quietly; and Brand sat down again.

A silence fell, during which the four persons present seemed all to be listening for the sound of a step; but none was heard, and after a minute or two Mrs Rutledge began to speak again.

'It's down by that old shack on Lamer's pond; that's where they meet,' she said suddenly.

Bosworth, whose eyes were on Sylvester Brand's face, fancied he saw a sort of inner flush darken the farmer's heavy leathern skin. Deacon Hibben leaned forward, a glitter of curiosity in his eyes.

'They – *who*, Mrs Rutledge?'

'My husband, Saul Rutledge . . . and her . . . '

Sylvester Brand again stirred in his seat. 'Who do you mean by *her?*' he asked abruptly, as if roused out of some far-off musing.

Mrs Rutledge's body did not move; she simply revolved her head on her long neck and looked at him.

'Your daughter, Sylvester Brand.'

The man staggered to his feet with an explosion of inarticulate sounds. 'My – my daughter? What the hell are you talking about? My daughter? It's a damned lie . . . it's . . . it's . . . '

'Your daughter, *Ora*, Mr Brand,' said Mrs Rutledge slowly.

Bosworth felt an icy chill down his spine. Instinctively he turned his eyes away from Brand, and they rested on the mildewed countenance of Deacon Hibben. Between the blotches it had become as white as Mrs Rutledge's, and the Deacon's eyes burned in the whiteness like live embers among ashes.

Brand gave a laugh: the rusty creaking laugh of one whose springs of mirth are never moved by gaiety. 'My daughter, *Ora*?' he repeated.

'Yes.'

'My *dead* daughter?'

'That's what he says.'

'Your husband?'

'That's what Mr Rutledge says.'

Orrin Bosworth listened with a sense of suffocation; he felt as if he were wrestling with long-armed horrors in a dream. He could no longer resist letting his eyes return to Sylvester Brand's face. To his surprise it had resumed a natural imperturbable expression. Brand rose to his feet. 'Is that all?' he queried contemptuously.

'All? Ain't it enough? How long since you folks seen Saul Rutledge, any of you?' Mrs Rutledge flew at them.

Bosworth, it appeared, had not seen him for nearly a year; the Deacon had only run across him once, for a minute, at the North Ashmore post office, the previous autumn, and acknowledged that he wasn't looking any too good then. Brand said nothing, but stood irresolute.

'Well, if you wait a minute you'll see with your own eyes; and he'll tell you with his own words. That's what I've got you here for – to see for yourselves what's come over him. Then you'll talk different,' she added, twisting her head abruptly toward Sylvester Brand.

The Deacon raised a lean hand of interrogation.

'Does your husband know we've been sent for on this business, Mrs Rutledge?'

Mrs Rutledge signed assent.

'It was with his consent, then – ?'

She looked coldly at her questioner. 'I guess it had to be,' she said. Again Bosworth felt the chill down his spine. He tried to dissipate the sensation by speaking with an affection of energy.

'Can you tell us, Mrs Rutledge, how this trouble you speak of shows itself . . . what makes you think . . . ?'

She looked at him for a moment; then she leaned forward across the rickety bead-work table. A thin smile of disdain narrowed her colourless lips. 'I don't think – I know.'

'Well – but how?'

She leaned closer, both elbows on the table, her voice dropping. 'I seen 'em.'

In the ashen light fron the veiling of snow beyond the windows the Deacon's little screwed-up eyes seemed to give out red sparks. 'Him and the dead?'

'Him and the dead.'

'Saul Rutledge and – and Ora Brand?'

'That's so.'

Sylvester Brand's chair fell backward with a crash. He was on his feet again, crimson and cursing. 'It's a Goddamned fiend-begotten lie . . . '

'Friend Brand . . . friend Brand . . . ' the Deacon protested.

'Here, let me get out of this. I want to see Saul Rutledge himself, and tell him – '

'Well, here he is,' said Mrs Rutledge.

The outer door had opened; they heard the familiar stamping and shaking of a man who rids his garments of their last snow-flakes before penetrating to the sacred precincts of the best parlour. Then Saul Rutledge entered.

As he came in he faced the light from the north window, and Bosworth's first thought was that he looked like a drowned man fished out from under the ice – 'self-drowned,' he added. But the snow-light plays cruel tricks with a man's colour, and even with the shape of his features; it must have been partly that, Bosworth reflected, which transformed Saul Rutledge from the straight muscular fellow he had been a year before into the haggard wretch now before them.

The Deacon sought for a word to ease the horror. 'Well now, Saul – you look's if you'd ought to set right up to the stove. Had a touch of ague, maybe?'

The feeble attempt was unavailing. Rutledge neither moved nor answered. He stood among them silent, incommunicable, like one risen from the dead.

Brand grasped him roughly by the shoulder. 'See here, Saul Rutledge, what's this dirty lie your wife tells us you've been putting about?'

Still Rutledge did not move. 'It's no lie,' he said.

Brand's hand dropped from his shoulder. In spite of the man's rough bullying power he seemed to be undefinably awed by Rutledge's look and tone.

'No lie? You've gone plumb crazy, then, have you?'

Mrs Rutledge spoke. 'My husband's not lying, nor he ain't gone crazy. Don't I tell you I seen 'em?'

Brand laughed again. 'Him and the dead?'

'Yes.'

'Down by the Lamer pond, you say?'

'Yes.'

'And when was that, if I might ask?'

'Day before yesterday.'

A silence fell on the strangely assembled group. The Deacon at length broke it to say to Mr Brand: 'Brand, in my opinion we've got to see this thing through.'

Brand stood for a moment in speechless contemplation: there was something animal and primitive about him, Bosworth thought, as he hung thus, lowering and dumb, a little foam beading the corners of that heavy purplish underlip. He let himself slowly down into his chair. 'I'll see it through.'

The two other men and Mrs Rutledge had remained seated. Saul Rutledge stood before them, like a prisoner at the bar, or rather like a sick man before the physicians who were to heal him. As Bosworth scrutinised that hollow face, so wan under the dark sunburn, so sucked inward and consumed by some hidden fever, there stole over the sound healthy man the thought that perhaps, after all, husband and wife spoke the truth, and that they were all at that moment really standing on the edge of some forbidden mystery. Things that the rational mind would reject without a thought seemed no longer so easy to dispose of as one looked at the actual Saul Rutledge and remembered the man he had been a year before. Yes; as the Deacon said, they would have to see it through . . .

'Sit down then, Saul; draw up to us, won't you?' the Deacon suggested, trying again for a natural tone.

Mrs Rutledge pushed a chair forward, and her husband sat down on it. He stretched out his arms and grasped his knees in his brown bony fingers; in that attitude he remained, turning neither his head nor his eyes.

'Well, Saul,' the Deacon continued, 'your wife says you thought mebbe we could do something to help you through this trouble, whatever it is.'

Rutledge's grey eyes widened a little. 'No; I didn't think that. It was her idea to try what could be done.'

'I presume, though, since you've agreed to our coming, that you don't object to our putting a few questions?'

Rutledge was silent for a moment; then he said with a visible effort: 'No; I don't object.'

'Well – you've heard what your wife says?'

Rutledge made a slight motion of assent.

'And – what have you got to answer? How do you explain . . . ?'

Mrs Rutledge intervened. 'How can he explain? I seen 'em. . . . '

There was a silence; then Bosworth, trying to speak in an easy reassuring tone, queried: 'That so, Saul?'

'That's so.'

Brand lifted up his brooding head. 'You mean to say you . . . you sit here before us all and say . . . '

The Deacon's hand again checked him. 'Hold on, friend Brand. We're all of us trying for the facts, aint we?' He turned to Rutledge. 'We've heard what Mrs Rutledge says. What's your answer?'

'I don't know as there's any answer. She found us.'

'And you mean to tell me the person with you was . . . was what you took to be . . . ' the Deacon's thin voice grew thinner: 'Ora Brand?'

Saul Rutledge nodded.

'You knew . . . or thought you knew . . . you were meeting with the dead?'

Rutledge bent his head again. The snow continued to fall in a steady unwavering sheet against the window, and Bosworth felt as if a winding-sheet were descending from the sky to envelop them all in a common grave.

'Think what you're saying! It's against our religion! Ora . . . poor child! . . . died over a year ago. I saw you at her funeral, Saul. How can you make such a statement?'

'What else can he do?' thrust in Mrs Rutledge.

There was another pause. Bosworth's resources had failed him, and Brand once more sat plunged in dark meditation. The Deacon laid his quivering finger-tips together, and moistened his lips.

'Was the day before yesterday the first time?' he asked.

The movement of Rutledge's head was negative.

'Not the first? Then when . . . '

'Nigh on a year ago, I reckon.'

'God! And you mean to tell us that ever since – ?'

'Well . . . look at him,' said his wife. The three men lowered their eyes.

After a moment Bosworth, trying to collect himself, glanced at the Deacon. 'Why not ask Saul to make his own statement, if that's what we're here for?'

'That's so,' the Deacon assented. He turned to Rutledge. 'Will you try and give us your idea . . . of . . . of how it began?'

There was another silence. Then Rutledge tightened his grasp on his gaunt knees, and still looking straight ahead, with his curiously clear unseeing gaze: 'Well,' he said, 'I guess it begun away back, afore even I was married to Mrs Rutledge . . . ' He spoke in a low automatic tone, as if some invisible agent were dictating his words, or even uttering them for him. 'You know,' he added, 'Ora and me was to have been married.'

Sylvester Brand lifted his head. 'Straighten that statement out first, please,' he interjected.

'What I mean is, we kept company. But Ora, she was very young. Mr Brand here, he sent her away. She was gone nigh to three years, I guess. When she come back I was married.'

'That's right,' Brand said, relapsing once more into his sunken attitude.

'And after she came back did you meet her again?' the Deacon continued.

'Alive?' Rutledge questioned.

A perceptible shudder ran through the room.

'Well – of course,' said the Deacon nervously.

Rutledge seemed to consider. 'Once I did – only once. There was a lot of other people round. At Cold Corners fair it was.'

'Did you talk with her then?'

'Only a minute.'

'What did she say?'

His voice dropped. 'She said she was sick and knew she was going to die, and when she was dead she'd come back for me.'

'And what did you answer?'

'Nothing.'

'Did you think anything of it at the time?'

'Well, no. Not till I heard she was dead I didn't. After that I thought of it – and I guess she drew me.' He moistened his lips.

'Drew you down to that abandoned house by the pond?'

Rutledge made a faint motion of assent, and the Deacon added: 'How did you know it was there she wanted you to come?'

'She . . . just drew me . . . '

There was a long pause. Bosworth felt, on himself and the other two men, the oppressive weight of the next question to be asked. Mrs Rutledge opened and closed her narrow lips once or twice, like some beached shell-fish gasping for the tide. Rutledge waited.

'Well, now, Saul, won't you go on with what you was telling us?' the Deacon at length suggested.

'That's all. There's nothing else.'

The Deacon lowered his voice. 'She just draws you?'

'Yes.'

'Often?'

'That's as it happens . . . '

'But if it's always there she draws you, man, haven't you the strength to keep away from the place?'

For the first time, Rutledge wearily turned his head toward his questioner. A spectral smile narrowed his colourless lips. 'Ain't any use. She follers after me . . . '

There was another silence. What more could they ask, then and there? Mrs Rutledge's presence checked the next question. The Deacon seemed hopelessly to revolve the matter. At length he spoke in a more authoritative tone. 'These are forbidden things. You know that, Saul. Have you tried prayer?'

Rutledge shook his head.

'Will you pray with us now?'

Rutledge cast a glance of freezing indifference on his spiritual adviser. 'If you folks want to pray, I'm agreeable,' he said. But Mrs Rutledge intervened.

'Prayer ain't any good. In this kind of thing it ain't no manner of use; you know it ain't. I called you here, Deacon, because you remember the last case in this parish. Thirty years ago it was, I guess; but you remember. Lefferts Nash – did praying help *him*? I was a little girl then, but I used to hear my folks talk of it winter nights. Lefferts Nash and Hannah Cory. They drove a stake through her breast. That's what cured him.'

'Oh – ' Orrin Bosworth exclaimed.

Sylvester Brand raised his head. 'You're speaking of that old story as if this was the same sort of thing?'

'Ain't it? Ain't my husband pining away the same as Lefferts Nash did? The Deacon here knows – '

The Deacon stirred anxiously in his chair. 'These are forbidden things,' he repeated. 'Supposing your husband is quite sincere in thinking himself haunted, as you might say. Well, even then, what proof have we that the . . . the dead woman . . . is the spectre of that poor girl?'

'Proof? Don't he say so? Didn't she tell him? Ain't I seen 'em?' Mrs Rutledge almost screamed.

The three men sat silent, and suddenly the wife burst out: 'A stake through the breast! That's the old way; and it's the only way. The Deacon knows it!'

'It's against our religion to disturb the dead.'

'Ain't it against your religion to let the living perish as my husband is perishing?' She sprang up with one of her abrupt movements and took the family Bible from the what-not in a corner of the parlour. Putting the book on the table, and moistening a livid finger-tip, she turned the pages rapidly, till she came to one on which she laid her hand like a stony paper-weight. 'See here,' she said, and read out in her level chanting voice: '*Thou shalt not suffer a witch to live.*'

'That's in Exodus, that's where it is,' she added, leaving the book open as if to confirm the statement.

Bosworth continued to glance anxiously from one to the other of the four people about the table. He was younger than any of them, and had had more contact with the modern world; down in Stark-field, in the bar of the Fielding House, he could hear himself laughing with the rest of the men at such old wive's tales. But it was not for nothing that he had been born under the icy shadow of Lonetop, and had shivered and hungered as a lad through the bitter Hemlock County winters. After his parents died, and he had taken hold of the farm himself, he had got more out of it by using improved methods, and by supplying the increasing throng of summer-boarders over Stotesbury way with milk and vegetables. He had been made a select-man of North Ashmore; for so young a man he had a standing in the county. But the roots of the old life were still in him. He could remember, as a little boy, going twice a year with his mother to that bleak hill-farm out beyond Sylvester Brand's, where Mrs Bosworth's aunt, Cressidora Cheney, had been shut up for years in a cold clean room with iron bars in the windows. When little Orrin first saw Aunt Cressidora she was a small white old woman, whom her sisters used to 'make decent' for visitors the day that Orrin and his mother were expected. The child wondered why there were bars to the window. 'Like a canary-bird,' he said to his mother. The phrase made Mrs Bosworth reflect. 'I do believe they keep Aunt Cressidora too lone-some,' she said; and the next time she went up the mountain with the little boy he carried to his great-aunt a canary in a little wooden cage. It was a great excitement; he knew it would make her happy.

The old woman's motionless face lit up when she saw the bird, and her eyes began to glitter. 'It belongs to me,' she said instantly, stretching her soft bony hand over the cage.

'Of course it does, Aunt Cressy,' said Mrs Bosworth, her eyes filling.

But the bird, startled by the shadow of the old woman's hand, began to flutter and beat its wings distractedly. At the sight, Aunt Cressidora's calm face suddenly became a coil of twitching features. 'You she-devil, you!' she cried in a high squealing voice; and thrusting her hand into the cage she dragged out the terrified bird and wrung its neck. She was plucking the hot body, and squealing 'she-devil, she-devil!' as they drew little Orrin from the room. On the way down the mountain his mother wept a great deal, and said: 'You must never tell anybody that poor Auntie's crazy, or the men would come and take her down to the asylum at Starkfield, and the shame of it would kill us all. Now promise.' The child promised.

He remembered the scene now, with its deep fringe of mystery, secrecy and rumour. It seemed related to a great many other things below the surface of his thoughts, things which stole up anew, making him feel that all the old people he had known, and who 'believed in these things', might after all be right. Hadn't a witch been burned at North Ashmore? Didn't the summer folk still drive over in jolly buckboard loads to see the meeting-house where the trial had been held, the pond where they had ducked her and she had floated? . . . Deacon Hibben believed; Bosworth was sure of it. If he didn't, why did people from all over the place come to him when their animals had queer sickness, or when there was a child in the family that had to be kept shut up because it fell down flat and foamed? Yes, in spite of his religion, Deacon Hibben *knew* . . .

And Brand? Well, it came to Bosworth in a flash: that North Ashmore woman who was burned had the name of Brand. The same stock, no doubt; there had been Brands in Hemlock County ever since the white men had come there. And Orrin, when he was a child, remembered hearing his parents say that Sylvester Brand hadn't ever oughter married his own cousin, because of the blood. Yet the couple had had two healthy girls, and when Mrs Brand pined away and died nobody suggested that anything had been wrong with her mind. And Vanessa and Ora were the handsomest girls anywhere round. Brand knew it, and scrimped and saved all he could to send Ora, the eldest, down to Starkfield to learn book-keeping. 'When she's married I'll send you,' he used to say to little Venny, who was his favourite. But Ora never married. She was away three years, during which Venny ran wild on the slopes of Lonetop; and when Ora came back she sickened and died – poor girl! Since then Brand had grown more savage and morose. He was a hard-working farmer, but there wasn't much to be got out of those barren Bearcliff acres. He was said to have taken to drink since his wife's death; now and then men ran across him in the 'dives' of Stotesbury. But not often. And between times he laboured hard on his stony acres and did his best for his daughter. In the neglected graveyard of Cold Corners there was a slanting headstone marked with his wife's name; near it, a year since, he had laid his eldest daughter. And sometimes, at dusk, in the autumn, the village people saw him walk slowly by, turn in between the graves, and stand looking down on the two stones. But he never brought a flower there, or planted a bush; nor Venny either. She was too wild and ignorant . . .

Mrs Rutledge repeated: 'That's in Exodus.'

The three visitors remained silent, turning about their hats in reluctant hands. Rutledge faced them, still with that empty pellucid gaze which frightened Bosworth. What was he seeing?

'Ain't any of you folks got the grit – ?' his wife burst out again, half hysterically.

Deacon Hibben held up his hand. 'That's no way, Mrs Rutledge. This ain't a question of having grit. What we want first of all is . . . proof . . . '

'That's so,' said Bosworth, with an explosion of relief, as if the words had lifted something black and crouching from his breast. Involuntarily the eyes of both men had turned to Brand. He stood there smiling grimly, but did not speak.

'Ain't it so, Brand?' the Deacon prompted him.

'Proof that spooks walk?' the other sneered.

'Well – I presume you want this business settled too?'

The old farmer squared his shoulders. 'Yes – I do. But I ain't a sperritualist. How the hell are you going to settle it?'

Deacon Hibben hesitated; the he said, in a low incisive tone: 'I don't see but one way – Mrs Rutledge's.'

There was a silence.

'What?' Brand sneered again. 'Spying?'

The Deacon's voice sank lower. 'If the poor girl *does* walk . . . her that's your child . . . wouldn't you be the first to want her laid quiet? We all know there've been such cases . . . mysterious visitations . . . Can any one of us here deny it?'

'I seen 'em,' Mrs Rutledge interjected.

There was another heavy pause. Suddenly Brand fixed his gaze on Rutledge. 'See here, Saul Rutledge, you've got to clear up this damned calumny, or I'll know why. You say my dead girl comes to you.' He laboured with his breath, and then jerked out: 'When? You tell me that, and I'll be there.'

Rutledge's head drooped a little, and his eyes wandered to the window. 'Round about sunset, mostly.'

'You know beforehand?'

Rutledge made a sign of assent.

'Well, then – tomorrow, will it be?'

Rutledge made the same sign.

Brand turned to the door. 'I'll be there.' That was all he said. He strode out between them without another glance or word. Deacon Hibben looked at Mrs Rutledge. 'We'll be there too,' he said, as if she had asked him; but she had not spoken, and Bosworth saw that her thin body was trembling all over. He was glad when he and Hibben were out again in the snow.

They thought that Brand wanted to be left to himself, and to give him time to unhitch his horse they made a pretence of hanging about in the doorway while Bosworth searched his pockets for a pipe he had no mind to light.

But Brand turned back to them as they lingered. 'You'll meet me down by Lamer's pond tomorrow?' he suggested. 'I want witnesses. Round about sunset.'

They nodded their acquiescence, and he got into his sleigh, gave the horse a cut across the flanks, and drove off under the snow-smothered hemlocks. The other two men went to the shed.

'What do you make of this business, Deacon?' Bosworth asked, to break the silence.

The Deacon shook his head. 'The man's a sick man – that's sure. Something's sucking the life clean out of him.'

But already, in the biting outer air, Bosworth was getting himself under better control. 'Looks to me like a bad case of the ague, as you said.'

'Well – ague of the mind, then. It's his brain that's sick.'

Bosworth shrugged. 'He ain't the first in Hemlock County.'

'That's so,' the Deacon agreed. 'It's a worm in the brain, solitude is.'

'Well, we'll know this time tomorrow, maybe,' said Bosworth. He scrambled into his sleigh, and was driving off in his turn when he heard his companion calling after him. The Deacon explained that his horse had cast a shoe; would Bosworth drive him down to the forge near North Ashmore, if it wasn't too much out of his way? He didn't want the mare slipping about on the freezing snow, and he could probably get the blacksmith to drive him back and shoe her in Rutledge's shed. Bosworth made room for him under the bearskin, and the two men drove off, pursued by a puzzled whinny from the Deacon's old mare.

The road they took was not the one that Bosworth would have followed to reach his own home. But he did not mind that. The shortest way to the forge passed close by Lamer's pond, and Bosworth, since he was in for the business, was not sorry to look the ground over. They drove on in silence.

The snow had ceased, and a green sunset was spreading upward into the crystal sky. A stinging wind barbed with ice-flakes caught them in the face on the open ridges, but when they dropped down into the hollow by Lamer's pond the air was as soundless and empty as an unswung bell. They jogged along slowly, each thinking his own thoughts.

'That's the house . . . that tumble-down shack over there, I suppose?' the Deacon said, as the road drew near the edge of the frozen pond.

'Yes: that's the house. A queer hermit-fellow built it years ago, my father used to tell me. Since then I don't believe it's ever been used but by the gipsies.'

Bosworth had reined in his horse, and sat looking through pine-trunks purpled by the sunset at the crumbling structure. Twilight already lay under the trees, though day lingered in the open. Between two sharply-patterned pine-boughs he saw the evening star, like a white boat in a sea of green.

His gaze dropped from that fathomless sky and followed the blue-white undulations of the snow. It gave him a curious agitated feeling to think that here, in this icy solitude, in the tumble-down house he had so often passed without heeding it, a dark mystery, too deep for thought, was being enacted. Down that very slope, coming from the graveyard at Cold Corners, the being they called 'Ora' must pass toward the pond. His heart began to beat stiflingly. Suddenly he gave an exclamation: 'Look!'

He had jumped out of the cutter and was stumbling up the bank toward the slope of snow. On it, turned in the direction of the house by the pond, he had detected a woman's footprints; two; then three; then more. The Deacon scrambled out after him, and they stood and stared.

'God – barefoot!' Hibben gasped. 'Then it *is* . . . the dead . . . '

Bosworth said nothing. But he knew that no live woman would travel with naked feet across that freezing wilderness. Here, then, was the proof the Deacon had asked for – they held it. What should they do with it?

'Supposing we was to drive up nearer – round the turn of the pond, till we get close to the house,' the Deacon proposed in a colourless voice. 'Mebbe then . . . '

Postponement was a relief. They got into the sleigh and drove on. Two or three hundred yards farther the road, a mere lane under steep bushy banks, turned sharply to the right, following the bend of the pond. As they rounded the turn they saw Brand's cutter ahead of them. It was empty, the horse tied to a tree-trunk. The two men looked at each other again. This was not Brand's nearest way home.

Evidently he had been actuated by the same impulse which had made them rein in their horse by the pond-side, and then hasten on to the deserted hovel. Had he too discovered those spectral foot-prints? Perhaps it was for that very reason that he had left his cutter and vanished in the direction of the house. Bosworth found himself shivering all over under his bearskin. 'I wish to God the dark wasn't coming on,' he muttered. He tethered his own horse near Brand's, and without a word he and the Deacon ploughed through the snow, in the track of Brand's huge feet. They had only a few yards to walk to overtake him. He did not hear them following him, and when Bosworth spoke his name, and he stopped short and turned, his heavy face was dim and confused, like a darker blot on the dusk. He looked at them dully, but without surprise.

'I wanted to see the place,' he merely said.

The Deacon cleared his throat. 'Just take a look . . . yes . . . We thought so . . . But I guess there won't be anything to *see* . . . ' He attempted a chuckle.

The other did not seem to hear him, but laboured on ahead through the pines. The three men came out together in the cleared space before the house. As they emerged from beneath the trees they seemed to have left night behind. The evening star shed a lustre on the speckless snow, and Brand, in that lucid circle, stopped with a jerk, and pointed to the same light footprints turned toward the house – the track of a woman in the snow. He stood still, his face working. 'Bare feet . . . ' he said.

The Deacon piped up in a quavering voice: 'The feet of the dead.'

Brand remained motionless. 'The feet of the dead,' he echoed.

Deacon Hibben laid a frightened hand on his arm. 'Come away now, Brand; for the love of God come away.'

The father hung there, gazing down at those light tracks on the snow – light as fox or squirrel trails they seemed, on the white immensity. Bosworth thought to himself: 'The living couldn't walk so light – not even Ora Brand couldn't have, when she lived . . . ' The cold seemed to have entered into his very marrow. His teeth were chattering.

Brand swung about on them abruptly. '*Now!*' he said, moving on as if to an assault, his head bowed forward on his bull neck.

'Now – now? Not in there?' gasped the Deacon. 'What's the use? It was tomorrow he said – ' He shook like a leaf.

'It's now,' said Brand. He went up to the door of the crazy house, pushed it inward, and meeting with an unexpected resistance, thrust his heavy shoulder against the panel. The door collapsed like a playing-card, and Brand stumbled after it into the darkness of the hut. The others, after a moment's hesitation, followed.

Bosworth was never quite sure in what order the events that succeeded took place. Coming in out of the snow-dazzle, he seemed to be plunging into total blackness. He groped his way across the threshold, caught a sharp splinter of the fallen door in his palm, seemed to see something white and wraithlike surge up out of the darkest corner of the hut, and then heard a revolver shot at his elbow, and a cry –

Brand had turned back, and was staggering past him out into the lingering daylight. The sunset, suddenly flushing through the trees, crimsoned his face like blood. He held a revolver in his hand and looked about him in his stupid way.

'They *do* walk, then,' he said and began to laugh. He bent his head to examine his weapon. 'Better here than in the churchyard. They shan't dig her up *now*,' he shouted out. The two men caught him by the arms, and Bosworth got the revolver away from him.

The next day Bosworth's sister Loretta, who kept house for him, asked him, when he came in for his midday dinner, if he had heard the news.

Bosworth had been sawing wood all the morning, and in spite of the cold and the driving snow, which had begun again in the night, he was covered with an icy sweat, like a man getting over a fever.

'What news?'

'Venny Brand's down sick with pneumonia. The Deacon's been there. I guess she's dying.'

Bosworth looked at her with listless eyes. She seemed far off from him, miles away.

'Venny Brand?' he echoed.

'You never liked her, Orrin.'

'She's a child. I never knew much about her.'

'Well,' repeated his sister, with the guileless relish of the unimaginative for bad news, 'I guess she's dying.' After a pause she added: 'It'll kill Sylvester Brand, all alone up there.'

Bosworth got up and said: 'I've got to see to poulticing the grey's fetlock.' He walked out into the steadily falling snow.

Venny Brand was buried three days later. The Deacon read the service; Bosworth was one of the pall-bearers. The whole countryside turned out, for the snow had stopped falling, and at any season a funeral offered an opportunity for an outing that was not to be missed. Besides, Venny Brand was young and handsome – at least some people thought her handsome, though she was so swarthy – and her dying like that, so suddenly, had the fascination of tragedy.

'They say her lungs filled right up . . . Seems she'd had bronchial troubles before . . . I always said both them girls was frail . . . Look at Ora, how she took and wasted away! And it's colder'n all outdoors up there to Brand's . . . Their mother, too, *she* pined away just the same. They don't ever make old bones on the mother's side of the family . . . There's that young Bedlow over there; they say Venny was engaged to him . . . Oh, Mrs Rutledge, excuse *me* . . . Step right into the pew; there's a seat for you alongside of grandma . . . '

Mrs Rutledge was advancing with deliberate step down the narrow aisle of the bleak wooden church. She had on her best bonnet, a monumental structure which no-one had seen out of her trunk since old Mrs Silsee's funeral, three years before. All the women remembered it. Under its perpendicular pile her narrow face, swaying on the long thin neck, seemed whiter than ever; but her air of fretfulness had been composed into a suitable expression of mournful immobility.

'Looks as if the stone-mason had carved her to put atop of Venny's grave,' Bosworth thought as she glided past him; and then shivered at his own sepulchral fancy. When she bent over her hymn-book her lowered lids reminded him again of marble eyeballs; the bony hands clasping the book were bloodless. Bosworth had never seen such hands since he had seen old Aunt Cressidora Cheney strangle the canary-bird because it fluttered.

The service was over, the coffin of Venny Brand had been lowered into her sister's grave, and the neighbours were slowly dispersing. Bosworth, as pall-bearer, felt obliged to linger and say a word to the stricken father. He waited till Brand had turned from the grave with the Deacon at his side. The three men stood together for a moment; but not one of them spoke. Brand's face was the closed door of a vault, barred with wrinkles like bands of iron.

Finally the Deacon took his hand and said: 'The Lord gave – '

Brand nodded and turned away toward the shed where the horses were hitched. Bosworth followed him. 'Let me drive along home with you,' he suggested.

Brand did not so much as turn his head. 'Home? What home?' he said; and the other fell back.

Loretta Bosworth was talking with the other women while the men unblanketed their horses and backed the cutters out into the heavy snow. As Bosworth waited for her, a few feet off, he saw Mrs Rutledge's tall bonnet lording it above the group. Andy Pond, the Rutledge farm-hand, was backing out the sleigh.

'Saul ain't here today, Mrs Rutledge, is he?' one of the village elders piped, turning a benevolent old tortoise-head about on a loose neck, and blinking up into Mrs Rutledge's marble face.

Bosworth heard her measure out her answer in slow incisive words. 'No. Mr Rutledge he ain't here. He would 'a' come for certain, but his aunt Minorca Cummins is being buried down to Stotesbury this very day and he had to go down there. Don't it sometimes seem zif we was all walking right in the Shadow of Death?'

As she walked toward the cutter, in which Andy Pond was already seated, the Deacon went up to her with visible hesitation. Involuntarily Bosworth also moved nearer. He heard the Deacon say: 'I'm glad to hear that Saul is able to be up and around.'

She turned her small head on her rigid neck, and lifted the lids of marble.

'Yes, I guess he'll sleep quieter now. – And *her* too, maybe, now she don't lay there alone any longer,' she added in a low voice, with a sudden twist of her chin toward the fresh black stain in the grave-yard snow. She got into the cutter, and said in a clear tone to Andy Pond: ''S long as we're down here I don't know but what I'll just call round and get a box of soap at Hiram Pringle's.'

The Welcome Visitor

DAVID STUART DAVIES

The evening shadows lengthened on the blind and although she was content to sit in the dark, Dorothy switched on the small lamp by Emily's bed for her sister's sake. She thought the artificial illumination might help Emily to rally a little – but it did not. The bright light illuminated her sister's gaunt features: the grey cheeks were hollow, the skin like ancient parchment and what once had been wide lustrous blue eyes, full of vibrancy and life, were now small misty orbs which stared vacantly ahead of her. Dorothy took her sister's wrist and felt for a pulse. It was feeble and irregular. Death was but a whisper away.

That it should come to this. After all these years, thought Dorothy. All these years together, sharing. Sharing everything, including their terrible secret. But now it looked like it was going to end. It had been unthinkable once upon a time: that life, that everlasting road down which they travelled, should come to an end. But now, for Emily, it had turned into a cul-de-sac. It seemed that there was no way out and certainly no turning back. Dorothy was well aware that when Emily died, she would follow very quickly. Already she felt weak and emaciated. It was only her concern for her sister that kept her going. Every action was an effort. Every movement fatigued her. It seemed such a long time since they'd had sustenance. With their infirmities, the infirmities of great old age, they were no longer able to go out and obtain the necessities as they had in their glory days. They had become prisoners of their own nature.

Dorothy had often wondered whether their move to this cottage some two miles from the nearest village had been wise. They were so isolated, but of course that had been the plan. Emily had always been keen on living as far away from people as possible, 'to prevent discovery'. But since they had come to the cottage and age had begun to catch up on them, the effort of travelling for supplies grew more onerous every time. Their old bones and tired bodies were not up to it. And so they were forced to fast until the situation became almost desperate and then they would make the effort once more. But this time they had waited too long and Emily had slipped into illness almost with a welcome resignation. They had both agreed that now life, their strange life, had become intolerable. Never before had they contemplated dying. Dying finally that is. It had been unthinkable, but now it seemed so real and so close. Dorothy shuddered at the thought, the thought of that eternal darkness from which there was no waking up.

She ran her fingers over Emily's icy brow. 'Oh, my dear sister,' she said, a tear rolling its way down her grey wrinkled cheek.

Just them something highly unusual occurred, something so rare that for a moment Dorothy was not quite sure what was happening. The doorbell rang. Its ancient clang vibrated through the house and then it fell silent. Surely it can't be a visitor, thought Dorothy, rising uneasily to her feet. They never had visitors.

They couldn't.

More than once she had thought of contacting a doctor when Emily finally took to her bed, but she knew that would be impossible. If they were going to die, it had to be on their own terms.

And then suddenly there it was again, the metallic cacophony of the doorbell; insistent and raucous. It reminded Dorothy of the bells those creatures rang as they patrolled the streets pushing their unsavoury carts with cries of 'Bring out your dead'.

She had better answer the door in case whoever it was ringing the bell took it upon themselves to break in. 'I knew that two old ladies lived there and when they didn't answer . . . I thought the worst so I thought it best if I . . . ,' she could hear the explanation in her head as she approached the door. Pulling back the rug that was rolled up on the floor to prevent the cold air seeping in, she pulled back the bolts and unlocked the door.

The feeble hall light shone upon the visitor. It was a young man, not yet twenty. He was dressed in blue jeans and wore a brightly coloured shiny blouson jacket with the words 'Pete's Pizza Parlour' emblazoned on it. He grinned a well-practised grin.

'Good evening,' he said grandly, as though he was introducing a show or a concert. 'I'm from Pete's Pizza Parlour which has just opened in the village. We deliver pizzas and burgers within a five-mile radius and we have a special opening offer: two pizzas for the price of one.' He thrust a leaflet at Dorothy. 'Choose one off the list and I'll phone through to the shop and it'll be here in under the hour.'

Dorothy, temporarily overwhelmed by this animated perform-ance, was about to thank the young man for the information and then ask him to leave when an idea struck her. With a gracious smile and a 'thank you', she took the leaflet and pretended to read it. Without her glasses the print was just a multicoloured blur.

'Oh, these are really nice,' she said, mustering some coquettish charm. 'I think I'd like one of those and I'm sure my sister would like one, too. She's not well you know.'

'Sorry to hear that,' said the youth easily, without any conviction in his voice.

'She's in bed upstairs. I'm sure one of these pizza things would help to raise her spirits. I'll go up and see what flavour she'd like.'

'Righto.'

'Oh, I say, would you be a dear and come up with me and then when she's decided which flavour, I can pay you and it'll save me coming downstairs again.' Dorothy affected a little laugh. 'My old legs are not what they were.'

The youth seemed a little uncertain about this request, but he didn't want to lose a customer – and his commission - so he nodded in agreement. 'Sure,' he said.

He trailed behind the old girl as she mounted the stairs slowly and laboriously. He had no idea that it was now her turn to put on a performance.

'In here,' Dorothy said on reaching the landing. She opened the bedroom door and the youth walked in. It was cold and musty, with a weird smell that assailed his nostrils. He saw what appeared to be a corpse in the bed: a grey, skeletal face with glassy eyes and thin lank hair peeped above the bedclothes. It was like an exhibit in the chamber of horrors. On seeing this apparition he gasped and swore. Hearing the strange new voice in the room, Emily slowly swivelled her head in the youth's direction and grinned. He swore again, his blood running cold with fear. He felt the dank atmosphere of the room rush in upon him like the beating of shrouded wings. What on earth was going on, he wondered. That was all he wondered for at that moment Dorothy hit him hard on the back of his head with a large brass candlestick, one she had bought in a German Market in 1867.

The boy toppled forward on to the bed.

By now saliva was drooling down Emily's ancient chin.

'Sustenance at last,' crowed Dorothy, stepping forward and with renewed strength hauling the body further up the bed so that the youth's neck was within easy reach of Emily.

'You first, my dear. Your need is greater than mine,' she said.

Emily, her eyes now smouldering with desire, leaned forward over the youth's smooth neck. 'Thank you, sister dear,' she said. Her first words in many a long day. Then she sank her ancient fangs deep into the boy's flesh and began to drink noisily.